THE
SECRETARY

BOOKS BY CATHERINE HOKIN

The Fortunate Ones
What Only We Know
The Lost Mother

CATHERINE HOKIN

THE SECRETARY

GRAND CENTRAL

NEW YORK   BOSTON

Grand Central Publishing
Hachette Book Group
1290 Avenue of the Americas, New York, NY 10104
grandcentralpublishing.com
twitter.com/grandcentralpub

Originally published by Bookouture, an imprint of Storyfire Ltd., in 2021
First Grand Central Publishing edition: January 2023

Grand Central Publishing is a division of Hachette Book Group, Inc. The
Grand Central Publishing name and logo is a trademark of
Hachette Book Group, Inc.

The publisher is not responsible for websites (or their content) that are not
owned by the publisher.

The Hachette Speakers Bureau provides a wide range of authors for speaking
events. To find out more, go to www.hachettespeakersbureau.com or email
HachetteSpeakers@hbgusa.com.

Grand Central Publishing books may be purchased in bulk for business,
educational, or promotional use. For information, please contact your local
bookseller or the Hachette Book Group Special Markets Department at
special.markets@hbgusa.com.

Library of Congress Control Number: 2022943588

ISBN: 9781538725733 (trade paperback)

Printed in the United States of America

LSC-C

Printing 1, 2022

For Shiralee,
the best cheerleader to have in your corner

THE
SECRETARY

PROLOGUE

December 24, 1941

Why had he given her a drawing? Why had he given her a gift at all? And why was he even here? His datebook placed him at the Eastern Front for at least another week.

Magda couldn't concentrate—her head was filled with lists. She had been so careful: she had replaced every letter and document his absence had allowed her to sneak a glance at, even though she hadn't expected him back. She was methodical; she was never careless; she never assumed she was safe. So why was her heart pounding?

A sudden cough—the low bark she knew as a signal—pulled her back into the room. Walther. Magda caught his eye, and the brief nod that meant *switch on your smile, straighten your shoulders.*

A second later, she realized that Elsa had been alerted too and had followed her father's gaze, her face twisting when she saw where it had landed. Elsa was a hawk, eyes everywhere, especially when it came to Magda. Magda knew she needed to make a better friend of the girl; the problem was how.

"Fräulein Aderbach, look at the camera and hold your frame steady!"

Magda snapped her attention back to the photographer and smiled her best smile. It wasn't until he was done positioning and repositioning his subjects that she managed to take a proper look at the drawing itself. It was a pen and ink sketch of a house, with an address and her name picked out in a gold scroll in the top corner. She had no clue what it meant, or why the men to her left and right were holding similar drawings. Her boss—Reichsführer-SS Heinrich Himmler—had distributed his gifts to her and the others without explanation.

Magda forced herself to concentrate as Himmler began talking again, living up to his reputation for being long-winded. The first part of his speech had dragged on for an hour; the second could easily last as long. The special ceremonies Himmler had concocted to honor his beloved SS ran to timetables only he knew, and followed rituals he said harked back to the knights and quests Germany's heroic past was filled with. Magda didn't know if tonight's Yuletide celebration—Himmler had forbidden his "family" from calling it *Christmas*—was historic or not, but it was certainly macabre.

Himmler's villa on Hagenstraße in Grunewald—a wealthy suburb of Berlin tucked into the edges of the thick forest from which it took its name—had always struck Magda as a far colder place than it looked from its elegant exterior. Tonight, it was particularly austere. Himmler had removed the name from the holiday season and all the trappings that went with it. There was no tree weighed down with baubles, no gingerbread scenting the house, no carols. Himmler had instructed his guests to enter the wood-paneled reception hall in silence. He had left them there in a darkness so complete, Magda could barely see her own hand. By the time his carefully stage-managed theatricals had started—on the stroke of a gong whose loud bellow resounded through her body—the tension in the room was sharp enough to taste.

As the gong faded, a candelabra had burst into life, its flames welcomed by a ripple of voices too low for Magda to make out what was said. When it rang out again, a second set of candles had flared. This time, the murmur had separated itself into words, although Magda quickly wished that it hadn't.

Let his, and our, light shine. Let his, and our, light shine.

The chant had whispered on and on, creeping out of the shadows and into the room. And then the third set of tapers had burst into life, and Magda finally saw them. The men in their black SS uniforms appearing like wraiths, intoning the chorus their wives and children instantly echoed. Soon, so many candles were ablaze, the room glowed a dull gold and some of the guests were discreetly loosening their collars. Magda, by contrast, was chilled to the bone. She had been edging away when Himmler had invited ten of his most "valued and trusted servants" to step forward and had included her name with the chosen.

Walther coughed again. Magda refocused. Himmler was still speaking, his voice stuck in the monotonous drone his lackeys told him was melodic.

"These houses whose portraits you hold are your new homes. Treasure them: they are symbols of what this country will soon be. Every one of them once belonged to a Jew. Every one of them is cleansed by their removal. These streets are no longer defiled; this beautiful corner of Berlin is returned to us. As Germany will be returned to us, city by city, field by field, as our light—the Führer's light—shines on in our hearts, and in our hands."

He stopped. There was the briefest pause and then applause rang out, led, as Magda knew it would be, by Walther.

Himmler bowed and stepped forward, his too-eager beam fixed on his "lucky faithful."

I have to thank him. I have to praise him to the skies or he will take offense and be done with me.

Magda knew what she needed to do, but her brain was stuck on *cleansed* and *defiled,* and when she opened her mouth, it refused to cooperate.

"I can't accept this. I can't possibly—"

"Believe my good fortune."

Walther was at her side, his hand pressing onto her shoulder. Magda knew it was there to calm her, although it felt as if he was holding her in place.

"And, given that you were my secretary before the Reichsführer's, I am adding my thanks to yours. This is an honor for us both, wouldn't you agree, Magda dear?"

Somehow she found the right words. Himmler lapped up her delighted performance and swept on to bask in the next.

Magda couldn't move.

"He trusts you. This is proof. You did it, Magda; you are where we need you to be. You should be proud."

Walther's whispered words as he steered Himmler away had pinned her to the spot as surely as his hand.

Proud?

Magda stared around the room as the guests mingled, their diamond earrings and silver shoulder-flashes gleaming. She knew that Walther was right—that she had done her job well and convinced Himmler she was loyal—but the result of that was unbearable. The discreetly made-up women fawning over their uniformed husbands disgusted her. The scent of victory they wore turned her stomach.

We have played our parts so perfectly, they believe we're the same as them.

Tears she didn't dare shed pricked at her eyelids.

What if no one ever believes we were not?

PART ONE

CHAPTER ONE

Nina, October 1975

The day of her great-grandmother Herthe Aderbach's funeral was a day of firsts for seven-year-old Nina Dahlke.

It was the first time she had been in a graveyard, an event she quickly realized she did not want to repeat. It was the first time she had ridden in a car. It was the first time she had come face to face with the wall that divided Berlin into the East, which was her home, and the West, which was a blank to her. And it was the first time she saw her unflappable grandmother Magda not only unsure of herself—a state of affairs that would have been strange enough on its own—but also utterly and unmistakably afraid.

The day had started with the car or, to be more accurate, her parents' ridiculously childlike excitement about their new acquisition that not even a funeral could dim. Unlike her mother and father, Nina had no interest at all in cars. As far as she could see, the only remarkable thing about the boxy brown Trabi was the effect it had on her parents. If Nina had known the word, she would have described their mood as giddy. Her father Holger had polished it twice from tip to stern in the three days he had owned it. When they climbed into its chemically scented interior to drive to the cemetery, her normally undemonstrative mother Britte had caressed its thin roof.

"Five years we've been waiting for this, Nina. Five years to get to the top of the list. Can you imagine?"

Given that it was identical to all the other cars that spluttered round their neighborhood, Nina couldn't. More than that, however, she had been confused by the question. Her parents had never asked her to use her imagination before; they normally begged her to stop. *Good citizens* of the German Democratic Republic—which both Britte and Holger Dahlke were determined they, and Nina, would be—were sensible people. *Good citizens*, as her mother constantly reminded her, were not given to flights of fancy, which were of no practical use. Her teacher had said the same thing when she handed back Nina's last story assignment—which was, admittedly, rather more magical than the theme "The Good Child of the Factory" had requested—soaked in red pen. As far as Nina could see, and as she had explained to Frau Maier when she saw the *D* scrawled across her hard work, what the phrase *good citizens* really meant was dried-up and dull.

The memory of Frau Maier's plump face reshaping from cozy to pursed wasn't a pleasant one. Neither was the memory of sitting in Principal Huber's office while he angrily invited her parents to explain why they were raising a child who "believed she had the right to question authority" and "what was going so wrong with their parenting?" All three of them had had to write letters of apology to the school, an instruction Nina had struggled to understand, given that the "crime" in question was hers.

"It's the way things are done, chicken. Everyone is responsible for everyone around them. That means that there are thoughts that are better to keep private, rather than letting everything that pops into your head pop out on your tongue. It isn't always easy, Nina, hiding who you are—I know that, I really do. But, trust me, sometimes it's the safest thing."

Grandma Magda had dried Nina's tears with that advice; Nina hadn't admitted how much it disappointed her. Although she hadn't fully understood everything Magda had said, she knew it wasn't a million miles away from her mother's tight-lipped "learn to be quiet and learn that quickly before you mess everything up."

What Nina had really wanted when she crawled wet-eyed onto her grandmother's knee was for Magda to defend her. To march into school waving the red-inked assignment as if it was one of the scarlet flags the whole building was festooned with and demand the grade A Nina knew it deserved. It was Magda, after all, who had introduced her to the fairy stories packed with princesses and curses and magical creatures that Nina had been trying to copy. The stories Frau Maier had dismissed as "empty capitalist nonsense you have no business reading." And it was her grandmother who always insisted that everybody had the right to fair treatment—it was one of her favorite sayings—and Nina having her best story covered in red definitely wasn't fair treatment.

Nina had been about to beg Magda to do just that, and then it had dawned on her that perhaps her grandmother had no business reading the stories either. That Magda would also get into trouble if she admitted she was the source of Nina knowing them. It was, admittedly, hard for Nina to imagine Herr Huber demanding a letter of apology from someone as well respected as her grandmother.

Until her retirement, Magda had held some kind of job with the government that Nina didn't understand but knew was important because everyone had told her so. She still sat on a lot of what sounded like very boring committees. And she had done something heroic in the war, although the war—and everything associated with it, including the death of Nina's never-discussed grandfather—was a time in her life Magda refused to speak about. But then Nina's mother was a teacher, and her father worked in an office, which were also respectable jobs, and the principal had still managed to reduce them to the status of naughty children. Instead of arguing, therefore, Nina had tried out the art of holding her tongue that everyone had suggested she practice. It hadn't come easily.

"Remember, Nina, this isn't a place for children. I don't know what Mother was thinking letting you come, but it's on her head not mine. There's to be none of your nonsense today."

Britte's terse command broke into Nina's meanderings as the car made its slightly jerky way round the edge of Friedrichsfelde Cemetery. If she had been looking at her daughter as they drove through the narrow gateposts, Britte would have realized that the order wasn't necessary. Nina was staring out of the window at the bare lifeless trees and the crumbling weather-beaten statues feeling suddenly very small. Wishing she had listened to everyone, including her mother, who had told her she was too young to go to a funeral, and not begged Magda to let her attend.

Everyone had talked about the importance of "saying a proper goodbye" and how comforting that was. Nothing in the cemetery, however, was comforting. The rows of headstones sticking up like graying teeth upset her. So did the damp-smelling earth piled up beside the grave, and the coffin that was too solid and too final and far too small to contain her big-hearted great-grandmother. Nina pushed her shaking hands deep into the pockets of her scratchy wool coat and squeezed her eyes shut as the casket was lowered into the grave. Then the first clod of earth thumped onto the lid and her knees turned to water.

"She's been very brave, but that's enough now, Holger. Why don't you take her home or, better still, given that we'll be here a little while yet, take her for a drive in that new car of yours. Show her a bit of Berlin."

Nina was more than happy to obey her grandmother's quietly made intervention. Holger was more than happy to follow his mother-in-law's bidding and lead his family away. Within moments, Nina was back in the car, curled up with the doll she wished she hadn't left behind on the back seat during the funeral, as her parents reeled off street names and landmarks and tried to work out a route. Nina didn't mind where they went, as long as it was away from the cemetery. Her ears pricked up, however, when Holger mentioned the Brandenburg Tor. None of her classmates had been to see that yet, and a trip to the Tor, with its enormous chariot and horses, would be quite an adventure to boast about.

It soon became clear, however, that neither of her parents possessed the knowledge of the city's streets they both claimed. The wedding-cake houses on Karl Marx Allee did not lead into Alexanderplatz with its needle-shaped television tower, as Holger had confidently promised it would. Instead of the broad tree-lined sweep of the Unter den Linden, which Britte had said Nina would love, the Trabi was locked instead inside a labyrinth of increasingly narrow gray streets. Nothing outside the windows looked different enough from the roads round her home in Oberschöneweide to grab Nina's attention. If anything, the district they were in was less interesting—at least there were pretty parks where she lived and it was within walking distance of the river. Nina stopped imagining the tales she would take into school. She was tired, and slightly sick from the car's constant bumping. She closed her eyes as her parents continued to bicker. Then Britte's moaning turned into a wail.

"Where have you brought us? Oh dear God, that's a guardhouse. It's a checkpoint. Are you mad?"

Nina snapped awake. The car's back window didn't open, but she pressed herself up against it as hard as she could and peered out. The street ahead was blocked by a slab of concrete whose dinginess made the red and white barrier stretched in front of it seem unnaturally bright.

"Is that it? Is that the Wall?"

Britte sprang round and pulled Nina back from the glass as if it was paper-thin. "Don't call it that, especially not here where you've no idea who could be listening. Do you want to get us arrested?" She kept one hand on Nina's chest and punched Holger's arm with the other. "Don't just sit there—turn round or reverse."

Holger tried, but his feet were too heavy, and the gears crunched. As he tried again, the hut door flew open and two soldiers came running, their rifles lifted and trained on the Trabi.

"Cut the engine! They must think we're trying to escape."

Britte's piercing shriek bounced round the car; Nina flung her hands across her ears. The guns were coming closer, slick and black and mesmerizing.

"Mama, what do you mean? Escape from where? And why would we be arrested?"

Her mother either couldn't hear her or didn't want to.

The soldiers flanked the car and drummed their fists against the front windows.

"Don't open them, Papa, please."

But Holger didn't have time to register her tears: he was already half out of his seat, dragged out by one of the gun-wielding guards.

Britte turned round again to Nina. Her pale skin was scarlet, and her thin lips were white. Her face looked all the wrong way round. "Get out, Nina, before they make you. Whatever they ask you, answer them. And, for God's sake, don't call it what you called it before: remember the right name."

Nina scrambled out of the car behind her mother, scuffing her shiny brown shoes on the cobbles.

One of the soldiers waved her onto the pavement.

The Anti-Fascist Protection Barrier. Only Westerners call it the Wall.

The Barrier: that was the name Britte wanted her to use—the one that had been drilled into Nina since her first day at school.

As the soldiers began grilling her parents, she dug round for all the other facts she had had to learn and regurgitate in tests and essays, terrified she might make a mistake and get her parents into more trouble than they were in already: 1961—it had been built in 1961. And it was there for the GDR's protection, to keep out the capitalists and the criminals from the wicked other side. What was it Herr Huber always said, in his never-ending assemblies at the start of each term? Nina scrabbled round, trying to hear his voice over the blood drumming in her ears. *We're not meant to go near it.* That was it. *In case Westerners get close enough to tempt us into wrongdoing. And terrible things would happen if it wasn't there.* She could picture him now and hear his voice booming through her head the way it had in the school gymnasium.

"The West doesn't respect our way of life and they are jealous of our excellent workers and would steal them all if they could. And worse, far worse, without that barrier, the West would wage war on us, with all the terrible suffering that would bring. Our government loves us too much to permit that and so it protects us. And we love our government, don't we?"

Nina always shouted back *yes* along with the rest of the school, even though she didn't really know what he meant by war and suffering, and she wasn't sure how to love something as faceless as a government. And she had stopped putting her hand up to ask because Frau Maier said there was no need or place for questions, and only naughty children asked them. Instead of sharing her confusion, Nina had done what everyone else did and agreed that, yes, she was privileged to live in a country that truly cared for its citizens. It was hard, however, to feel privileged while soldiers brandishing rifles screamed at her parents and threatened to take them away.

In the end, the border guards didn't speak to her. After they had checked the car and found neither the suitcases or the money they were apparently looking for, they seemed to accept that Britte and Holger were hopeless navigators, not escapees, and released them. Holger drove jerkily away; neither Britte nor Nina mentioned the rip in the shoulder of his tweed coat. Nobody mentioned anything about the incident at all. The only thing Britte said to Nina was a curt, "Don't tell your grandmother—I really don't need my mother's commentary on this."

Nina didn't answer; she was too busy trying to make sense of the guns and the threats.

*

The journey back to Magda's two-story home in Triniusstraβe, a
ten-minute walk from the Dahlkes' apartment building in Kottmeier Allee, was completed at an uncomfortable bone-jarring speed.
By the time they arrived, the house was crammed with people.
Holger and Britte disappeared into the forest of black coats, but
Nina was too shaken to weave her way through them. She slipped
away instead, first to the kitchen where she helped herself to a slab
of almond-studded sugar cake, and then upstairs to the back of the
house and her great-grandmother Herthe's bedroom. The room,
however, wasn't a sanctuary anymore: it was too hollowed out. The
sturdy furniture was all in its right place. Herthe's collection of
silver-framed photographs still hung on the wall; her tortoiseshell
hairbrush was still on the dressing table. The right things were
there, but Herthe wasn't and so none of them breathed. The bed
Herthe had spent her last year in, where Nina had curled up in the
afternoons after school, wasn't a boat or a magic carpet; it was just
a bed. Without the stories that went with them, the faces staring
out from the photographs were meaningless shadows.

Nina put her cake down, her appetite gone. It had barely been
a week since Herthe had died—there must surely still be a trace
of her somewhere?

Where's the treasure tin? It isn't her room without the treasure tin.

Nina spun round to the nightstand, fingers crossed that the
floral tin brimming with buttons and coins and cast-off bits of
jewelry would be sitting there waiting. Ever since Herthe had
been bedridden, she had insisted on keeping it close by, ready
for Nina to play with. In the last weeks before her death, when
Herthe had been too weak to do anything except hold Nina's hand,
Magda had picked up the game her mother had started. The three
of them had settled themselves against the thick pillows, Magda
had cast the spell Herthe was too tired to manage—*Pick out one*

piece and I'll spin you a story—and Nina had opened the tin and plunged in, pulling out a broken chain, or a pendant that had lost its setting, or a key that had long lost its lock, to weave a tale out of. It was their special thing: mother and daughter and granddaughter all in love with storytelling. Except now the nightstand was empty and the stories were gone.

Nina panicked. She blundered round the room blind as a moth, rummaging behind the curtains, checking under the bed. There was no tin to be seen. The drawers in the nightstand and dresser were too narrow for it to be stowed in there. The only piece of furniture where it might possibly be hiding was in the bulky, double-fronted wardrobe. Nina hesitated: she had a feeling that her grandmother wouldn't be happy with her opening doors and digging. Magda was a stickler for something she called *privacy,* which Britte had explained, somewhat confusingly, as "keeping your hands to yourself and your nose well out." Nina knew she should really ask first, but her grandmother was busy, and she needed to find it. She reached up, gripped the two dangling brass rings and pulled.

The doors swung open with a pop and a whoosh of dried-out musty lavender. It had been such a long time since Nina had seen Herthe in anything but a high-necked white nightgown and a washed-out woolen bed jacket, it was a shock to see the flower-sprigged skirts and dresses that filled the deep space.

Nina stepped back. She didn't want to touch them. They looked too stiff to have ever contained her great-grandmother's body. And so old, she was scared the tiniest knock would crumble them to dust. But she wanted the treasure tin, and all storytellers knew that missing things always ended up in places that were frightening. Holding her breath, Nina bent down as far as she could, making sure that only the bottom of the clothes were in her eyeline. She wriggled a careful hand under the rigid rows of material, stretching until her fingers found a line of boxes at the back.

The first two were cardboard and gave when she pressed them, but the third one was cold and rattled when she pushed. Taking a deep breath, Nina grabbed hold of it and pulled. The tin slid out. As it did so, it dislodged a tightly coiled scroll, which rolled out onto the floor in a puff of dust.

Nina instantly forgot about the treasure and grabbed for the scroll. The paper was thick and had yellowed in patches and was far more exciting than broken bits of jewelry—it could be a map, or a letter, or a long-lost painting hidden since the war that the government would thank Nina for finding and maybe even give her a medal. She tugged the roll open, smoothed it out, and then sat back on the carpet and gasped.

It was a drawing, done in black ink, of the most wonderful house Nina had ever seen. The delicately sketched building was like an illustration from a picture book; it was certainly nothing like the houses in Oberschöneweide. The homes crowding those streets were either apartment blocks of the sort Nina lived in, which were all sharp edges and identical rooms, or small and square like her grandmother's, which had been built for loyal party workers after World War Two's air raids had devastated the area. Nothing on this house, however, was simple or plain. The doorway was arched and ornate and had a circular clock and a carved shield set above it. The tiled roof curved in swoops and dips. There was a round tower on one corner, and shuttered windows with small hearts carved into them, and what appeared to be a covered walkway or balcony wrapped round one side. It was jumbled and chaotic and enchanting. It looked like the kind of house a magician would live in with a family of owls, or where a princess would hold parties for a court full of elves.

Nina's imagination was already soaring, and then she noticed the lettering in the top right-hand corner. It was printed in gold and in an elaborately curly style that made the inscription difficult to read, but, on the third go, she got it:

The Tower House, Erdener Straße, Berlin-Grunewald.
For Magda Aderbach from HH, a gift.

"Where did you find that?"

Nina had been so entranced, she hadn't heard the bedroom door open or her grandma come in. If she had been paying more attention, she might have noticed that Magda's tone was oddly clipped.

"It was in the back of the wardrobe. It fell out when I was looking for Great-Grandma's tin. It's so beautiful, Grandma—as pretty as a castle from a fairy tale. And it's got your name on it. Did you really live there? Was it really yours?"

Nina looked up at Magda, expecting her face to shine with excitement. She didn't recognize the woman staring down at her. Nina knew her grandmother was old, at least sixty, but she had never thought of her that way. When Magda picked Nina up from school—which she did every afternoon now she had retired—she never complained that she was too tired to play, the way Nina's mother always did. She didn't even complain when Nina begged to stay out in the park on chilly days when the wind made Magda's damaged hand ache. Magda had always been solid and reliable and steady. Now her body was drawn in and hunched and Nina couldn't imagine her walking anywhere, never mind playing chase. As for her face. Nina had heard the phrase *as white as snow* before, but snow was real and it sparkled. Magda's skin had turned the color of the putty her father used to mend holes with.

She's afraid.

The thought came from nowhere and made Nina shiver. Her grandmother was capable and certain; she was never *afraid*. And yet even that unthinkable word wasn't strong enough to explain the distortion in Magda's face. Her mother had been afraid at the checkpoint, and so had Nina. But there had been guns and soldiers and shouting there, and fear that was noisy and messy, that spilled out in begging and tears. There was nothing here but a piece of paper, and the fear Nina could sense swirling round Magda wasn't noisy; it didn't spill out. It was cold and solid, and bigger than the room.

"What's the matter?"

Magda replied as if she hadn't heard the question. "I had no idea she'd kept it. I told her to get rid of it; I told her to burn both of the pictures I was stupid enough to bring back. She promised me she had. I should have realized she could never resist anything *pretty*."

Nina didn't know how she was supposed to react. Magda had spat out the last word. Now she was staring at the drawing as if she expected it to burst into flames.

"Don't you like it?"

Magda looked at Nina blankly, and then her eyes suddenly filled. Although Magda upset and crying was as unthinkable to Nina as Magda afraid, it was an easier thought to latch on to.

Maybe she's sad. Maybe she loved living there as much as I know I would and she's miserable she doesn't anymore. Maybe HH was a prince she once loved and he had to go away, on a quest.

"Can I have it?"

"What?"

Nina picked the sketch up. "You're sad to see the house again, aren't you? Because you miss it and the person who gave it to you. But I love it, I do, and I'd take care of this, and I'd write stories about it. And maybe, in a bit, if you stopped feeling upset, you could tell me what it was like living there." Nina smiled at her grandma, confident she had worked out the problem. "It's a princess's house. You're so lucky."

There was no answering smile. Magda's body stiffened; her mouth went slack.

Nina scrambled to her feet, still clutching the drawing.

"Grandma, what's wrong? Are you sick? Should I go and get Mama?"

"A princess's house? Is that what you think? My God, how must it feel to be this innocent?"

Magda's tone was so harsh, so unlike her, Nina started backing away.

"Take it if you want. No, don't. Tear it up and forget it, and never mention it to me again."

Magda was shouting. She never shouted. Her eyes were black and hard, as if someone else were using them. And the hand with its stumps where the middle fingers should be—an injury that Nina rarely noticed because it was just part of Grandma—had twisted itself into a cruel and mangled claw.

"I mean it, Nina—get rid of the damn thing."

Whoever this woman was, Nina didn't like her, and she didn't want to be near her. She had tried so hard all day, at the funeral and at the checkpoint, to be grown-up and not cry, but this was too much. Nina burst into the tears she'd been storing up since the cemetery and—clutching the drawing tight to keep it safe from this nasty new grandmother—she fled.

CHAPTER TWO

Magda, June 1935–June 1937

Walther Tiedemann was the shiniest man twenty-year-old Magda Aderbach had ever seen. Everything about him—from his soft blond hair and his sapphire blue eyes, to his impeccably cut gray suit—gleamed. The sight of him could have swept Magda away, except the most polished thing about him was his swastika pin.

Magda, and all the other girls in the final year of studying for their secretarial exams at the Technische Hochschule Berlin, had spent the past week in a state of excitement more suited to the arrival of a movie star in their midst than a businessman in his forties. The teachers were no better. They were breathless with the great man's coming and had used production statistics for the Tiedemann Electric Motor Company as the basis for too many lessons. They had also—to the unconcealed amusement of their pupils—invested in glossy new haircuts and dresses with deeper necklines than any of them normally wore.

Their excitement, however, was understandable: Walther Tiedemann—who had inherited the thriving family business from his father—was Germany's most well-known, and most glamourous, businessman. He was rarely out of the newspapers. A small forest's worth of print had been devoted to the company's soaring profits and dazzling takeover deals and—since the death of his wife five years previously—Walther's equally dazzling social life. When the news of a secretarial vacancy at his Spandau headquarters was announced, Magda had been as eager as the rest of her classmates to secure the position. And now she was within a clever answer or two's reach of the job, and she didn't want to work for him at all.

"Here she is, Herr Tiedemann, our star pupil. In you come, Fräulein Aderbach, in you come. We don't want to keep our honored guest waiting."

Frau Kuechler, the directress of the school's secretarial division, had waved Magda into the room with a smile that was far too wide for her narrow face. Herr Tiedemann had risen rather more gracefully and offered her a slight bow. Magda could have sworn she heard Frau Kuechler sigh as he held out his hand.

She's acting as coy as a moonstruck teenager.

That was a daunting thought. Frau Kuechler was normally as far from that description as a grizzled army general. Now, however, she was breathy and blushing and her stocky chest was positively quivering beneath its tightly buttoned tweed. Magda hastily averted her eyes from what was a deeply alarming spectacle and took the businessman's outstretched hand, touching it with as little of hers as she could. She intended her distance, and the speed of her handshake, as a snub; Tiedemann didn't, however, appear to notice.

"It is a pleasure to meet you, Fräulein. Directress Kuechler has waxed quite lyrical about your abilities. I must confess, with the pedigree she outlined, I was expecting someone older."

Tiedemann gestured for Magda to sit down and followed suit, stretching his long legs out in front of him until they occupied the bulk of the flower-patterned rug.

He's too used to this. Being charming, making women flutter.

Walther Tiedemann was seriously attractive; even with her eyes firmly opened to his political leanings, Magda couldn't deny that. She could imagine most of her friends flirting and flattering and competing for a date with him, even if he was old enough to be their father. Magda hadn't been immune to the businessman's charms herself when she and the other girls had pored over the latest press photographs of him in a sharply tailored tuxedo. And—although she had not long met a man who had stolen her heart—she had joined in with the classroom giggling as some of the bolder girls described how they planned to use his typing pool as a stepping stone to his bed. Now, however, it didn't matter how handsome Tiedemann was: his bright eyes and square jaw were ruined by the red and black badge fastened to his jacket. Magda kept her response, therefore, to a coolly polite "thank you" and was taken aback when he grinned.

"Intelligent and reserved, an excellent combination. So, given that I have all your predicted examination scores and sample pieces, and I know you are—as your director put it—a 'star,' why don't you tell me something about yourself, Fräulein Aderbach? Something more personal than your dizzying shorthand and typing speeds."

It was a test—everything about his steepled fingers and his cocked head told Magda that. And if passing it meant being offered a position working for a man who was a National Socialist, it was a test Magda was quite happy to fail.

She squared her shoulders, folded her hands neatly in her lap and looked him straight in the eye.

"I was born in Oberschöneweide and I'm proud to still live there. My father is a manager at the Oberspree Cable Works."

The name of the Berlin neighborhood she came from, never mind the factory where her father worked, should have been enough to switch off his attention. Instead, Tiedemann further confused Magda by bursting into an unmistakably delighted laugh.

"Intelligent, reserved and fearless: who cares about typing speeds with qualities like those? So, you hail from Oberschöneweide? Such a fascinating place. Perhaps not quite as street-thumpingly left-wing in its politics as 'Red Wedding' claims to be, but a hotbed of socialism nonetheless. What is it they say about your district? Ah yes: 'Never walk through it wearing a brown shirt: even the babes in their prams are trained to attack.'"

His response was completely unexpected; Magda had to bite her lip rather than risk the smile that was pulling at her mouth. Everyone in Oberschöneweide was deeply proud of their commitment to keeping fascism off their streets, and also of that saying—and the National Socialist bully-boy brownshirts had felt the force of it and learned to beware.

Frau Kuechler, however, was far less entertained and broke into a horrified coughing fit. Tiedemann poured her a glass of water and passed her his handkerchief—a square of white silk the directress clasped to her chest as if it was an icon—but he kept his gaze on Magda.

"So, Fräulein. I assume from the information that you chose to share, out of all the things that you could, and from the way you keep frowning at my lapel, that you're no lover of the Party?"

The Party. Magda hated the way he said it, as if there was no other. She hated more that he was right. No matter the old loyalties her family and friends clung to, the rise of National Socialism had meant the end of democracy in Germany. In the two years since their leader Adolf Hitler had swept to power in 1933, all opposition to the fascists' way of defining the world had been banned. The German Communist Party, the KDP—which drew huge support throughout Berlin's working-class neighborhoods, such as Wedding and Oberschöneweide—was the regime's first victim. Magda was fully aware that to admit to having any trace of socialist sympathies, or any ties, no matter how slender, to what was now a banned and underground organization, was a dangerous act. The question she had just been asked, therefore, was a loaded one, and both she and Tiedemann knew it. Magda also knew, given his political affiliation and—as was clear from the fresh bunch of edelweiss placed beside the photograph of Hitler on the sideboard—Frau Kuechler's, that a cautious answer was the only sensible one to offer. Given, however, that Magda had no intention of ever seeing him again, that wasn't the one she gave.

"No, I am not. I can't be. I was brought up to believe in equality. In the same laws and standards applying to everyone in our country, regardless of their religion or their politics. But that view, unfortunately, doesn't seem to be the National Socialist way. From what I can see, the Party only believes in two kinds of people: the ones who are the same as them, and the rest." She stopped, conscious she was slipping into a more dangerous speech than she had initially intended.

Tiedemann, however, was looking at her so intently, it was as if the rest of the room had disappeared.

"Go on, Magda. There's more you want to say—I can see it in your face. Whatever it is, I want to hear it, trust me."

Trust me. It was an odd choice of words. Even odder was that Magda realized, in that moment, that she did.

Tell him what you really think, what everyone who matters to you would expect you to say.

She kept her eyes firmly on his as she continued.

"All right. Then I should have said that there are three kinds, not two: the ones who are the same as them, who are the most important group; the ones they haven't persuaded to their way of thinking yet, who they tolerate for now; and Jewish people. I hate a lot of the things Hitler and his party stand for, but I really hate the way he and his cronies talk about Jewish people. As if they're not people but *other*, as if they're inhuman. It's not right to treat anyone that way. So, no. I'm no fan of the Party. I'm better than that."

It was a brave speech, and, however Tiedemann chose to respond, Magda was proud of it. Before he could say anything, however, Frau Kuechler roared in.

"Fräulein Aderbach, you will apologize for your rudeness at once." The directress was no longer coy—she was bristling with fury. "Herr Tiedemann, I am mortified that one of our students could address you in such an insolent way. I hope that you won't judge us all by her appalling behavior. And I will, of course, find another candidate for your vacancy immediately. This one is clearly unsuitable."

Herr Tiedemann shook his head. "No, Madame, you won't. There is no other candidate. This one's my girl."

His attention was all on Magda. When the directress started to argue, he flicked her protests away. Magda didn't understand what was going on, but she knew instinctively that there was far more to Walther Tiedemann than the façade he presented. When he smiled at her this time, the warmth in his face far outshone his badge.

"He used those exact words—*this one's my girl*? Even though you told him you loathed Hitler?"

"Not just Hitler, 'all his cronies' too." Magda grinned across the kitchen table at Christoph. "Honestly, I was as surprised as you are when he didn't bawl me out. When I saw his lapel pin, I had him down as a fully paid-up Party lover. But now . . ." She stopped, unsure how to finish. Her sense that Walther Tiedemann was far more than he seemed was still too unformed to put into words.

Christoph stopped checking the collated pamphlets off on his list and frowned. "But now what? You've fallen for his playboy charms?"

Magda wasn't sure if it was her father Ernst's low whistle or her clenched jaw that Christoph caught first. Whichever it was, he fell over himself to apologize.

"That was uncalled for. I'm sorry. And I get that it's an amazing offer—you could never earn a salary as high as the one he's offering you working at the Oberspree. But it's hard to reconcile what I know of him, and what I know of you, and this." He gestured to the stacks of pamphlets covering the table and the long list of drop-off points, all of which were potentially under surveillance, all of which the four of them—Magda, Christoph, and her parents —would deliver whatever the risk.

It was hard to argue with his reasoning. Magda might not be convinced any more that Walther Tiedemann was devoted to Hitler, but it was still too big a stretch to imagine him sitting down with his morning coffee and opening a copy of *The Red Flag*. Back in her own home, and away from Tiedemann's warm gaze, it was easier to see what Christoph saw—the National Socialist-supporting businessman denouncing the entire Aderbach household for keeping copies of the banned newspaper in their home.

And if he knew we weren't only reading it but were the core of the network responsible for distributing it throughout the city...

Her father cut in as if he could read Magda's thoughts. "Do you think he's got wind of what we're doing here?" He fastened his last bundle and pushed it over to Christoph. "We've taken every precaution I can think of, but anyone could be an informer. Anyone could have leaked that it's us acting as the Berlin distribution hub. Could Tiedemann be using you as the bait to reel in bigger fish?"

Magda's first impulse was to dismiss the idea that Tiedemann was working for the Party to root out resistance—or that she could possibly figure on anyone's radar as a troublemaker—as ridiculous. For all her brave words at the interview, she was not, yet, a fully active member of the anti-fascist resistance. Magda, to her annoyance, was kept so far on the edge of the activities her parents and Christoph were engaged in, she was practically in a different country. She was little more than a bag-carrier when it came to distributing the pamphlets, staying in the shadows while Christoph knocked out the night's codes on the faithful's doors. Every word of the beliefs she had so determinedly explained to Walther Tiedemann were, however, true: Magda had been raised in a household that was dedicated to building a world that was fair.

Ernst Aderbach had emerged from the horrors of the Great War as a pacifist, and his wife Herthe shared his ideals. They both believed that the devastation wrought by the war could only be atoned for if a kinder, more just way of life came out of it, and they were both determined to do whatever they could to create that. Magda's childhood meals had been eaten at a table littered with protest leaflets. She had gone to sleep soothed not by lullabies but by voices rising and falling as arguments over galloping inflation and war reparations and the possibility of rebellion flared in the kitchen below. *How can we make life better for everyone?* was the rhythm of her home, and all those around it. And then Hitler stormed into power with his brown-shirted thugs and his black-uniformed security police and fear became her streets' new pulse. Old friends came to the house less often, and only under the cover of night. Discussions became quiet things, muffled by drawn blinds and locked doors. Magda walked into conversations spiked with *resistance units* and *how best to fight back* and her once too talkative father clammed up.

"It's not because he doesn't trust you; it's to keep you safe."

Her mother had offered that apology after Magda had spent a wound-up night complaining about being kept in the dark, and being kept away from the fight against the fascist movement she had been brought up to loathe.

"These are dangerous times, Magda, especially for people who think the way that we do. Every leaflet we write or pamphlet we deliver could send us to jail. Every strike your father agitates for could end up with him being beaten, or worse. There are watchers everywhere. Even the children, God help them, are taught to tell tales and ruin their families. If Kiefer was to find out the half of what we are doing…"

Herthe hadn't been able to complete the sentence; she hadn't needed to. Both women knew all too well what she meant.

Magda had forced herself to stop asking, but she hadn't stopped listening, or wanting to play her part. Her father might not want her marching in the street, but he couldn't argue with her getting her secretarial qualifications and working her way up through the union ranks he respected. He couldn't argue if she was the one organizing the strikes to improve wages and conditions. She had been prepared to study and work and wait for as long as it took to show him that she wasn't a child anymore, but a capable and brave and trustworthy woman. And then Ernst had brought Christoph Traube home one snowy night in December 1934 and Magda was no longer prepared to wait for anything at all.

The attraction between the two of them was immediate. Herthe had climbed into bed with Ernst, after a meal full of discussion and laughter that had made them feel both nostalgic and twenty years younger, and prophesied a wedding. Christoph was passionate about politics and a born raconteur. Ernst was too entertained by his junior manager's enthusiasm to hush him, especially as Magda's younger brother Kiefer was away for the night. As for Magda, she had never met a man with such life in him. Christoph was only two years older than her, but he had packed so much living into that extra time that Magda wasn't sure at first if the emotion pinking her cheeks was pleasure or jealousy.

Everyone in the Aderbachs' circle, including Magda, nursed romantic dreams of traveling to Russia, even though the country was secretive and largely unknown outside the myths they wove round it. None of them had ever been, but Christoph had. He had spent a year at the International Lenin School in Moscow and was, therefore, the nearest thing anyone in Oberschöneweide had to an authority on the country's workings.

Magda also nursed dreams about fighting injustice. They were still dreams, but Christoph had already organized strikes against grasping bosses in a dozen factories and written a sheaf of articles for *The Red Flag*, and far older men than him sought out his advice. By the time he left the house that night, Magda was dizzy from talking and arguing and laughing, and headfirst in the middle of an infatuation that was clearly returned. That had matured over the six months since their first meeting into love. And that had finally brought Magda at least into the fringes of the resistance work against Hitler and his party that she was desperate to do.

Which Father will ban me from if he scents danger.

Mindful of that, Magda added her last stack to the tally pile and shook her head.

"It's possible, I suppose, although he could find a far better lure than me if that was his plan. But no, I don't think that's what Tiedemann's doing. I don't think he works for the Party, not in the way you mean. When I told him that I hated the way Hitler treats anyone who opposes him, especially the way he threatens anyone who is Jewish, I sensed he felt the same." She stopped as Ernst snorted. "But I'll take care around him, of course I will, the same as I've always taken care around the teachers and the other girls at the college. I know how to keep my mouth shut."

"We know that." Christoph stood up and began packing the bundles into a suitcase. "And this job could be useful. We've been trying to get a contact inside Tiedemann's Spandau complex for months. If you could get our message into their—"

"What are those?"

No one had heard the kitchen door open. No one had noticed Kiefer standing in the doorway in his brown Hitler Youth jacket and red swastika armband.

Everyone moved at once. Christoph swept the last pamphlets into the case and snapped the lid shut. Herthe put herself between Kiefer and the table and began bombarding him with questions about his cut-short night. Magda leaped up and started rummaging around the cupboards for her brother's favorite *lebkuchen*, keeping up a running commentary as she searched for the biscuit tin. Anything to divert him, and the danger his new loyalties carried. Only Ernst stayed where he was, deliberately refusing to look at his son.

Kiefer took no notice of any of them.

"I could see red and black writing, and a hammer. Are they *communist* leaflets?" The sneer underpinning the word was unmistakable.

"And what would you do if they were? Report your whole family? See us all marched away to a camp?" Ernst had finally turned to face his son. It was obvious from his clenched fists that he was trying for menace, but the pacifist in him won and all Magda could hear was his pain.

"Father, don't. There's nothing to be gained from fighting." She wanted to add *because Kiefer will enjoy it*, but she held her tongue. There was too much at stake to risk a confrontation. Whatever lessons in tolerance Kiefer had learned in his home had long since been buried under the weight of classroom propaganda. He was all bright-eyed and twitching now and scenting disloyalty, watching the four of them as if they were strangers he would happily crush. Fired up with the oath he had sworn on joining the Hitler Youth to denounce any trace of anti-Party behavior, no matter the source, no matter the consequences.

"You overestimate how interesting we are." Christoph caught Magda's eye and dropped the closed suitcase onto the table. "Have a look inside if you want. What you saw were instruction manuals for a new electric motor the Cable Works has bought from the Tiedemann Company. Where your sister has just got a job by the way." Kiefer stopped in the act of reaching for the case. "She's going to work directly for the main man himself, as one of his secretaries."

"For Walther Tiedemann?" Kiefer stepped back from the table and stared at Magda. "Really? But he's one of the Party's biggest supporters. And he's friends with Himmler, the Chief of Police. He spoke to me once, at the SS headquarters in Prinz Albrecht Straße when my youth group went there on a tour. He's really cool, and crazy rich." Kiefer's eyes were still shining, but he had forgotten all about the case. "When you start work, do you think I could meet him?"

Magda felt Christoph's hand slip into hers and she nodded. "Of course." That was all she could manage—the sight of her adored little brother dressed in an enemy uniform, trying to be a man at fifteen, and the thought of her new employer hobnobbing with the SS had choked up her throat.

Kiefer, however, was happy and distracted and went to bed full of "how loyal this proves my family is." Everyone held on to their rigid smiles until he left the room.

"Well, you've thrilled our Hitler-lover. Which should be a warning."

Magda spun round, ready to snap back at her father, but his face was crumpled and old and shouting her frustration at him would have been too cruel.

"He'll grow out of it, Papa; he'll come back to us. And Tiedemann isn't who you think he is. I don't know how I know that, but I do." She stopped. She was trying to knit certainties out of mist.

Not even Christoph could conjure up a reply.

When I saw his lapel pin, I had him down as a fully paid-up Party lover.

If Magda had ever needed an argument in favor of trusting her first instincts, Walther Tiedemann was it. It had taken her six months to rise from the typing pool she had joined in June 1935 to the management secretarial floor. It had taken a further six to snag the position as his personal assistant, the holy grail she'd been aiming for since she'd been accepted into the company. She had sat at the desk in the office adjoining his on her first day in her new role, eager to renew her acquaintance with the Herr Tiedemann who had interviewed her. He had breezed in full of smiles. He had been charming, overflowing with appreciative comments about her unerring eye for detail and her faultless hard work. Twelve months later, he was still charming and still appreciative, but that was it. As far as Magda was concerned, Herr Tiedemann had proved himself to be not so much a man of hidden depths as a crushing disappointment. And his workers had proved as hard to get close to as their boss: every tentative approach Magda had made to interest them in the socialist cause had met with shrugs.

The man who had looked into her eyes and said "trust me" had disappeared back behind his swastika pin. Whatever sympathy for a more tolerant world Magda had glimpsed in him at the college had never resurfaced. The man she worked for and the man he presented to the world were cut from exactly the same cloth: that of a committed and loyal National Socialist member. His check stubs were fat with donations to the Party's various money-grabbing initiatives. His diary was stiff with the Party's grandees. Magda filled its spaces each week with a roll call of the Führer's inner circle. Lunches hosted by Hitler's secretary Martin Bormann. Dinners with Propaganda Minister Goebbels. Drinks with the Führer himself. Magda juggled Tiedemann's business and social appointments along a network of contacts she had hoped—against all the evidence—he did not really mix with, a network that stretched through each of the Reich's multiplying ministries. Tiedemann's appetite for involvement at the heart of them all was, apparently, tireless. One name, however, appeared with more frequency than any of the others: Reichsführer-SS Heinrich Himmler.

Himmler was, according to Magda's boss, obsessed by organization—how processes could be streamlined and made more efficient; how money could be saved. He was, therefore, a frequent visitor to the Spandau factory complex, taking endless tours and drilling Walther. "Picking the country's best industrial brain," as Himmler himself always extravagantly put it.

Given his position as head of the *Schutzstaffel*—or the SS as they were better known, the Party's brutal private army that, by 1937, operated outside any codes of behavior most Germans would recognize—Magda had expected Himmler to be a fearsome figure. She knew—because he had told her—that, since he had taken over the SS in 1929, Himmler had built the organization from being essentially Hitler's bodyguard into an elite force of over 50,000 men. She also knew that his ministerial responsibilities extended to control over the Gestapo, the Party's equally brutal and all-powerful secret police.

The first time she had entered the Reichsführer's name into the daily diary as a visitor, her stomach had flipped. The man who climbed out of the gleaming Mercedes, and waited for the factory's management to line up in grateful rows was, however, completely nondescript. He was paunchy and bow-legged and slightly hunched over. He blinked over his spectacles in a manner more suited to a hesitant schoolteacher than one of the Party's rising stars. Despite his best efforts to grow a distracting mustache, his chin was receding, as was his voice: he shouted rather than spoke, but the volume added no substance to his words. He was also—as Magda realized when he took her hand in his damp one and labored his way through an overdone compliment—a fumbling boy around women. Magda couldn't understand how such an insignificant man could have risen as high, and as quickly, as Himmler had. As the rest of the factory fawned, she had felt—as she described the day later to Christoph—like the child in *The Emperor's New Clothes*, desperate to shout out, "But why can't you see what he really is?"

Walther Tiedemann clearly couldn't. As well as their shared fascination in the minutiae of workplace organization, the men were close neighbors in Grunewald, and Tiedemann—adding another black mark to his increasing tally—devoted hours to courting Himmler's favor. The activities Magda was asked to coordinate caterers and florists for were never-ending. Card-playing evenings at Tiedemann's Winkler Straße villa, luncheon parties on the lake shore at nearby Krumme Lanke, and, on one memorable occasion, an elaborate masked ball in the rose gardens of the summer palace on Pfaueninsel, an island in the River Havel reserved for Party use. Whatever the occasion, or the numbers gathered, the title "guest of honor" always appeared by Himmler's name. And every socialite and film star and businessman who made it onto the coveted guest lists boasted a pedigree that was, at Himmler's insistence, resolutely "German."

"What did you expect? A whole tribe of Israels and Samuels and Blumensteins driving up to the hallowed gates? You've been working for the playboy too long. Maybe there's still some rich Jewish residents left in Grunewald, but I'm pretty certain they're as banned as the poor ones from anything approaching a life. Unless, of course, that's the one place in Berlin not plastered with signs proclaiming *Jews Forbidden* and everyone's running round holding hands."

Magda had managed to bite back her angry response to Christoph's sarcasm, although she'd had to walk away from him to do it. His mood nowadays was permanently raw, his good temper frayed from the six months he'd spent imprisoned in Berlin's Columbia House for protesting against the Nuremberg Laws, a set of decrees that cruelly defined what being Jewish meant. Although Christoph was tight-lipped about the time he had spent there, the prison—which was run by the Gestapo and housed mainly communists and Jews—was notorious for its vicious interrogation methods. Magda had seen the ragged scars on his back, which he had admitted had been carved into it with lead-tipped whips. And the lightning flashes branded into his upper arm. After what he had suffered, she could bear a little sarcasm. Besides, Christoph was right: Grunewald was no better in its treatment of its Jewish population than most of Berlin. Although some of the stately villas that graced its streets were still in the hands of the Jewish families who had lived in them since the colony was founded, their owners were not faring well.

The racial laws passed by the Party in 1935 had split Germany's Jewish population off from the rest of their countrymen as effectively as a wall. Jews were no longer classed as citizens. Jews were no longer allowed to marry outside the rigid classifications they had been forced into, which had nothing to do with Jewish customs or beliefs and everything to do with hatred. Jews were no longer allowed to work in the civil service or medicine or in any branch of education. The shops they owned were no longer frequented; their children were no longer welcome in the schools that had previously admitted them; parks and cinemas and swimming pools no longer opened their doors. The only thing rich Jews could do that poor ones couldn't was to pay the huge fees the Party demanded from them to emigrate, and they could only do that if they could persuade anyone in a rapidly retreating world to take them in.

Some areas fought back and tried to protect their neighbors, at least in the early days—Oberschöneweide among them—but most rolled over. Grunewald, at least from what Magda had gathered by listening closely to her boss's conversations, had capitulated quickly, perhaps because of the high numbers of Party officials who had flocked to the suburb's clean air and elevated social status.

Before she knew the area, everything Magda had heard about Grunewald's forests and lakes and palace-like villas had made the place sound magical. When she had first joined the Tiedemann Company in 1935, she had longed for an invitation to Tiedemann's famous Winkler Straβe villa. After a year of organizing guest lists whose names made her skin crawl, however, Magda had long lost the desire to go. She had also long lost the desire to work for her famous boss. So, when he did finally summon her to his home, on a Friday in May 1937—to drop off papers for signing that were too urgent to await his return from a last-minute trip—Magda realized that she was more on edge than excited. She sat on the train worrying about who she might meet, with *Why don't you resign?* running through her head and, for the first time, sticking there.

Nothing about the day she spent in Grunewald turned out to be magical. The tree-lined streets and pastel-colored mansions were certainly beautiful, but the swastika-crested Mercedes idling outside them muted their charms. Within five minutes of exiting the train station, whose flower-hung archway was reminiscent of a castle, Magda had seen more *Jews Forbidden* signs stuck on benches and park gates and shop doorways than she cared to count. More chilling even than those were the guards stationed outside the Goldschmidt Jewish School in Hagenstraße and the nervous children being hurried up the steps by teachers who as good as sniffed the air for danger. When she mentioned the strangeness of guards outside a school to the maid who answered Tiedemann's door, and was told that Himmler refused to let his chauffeur drive in that direction from his house in the same street, Magda could have wept.

The Winkler Straße villa was a three-story confection of lemon paintwork and white stucco work that billowed around the walls like whipped-up meringue. Magda had walked up the driveway trying not to think about Hansel and Gretel. Once Tiedemann had explained that his extended weekend vacation would be spent at Hitler's Bavarian mountain retreat, the *Why don't you resign?* that had been tormenting her quickly turned into *You must.* After his revelation, Magda had refused his offer of tea or a tour of the house. She had hovered instead in the freesia-soaked hallway, her hand outstretched for the signed papers. If Tiedemann was offended by her lack of interest in his hospitality, he didn't show it. Magda wouldn't have cared if he had.

The paperwork completed, she had burst back out of the house desperate for fresher air. The afternoon was still early; the sun was still warm. Her map showed an easy walk down Koenigsallee to the Krumme Lanke and her shoes were sturdy ones. She set off imagining crystal-clear water and a quiet lake shore and was soon inside the fringes of a wood filled with the spikily fresh scents of mint and pine. The ground was carpeted with a mix of purple and white flowers she was too much of a city girl to recognize but knew would make a bouquet her mother would love.

Magda was so absorbed in her picking and wandering, she didn't notice she had reached a row of houses until the grass under her feet gave way to gravel. She stopped, thinking she had taken the wrong path and accidentally walked out of the forest. The little enclave of houses she had stumbled into, however, was nestled inside the bower made by the trees' branches as if they had been deliberately hidden there. The crescents they occupied were peaceful and, on the surface, beautiful, and yet…

She looked at the map she had brought with her, but there was no mention of a housing estate. There was, however, a signpost a few steps away from where she was standing. Unable to pinpoint why she felt uneasy, Magda walked toward it, hoping to get her bearings.

The first thing that struck her was that the houses edging the neatly swept roads were completely different to the deliberately distinctive villas surrounding Tiedemann's. Unlike those, these homes were all identical in shape and size, were painted a uniform pale cream, and had swooping roofs and gabled windows set off with green wooden shutters. They wouldn't have looked out of place in an Alpine-set folk tale, except each of them was flying a swastika flag from a pole on its neatly clipped lawn. There was also a swastika and an eagle carved onto the top of the signpost.

Magda peered up at the street names picked out in a flowing gothic script. *The Loyalty Path, The Ancestral Way, The Führer Platz.* She stopped reading.

As she stepped back, her neck prickling, she stubbed her heel on a sharp stone and cried out. A dog immediately began barking and throwing itself against a fence in a frenzy of leaden thumps and clashing chains that made Magda's whole body shiver. She gave up any thought of the lake and sped back instead through trees that no longer looked welcoming and into the first station she stumbled across, desperate for the city's busy pavements and people. Two weeks later, when Himmler, demanding her company and her notepad on a factory visit, began extolling the wonders of the SS estate he had designed and had built in the Grunewald forest, whose model he intended to be "the pure heart of all our future communities," she knew her time in Tiedemann's employment was done.

Which is why I need to finish my letter and go.

Magda had started writing her resignation letter the night of her Winkler Straße visit, but it was still sitting in her bag. It was stilted and overly formal, citing family reasons for her leaving. It didn't say what she wanted it to say: that she was done working for a man with no morals.

Which I could write if I wanted—it's not like I need him, or care a fig about his feelings. And getting closer to his Nazi friends can't do my family any good. I don't imagine Himmler would be particularly impressed with where, or who, I'm from.

Magda put down her pen and glanced at the clock. It was 4:45 p.m. Her work was completed; Tiedemann was gone for the day. She could write her letter, leave it on his desk, and be done. And she could say whatever she chose. She didn't need a reference—there was a job waiting for her at the Cable Works whenever she wanted it. She would miss the salary but not enough to swallow her contempt and stay. She wouldn't miss the commute between Oberschöneweide and Spandau, which could take up to an hour each way and had made her bones ache in the winter when the winds swept so much ice through Berlin even the stones throbbed with cold. And she would not miss Walther Tiedemann, with his too bright smile and his too thick charm and his nonexistent conscience.

Filled with an energy she hadn't felt for weeks, Magda jumped up and ran to the cupboard where she stowed her handbag during the day. Ten minutes typing and she would be free. She was laughing when she pulled the bag out, imagining the relief on her father's face when she told him. Although Ernst had understood Christoph's desire to get one of their people into the factory, he had never been happy that Magda had taken the Tiedemann job and put herself into the danger he had feared that would involve.

As the businessman was photographed more and more often at the center of Party circles, Ernst's worries had only increased.

Well, tonight he can celebrate!

That was all Magda was thinking about as she opened her bag. When she dumped its contents out because she couldn't immediately find the letter and was impatient to be gone. She wasn't, unfortunately, thinking about what should have been at the front of her mind: that she had spent the previous night slipping in and out of the shadows in Friedrichshain and Prenzlauer Berg pushing anti-Party leaflets through letter boxes. She had forgotten that—when the three low whistles alerting her to a patrol had rippled down the street—she had stuffed the last two leaflets into her bag and hadn't removed them again when she ran home, as exhilarated as she was frightened by the close call. She hadn't remembered that mistake at all. Until the office door suddenly swung open. And a flimsy sheet bearing the slogan *Support Your Jewish Brothers* sailed off the cupboard and danced down onto Walther Tiedemann's expensively shod feet.

"My office, now."

He had the leaflet, and he was blocking her exit. With no other option, Magda did as she was told. Tiedemann followed her and locked the heavy door behind them. Magda didn't sit. She assumed the SS, or the Gestapo, or whoever he chose to call, would come for her quickly.

"You don't care for me very much, do you?"

The question caught Magda—whose head was full of how to keep her parents and Christoph safe from whatever trouble she was in—completely off guard. Her mouth flared into action before her brain could catch up.

"No, I don't. I don't care for you at all."

And there it was again, that smile that had fooled her two years ago. As unexpected now as it had been then. Magda resolved not to be swayed by it this time.

"Do you want to tell me why?"

He hadn't reached for the telephone yet. That didn't mean he wouldn't.

But so what if he does? You're finished, so why stay silent now? Why not tell him the truth, the way you were going to do in the letter, especially if it stops him asking about who else is involved?

Tiedemann had sat down. He looked perfectly at ease. Magda decided to copy him. She pulled out a chair and took her time settling into it. She wanted to get these words right.

"Okay then. I don't like you because I thought you were a better man, and you're not." She paused to gauge his reaction. He carried on silently watching her. "When you interviewed me, when I made it clear how I felt about the Party, and its treatment of Jewish people, I thought I detected some sympathy in you that outweighed the badge you were wearing. I was wrong. You've sold yourself to the National Socialists body and soul. You might as well be wearing a uniform." She stopped. He wasn't smiling anymore, but he didn't look angry either.

I can't read him. I haven't a clue what he's thinking.

His next question confirmed that instinct was right.

"I presume you organize your leafleting and whatever other activities you engage in through small cells, where a tight bond of trust is essential. How long does it take you to build that? How long is it before your organization, whatever form it exists in, takes someone new on board?"

"Years." Magda had answered him immediately again—there was a calmness in his manner that was disarming. And, once again, she had told him the truth. She decided, therefore, to carry on. "I was on the fringes for a long time before I was allowed to even sit in on discussions or do the most menial tasks, although everyone involved knew me. It was over a year after that before I was allowed to be active, and that was only because—" She stopped. She had been about to say *because my boyfriend was imprisoned and I was the only one close enough to step into his shoes.* That, however, was too intimate and too dangerous to share; she settled instead for, "Because there was a gap I was best placed to fill."

"Years." Tiedemann nodded. "I hoped you would say that. It means you are not as impulsive, or careless, as dropping this leaflet suggests." He picked it up from the desk where he had put it and turned the cheap paper over, scanning the headline and the long list of names printed on both sides. "*Support Your Jewish Brothers.* It's a worthy sentiment, but, with all these addresses you've given, it's also a perfect shopping list for the SS. There won't be a single one of these businesses still standing by the end of the week."

The words sounded as if he was making a threat; the tone didn't. The thought that he could be right—that they could have accidentally been doing the SS's work for them—stole Magda's voice. Tiedemann carried on.

"There are better ways to help, Magda—ones with more meaningful results. There's definitely no future in encouraging people to cling on to their livelihoods for a few more fear-filled months. Nothing is going to get better: the Party hates Jewish blood too much to return Germany to tolerance." He shook his head as she started to speak. "I know you know that; I'm not trying to patronize you. But what you can't know, unless you walk in their midst the way I do, is the depth of that hatred. The race laws are only the start of this separating out—there's a purge coming, all of them hint at it, which is going to run deeper than restrictions on schools and marriage. People can't afford to live their old lives anymore; they're no use to them. They need new ones they can be safe in." He took a key out of his inside pocket and unlocked the top drawer of his desk. "That is what they need help with, from those of us able to provide it. Here, take a look."

The document he pushed toward her was a worker's identity card for Tiedemann Factories, made out in the name of Konrad Bauer. It carried a photograph of a serious-looking young man, together with his address, the date and place of his birth and the day he had started his employment. It was no different to a dozen others Magda had seen.

"I don't understand. Why are you showing me this?"

Tiedemann smiled. "Because it's good, isn't it? You couldn't tell it apart from the cards all our workers carry, but it's a forgery." Tiedemann picked the card back up and returned it to the drawer. "Herr Bauer was born Daniel Aaronsohn. He isn't from Munich —he's never been there, or to the tenement address where this says he currently lives in Neukölln. But the people who do live there will vouch for him if needed. And everyone in his section has a forged identity, including his manager, which means he will keep his job when the prohibitions against Jews shift down from the professions to the factories, which, believe me, they will."

"Why have you done this for him?"

There were a dozen other questions crowding Magda's tongue as she tried to make sense of what Tiedemann seemed—so improbably— to be doing, but that was the first she could settle on.

Tiedemann shrugged. "Because he's one of my best workers. His production rate sets the standard for everyone else. And he's a good man—they all are. Why should I lose any of them because the fanatics in power are obsessed with 'pure blood'?"

The fanatics in power? Magda was beginning to wonder if she had dreamed the last two years.

"But aren't you worried about the danger? Anyone could report this."

Tiedemann took another document out of the drawer.

"The men who work for me wouldn't. Besides, is that what matters—being worried? Are you worried when you post your leaflets? Enough to stop I mean? And are you worried when you stand in front of Himmler and can barely conceal how much you dislike him?" He smiled as Magda blushed. "Don't. I admire you for it, and he thinks you are quiet and aloof around him because you are overawed, which flatters his gossamer ego. You are, however, going to have to learn to hide your feelings better if you are going to be of use to me, and also not a danger to those you love."

Before Magda could ask what on earth that meant, he pushed a second document across the desk. This one was headed *The American Consul in Berlin* and was a visa application for entry into the U.S. made out in the names of the Lechenich family of Bettinastraβe, Grunewald.

"A lovely family, and old friends of mine. The father is one of the best perfumiers in Berlin and the son is a talented violinist who could have had his pick of the city's orchestras. But their prospects are gone, and their property is under threat, and they cannot stay. Hopefully, the visas will come through before this year's quota to enter the United States is filled up, or before the Party finds some new way to relieve them of all of their savings. If not, well, there are still strings I can pull to set things faster in motion."

"Why are you doing all this?" Magda had finally recovered her voice and the questions came pouring out. "Why are you helping people everyone you mix with hates? And why are you mixing with those men at all if this is what you actually care about? How can you play cards with Himmler and spend your weekends with Hitler and then tell me about the Jewish workers you have rescued? How am I supposed to know which side of you is real?"

"Because you already do—because you knew two years ago, the same way I knew who you really were." Tiedemann folded the application form up and dropped it back inside his desk. "Whatever is different in our lives, I was raised the same as you. To believe that every life is precious and deserves to be treated the same. To believe that nobody is worth more than anyone else on the basis of birthplace or wealth or blood, or any of the other worthless excuses men think up to put themselves higher than they ought to be. As to why I am doing this? Does there have to be only one reason? Do you have one burning emotion that drives you? Or are you the same as me? Reacting to injustice from a muddle of fury and disbelief, and fear of what worse things could follow?"

Everything he said made sense. Everything he said had been expressed a dozen times around her family's kitchen table. But he still hadn't explained how he could live so comfortably inside the hornets' nest, and Magda needed answers to it all.

"I agree with all that. I resist, on what small level I do, because I don't have a choice if I want to look at myself in the mirror. But I'm not a hypocrite. I don't seek out the circles that sicken me. I don't embrace them."

For the first time since she had dropped the leaflet, Tiedemann frowned.

"Where do you think it's easier to get information from, Magda? From inside and close up, or from miles away? And who do you think gets scrutinized the closest—the friend or the foe?" He stopped and sighed, and rubbed at a face that had suddenly grown weary. "I don't expect you to answer. I don't expect you to be impressed. I didn't start all this because I'm a saint. If anything, I was a fool. I'm a businessman, driven by bottom lines and profit. After 1933, if I wanted my factories to stay in work, I had to work with the Party, so that is what I did. I didn't give it much thought at first—I thought they were all slogans and bluster. But then I got closer, and I didn't like anything I saw. They are evil men, and, as close as I am, I don't think I've grasped half of what they are capable of. Maybe I should have taken a stand—I thought about it—but what if they had shut me down? What if all my workers had lost their jobs? Maybe I'm a coward, trying to justify the road I chose, but I *embraced* them, as you put it, to learn them, to see where I could get around them. It's come at a price, believe me—being with men whose values are as twisted as Himmler's corrodes a little piece of your soul. But if it means I can help decent men keep their jobs and old friends get to safety, close is where I have to be."

It was clear from the sudden lift in his voice that he was telling the truth.

He is who I thought he was, who I said he was. He wants to live in the same world that I do.

The realization that she hadn't been wrong about him, and that he had allowed her finally to see behind his mask again, took her breath away. She wanted to laugh, and to curse him for keeping secrets. She wanted to spill out all the frustrations his hiding had caused her. All she could manage, however, was a rather shaky, "How do you do it?"

Tiedemann had turned away from Magda to stare out of the window across the factory complex's maze of sheds and chimneys. His eyes when he focused back on her were bleary and tired; she had to fight the urge to grab hold of his hand and pat it.

"How do you fight the corrosion?"

His face finally relaxed.

"I surround myself with the right people. People who I watch for a long time, and who I disappoint for a long time, until I know them down to their core. And then, if they haven't completely given up on me, I warn them that there is going to be far more to do than has already been done, and I let them in."

This isn't leaflets and dodging from patrols in dark streets. This is the eye of the storm. This is dangerous beyond any level I've known if I choose it. And not just to me.

But this is real; this could matter.

Magda only realized she was smiling when Tiedemann looked into her eyes and smiled back.

CHAPTER THREE

Nina, July 1984

It was a short shopping list—an inkpad, a set of rubber letter stamps, and two pads of paper—but Nina still went to three different shops to collect them. *Keep your head down and don't attract attention.* She had been listening to that lesson for as long as she could remember. At ten, its meaning—that *curious and questioning* meant *difficult and troublesome*—had been hard to follow. By sixteen, however, Nina had learned the lesson's value, although the way she chose to apply it as she made her careful purchases was definitely not what her parents and teachers had intended.

"Why can't you be a good girl? Why do you have to go looking for trouble?"

Britte's voice chimed through Nina's head as she pushed the coins across the counter and picked up the paper, being careful to mention the long essay she had to write in case anyone cared. She had heard that complaint from her mother as often as the instruction to *keep your head down*; the two usually went together.

At least this time I'd deserve it.

The thought brought Nina no more pleasure than knowing that, six years ago when all her problems had started, she hadn't been looking for trouble at all.

What do a GDR shop assistant and an astronaut have in common? They both work in empty space.

It was a joke. A not particularly funny one perhaps, but it was still nothing more than a joke that ten-year-old Nina had overheard one sunny afternoon in the park and retold the next day in the classroom. She had barely understood what she was saying; she had been far too innocent to worry if a teacher was listening. The only thing in her head was that the joke was about space, and everyone in her school in 1978 was obsessed with space because the East German cosmonaut Sigmund Jähn had become the first German to fly there. Jähn had been declared a national hero and every lesson for a week had been shaped around him and his exploits. So Nina, as obsessed as the rest of her country, had told a joke she assumed would be met with gales of laughter. Six years later, its telling still haunted her.

"Who told it to you? One name and this all goes away."

Principal Huber had asked her to "reveal her source" as he put it kindly at first, before he lost his temper and called her a "disgrace." Then her teachers had tried to persuade her, and then her parents, and finally her classmates when they were all given detention, "because one person hurting our country hurts us all." Nina's honest response—that she couldn't give up a name she didn't have—fell on deaf ears. And then her exasperated, "You're all such miseries; when I'm big enough, I'm getting out of here and going back to our big house in the West," fell on angry and shocked ones.

In the end, Magda had stepped in and used her good name to prevent her granddaughter gaining a bad one. It was her clenched face and hissed, "Don't you dare mention that damn place ever again," that had, however, frightened Nina into silence and then into the apologies everyone was demanding. Thanks to Magda's intervention, the detentions stopped, but the sin clung. Nina—unnerved by her grandmother's fury—tried her best to do what everyone wanted and consider the consequences before she opened her mouth. When one teacher after another had snapped that "her kind of questions weren't wanted," she stopped putting up her hand and annoying them. When her history lessons descended, as they always did, into *East is good and West is bad*, she learned to bite her lip. None of it mattered. Nina worked hard and kept quiet, but none of her papers ever received a grade higher than a very low C again, even though she knew they deserved better.

Eventually, after all her hard work and, mostly, spotless behavior had brought nothing but poor grades and black marks, Nina stopped listening. She went through the motions of being a good citizen. She saluted the GDR flag and parroted the GDR slogan *The Party, The Party Is Always Right,* along with her classmates on May Day and GDR Founding Day and Anniversary of the Russian Revolution Day. She still didn't understand how the German fascists who had wreaked havoc all across Europe in World War Two had come only from the West and never from the East, even though Germany had been all one country then. She didn't waste her time asking anyone the reason for that, not even her grandmother, who still wouldn't discuss the war, and her own part in it. She also didn't understand why the old gray men who ran the GDR were obsessed with building nuclear weapons, although they maintained that war was a horror the West wanted to unleash on the world, not them. She had no one to ask about that either. Above all, she made sure never to mention the big house in the West again. That didn't stop her dreaming about it.

By sixteen, Nina had learned nothing but lessons and not one of them had helped her: she was confused, and cut off, and lonely, caught up in the longing for a life in the West that was so far away it might as well have been on the moon.

And then Julia Voigt arrived at her school—wearing real Levi's, not GDR-branded cardboard-stiff denims—and Nina's life turned upside down.

"Did you get it all?"

Nina nodded and tipped the contents of her backpack onto the floor of Julia's bedroom, which was its usual colorful chaos of books and magazines and discarded clothes. Nothing in Julia's home resembled the dull brown safeness of Nina's. And nothing about Julia's parents resembled her own. The Voigts were both musicians, an occupation Britte and Holger refused to even accept was a job. When the Voigts were around—which their work meant wasn't often—they talked to Julia as if she was an adult and encouraged her to "express herself," a phrase that made Nina's heart leap. Nothing seemed to worry them—including the fact that they had both been arrested and were both, or so they said, on government watch lists. Nina found Julia's parents impossibly glamorous, but she kept them—and Julia—well away from her own.

"Yes. And I got rough-quality paper, not the best kind, and cheap ink. Nothing that stands out, or is easily traced."

Julia spread the letter stamps out, separating the capital letters from the smaller cases, forming them into a sentence.

"Stefan said we were to use the slogan *No More* Neues Deutschland—*We Demand a Free Press for a Free People*. He said the ND pretends to be a fair newspaper but it's really a government mouthpiece and prints so many lies, it's time it was brought down. This is going to be the first step in a much bigger campaign."

Julia's face was as lit up as if it was Christmas, the way it always was when she had a new cause to fight. Nina, unlike the rest of their classmates, found Julia's enthusiasms and her determination to—in Julia's thrilling words—"root out injustice" incredibly exciting. And it wasn't only Julia who had charmed her.

Nina rolled a stamp across the inkpad and made a test print on the cardboard back of one of the pads, hoping Julia wouldn't notice that the letter she'd chosen was an S. If Julia suspected Nina had a crush on her older brother, Stefan, Nina knew she would never hear the end of it. It wasn't as if she could help it. Nineteen-year-old Stefan had the bluest eyes, and the silkiest black hair, and the most wonderful smile Nina had ever seen—how could she not be a little bit in love with him? And he wasn't only handsome, he was clever. He and his friends—or the Treptow Civil Rights Collective, as they called themselves—could talk politics for hours when they gathered in Stefan's crumbling flat, and they weren't afraid of discussing anything, even the Stasi. Nobody else Nina knew openly mentioned the GDR's highly secretive state security police. Their slogan, *The Party's Sword and Shield*, made it perfectly clear where the organization stood in relation to the GDR and its government, and it certainly wasn't on the side of its people. If the Stasi were talked about at all, it was in hushed tones and in oblique references to "you never know who might be listening," when everybody clearly did. Stefan's collective, however, talked about the country's watchers and their surveillance methods with a depth of knowledge that thrilled Nina as much as it scared her.

It was Stefan who had agreed that the girls could finally get involved with the Collective's activities, albeit on the fringes. And it was him who had explained that rubber stamps had to be used for leaflets because access to printers and typewriters was deliberately restricted, and handwritten messages were too dangerous to risk.

"They probably have an example of my writing already. You wouldn't believe what those bastards collect. Smells are one of their obsessions—they wipe the chairs down after they've finished interrogating their prisoners and then keep the cloths so they can literally sniff us out. It sounds crazy, but it's true."

Stefan was right—his explanation had sounded crazy. But he and two of the other boys had been arrested and one of them had spent six months in Berlin's Hohenschönhausen prison, which no one could find on a map but everyone knew was a Stasi torture center. When the group talked about impregnated cloths, and mini-cameras hidden inside handbags and umbrellas, and how they could pick out a Stasi agent from a block away because they were the only ones with their eyes up and not down, Nina believed them.

The Collective were fearless; Julia was the same. She asked whatever she liked in class and didn't care what grades she got. She also refused to go to the Free German Youth meetings all Eastern teenagers were expected to attend because, as she put it to anyone who challenged her, "They're no better than a socialist version of the Hitler Youth movement." She was noisy, and argumentative, and Nina adored her. Which Magda, at least, understood.

"I can see the attraction. She's funny, and she's smart. But that tongue of hers is going to get her into an awful lot of trouble."

Nina had waited for her grandmother—the only one of her family she had introduced Julia to—to add "and you with her," but a waitress had appeared as she said it. Magda had immediately switched her attention to praising their meal and the argument, to Nina's relief, had been, temporarily at least, avoided.

The lunch Magda had arranged for Nina's sixteenth birthday treat was meant to be special not strained. The restaurant at the top of the Berlin television tower in Alexanderplatz was famous, and so overwhelmed with day tourists from the West, it was hard for East Berliners to get a table. Nina couldn't deny that it was an experience. Unlike most places in the GDR, the food in the restaurant was designed with Westerners in mind, and it even served real coffee, not the undrinkable pea-flour-filled Kaffee-Mix the government was trying to persuade everyone was delicious, rather than acknowledging the latest round of shortages. Most famously of all, the restaurant revolved once an hour, giving the diners a panoramic, and complete, view of Berlin. It was a thoughtful, extravagant place for a meal, and Nina had hated every minute of it.

As the waitress finally glided on to the next table, Nina pushed her plate away. She knew she should drop the subject of Julia, but she was tired of empty conversations.

"I know Julia's different, Grandma. And I know I'm not meant to think that different is good. But the thing is, I can talk to her. Properly. About the real stuff." She had looked out of the window—

she knew better than to point—and let Magda follow her gaze. "Like that."

Berlin stretched out below them, the city as complete as Nina could ever have imagined it, and as broken. This high up, the swooping jagged line of the Wall was unavoidable.

"That's what's been upsetting you all afternoon. I did wonder."

"I haven't been able to see anything else since we got here, and when the platform revolved..." Nina kept her voice as low as her grandmother's had been, but she didn't try to hide her despair. "I've seen diagrams. I knew it wasn't the simple slab of concrete I saw at the checkpoint when I was a child. But to see it so clearly laid out..."

"It's not as simple as a wall, is it?"

Nina stopped. Magda was blinking hard. Perhaps she didn't need to explain; perhaps her grandmother really did understand. That, up here, the name each side gave it didn't matter: that neither *Wall* nor *Barrier* were final enough to explain it. That both those words were narrow and navigable. Children hopped over walls and balanced on top of them. Barriers lifted. The scar running below them needed a name more suited to a siege or a battle.

Nina was too high up to pick out the guard towers, or the dogs that patrolled the length of it, or the guns and barbed wire. What she could see, however, was the true width of the city's separation: the stretches of bare concrete and sand and parched grass that separated the inner wall closest to the East from the outer that hugged the West. And that all the empty ground, and the dog runs and gun-wielding guards, were on the eastern side, with nothing to match them on the West. Magda was watching her closely, her face scrunched with worry.

I could try talking to her. If I don't get loud, if I don't accuse her of being part of the problem, maybe she could help me make sense of it all.

Nina took a deep breath and leaned across the table, so that she couldn't see the rest of the room, or the view.

"I could say to Julia that that thing down there doesn't look like protection. That, if it was meant to keep the West out rather than the East in, as we're constantly told, all the uncrossable spaces and the guns and the danger would be on their side, not ours. I could tell Julia that I don't believe anymore, or maybe I never did, that it's proof our government cares about its people. And that I don't want to live in a world run like this. She would get it. I'm not sure anyone else would."

"Not even me?"

The catch in Magda's voice had made Nina look properly at her grandmother. Magda's hands were shaking as she smoothed her salt and pepper curls.

"I want to listen to you, Nina, and to hear you; believe me I do. I know you are struggling and that I have been... perhaps too quick to side with your parents' obedient views. Maybe I could be braver and try harder to help you?"

Be braver was such an odd choice of words; offering help wasn't the response Nina had expected. Nina hadn't known what to say. She loved her grandmother dearly and had tried to share more of her confusions with her than she had ever dared to with her parents. She also knew that there was far more to Magda than the little she revealed to the world. Nina had already prized out the few scraps Britte knew about Magda's past—that she had helped communists and other persecuted people escape from Hitler during the last years of the war. As sparse as the details were, they—plus the house Nina still knew nothing about beyond its existence—suggested a very different woman to the one Magda presented. They suggested a woman who might truly understand Nina's frustration with her too-controlled life, but... A gap had opened up between her and her grandmother half a lifetime ago with the discovery of a picture, and that gap had never properly healed.

After the day of Herthe's funeral, neither of them had, directly, mentioned the drawing again. Nina had kept the sketch and spun her dreams; Magda had never asked what she had done with it. Nina, however, had never forgotten the fear or the tears or the fury the sketch had provoked, and she doubted Magda had either. That fear had been there again in the hissed command when Magda had stepped in to plaster over the joke-telling episode. But the silence Magda had forced on them both was impenetrable.

As Nina had grown older and more frustrated by the system she lived under, her anger had grown with her. She couldn't let that spill out at school, and her parents refused to engage with it, which meant that Magda—to Nina's shame—had increasingly become its target. After one too many accusations that usually began with "you're too old, you don't understand, you don't care," Magda had refused to stay in the room when Nina picked at the past or kicked against the present. That broke both their hearts, although neither would admit it. So Nina had sat in the restaurant and was about to shrug Magda's question off rather than confront it, and then the voice in her head that was tired of silences and secrets suddenly asked, *Why not just speak?*

"How can you live here?"

Magda's head shot up from the cutlery she'd been pointlessly straightening.

"You know what it was like before, living under the Nazis and having every aspect of your life controlled. Because that's what the Third Reich did, isn't it? Controlled people's minds and hearts, 'to make them fight on the side of an evil ideology'? It's what we've been taught at school anyway. But if what my mother said is true, you helped people escape from them. And that's where I get stuck. This is a dictatorship—our lives are just as controlled here as yours was by the Nazis, and yet you still choose it; you still stay. Why? Do you honestly think the GDR is perfect? That the West isn't better? You've retired—that means you could go there any time you want. You could go and find your old home. But you won't; you act like you never lived there. And even if for some reason that house is full of bad memories, there must still be people there you were once close to."

Nina stumbled to a halt, realizing she had turned a question into a speech full of accusations—the precise opposite of what she had intended to do—and that she had also hit a nerve. Magda had worked her napkin into knots. When she finally spoke, she kept her voice low, but her tone was as passionate as Nina's and her eyes were blazing.

"Dear God, the presumption of youth. A few garbled lessons and you think you know everything. You know nothing about the Third Reich, absolutely nothing. You think the Nazis *controlled* people? No, Nina, they didn't: they destroyed people. Not only the millions they killed—who, whatever they tell you in school, weren't all communists; they weren't even the main target—but the rest of us too, the ones who tried to stand up to them. They took our souls, and they ruined our lives."

As Magda stopped and took a gulp of water, a horrified Nina tried to break in, but Magda shook her head at the stumbling apology and carried on.

"You are so hot-headed, so quick to rush in without a care for the chaos you cause. I didn't choose to live under the Nazis, and I didn't choose to live under this regime we have now. Do you think anybody beyond a fanatical few chose to live under *this*? Believe me, whatever the GDR has become, back when it started, East Germany wasn't only meant to be better than what went before—it was our idea of a paradise. How could I know that would turn into watching and control, let alone a wall? But I'm not the fool I once was—I don't think I can change what people with power can do. And as for going to the West, to that house? You talk as though, just because my age allows me more movement, that's a simple thing. You don't have a clue what you're asking."

This time when Nina jumped in, she wouldn't let Magda stop her.

"Then tell me—help me understand. You think all I want is to hate things, but I don't. I want to make life better, for me, for everyone. I don't know how to do that, but you do. You've done it—even if it went wrong, you said you came out of the war and built a paradise. What if we could do that again, here, together?"

Nina reached across the table and grabbed Magda's hands. There was a nakedness to her grandmother's face she had never seen before, as if the skin had peeled back. It was disturbing to see Magda so revealed, but it was also strangely beautiful.

"You spent my childhood telling me wonderful stories, Grandma, but they're not what I need now. I need the truth. I want to know about the woman who stood up to the Nazis. I want to know why a woman who was once that brave can possibly be afraid of anything, never mind an old house."

She was too eager; her voice had risen far too high. Heads swiveled. Magda looked up and blinked and her shutters crashed down. She disentangled her hands from Nina's and reached for her bag.

"I'm not afraid. You insult me by saying that. And I have no interest in the West—why would I? The GDR has done nothing but care for me. I worked hard and I received fair rewards, exactly as the system promised I would. I have a generous home and a generous pension because I live in a country that values loyalty and commitment. I am not about to give all that up to go shopping."

Nina knew the tirade was meant for the listening tables, not for her, but Magda's sudden switch to cold and dismissive threatened to turn her into a bewildered child again.

"I didn't mean go to the West to go shopping; I'm not that shallow. I'm just trying to understand what changed for you. You lived in that house, Grandma, that beautiful house. You must have had a lovely life there, and then the war came and you stood up for what you believed in. And yet you won't go back and look for it, or look for anyone from before, although there must be people who would remember you, and want to thank you. You act as though your life then was some terrible secret."

Magda hesitated; she put her hand back in Nina's. Nina held on tight, as if she could squeeze out whatever it was Magda suddenly looked desperate to say. Then someone walked past their table a fraction too close and the moment passed. Magda pulled her hand back, reached for the bill, and got up.

"Life isn't a fairy story, Nina. Beautiful houses aren't always lived in by beautiful people, and the past isn't some star-sprinkled land I'm longing to share. This is where we are." She waved a hand at the view, which was once again slowly revolving. "Learn to live in it. No matter what you think of what's been done to Berlin in your lifetime, there's things I've seen here that are much, much worse."

"Wake up! You're going to waste all the ink."

Nina jerked back to her task, concentrating on stamping out the slogan until the stack of leaflets piled up between the two girls was satisfyingly high. When the last sheet was complete, Julia sat back on her heels and wriggled her cramped fingers.

"Thank goodness that's done—I can't feel my hands. Let's drop them over to Stefan and see if we can get dinner out of him. I'm starving and there's nothing edible here."

Nina waved the last few leaflets dry and began stacking them inside her backpack, more than happy to have an excuse to go to the flat. And then she stopped.

"They still think of us as kids, don't they? Your brother and the others. I'm tired of it, of always listening, of being an audience for them showing off. I want to do something real."

"What do you mean?"

Nina grinned: the idea had only just come to her, but she could feel it gathering steam.

"Why don't we do the leafleting ourselves? It's Productive Work Day tomorrow—we've both been put down to go to the concrete factory and learn about production improvement methods, which sounds like hell on earth. Why don't we take the leaflets there and make it more interesting?"

Julia's grin spilled all over her face. "That's brilliant! Direct action, that's what it's called—that's what we'd be doing. Stefan will be over the moon with us."

Direct action. Doing, not giving in and accepting. Nina loved the sound of that almost as much as *Stefan will be over the moon*.

"This is a management-only floor—what are you doing wandering about up here? And what's that you're holding?"

The angry-faced man had come from nowhere. It was too late to tear the leaflet up; there was nowhere to throw it. Nina panicked and couldn't keep track of her words.

"I don't know. I was looking for the toilets and I found it. It was lying on the floor."

She took a step back, but the man was already on her. He snatched the paper out of her hand before she could think up a better defense.

"What the hell is this? Did you bring this in? Do you have more?"

Nina's hand instinctively slipped to the pocket of her factory overall where she still had one last bundle. The man's eyes narrowed.

"Give them here, right now."

Nina stepped back. Julia was on the walkway below, probably already dropping her leaflets along it. They couldn't both get caught. She dodged his hand and sprang toward the balcony and—with a yell of, "Read these—they matter," which jerked Julia's head up—she flung the leaflets over the side. The gesture felt wild and heroic.

Not one of the open-mouthed workers below picked them up.

"You little bitch."

Before Nina could turn and protect herself, the supervisor grabbed her arm and wrenched it halfway up her back. Pain rushed through her, white hot and vicious, and she sagged. He began dragging her down the corridor.

"Are you really so stupid? Anyone who's handled one of your leaflets will be immediately under suspicion of bringing them in. That's working people with families who could be out of a job in seconds and their lives ruined, all because some idiot schoolkid decided to play the big rebel. What the hell did you think your little stunt would achieve?"

Nina couldn't give him an answer. Her mind wasn't blank the way stories always claimed minds went in frightening moments; it was racing, tumbling over all the consequences she hadn't thought about until this minute.

The supervisor didn't seem to care whether she answered him or not. He carried on twisting her arm, bombarding her with his questions and his fury until they arrived at a glass-paneled oak door bearing the title *Factory Director*.

"Stay there. Don't move."

He flung her into a chair, knocked on the director's door, and went inside.

Nina eased her aching arm in front of her body and tried to rub the life back into it. The pain throbbed through her side; the corridor blurred.

The next hour was a flurry of opening and slamming doors and telephone calls and overalled men trooping in and out of the director's office carrying piles of leaflets that were crumpled and torn and marked by what appeared to be footprints. Nina wondered if the workers had been asked to deliberately deface them; she wasn't foolish enough to ask. Nobody spoke to her; nobody came near her. It was as if the air she sat in was contaminated.

"Get up."

Nina snapped out of the dozing state she had fallen into. She had no idea how much time had passed; there was no natural light anywhere near her and she didn't dare look at her watch. The man standing in front of her wasn't wearing one of the blue jackets or gray overalls that marked out the factory's employees. He was dressed instead in a shiny brown suit that was as crumpled as his face. He was of medium height and medium build and his hair was thinning. He had the kind of pasty complexion that suggested long hours in dark rooms. He was so completely unremarkable, he didn't seem real.

"Follow me."

He moved so quickly, there wasn't a moment to ask *why* or *where*.

"In here."

The Stasi agent—which Nina was now convinced from his manner and his invisible appearance he must be—waved her into a room empty of everything except two plastic chairs set at either end of a narrow table. To her relief, Julia wasn't in it, which surely meant she hadn't been caught. The man sat down, gestured for her to do the same, and extracted a folder and a pad from his briefcase. He did not introduce himself.

"Tell me what you know."

Nina stared at him. She had expected to be asked specifics: her name and address, the details of her accomplices. The sweep of his question was confusing. Not knowing what to say, she said nothing. He made a note on his pad and he asked her again. With no clue still as to what he wanted, Nina settled on the only response she could think of.

"About what?"

If her non-answer had irritated him, he didn't show it. He didn't show anything at all; he simply repeated the same question. Nina's palms began to sweat. She wished she had listened harder when Stefan had described Stasi interrogation techniques, instead of simply admiring him. The agent continued to watch her and wait; he looked as if he could wait all day.

Nina took the quietest breath that she could and tried to speak more calmly than her thumping heart wanted her to.

"The leaflets were my idea. I made them; I brought them here."

Her voice sounded terribly thin. The agent opened the buff-colored folder he had placed on the table in front of him and consulted its contents.

"And were the leaflets a joke, Fräulein Dahlke?"

She heard the slight emphasis on *joke*, but she was still a step behind.

"Your file says you enjoy telling jokes. I was asking if this was another one?"

They've kept a file on that?

The thought was both absurd and terrifying, and momentarily loosened her tongue.

"Why would anyone still care about that? I was ten years old when that happened; I was a child."

The agent sighed. "So many people think that is a defense. They sit in front of me and they say, 'But I was young, I didn't know any better; it was a mistake I made years ago.' But do you see, they all, in the end, sit where you are: in front of me. An insulting joke at ten, an inciting leaflet at sixteen. The path always goes the same way. It always leads to traitor."

"*Traitor*? Are you serious?"

Nina couldn't believe she had heard him right. That was a word that went with spies and leaked secrets, with chases and guns. It made no sense stacked against ink pads and cheap paper.

The agent made another note on his pad. "You're not happy with that description? Then how would you describe yourself, with your—and let me use your own words—'big house in the West'? As a patriot?"

Nina knew better than to say yes. She stayed silent.

He leaned forward and switched to a softer tone, which was a long way from comforting. "Perhaps this is unfair. Perhaps you are not the failure here. Perhaps we are the ones at fault. The warning signs were already there when—as you have pointed out—you were a child. And yet, until now, we have let you remain in your school, and with your family."

Until now hung in the air. The skin on Nina's arms contracted.

The agent continued. "Luckily it is not too late to remedy whoever's mistakes these are. I am sure a place can be found for you at one of our special youth centers—at Hennickendorf perhaps, or, if that doesn't work, at Torgau. A little re-education might just do the trick."

She was going to be sick. She could feel her stomach churning, could taste sour liquid rising in the back of her throat. The Youth Work Centers for "ill-adjusted" teenagers were one of the GDR's worst-kept secrets. Everyone at school knew of someone who had disappeared inside one of those. The stories about Hennickendorf, the facility closest to Berlin, were bad enough. The center there was situated on part of an old World War Two prison camp and was reputedly run on the same military lines. As for Torgau, that was the nightmare, the threat every naughty child in the GDR was terrified of. The rumors about it were terrible: barbed wire and watchtowers and brainwashing; punishments so brutal that the center's whispered name was *the extermination camp*. Nobody came out of Torgau, or Hennickendorf, or any of the other Youth Work Centers meant to "turn anti-socials and hooligans back into valuable citizens," and lived any kind of a life.

Don't rile him; get through this. Until you can get out and get free.

For once she listened to the voice in her head.

"I don't want that. I didn't mean to do anything that would lead to that."

The agent nodded. "Excellent. Then tell me what you know, and let's see where that leads instead."

He wants Julia, or Stefan. One name and this all goes away. I can't do it. I won't.

Just as she was working up the courage to say it, there was a knock on the door. The agent frowned—the first real emotion Nina had seen him display. He opened it, held a muttered conversation with someone Nina couldn't see and left.

When the door eventually reopened—after an interval that seemed far longer than the half-hour recorded by Nina's watch—it was Magda who entered.

"What are you doing here?" Nina wanted to fling herself into her grandmother's arms, but Magda's frigid expression kept her firmly in the chair.

"Getting you out. Trying to hold on to some kind of a future for you again, despite your best efforts to wreck it."

Magda's voice was as sharp as her face. It made Nina want to curl up or run away.

"I'm sorry…"

Magda dismissed the apology with an abrupt wave. "That can keep. The main thing now is for you to stay quiet and not argue with what's been agreed."

"What do you mean?" Nina could see that Magda was holding tight to her temper, but being told not to argue surely meant there was something she would want to argue with. "What have you done?"

Magda's voice was so cold, Nina struggled not to recoil.

"What I had to. I gave them information. I put the blame for this on the Voigts' bad influence—with their past history, that's plausible enough. And I did what I did last time: I used my reputation as a loyal Party member, a currency that is probably worn out by now, to make a bargain. There'll be letters of apology, and some kind of community work as a penance. But there won't be criminal charges or prison. And there's a slim chance—the slimmest—that you'll get to sit your *Abitur* examination and complete your education. I made sure you walk away from this, Nina. That's what I've done."

Nina was still frozen at *bargain*.

"You gave them Julia's parents? How could you? I didn't ask you to do that; I didn't want it."

"I don't care."

Nina recoiled as Magda hissed and turned into the hard-eyed grandmother from Herthe's bedroom again.

"What did you think was going to happen, Nina? Was this how you were planning to make the GDR great again? Did you imagine you could carry out an operation like this—with no skills and no training—and not get caught? Or did you imagine your leaflet was going to raise up a rebellion? To do what? To go where? Did you think for one moment about the danger your actions exposed all the workers here to, never mind yourself or your family?" Magda shook her head as Nina gaped. "You thought you were a hero. You weren't: you were selfish and stupid, and now someone—as someone always does—has to pay."

"But Julia's my friend. If her parents get in trouble, she could be…" It was too much. Nina could no longer hold back the tears she'd been fighting to contain since her arm had been wrenched half out of its socket. And she couldn't—although she wanted to—push Magda away when she finally gathered her frightened granddaughter into the embrace she desperately needed.

"Hush now. I'm sorry for Julia, sweetheart, really I am. But her parents' behavior had already put her at risk. There were bound to be consequences at some point."

Nina wriggled away from Magda's tear-stained coat. "Can't you do anything? To help Julia, at least?"

The sadness in Magda's eyes was unbearable.

"No, I can't. That's her parents' job, not mine. Mine is to protect you. That's the worst of these things, Nina; that's what I never wanted you to have to learn. There's always a choice that isn't a choice. It's always impossible to save everyone."

She's talking about something deeper than this.

Nina didn't know where the feeling had come from, but she was certain it was true.

"What do you mean by that? Is this—having to choose who to keep safe—what it was like before?"

Magda flinched. Before she could answer, however, the door opened, and the Stasi agent reappeared.

"Well, isn't this touching. You should be grateful to your grandmother, Nina. She has stepped in to keep you back from the brink once again."

Magda loosened her hold on Nina and straightened her coat.

"She is grateful. To you as much as to me. And now this matter is over, I think I should take her home. I am sure you want her to reflect on the day."

How is she managing to sound this composed when I swear she was heartbroken a moment ago?

Nina knew better than to ask. She got up and moved behind Magda toward the door. Her legs were shaking so hard, the few steps may as well have been a mile.

"I am interested that you think the matter is *over*."

Magda paused; her arm shot back round Nina. The agent continued to lean against the wall as casually as if they were discussing the weather.

"It seems to me that it is anything but. Look at it from our point of view, Frau Aderbach. Your granddaughter doesn't seem to learn from one mistake to the next. And, as for you, what secrets are you hiding?" He made a show of opening his file again. "I keep going back to that little gem from Nina's joke-telling days. A house in the West we don't seem to know about. Unless you want to tell us, of course?"

Magda's hand was as tight as a vise on Nina's waist, but her voice was perfectly steady. "There is nothing to tell. My good name, and my years of loyal service to my country are what counts here, not a child's nonsensical story."

For the first time since he had made an appearance in the factory, the Stasi agent smiled.

"Your good name. Yes, I've heard a lot about that. And how loyal you've been for the last forty years. That's admirable, but I can't help but wonder what came before. I've heard the story, about the lives you saved with your factory owner. But I've only ever heard the version you made sure was told." He paused.

Nina looked at Magda: there wasn't one flicker of emotion on her face.

She's totally controlled; it's as if she's not here.

The agent could clearly see it too.

"You are an interesting woman, Frau Aderbach. So calm, so in control, it's as if you've been trained. What a useful skill; I'm surprised we haven't made better use of it. And your granddaughter here, messier maybe, but as fearless as you." He stood up straighter. "Well, perhaps you are as straightforward as you say you are—I've been told I take too much notice of history, but, as I explained to the *fräulein* earlier, I do like to see where the pathways start." He leaned across Magda, who managed not to recoil, and opened the door. "Go home, reflect if you want. But don't think this matter is over. This is the GDR, Frau Aderbach: nothing here is ever over at all."

CHAPTER FOUR

Magda, December 1938–March 1940

"The Jews are the essence of everything that is wrong; they cannot be allowed to remain under the same skies as our people. We will drive them out from wherever we go—with whatever methods are needed. We will not shirk from our duty, no matter what that duty demands."

The applause that greeted Himmler's speech set up a breeze that made the candles dance. Magda stood in the center of the clamor, her hands doing what they had to do, her brain trying not to scream. She wanted to slap her hands across Himmler's mouth. She wanted to yell the word *evil* until everyone opened their eyes and stopped clapping. She swallowed hard instead and switched her attention away from the Reichsführer, trying to drown him out with the beauty of the white lilies filling the room. The contrast between the cruel words and the softly lit ballroom they had been unleashed in was, however, too harsh. Magda's bones began to feel brittle.

"Goodness, is that a smile or a grimace? It's hardly flattering—it makes your neck look stringy and old."

It was Elsa, of course—who but Walther's impossible daughter could deliver such a nasty barb from behind such a pretty smile —pausing on her way to the stage, where Himmler was finishing his speech and waiting to wish her a happy nineteenth birthday. Elsa looked beautiful. She always looked beautiful—there wasn't a woman in any room who could outshine her. Her blonde finger-waved hair was caught back from her delicate face by two crescent moon clips; her blush-pink gown skimmed her shoulders and curtained her milk-white back; the diamond stars dangling from her earlobes elongated her elegant neck.

It would be more honest if she had come dressed in a black SS uniform.

Magda took a glass of champagne from a circling waiter and unclenched her smile. "That is unfortunate. The Reichsführer's speech was such an inspiring one, I was actually on the verge of tears and trying to contain them."

Anyone who knew Magda at all would have seen straight through that comment, but no one in the room, apart from Walther, knew Magda at all. Least of all—Magda hoped—Elsa, who, from her shining eyes, genuinely felt the inspiration that Magda most certainly didn't.

"Make a friend of her. She needs someone around her to temper her views."

Walther's request was as impossible to fulfill tonight as it had been six months ago when he had made it and finally introduced Magda to the daughter "I've totally spoiled." He had not only spoiled Elsa; he had also, unfortunately, overpraised Magda and, in doing so, turned the motherless and attention-craving Elsa green-eyed. Now there was nothing between the girls but dislike. Elsa, however, was very skilled at hiding that from her father. She was also perfectly suited to the world Walther had created around her. Like Kiefer, whose age she shared, Elsa had been educated in a school system shaped by the National Socialists. Unlike Kiefer, however, there had been no counterbalancing influences to hold her—even as loosely as they held Kiefer—back from a deeply committed loyalty to the Party, and to the SS officers her social circle was filled with. Magda knew that wasn't entirely Elsa's fault—she had been barely a teenager when Walther had started his flirtation with the regime, far too young to understand the nuances of what he was doing. Now she was too soaked in Party rhetoric for anyone to convince her that the men she made eyes at were filled not with glamour but poison.

Magda stepped back as Elsa brushed past. She was barely three years older than Walther's only daughter, yet tonight—as Elsa blew kisses at the guests Magda loathed—that gap may as well have been a hundred. She put her unfinished drink on another circulating tray, the champagne turned sour, as Elsa tripped up the stairs to the stage and kissed a delighted Himmler on the cheek. Seeing his blush, she did it again, before inviting her guests to turn their applause on her beaming father.

He has such a blind spot for her. Please God he hasn't created a monster.

The ballroom was too hot, the company was too wrong. Magda left the room as Elsa continued to sparkle, with no care at all that her witty *thank you*s followed immediately on from a speech promising the destruction of an entire race of people. She hurried down the silk-carpeted corridor, dodging the ranks of white-jacketed waiters, and out through the veranda doors into the villa's sweeping gardens.

The December night was thick with a frost that cut through Magda's chiffon dress and beaded slippers the moment she stepped into it. She didn't care. At least the air outside was clean and crisp and she could breathe in it.

Which I couldn't have done a month ago, not with the fires that burned then.

The memory made her shiver more than the biting cold. A month ago, the air hadn't been clean at all. It had stunk of petrol and charred wood, and the ash in the wind had coated her hair and her throat when she had run out of the villa into it, terrified the forest was on fire. Except it hadn't been the forest; it had been the streets, and not a single fire engine had come to hold back the inferno even though she, and then Walther, rang for them. The two of them had stood together, watching the flames dancing, refusing to believe that no one would at least try to stop them. And then Himmler had appeared in the early hours of a morning that was orange and smoke-laden, clutching cigars and talking about "victory," and it was clear no one would.

None of them had foreseen the orgy of violence that had erupted across Germany on November 9, 1938. Despite the increasingly savage attacks on the Jews in Austria since Hitler had annexed the country the previous March, despite Walther's extensive connections, despite Christoph's permanent ear to the ground. Even in the midst of it, none of them had guessed its scale. In one perfectly choreographed night, thousands of Jewish men were beaten and arrested. Thousands of Jewish businesses and homes were ransacked. Hundreds of synagogues were destroyed. So much broken glass had littered Germany's streets on the following morning, the destruction had been immediately dubbed *Kristallnacht*. In Grunewald alone, the synagogue that had stood on Franzensbader Straße since 1895 had been burned to a ruin. Two pastry shops, three tailor's workrooms, and half a street's worth of cafés had also been reduced to rubble, and a dozen families had been chased from their houses. Himmler had already moved his men into those.

"It was a purge, the one they've been planning for, or the start of it. And all of it executed with the attention to detail Himmler revels in. Every business smashed and every place looted was deliberately chosen. And yet not a single word of their intentions leaked out."

Walther had sat in his office with Magda in the days after the disaster, white-faced and shaking, trying to work out what clues he had missed. He couldn't find a single one. He was right, however, that the Party had moved from persecution to purge. Two days after the violence, Hitler issued orders that closed all remaining Jewish businesses. In the days after that, the Party began sweeping up all the property that Jewish homeowners had been forced to register the previous April, and the last savings Jewish families had managed to hold on to. The campaign had been rapid and unavoidable and brutal. Given Himmler's speech tonight, Magda suspected even that was not as brutal as what might be coming, although she couldn't imagine what there was left to take.

"We have to work faster; we have to get more people out or renamed" became the goal Magda and Walther set their days by. Magda visited the network of forgers they had established in the Berlin suburb of Moabit so often, Walther was sure she would get herself caught. That didn't stop her pushing her limits—or theirs. In the month since *Kristallnacht*, the tiny printshop secreted in the back of a bakery had doubled its output. It wasn't nearly enough. The surge in arrests had hit Tiedemann Factories as badly as all the other workplaces targeted in Berlin and—although Walther protested as vocally as he dared about the damage done to his production lines—it had led to the loss of too many workers they hadn't had a chance to protect. It was the sight of those men—men Magda knew by name, whose children she had given gifts to at the company's summer party—being led away, spat at and prodded by guns that had tipped her into haunting the streets of Moabit. It was the frayed-nerved exhaustion of that that had driven her to break her promise not to reveal the truth about Walther to anyone and to share with Christoph, for the first time, what kind of man her boss really was.

Christoph had been furious at the secrets she had kept from him and her family, and the danger she had courted. Walther was equally furious she had told anyone what they were doing. In the end, Magda had forced the two men to meet and—with a parting, "You're exactly the same, go and sort out your differences"—had left them to shout out their anger, while she scoured Berlin for new sources of paper, her excuses for needing it growing as flimsy as the supplies she paid too high a price for. The gamble with the two men at least, however, had paid off. Christoph had joined Walther's staff at the Spandau headquarters at the start of December, although he had refused to mix in any of Walther's social circles.

Which is a blessing, especially tonight. He'd be holding a gun, not a glass of champagne.

As a frozen Magda reluctantly re-entered the ballroom, preparing her excuses to leave, Elsa swept past in an SS officer's arms. The dance ended and the next one began, and a crowd of uniforms engulfed the giggling birthday girl. When Elsa re-emerged—with another suitor clinging to her waist as if he had unearthed a lost pot of treasure—she was starry-eyed and radiant, and clearly delighted that Magda had seen her success. She didn't, however, take to the floor. Keeping Magda firmly in her sights, she stretched up instead and whispered in her partner's ear, pushing him away with a winsome smile when he frowned. Magda's heart sank as the man strode stiffly toward her.

"Fräulein Aderbach, may I have the honor?"

Elsa was watching; Walther was too far away to step in. Magda had no choice but to accept the proffered arm. He led her onto the floor; Magda fixed her best smile in place. The music began. He rested his hand on the thin material covering her waist; she rested her hand on the silver flashes decorating his shoulder. The waltz continued its stately progression. Magda switched off her feelings and trusted that her body would move on without her, offering a silent prayer of thanks that Christoph wasn't there to see exactly how accomplished an actress she had become.

"It's getting late—you need to go."

"Which I would. If I thought you meant it. If your arm wasn't pinning me to the bed."

Magda laughed as Christoph's mouth found hers again and deliberately held him tighter to her. Since she had moved, a few months after Elsa's birthday, into the relative privacy of the guest house on Walther's estate, it was easier to conduct their affair. Her new home wasn't a perfect solution: sometimes the secrecy they lived under, hiding their relationship in case one of them was caught, irritated Magda. Sometimes she wondered what a simpler life would have been like, one where politics and war hadn't got in the way of weddings and home-making and the children they didn't mention but both of them craved. Today, however, from the soft shelter of the bed, their secret felt romantic, on the pleasurable side of illicit. Besides, it was Sunday—nobody needed them. Why shouldn't they enjoy a whole day together, rather than the few snatched hours that was all they could normally find? It wasn't as if the world waiting outside the cottage's ivy-clad walls was a welcoming one.

Don't think about that—not now, not with his arms still around you. There'll be time enough tomorrow to worry about armies and battles and loss.

She returned Christoph's kiss and tried to feel nothing except his cool hands on her skin, but the moment was gone, and Christoph could sense it.

"He's a bright boy—he'll stay safe. And all the early reports said there was almost no opposition when our armies marched in."

"Which is exactly what they would say."

Magda threw back the quilt and crossed to the window. The September sun streamed through the open sash, dappling her skin. The sky was washed with blue and dotted with cotton-wool clouds. The only sound breaking the silence was birdsong. And yet somewhere out there, far away in the forests of Poland, there was gunfire and bloodshed, and Kiefer was caught up in the middle of it.

"You couldn't have stopped him, Magda. Nobody could. He was all fired up for the Fatherland and desperate to go off and be a hero."

Just because Christoph was right didn't mean Magda wanted to hear it. Or to remember how proud her brother had been when he'd burst through the Aderbachs' door in his field-gray Wehrmacht uniform, bright-eyed and grinning and looking—in her eyes at least—not twenty years old but thirteen. Or to remember how sickened her parents had been when they saw him. Kiefer had stormed out of the house on the crest of a furious row neither Herthe nor Ernst would back down from and returned to his infantry unit. And now he was somewhere in Poland, part of an invasion that had begun two days earlier on the first of September 1939. One of thousands of Hitler Youth-indoctrinated boys feeding their leader's insatiable hunger for land.

"We've both disappointed them." Magda left the window's too perfect view and sank back onto the bed. "My parents think I'm as committed to fascism as he is. Kiefer's out there fighting for the Führer, and I'm working for a factory that churns out the shells and the bullets that let him. There's no difference between us as far as they are concerned. No, actually that's not true. I not only work for Tiedemann, the arms-contract-chasing bogeyman, I live on his fancy Grunewald estate, in his guest cottage, and I mix with his Hitlerite friends. If anything, I imagine they despise me the most."

"Stop it." Christoph pulled Magda into his arms and unwrapped her furious fingers from her hair. "You know why you live here: to keep your real work away from them, to keep them safe so that if, God forbid, you get caught, they don't fall with you. And you mix with who you mix with to stay above suspicion. One day, you'll be able to tell them all of that."

"Will I?" She pushed him away, in no mood to be consoled or solved. "You don't mix with any of Walther's circle, and you do as much good as me, so that's a poor excuse. And what if this never ends? What if the wider war that Hitler keeps threatening—that invading Poland has surely started—is unleashed and he wins? Who will I be then?" She broke off as a sudden thump echoed up the stairs. "What was that?"

Christoph leaped out of the bed and into his clothes, his senses as alert as hers.

"Magda, are you up there? It's almost lunchtime—please tell me you're not still in bed?"

"It's Elsa." Magda dropped her voice to a whisper. "Get into the bathroom and hide."

Christoph grabbed his shoes, his face creased in a frown.

"Surely she won't come upstairs? It's your house."

"Not in her eyes." Magda hurried him through the door into the small room nestled under the cottage's eaves. "As far as she's concerned, it's her father's house and I've no business being in it. She treats it like her own." She wriggled into her dress and hurried out onto the landing. Elsa was already halfway up the stairs.

"Well don't you look a fright. Who've you got hiding in there?"

There was no warmth in Elsa's tone; there never was when the two of them were alone. Magda kept her back firmly against the closed bedroom door. She had no intention of providing Elsa with an excuse for branding her as *immoral*. Even Walther would struggle to defend her against that charge in the National Socialists' puritanical—and, given how many of its ministers kept both a mistress and a wife, hypocritical—family-first world.

"What an odd question. Who could I possibly have in my bedroom? I've been working long hours and it's Sunday—I slept late. Why do you want me anyway?"

"I don't." Elsa's gaze traveled up and down Magda's crumpled dress and she sniffed. "But apparently Father does. He wants us at the house for some announcement he's expecting that's got him all worked up and annoying. Go and repair yourself." She stared around the upper landing, at the vases of wild flowers and the jewel-colored scarves Magda had draped across the old-fashioned bureaus that lined it. "I'll try to find somewhere less bohemian to wait."

Magda dressed and calmed her hair and face as quickly as she could, an inventory running through her head as she juggled hairbrushes and lipstick, and tried to calculate how much danger Elsa's appearance had put them in. Christoph wouldn't stir until he was certain the coast was clear. There were no details of the counterfeiters she had visited the day before anywhere in the house—those details were all stored in her head. The pitifully small batch of identity cards she had collected—a fraction of what was needed to safeguard the jobs of the Jewish workers employed at Spandau—were locked in a strongbox at the back of her wardrobe. Her KPD membership card—which she should have got rid of but had held on to as a reminder of who she really was—was sewn into the hem of her second-best winter coat. There was nothing for Elsa to find, no matter how many cupboards she opened or books she shook out—which she would do, looking for anything she could turn into a weapon to rid herself of her father's "infuriating favorite."

Magda went down the stairs in a far neater blue frock, her mental checklist all ticked, convinced she was as safe as she could be. And then Elsa turned round at precisely the moment Christoph twitched aside the bathroom curtain and burst into a laugh that grated over Magda's skin as if she had rubbed it with gravel.

"We are here, Papa. And you must blame Magda, not me, for the time we took. She is a little too fond of her bed today."

Elsa's switch from cold to warm as she entered her father's study was too commonplace to surprise Magda. She didn't, however, need to offer the apology Elsa had set her up to make. Walther, for once, wasn't listening to his daughter. He was curled instead around the radio cabinet, with his housekeeper Frau Klepper and Herr Bühl, the Tiedemann Company's Technical Director and one of Walther's tight circle of confidantes, hovering by his side. Magda didn't recognize the voice that had captured their attention—she also didn't fully understand what the reedy-sounding man was saying.

Elsa, however, did.

"Is that the BBC? Why on earth are you tuned into that? It's nothing but anti-German lies and propaganda."

"Hush."

The shock on Elsa's face at her father's curt command would ordinarily have made Magda laugh, but some of the words coming out of the mesh had started to make sense and Elsa's upset was no longer important. Magda ignored Elsa's aggrieved pout and focused, trying to unpick the broadcast from the English she had learned at school. When it finished, she was only half there, and hoping she had misunderstood.

No one spoke. Frau Klepper crossed herself. Herr Bühl slumped in his wing-backed chair and closed his eyes.

"Did I get that right? Has Britain declared war on us?" Magda's voice came out in a squeak she barely recognized.

Walther nodded.

"That was Neville Chamberlain, the British Prime Minister. He gave the Führer an ultimatum earlier this morning to move German troops out of Poland or face the consequences of Allied reprisals. The Führer ignored it."

"Of course he did." Elsa's snap woke up the room. "What did you expect him to do? His actions are completely lawful—Poland doesn't deserve to be Poland. You know as well as I do that the land they claim as their country, the land our troops have gone to take back, was stolen from Germany at the end of the last war, when our politicians didn't have the nerve to fight for our rights. The Poles are thieves. They deserve to lose what they stole. And they are brutes—they treat the poor Germans who stayed on and are trying to uphold a decent way of life there worse than animals."

"You don't know that's true, Elsa. You've never seen any evidence of mistreatment."

Walther stopped. Elsa's face had formed into harder lines than he—or Magda, who was far more familiar with Elsa's darker moods—had seen it shape into before.

"Why do I need to see evidence when the Führer tells me it is so? And what business is it of Britain, or France, if Germany decides to defend its own people? The Allies are the warmongers in this. Please God they will get what is coming to them."

"You don't mean that." Walther stretched out his hand to take hold of his daughter's, but Elsa held her slim fingers firmly away. "You wouldn't talk so easily about war if you had fought or lived through one the way I have. Nothing comes out of war except misery and suffering."

Elsa settled her hands in her lap and looked first at Herr Bühl and then at her father.

"And contracts, Papa. Don't forget those. Contracts you have already done pretty well out of since you, rather quickly, I might add, switched the factory over to armament production. Or are you going to join the pacifists and start turning those down?"

Walther shriveled.

Magda opened her mouth to lash out, but Herr Bühl shook his head. Elsa watched them all sink back into silence and switched on her most radiant smile.

"Frau Klepper, could you pour us all a glass of Father's delicious sherry?" She clicked her fingers at the woman who was still staring mutely at the radio. "There is so much to toast. A new Germany ready to take its rightful place in the world. The certain destruction of our enemies. The end of the Jews in every place that we conquer. That's a list worth celebrating, don't you think?" She turned to Magda as the housekeeper began handing out the thin-stemmed glasses with a shaky hand. "And what about love, Magda, shall we drink to that too? Or maybe to secrets—would you prefer that instead?"

Magda smiled, although it was a struggle. "To love, why not? The world will surely need it now."

She raised her glass and sipped her sherry. And kept her hand well away from the decanter she longed to fling into Elsa's self-satisfied face.

*

"They're from Poland. Kiefer brought them back as 'souvenirs.'"

Magda dropped the envelope of photographs onto Walther's desk and returned to her own office. She unwrapped herself from her scarf and a coat that was as thick as a quilt but felt paper-thin against the cruel winter that continued to torment Berlin. She tried not to listen as he opened the packet. She didn't need to see his reaction—she knew it would be as sickened as her own. She certainly didn't need to see the images again; the details were seared on her brain. The line of women, young and old, arranged along the top of a snowy slope as if they were waiting to be chosen at a dance. The same women lying in a tangled heap at the bottom, their dresses patterned with dark splashes. The line of men kneeling, guns pressed into their necks. The same men fallen face forward. The one with the child staring up at the camera, whose eyes had died before she did.

"Why would you bring such dreadful things home?"

Magda had asked her brother that question hoping to hear "to bear witness" in Kiefer's answer. When his response included "pride" and "deserved it" instead, she had walked away and sobbed. Now she could hear Walther doing the same. She gave him a few moments to compose himself and then went back in, a glass of whisky poured ready. He was as color-leached and shaken as she had expected him to be.

"They're Poles, mostly Jewish, if Kiefer's crowing is true, but I suppose you guessed that. There are more, there are worse. And the numbers he talks about are terrifying." Magda handed Walther the whisky and carried on talking, knowing some things were easiest said quickly. "Ten thousand in Schwetz, shot and buried in gravel pits. The same in a forest in Piaśnica. Psychiatric hospitals raided in every Polish city German soldiers entered and the patients all killed. Even if Kiefer is exaggerating—and God knows he's prone to—if that's been repeated all over Poland, the numbers of the murdered could run into hundreds of thousands. And it's only March. We've only been there six months. What will it look like a year from now? Will all the Polish Jews be dead? Is that the intention? Are the German Jews next?"

Walther stuffed the photographs back into the envelope.

"Yes, if you believe what Himmler said months ago at Elsa's party, although God knows how they could kill so many. That's not fighting—that's not what ordinary soldiers are trained to do. Does Kiefer know who's in charge? Where the orders came down from?"

Magda sat down on the other side of Walther's desk. "He's only a junior officer; he doesn't know much, but he's never done talking about the Reichsführer, so I think we can guess. Himmler has been traveling round the whole area in that personal train of his, making rousing speeches my brother has memorized and particularly loves for the orders to *shoot on the spot* and the all-inclusive *it's your duty to execute anyone who isn't as Aryan as you*. And he puts the SS—who he's desperate to join by the way—at every massacre location he boasts about."

Walther shuddered. "I was with Himmler at the weekend. All his talk of Poland centered on *our brave boys* and their *dignity*. This is *Kristallnacht* again—they gather up each tiny scrap of information they need to strike at their targets, but their own plans are so tightly guarded, no one can get wind of them."

"We have to do better. And we have to get these out to the world." Magda jumped up and began stalking the office. "Maybe I could look up the contacts in Prague who used to print *The Red Flag* for us. I could send the pictures and the numbers to them." She stopped. Czechoslovakia was under Hitler's control—the chances of any of those contacts still being alive was a slim one. "Or, if not them, someone. Anyone. People have to know." She was grateful when Walther ignored the tremor in her voice and nodded.

"Let me speak to Bühl—he has connections in Britain and America through the factory supply chains. Maybe he'll find someone who'll listen. In the meantime, we keep going. We can't stop killings on this scale—and God help us if they bring the same zeal to Germany—all we can do is help individuals escape and maybe they can go on and help others. One day, maybe enough people will have been helped that they can stand up together and say stop. So we keep going and, yes, we do better. We bury ourselves in Hitler's world so we are in step with them, not running behind. You're with me, aren't you? Whatever the cost."

Magda stopped pacing. Closer meant more danger, more risk, but there was nowhere else they could be. Before she could agree, however, the door between her office and Walther's burst open.

"Forgive me. This couldn't wait."

It was Herr Bühl, but not as Magda had ever seen him before. The normally unflappable director's face was covered in a slick of sweat that had turned its high color sickly.

"What's happened?"

Walther sprang up as he spoke and guided Bühl to the leather sofa that filled one of the corners of the room. The director—who Magda had always thought of as a big man—looked lost against the couch's wide expanse.

"Christoph has been caught by the Gestapo. He was picked up in Moabit carrying forged identity cards."

And now Walther was at Magda's side and she thought she heard herself moan.

"Where's he been taken?"

Bühl shook his head. "I don't know, Walther, I'm sorry. My guess is Columbia House or SS headquarters at Prinz Albrecht Straße. None of the eyes I've got looking can find him."

Magda was vaguely aware of Bühl's hand on her shoulder, and Walther telling her he would start pulling strings, but the edges of the room had dissolved and nothing he was saying would stick.

She was trying to get her limbs to work and take her home when the telephone rang.

"Magda, you need to listen." Walther was crouching by the side of her chair. His voice was so urgent, Magda forced herself to pay attention. "Himmler is coming. Someone has made a connection between Christoph and the factory and he's 'doing me the courtesy,' as he put it, of coming here himself and not sending the Gestapo in. You can't be here when he arrives."

"Why can't I?" Her head cleared, although there was pain in that she couldn't face. "I'm your secretary—where else would I be?"

Walther caught hold of her arm as she struggled up. "Don't be foolish. We don't know how long they've had Christoph. They could have broken him—he could have told them he's working for me. Himmler could be coming with orders for my arrest."

Magda shook him off. If Himmler was coming, that meant news, and news was what she needed, no matter who brought it or what the result.

"If they have broken Christoph—which I don't believe—Himmler will be coming for me as well. And if he's not and I'm not here, where I always am, he'll ask questions. He wouldn't overlook a detail as important as that. We can't give him any more threads to pick at than he already has. Not if we want to stay on the right side of him and stay safe."

Before Walther could argue, the telephone shrilled again. The door opened while the handset was still ringing.

"Herr Tiedemann, Fräulein Aderbach. A pleasure to see you as always, even in such peculiar circumstances."

Walther nodded to Bühl to leave, which he did at speed.

Himmler crossed the room as if he owned it and settled himself opposite Walther's desk. He did not remove the high-peaked black cap that added the valuable inches his short frame lacked; he never did in Walther's presence.

Don't do anything different. Treat him the same as you always do. Make this an ordinary day.

Magda offered her hand and let Himmler kiss it. She smiled her usual polite but not over-friendly smile and sat down with her dictation pad and her pen, letting Himmler, and then Walther, do the talking.

"As I explained on the telephone, my men have picked up one of your managers in possession of, shall we say, some rather disturbing papers. Nothing to do with you, Walther, my friend, I'm sure. How could it be? Who is more loyal than you? But tongues are wagging and it's my job to still them."

It's as if he learned how to interact from a book. He knows what amiable looks like but hasn't a clue how it feels.

Walther, who was as nimble at avoiding danger as Magda, smiled his usual smile and pulled a piece of paper from his drawer, glancing through it as if it contained something relevant.

"Christoph Traube is the man you've arrested? According to this, he joined us in December 1938, on a recommendation. A decent sort, according to my staff. I hope I haven't placed my trust foolishly."

Himmler sighed and shook his head. Magda assumed he thought he was being fatherly.

"You may well have done, I fear. You didn't check his references? You weren't aware Traube was in the KPD? That he had been imprisoned in 1936 due to his pro-Jewish sympathies?"

Magda thought Walther would act horrified, or lose his temper. Instead, he shrugged, which was far more effective in relaxing Himmler's guard.

"That is an unfortunate oversight. KPD men certainly aren't wanted here. I have people I entrust with checking everyone who comes to us, and I will speak to them, but I'll be honest, Heinrich, that wasn't an easy time for us. What with the changeover of the production lines to meet the demands of the armament contracts—

which we were obviously delighted to take on—and the loss of so many valuable workers after the trouble with the Jews in November." He spread his hands and assumed a more apologetic expression. "Politics. Isn't that always the problem? As essential as it may be, it's no friend to the businessman. We grabbed who we could to get the job done and this Traube must have slipped through the cracks. I am ashamed to admit it—you know me and detail—but there we are. Now, tell me my penance and I promise I'll do it."

There was a pause. For a moment, Magda wondered if Walther had overplayed his hand. And then Himmler laughed his dry laugh.

"This Traube has as many lives as a cat. He survived Columbia House. You gave him a job when, by rights, he should have been left on the streets to rot. And now he has been caught in possession of forgeries. At any other time, that would have merited the guillotine. But, apparently, he proved himself to be quite a fighter—he laid three of my men out without sustaining a bruise—which means he is headed for the army instead. Hopefully the bullet he richly deserves will find him there."

He's safe. They're not going to shoot him. He's safe.

It took all Magda's self-control not to slide off the chair. She caught Walther's eye and managed a nod of thanks as Himmler carried on talking.

"A coincidence then, let us call it that. No need to sully your good name, or interfere with your essential work here. I will, however, ask that you carry out a thorough review of your hiring practices and send me the report. Someone's head needs to roll."

Walther nodded, although Magda knew nobody's head would.

"As for a penance..." Himmler reverted to the smile that was empty, not charming. "If you could manufacture me some extra hours in the day on one of your conveyor belts, I would be delighted to take those." He turned the smile onto Magda. "Or make me a secretary as capable as yours—that's an area where I am sadly lacking."

Because you're sleeping with your current one and, rumor has it, she's pregnant, so you need to get her clear of your wife.

"I could work for you."

The words were out of Magda's mouth while her brain was still occupied with Hedwig Potthast and how such a sweet-looking little thing could climb into bed with a man as soul-sick as Himmler.

Both men frowned. Magda ignored that and rushed to finish the idea that suddenly struck her as perfect.

"If you need help, I am sure Herr Tiedemann could spare me, if it was for the Party and the war effort, that is. I could train an assistant to do most of my work here and—if the arrangement was suitable to your needs, Herr Reichsführer—perhaps I could stay with Herr Tiedemann one day a week, for a while, to make sure everything here also runs smoothly."

"An excellent suggestion, Magda; I should have proposed it myself. What do you think, Heinrich? Trust me, a week with this one by your side and your life will run easier than you ever imagined."

Walther was as exactly in step as Magda needed him to be, landing the catch she had visibly snared.

Himmler left the office thrilled to be "treated with such generosity," with all thoughts of Christoph's connections to the Tiedemann Company forgotten.

"Can you do it, Magda? This isn't putting on a face and socializing for a few hours—this is in the heart of his dealings. You've seen Elsa, and Kiefer, and me. You know what it costs to be near them."

Magda watched the black Mercedes swing out of the gates and nodded. She didn't trust her voice. She stood in silence until the car was out of sight, trying to hear Walther's "I'm proud of you" over the warning he had once given her. A warning she had barely noted then but was drumming through her head now: *Being with men whose values are as twisted as Himmler's corrodes a little piece of your soul.*

CHAPTER FIVE

Nina, November 1987–April 1988

The bang tore them out of bed, convinced the door was coming in. They rolled onto the floor, scrabbling for the jumpers and jeans they had discarded in a muddle the night before. Instead of the pounding footsteps they expected, however, there was silence.

Nina put down the one sock she had managed to find and sat back on the bed.

"Perhaps it was thunder—maybe there's a storm coming."

As much as she wanted that to be true, the second burst of noise wasn't a bang but a sharp rattle neither of them could pretend was hailstones. Nina raced to the window and shoved at the stiff sash.

"Can you see anything?"

She shook her head, wincing as the window flew open and an ice-sharp wind rushed in. A second wave of machine-gun fire split the air. Nina squinted into the darkness, trying to find an answer for Stefan's, "Which direction is it coming from?"

"It's the Sonnenallee crossing point. Look."

She shifted over to make room for his still sleep-warm body.

The sulfur-yellow watchtower lights had been joined by a string of bright flares that lit up the Wall like a sports stadium. As she opened the window wide enough to lean out, the burst from a third volley of shots flew up at them.

"Someone must have tried to get across." Stefan stopped. They could hear the dogs now, their howls rippling through the cloudless winter sky.

"Did you hear that?" Nina jumped back from the glass as a cry floated up above the barking. "We need to go. Someone might need help."

They tore round the small flat, gathering up warm coats and boots with thick rubber soles that wouldn't disturb the pavements. Neither spoke as they pulled their clothes on—they were both focused on the streets outside, listening for sirens and engines. There wasn't a sound to be heard; neither of them took that as a good sign.

The night they stepped into was a bitter one. Snow flurries blanketed the parked cars; litter lay frozen into spiky-edged clumps. There wasn't a soul to be seen anywhere in Kiefholzstraße. Nina wasn't surprised—5 a.m. was too early for the street to be up and, even if it wasn't, gunfire wasn't an alarm clock many would rise for. She buttoned her coat tight and jammed her hands in her pockets before the cold could catch them.

"The quickest way is straight down Baumschulenstraße. Let's see how close we can get that way first rather than ducking in and out of the backstreets."

Nina nodded and they set off. They didn't waste time discussing a plan. Their remit was a simple one: help if there was help they could give; bear witness to what the soldiers did; report whatever had happened to one of the Western media contacts they knew only through code names. They had done it before; they had got away with it before. Both of them knew that didn't mean a thing.

For all Magda's efforts at the cement factory, the life Nina was living now at nineteen bore no relation to the one her grandmother had bargained with the Stasi to hold on to. Nina wasn't unhappy with that, although there were plenty of reasons why she could be. There was no Julia anymore, which was a huge gap in Nina's life, but at least she and her parents hadn't been captured: they had escaped to the West, something, apparently, they had long been planning to do. There had also been no *Abitur*, which had been an equally hard loss. Principal Huber had laughed when he read her application.

"Why would we let you sit an examination that opens the door to occupations you will never be allowed near? Nothing in your conduct merits it. And as for the profession you imagine yourself working in... Broadcast journalism? My dear girl, you're deluded. With the way you have behaved, you'll be lucky to pick up the lowliest apprenticeship."

Whether his words were a prophecy or a promise, Nina never knew, but he had been proved right. The only opening she had been able to find was a job stacking shelves in one of the *Konsum* state-operated food stores that rarely had any produce to stack. It was miserable work, filled with angry customers, tired of queuing for staples that were never in stock or government-engineered substitutes whose prices kept climbing. There was no consolation for her lost future to be found at work, and none at home either. Although Nina had assumed the Stasi would drag her in and order her to become an informant, they didn't, but they did insert themselves into every corner of Magda and the Dahlkes' lives, to prove that they could. Nothing was overt, nothing was obvious. The Trabi's tires developed endless punctures. Britte's bike saddle routinely disappeared. Magda came home one afternoon and found the contents of her cupboards rearranged. The electricity went on and off in the Dahlkes' apartment while the rest of the block worked more smoothly than it ever had. After six months of subtle intrusions intended to prove exactly who was in charge, the family were blaming each other for attracting unwanted attention and torn up by arguments.

It was a load Nina could have crumbled under, but she didn't. Julia had escaped—Nina counted that as a victory. And because she had kept her mouth shut at the factory, Nina had a cause, and Nina had Stefan.

In the brief time she had to explain anything at all before the Voigts fled, Julia had told her brother that it was Nina who had

kept her out of the Stasi's hands. Because he was far more interested
in fighting for the East than fleeing with his parents to the West,
Stefan had gone temporarily to ground and stayed safe. When he
re-emerged, he sought Nina out. They had been inseparable from
the first night they ran through Treptow together pasting up peace
posters. Now Nina spent her days organizing concerts for punk
bands who sang about rebellion and writing anonymous reports
about Stasi brutality, which the Western papers lapped up. They
both knew they were on watch lists; they both refused to believe
they were on borrowed time. And every time Magda threw that at
Nina and begged her to stop, the gap between grandmother and
granddaughter grew.

*So God knows what she would do if she could see me now, running
through the dark toward bullets.*

"We need to get off the main street."

Stefan's sharp command pulled Nina away from thoughts of
Magda and back to the street. A black van had eased to a silent
stop a few hundred meters in front of them; black-clad soldiers
were spilling silently out of it.

"Wohlgemuthstraße will take us round to the derelict houses.
We've our best chance of seeing what's going on from there."

They moved silently, skirting the curving backstreets until they
reached a patch of wasteland that was as desolate as it had been
when it was cleared of people in 1961. Most of the properties
flanking the border had been demolished when the Wall was built,
to prevent their windows being used as escape routes. One or two
houses had remained, however, shuttered up and forgotten as the
money to deal with them ran out. The first had iron plates, thick
with graffiti, secured across its doors. The second had crumbled
enough around the lower windows to offer a way in. The smell as
they scrambled through was rank with ammonia and rot. Nina's
eyes streamed—she had to fight the urge to gag. Stefan wrapped

his scarf round his mouth and nose and gestured to the staircase leaning drunkenly against the wall.

It wasn't an easy climb: most of the stairs had jagged ankle-sized holes in their middles and, when Nina tried to grab hold of the banister to steady herself, it swayed nastily away.

"This is high enough."

Nina bent down in front of a window that had been lazily and only partially bricked up. Stefan kneeled beside her. Unlike the quiet streets, the checkpoint they could see through the gaps was alive with movement. Soldiers filled the stretches of grass and sand between the inner and outer walls. Some were crouching, rifles ready. Some held straining dog leashes. The only sound, however, came from the western side.

"*Murderers.* They're shouting *murderers.* Why?" Their vantage point was too narrow. Nina eased out a brick as she whispered and widened the hole they were watching through. "And what on earth is that doing parked over there?"

There was a truck—not a military one, but an everyday tail-lift type—pressed hard against the outer wall.

"It's not parked; it's crashed." Stefan's voice hardened. "And there's someone on the ground next to it."

Nina could see clearly now. Steam rose from the engine, metal was strewn across the sand and—exactly as Stefan had said—a body sprawled beside one of the wheels, a stain spreading round its head like a pillow. As they watched, a group of soldiers moved forward. The cohort circled the vehicle and then one of them squatted down and tugged a second body out from beneath the chassis.

"Why do they have to do it that way? Drag him across the ground as though he's a lump of meat, not a person?"

Fury made Nina clumsy. As she leaned forward, her elbow caught the loosely cemented bricks in the window space. Slowly, one after the other, half a dozen dislodged and tumbled to the ground. The crash carried through the crisp air as loud as the dawn's gunfire chorus. A soldier turned, and then another.

"Move!"

Stefan was on his feet, dragging Nina behind him down the staircase. They crashed across the stairs, not caring whether the planks broke or not, and landed on the stone floor in a cloud of dust and splinters. As they pushed back through the window, an engine spluttered into life. As they tumbled out onto the wasteland, the footsteps they had expected to hear earlier that morning pounded into life. They ran, faster than they had ever run in their lives. It wasn't fast enough.

Keep to the shadows. Keep your head down. Check every vehicle twice.

It had been three months since the Sonnenallee shooting and the horror of Stefan's death in a hail of bullets. Three long months that Nina had spent in hiding, moving between safe houses, avoiding daylight and terrified of a knock on the door. All that time avoiding danger and still the numbness of loss and her fear over Magda had wiped every carefully learned instruction away. When the news of Magda's arrest had seeped through to Nina's burrow, it had forced her, against every advice, back into the light. Nina knew that Magda's detention—which had lasted less than a day if the source had it right—could be a trap to smoke her out. So could the source. It didn't matter. Nina left her attic space. She hurried down streets that were far too bright. She didn't pause to look around, so she didn't notice the van. Even though it was a fish delivery van, and anyone who knew anything about the Stasi knew all about them. She didn't hear its doors slide open. She didn't hear the man who crept out of it. She didn't feel the hand that reached for her until it fastened to her mouth like glue. They caught her as easily as the fish they never carried.

*

"Hands under your thighs, palms up. Back straight."

The stool was too low. The position it forced Nina into—knees jutting up to her chin—stabbed pain through her legs and lower back. She didn't dare move. This interview bore no resemblance to the one the leafleting episode had led to. She had no idea where she was, although—after the first few days followed the patterns she remembered from Stefan's stories—she was as certain as she could be that it was Hohenschönhausen Prison.

Nina had been snatched from the street so quickly, she had lost any sense of time and place from the moment she had been hauled into the van and dragged back out from that into what she assumed, from the smell of petrol, was a garage, although the lights were too dazzling to make anything out. She was no longer in her own clothes—they had been stripped roughly from her in front of an audience she refused to see and replaced by a scratchy blue tracksuit. She no longer had a name—she was Prisoner 622. Beyond commands to "strip" and "stand still" and "keep your head down," no one had spoken to her. Time had grown elastic. She had barely slept. The lightbulb burst into life without warning during what was meant to be the night. Someone yelled at her if she slipped into sleep during the day.

Other than the uniformed men shouting and pushing at her, Nina had seen no one. She had heard footsteps twice as they moved her down the narrow empty corridors. She had turned frantically both times, convinced Stefan would be there, momentarily forgetting that the last time she had seen him he was more bullet holes than skin. Instead, red lights had flashed and an alarm had started furiously buzzing and she was pushed face-first into the wall before she could get a glimpse of anyone at all. The same routine had been repeated on her way to the room she now sat in. She could still feel the print of the rough wallpaper indenting her skin.

"Sit straighter."

The man facing her this time was in uniform and his questions were relentless.

"What was your role? Who were your accomplices?"

Nina kept giving the same answer: "In what?" All he did was keep asking. In the end, she slid off the stool, her legs and her back too numb to support her. She was taken back to her cell. The light went on and off; the guard outside yelled whenever she turned from her back to her side on the hard bunk, which she did without fail at least twice an hour. She was returned to the interview room. The cycle went on, and on.

On the fourth, or perhaps the fifth, night, Nina broke. She shouted at her interrogator, demanding to know how he could expect her to tell him about her role in an escape attempt nobody had ever reported. The officer simply added, "Then how did you know about it?" to his two original questions.

On the sixth, or possibly the seventh, night they tried a different tactic.

"Why do you keep resisting? You know that we know all about you. Your boyfriend is dead. Your grandmother, as I am sure that you are aware or why would you have broken cover, was arrested. Perhaps she will be arrested again. Who knows what we might need to do? What is certain is that you aren't going anywhere until you talk."

Nina had promised herself she wouldn't react if they spoke about Stefan, but at the mention of Magda, her head shot up.

"If you have hurt her in any way..."

Her interrogator laughed. "What? What will you do, Nina? Do you want to help her?"

The pivot caught her off guard—as the officer intended it to. "How?"

He smiled. "It's easy. You stop all this pointless resistance and you work for us. You keep an eye on your neighbors. You keep promoting those ridiculous bands. You tell us what is happening. And you tell us about your grandmother."

Nina's neck prickled. There was danger here, but there was also a way out.

"What do you want to know about her?"

The officer closed his file. "Whatever you think we would like to hear. She has secrets, Nina, you know that as well as we do. Help us make sure they aren't dangerous ones, and then your parents keep their jobs and their homes and maybe we can find you the college place you wanted. Refuse and, well, you're a bright girl: I am sure you can imagine how that choice would play out."

They haven't got anything on her. If they had, they wouldn't need me.

The certainty of that sat Nina up straight without any jabbing reminders.

And if I'm the one watching her, they won't get anything on her at all.

She nodded. She signed the papers. She was back in a van and out on the streets again before the day was done.

"I'm leaving for the West tonight."

Magda sank onto the sofa, her whole body trembling, as limp as if all the breath had flown out of her.

"Leaving? How? You don't have permission; you don't have a permit. What are you planning? What are you going to do?"

Nina's instinct was to run to her grandmother and soothe Magda's fear; she held herself back. She could be too easily persuaded out of what had to be done.

"I can't tell you—it's not safe."

Nina stopped. The truth was that she had told Magda so little about the events of the previous November, or her subsequent three-month disappearance, that she didn't now know where to start. She hadn't explained her sudden reappearance six weeks earlier in the last week of February beyond, "It was time to come home." She hadn't told Magda about her own arrest and neither of them had mentioned Magda's. She hadn't told her about Stefan's death.

Not that she had told anyone about that: the only way she could deal with his loss was to keep it firmly locked up inside her. And she hadn't breathed a word about her deal with the Stasi.

All I've done is build another layer of secrets. I can't leave without remedying that.

"All right, the truth then. The Stasi caught me, last November, when I got too close to a shooting they wanted hushed up. I kept away after that because I thought I was a danger to everyone, especially to you. I know they pulled you in, and I know I should have asked why, although I suspect it was more about me than you. It's all been such a mess." She shook her head as Magda tried to speak. "Let me get this out while I've still got time. I knew trouble was coming. You and I both know I'd been on the Stasi's radar since I got involved with—" She stopped again, unable to say his name and keep talking. "Anyway, the Stasi knew I was passing stories about the repressions here to the West. And then I heard you had been arrested, so I broke cover, and I was foolish, and I was caught. I made a bargain with them—there was no other choice—that's how I got out. But I didn't keep my end of it, so now when they catch me, it's prison. I can't face that, so I'm leaving."

"What did you promise them, Nina?"

It was obvious from Magda's flat tone that she had already guessed. Nina looked away.

"To inform on our neighbors, and some of my friends. And on you, which was what they really wanted. They wouldn't say why they had arrested you. I think it was about flushing me out, unless they've still got a bee in their bonnets about the house in the West. The reason didn't matter: I agreed so they wouldn't give the job to anyone else. It was the only way I could think of to protect you."

Magda's perfectly still face gave nothing away. "But they released me almost at once; if you knew they had arrested me, you must have known that. And they have nothing on me, because there is nothing to get."

The same old story. Nina wondered if Magda still thought Nina believed it. That didn't matter either.

"They think there is. Which is the other reason why I'm going. When I'm settled, you have to come and join me: whatever the truth of this is, we both need a safe home. So give me a few days, give me until Thursday, and then I'll be waiting at the crossing point at Friedrichstraβe station. I'll wait all day. You'll have no problem coming through and, at your age, no one will question your plans or care if you stay."

Magda drew herself in so tight, she looked half her size. "Even if that wasn't an impossible idea, what about your parents? Do you think leaving is an option for them?"

And this was the hardest bit, the bit that had sounded wrong whenever Nina imagined saying it.

Do it fast. Don't stop.

"No, I wouldn't ask them to. They'll stay here, and they'll survive because they believe in the system. Even if they are punished because I ran, they'll accept it." Magda started to protest; Nina refused to hear her. "It's not fair, I know that, and I'm sorry, but it can't be helped. You said it yourself—*there's always a choice that isn't a choice; it's always impossible to save everyone.* The Stasi are after me, and they are after you. I don't even care anymore why, or what you did or didn't do, but I won't leave you here to face them."

Magda's face was no longer still: it had collapsed as if there was no life left to hold it.

"But what if it is time that I did face them, or face someone? Have you considered that? Have you considered that perhaps I should be investigated and held to account? That there are things I have done that warrant it? And what about your mother, my daughter? Yes, she can be foolish and over-obedient, but she isn't a bad person. Neither is Holger. They aren't the ones who deserve punishing. When I said that to you about choices, I didn't mean this. I didn't mean you were ever supposed to be the one making them."

Nina glanced at the clock and realized she only had minutes left. How was she supposed to unpack *held to account* and *the ones who deserve punishing* in minutes?

"Fine, then tell me, once and for all: what do the Stasi suspect? What is this big secret?"

Magda continued to stare at her, but she said nothing.

Nina shook her head. "Fine. Don't tell me. What does it matter. I've thought about this; I've got a plan. We need a safe home, where we can stay for good if we want to—well, maybe we've already got one. I'm going to go to Grunewald; I'm going to find Erdener Straße and see if the Tower House is still standing. Maybe we can live there. And maybe I'll find out for myself what you're so determined to keep hidden."

"No." It was more of a sound than a word. "You can't. You have to promise me that you won't do that."

Magda's voice was suddenly that old strangled mix of horror and fury that made Nina's neck prickle.

"Ignore what I said: I don't want my past dug up. There's things I've done, Nina. For the right reasons but that...went wrong, or might look wrong to someone who wasn't there. Things I don't want stirred up again."

"What *things*, Grandma? You can't keep leaving me with veiled hints like this."

But even if Magda had wanted to tell her, it was too late. There was a soft rap on the door Nina knew meant *come now or don't come.*

"I have to go. Here, I can't take this; it's got my old papers in it. Bring it with you when you cross over."

Nina dropped her black leather handbag—the one she knew Magda had spent far too much money on the previous Christmas —onto the table. As Magda clutched it to her, Nina's resolve almost broke. There was nowhere she wanted to be except tight inside her grandmother's embrace. Holding her body back was an agony.

What if I never see her again? What if she doesn't follow me?

The pain of that thought was crippling, but Jannick's instructions had been brutally clear: "One knock, I wait two minutes; if you don't appear, we're done."

"I'll be there, at the station, on Thursday. I'll wait all day for you."

"Nina!"

She ran to the door and wrenched it open. By the time Magda caught up with her, Nina was gone.

Jannick hustled Nina into the car before she had a chance to change her mind. He didn't comment on her distress.

"Stick this inside your coat where it won't be visible. It will see you through the first few days until our contact gets you settled."

He handed her a waterproof packet containing a passport stamped with the Federal Republic's crest and a small amount of West German Deutschmarks and switched his attention back to the road. Nina had no idea where they were going, or whether she could bear to leave anymore. She had no idea of his plan either, beyond the fact that he had told her to wear a thick coat, even though spring had finally arrived and the days were getting warmer, and sturdy boots.

"He doesn't say much, I know, but he's one of the best. If you ever need help, he's the one to ask."

Nina stared out at the sparsely filled streets, trying to take confidence from what Stefan had told her about his friend when he had first introduced her to Jannick. It was hard not to start crying again at the thought of him. Over five months had passed since his murder and she could still feel every second of that night. She had left him dead in the street—the misery of that still haunted her. There had been no funeral. There had been no memorial except the long nights she had spent crying in a series of tiny rooms. And now she had to leave any trace of him behind for good or face years lost in a prison system she knew would destroy her.

It was Jannick who had made her face up to that truth, after the second time she had been hauled in front of a Stasi agent whose patience with her lack of reports was snapping. His, "You have to get out; I'll organize it," had made the task of escaping seem far simpler than Nina knew it would be.

"We're doing this the old-fashioned way."

It was so rare for Jannick to volunteer information, it took Nina a moment to register that he was speaking.

"You can't risk a false passport at a crossing point—your photo will have been circulated as a flight risk. The border's tightened up too much after the truck attempt to risk sticking you in the boot of a car, which means you're going across through a tunnel."

"What?" Nina momentarily forgot all about Stefan and Magda. "How? I thought all the tunnels had been found and blocked up years ago."

Jannick shrugged. "Some of us have been opening them up again. Since December we've got two big groups through, so the six of you tonight should be plain sailing."

The car was already slowing down, although they'd only been driving for twenty minutes or so. Jannick parked in an empty side street, told Nina to keep away from windows and lamp posts, and led her silently through a bunch of short alleyways to a row of what appeared to be disused warehouses.

"The tunnel you're going through is in the basement of the middle building. It was built in the sixties and leads out into Kreuzberg. It's not unmanageably long, but it will be cold, and the floor will be sodden. You'll have to crouch through most of it. Keep your breathing steady, keep going and you'll be fine."

There was another figure approaching, sticking as tightly to the shadows as they had, only visible because Nina was looking. She focused on their zigzagging movements, rather than *sodden* and *crouch*.

"One more goes in, and then it's us. Get ready."

Nina was halfway across the road when the spotlights bloomed.

"Down on the ground, arms splayed!"

She stumbled forward as the spray of light hit her. The figure she had been watching made a dive for the warehouse. A single—and, from the scream that followed it, accurate—shot rang out.

"Get down!"

Nina couldn't see Jannick; she couldn't see anyone. She threw herself to the ground as another bullet whistled past. Her knees cracked into the cobbles, and her chin followed. A searing pain ran through her bitten lip and bruised legs. And then they went numb and she could feel nothing at all, except the muzzle of the gun jammed into the back of her head.

CHAPTER SIX

Magda, August–October 1941

It wasn't until he said her name that Magda knew it was Christoph. Then she was able to see past the sunken cheeks and purple-shadowed eyes, and imagine flesh once again coating his bones. She pulled him inside, so desperate to hold him she barely noticed his animal smell. When the next words out of his mouth were, "I couldn't do it; I couldn't kill like that," she wouldn't let him speak again until she had drawn him a hot bath and found him clean clothes and watched him devour two bowls of chicken-rich soup with a ferocity that made her want to weep.

In the seventeen months since he had been arrested and had disappeared from her life, Christoph had aged beyond anything natural. He was twenty-eight years old: his haggard face looked twice that; his haunted eyes looked older still.

"They sent me to the Western Front first." His voice was rusty, as if he hadn't tried it out in a while. "The fighting was hard, but I got through it. By last July, I was in Paris. We completely overran it: if you saw the place now, you would think it was German. That was where we finally got a break—the commanders let us roam around as if we were tourists. It's so beautiful, Magda; once this is done, I'll take you there, I promise."

He smiled at her then, for the first time since he'd stumbled through the cottage's now firmly locked door. It was a fleeting thing that barely touched his lips, but it made Magda's heart lift in the seconds before it vanished.

"I really thought I had landed on my feet. I was hoping for a few quiet months patrolling, planning to keep my head down and talk my way into some leave, then come back to you and be done with it. Trouble was, I was a marked man—a communist and a 'Jew lover,' the two worst sins—and there was no chance of me slipping anyone's notice. I managed a week in Paris and then I was shipped out on a transport east. It was the last place I wanted to go, especially after Kiefer's photographs, but I wasn't surprised at the posting. We'd heard the reports that Russia had stopped pretending to be our ally and was pushing at Poland, threatening to take back the territories Germany had won. I wasn't surprised at that either, to be honest. I never believed the non-aggression pact Stalin signed with Hitler back in '39 would stand—how could it? In what world could communism and fascism ever sit comfortably together?"

He rubbed a hand across eyes that had finally caught a spark. Magda leaned forward, hoping he was about to launch into one of the tirades that had fueled him in the early days of the war. Hoping he was about to return to himself. He didn't. He slumped in his chair instead, his flickering eyes seeing things she knew she did not want to.

"Anyway, they moved me out of Paris and on to Poland. I wasn't ready for that, I really wasn't. The cities there weren't beautiful anymore; they were barely even cities." His face darkened; he didn't appear to notice that Magda had taken his hand, or that she was silently weeping. "One place we were quartered near, Wieluń, was totally flattened, the buildings heaped on top of each other like kindling. Nearly a year had passed since we bombed it, and the air still tasted of dust. As for Warsaw... One of my comrades had been there before the war—he described it as the most elegant city he'd ever seen. It wasn't elegant when we marched in. There wasn't a street without shell damage. Some of the walls had no more substance than lace." He paused. "Except for the ghetto. The walls around that were solid enough."

Which they would have to be. How else do you cut almost half a million people out of their lives, if not with thick walls and fear?

Magda stayed quiet. Christoph wasn't ready to hear that she knew what had been done to the Jewish population in Warsaw: he would only ask how she knew it. She let him continue wandering through his memories instead.

"They put me on ghetto duty of course, because patrolling its walls 'was the perfect job for a Jew protector.' Except protecting wasn't what they wanted me to do. My main—my only—duty was to shoot anyone who escaped, including the children, who were the only ones with the nerve by that point to try. 'Shoot to kill and leave the bodies where they fall' was the order, the way farmers tie dead crows to a fence to act as a warning."

She didn't want to ask, but she had to know how deep his scars ran. "Did you do it?"

Christoph looked at Magda as if he had forgotten she was there.

"No, of course not. I would have taken a bullet myself first. More of us would have than you would think if you listen to Kiefer. Not that it mattered, because there were far more who were happy to oblige—who held shooting parties if as much as a shadow moved."

He suddenly gripped her hand so hard she could feel her bones grating. "I still see them, Magda, when I sleep. I can't make the images stop. Children so hungry they were desiccated, their faces turned old. I can still smell the stink of the place." He pulled away from her and reached for the schnapps bottle, pouring a measure that filled up his glass. "It's a sport to the SS. Funneling Jews into a ghetto, pinning stars on their arms like targets. It's all about making them easier to hunt. I'm surprised Hitler doesn't have them wearing markers on top of their hearts and be done with it."

"That's coming." Magda shook her head as Christoph stared at her, his face creased in confusion. "It's nothing, forget it. I'm so sorry you've seen what you've seen; I wish I could wipe it all from your memory. And I'm glad you walked away, no matter how much danger that puts you in. Was that it? Was Warsaw the reason you left?"

"No." He took another deep drink. "It should have been, but I had comrades I thought I owed some kind of loyalty to. I was there for a month, and then we were moved on again farther east. I don't know where to; the place names stopped meaning anything after a while. We mopped up partisans, we were sent on exercises, we were constantly practicing for what the officers kept referring to as 'the next big push.'"

"The attack against Russia?"

He nodded. It was what Magda had suspected had broken him since the disheveled stranger banging at her door had turned into Christoph. It was what she had been praying that he—with his long love of the country—wasn't involved in since Goebbels had announced the invasion of Russia across German airwaves on the twenty-second of June. The way the Party-faithful newspapers and newsreels, and the staff in Himmler's Prinz Albrecht Straβe office— whose typists and secretarial assistants were now under Magda's firm hand—had reacted, anyone watching would have thought the destruction of Russia was the only reason Germany had entered the war. All through July, the press had fattened their readers on a diet of Russian atrocities and Germany's moral obligation to subdue the "savages" and "sub-humans" who threatened the Reich. The last time Magda had seen her parents—when she had accidentally confessed who she now worked for but couldn't explain why for fear of embroiling them, and had therefore been met with horror and disgust—they had been weeping over the hate-inflamed headlines. And now it was clear from Christoph's tortured face that the reality of the invasion had been even worse than the promises the papers had made.

"What we have done there...it will come back to haunt us, Magda—it must."

He began to cry, noiselessly and without seeming to notice the tears falling down his thin face. Magda couldn't move; she thought her heart would break at the sight of his misery.

"The Russian people are being slaughtered, not just the soldiers. Russian Jews are being hunted down and butchered. I saw men driven into a synagogue and burned alive. I saw mothers shot as they tried to wrap their bodies round their children, and those children dragged out from beneath their dead mothers and shot too. Thousands of them, rounded up and exterminated, as if they were lice or ants. The hatred is past anything human."

Thirty million are to be eradicated. The Russians are to be wiped from the earth, the Jews first among them.

Himmler's words. Magda had typed them a month ago, just before he had embarked on a tour of poor crushed Lithuania to ensure his—and Hitler's—dream of Russia's enslavement was being properly carried out. She had copied them out and sent them to Eckhart Bühl, in the vain hope that this time they would reach one of his contacts in America or Britain, and not fall into the silence that had apparently swallowed every one of their attempts at communication.

Christoph's voice had almost petered out; she forced herself to focus.

"I couldn't stop it. I couldn't be a part of it. I walked away. I walked for weeks, making my way back to you."

Magda wanted to ask him, "And what now?" but he was drained, and, besides, there was only one answer to that question. Christoph was a deserter: he had been in danger before he was conscripted; now there was no safe way of re-entering the world unless he could reinvent himself.

She got up and wrapped her arms around him, kissed the top of his beaten head.

"Stay here tonight, with me, where you belong. It isn't safe to stay longer, not with Elsa and so many Party officials prowling around Grunewald, but I'll talk to Walther. I'll find you a better cover, where you can get back to yourself." She didn't add "if you can"; she had to trust that he could.

He leaned back into the comfort of her arms. "I could go to Oberschöneweide. Your parents would shelter me, and we could meet easier there."

Magda smiled and took his hand and led him upstairs to bed. There would be time enough when he had slept to explain why, for her, that door was firmly shut.

I should turn their own tactics against them—bolt the doors and throw in a match.

Magda ducked as another camera bulb flashed. Photographers had swarmed all over the ceremony in Berlin Cathedral; now they swarmed all over the reception at the Kaiserhof Hotel. Elsa wanted every moment of her wedding day captured. If Magda ever hoped to hold her head up in Oberschöneweide again, however, she couldn't afford to be caught among the uniformed guests. Keeping the nearest cameraman firmly in sight, she weaved her way through the stragglers still milling around the ballroom, despite the hotel manager's best efforts to move them out and his orchestra in.

The wedding breakfast and the speeches were done. Hitler, thank God, had left before Magda had been summoned to hold down her stomach and meet him. There would be an hour before the syrup-soaked sponge cake—whose triple layers and intricate icing made a mockery of the rationing starting to bite in the rest of Berlin—was cut and the dancing began. Time enough for her to find Walther and pull him away from the froth and the flowers and back into the real world.

Not that I have much claim on that anymore.

Since joining Himmler's staff as his personal secretary, Magda's life had grown even more comfortable than Walther had made it.

She spent her days in the back of polished limousines and in offices and homes that were warmly lit and well stocked. Himmler paid her far more than he needed to ensure she was at his permanent beck and call. She had a dress allowance to ensure she always looked as smart as he demanded her to be. He had even started to grumble that the small guest cottage she lived in did not reflect well enough on her new status, and therefore on his. The privileged life Magda lived was not one she wanted, and the cost of living it was high. She knew, however, it was a life most of the tired and hungry citizens of Berlin would have stepped gratefully into. The city outside her comfortable world, the city Christoph and her parents lived in, was feeling the pinch of a war that, despite two hard years and too many promises, showed little sign of ending.

Most people's daily pattern was standing by empty shelves and in long queues. Most people's reality was dealing with the increasing shortages of everything their daily lives needed—from leather to sole their shoes with, to ink and candles and paper—and permanent shortages of coal. Unlike Magda, who never had to think about what was in her larder, Berlin's citizens—or at least the ones who weren't Jewish, who could starve as far as the Party was concerned—juggled ration cards and the burgeoning black market and were still left with growling stomachs. Wedding breakfasts outside the Kaiserhof weren't three-course affairs that finished with platters of honey-soaked pastries. Wedding guests outside the Kaiserhof weren't draped in pastel-colored bias-cut silk and silver-set gemstones. For some of the women marrying on the same blue-skied October day as Elsa Tiedemann, the only ornament they wore would be a six-pointed yellow star.

I'm surprised Hitler doesn't have them wearing markers on top of their hearts and be done with it.

Magda clutched at the swastika-draped banister as Christoph's words flew back. Well now Hitler had: since September, all Jewish people over the age of six had been ordered to wear the star on their lapels, and God help anyone who defied that.

"Are you all right?"

Walther had found her. Magda let him take her arm and settle her at a spindly gilt table with a gin fizz in her hand. She collected herself quickly, making sure to laugh if anyone looked their way.

"You haven't visited Spandau in weeks. I was beginning to worry."

Magda sipped at her drink, her mouth puckering at the sharp lemon juice, and accepted a cigarette from Walther's monogrammed case.

"I couldn't get away—he's got me working round the clock. There's something coming, Walther, but, no matter how many confidential memos I file—and copy—I can't work out what it is. I know it's worse than ghettoes. There are reports coming in daily from Heydrich and that uptight logistics man of his, Eichmann, about the extension of labor camps and new 'detention facilities' that they seem to be planning to build on a gigantic scale. And they've got me doing these costings..." She stopped and checked the nearby tables. There was nobody close to them, but she dropped her voice anyway. "I've got such a bad feeling about them. Himmler used bland words—*cargo* and *collection facility*—when he briefed me, and I have to do the same when I write the report, but I know they don't tell the real story. I've got all these figures for different sizes of *freight*—which is another word he's very insistent on—that needs moving, although I don't know where to. Four pfennigs for large units, two for smaller ones; a discounted rate if more than 400 are moved at one time." Her hand had started to shake.

Walther gently removed the cigarette from between her fingers and stubbed it out.

"What do you think it is, Magda? Food for the troops? Livestock? Some of the art they've been looting from Paris?"

The orchestra had started up. Magda could hear the first notes of Lehár's "Gold und Silber" waltz spilling out of the ballroom.

"I wanted to think that. If the trains I had to calculate the loads for had been cattle trucks or goods wagons and nothing else, I might have believed it. But part of the exercise was a cost comparison and—when Himmler told me not to bother checking the engine types and simply call them Model A and Model B—I got suspicious. Some of the letters hadn't been completely erased from the forms, so I looked up the locomotive descriptions. Model B was a freight train like I expected, but Model A was the passenger kind. Which suggests that at least some of the *cargo* they are so carefully costing isn't animals or paintings but people."

She didn't need to add "and most likely the ones wearing stars"—Walther's tightened jaw told her he was already there.

"How many transports did he make you do the exercise for?"

Magda picked up her drink again. "He didn't give me a number. All he wanted was a formula for the cheapest way of doing things. And the calculations were done per kilometer of track, which means I couldn't work out the distances involved, or, therefore, the destinations."

Walther lit another cigarette, although his previous one was still smoldering in the ashtray.

"Eichmann was the officer they sent to Austria to take charge of the Jewish residents there after the *Anschluß*. By the time he had finished confiscating their businesses and legislating them out of existence, there were hardly any left. He moved onto Poland after that where—or so rumor has it—he's been moving Jewish families in from all over the occupied territories. What I don't know is why…"

"So this is where you've been hiding. Honestly, Papa, can't business wait, today of all days? Gunther and I are ready to start the dancing, and how can we do that without you there to applaud us?"

Elsa had appeared at Walther's elbow without either of them noticing. Magda couldn't tell if she had heard any of their conversation. She didn't look troubled, the way she surely would have if she had. Her eyes sparkled beneath the flattering frame of a floor-length lace veil and a diamond tiara that danced a circle of stars around her blonde hair. Her pale pink mouth was on the pretty side of petulant.

Walther immediately stopped talking and jumped to his feet, all kisses and apologies. He rushed off to the ballroom as soon as she shooed him away. Elsa watched him go, but she didn't follow. She flicked out the circular train on her figure-hugging satin dress instead and stared down at Magda with an expression that was uncomfortably predatory.

"I thought you had your sights set on a wedding day like this when Papa first introduced you. I assumed your intention was to marry him. I sometimes wonder if that's still your plan; you've got your claws in deep enough. Or are you aiming higher now that you've landed your shiny new job? Are you planning to become the next Frau Himmler? It's a higher-stakes play, but you could win it, if you made more effort on the sexy seductress front and less on the humble secretary. Dear Heinrich is awfully bored with his wife, but, as happy as he is to bed little Heddy, he's not in any hurry to divorce Margarete in order to marry the mistress, or not that one. So are you going to go for it? Are you going to smother Heinrich with your charms and hop in there first?"

The idea that Magda had wanted to marry Walther was absurd; the idea that she wanted to marry Himmler was repulsive. Magda, however, refused to take the bait and said nothing. When Elsa was in this catlike mood, it was better to let her run with whatever nastiness she was spinning.

"Sticking to silence, your favorite trick? That's a shame, because I could do with some help here to understand exactly what your goal is. You play the part of a respectable German *fräulein*, so when are you intending to complete the picture and snare a husband, produce a pack of children to serve the Reich? And if your hubby's not going to be my dear father, which, trust me, it's not, then who? Are you hoping Heinrich will find a suitable man for you, if you're not after him of course. Shall I ask him to start looking?"

It wasn't a genuine question—there was too much malice in Elsa's face for that. And there wasn't an honest answer Magda could give. What was she meant to say? *I would rather jump from the hotel roof than marry a man who wears a Death's Head ring and a skull on his cap and birth a generation of killers just like Daddy.* Or perhaps: *I would sooner cut out my heart than sign my life over to the care of a pack of murderers and promise to "consecrate my life to the SS" the way you did in front of Himmler this morning.*

Magda got up and smoothed the wrinkles out of her duck-egg-blue gown. She had no interest in playing games with Elsa; she had no interest in this wedding. She would dance one dance for appearances' sake, and then she was done with the day. Elsa, however, wasn't finished.

"I know that you hate us. That marrying an SS man would turn your stomach."

It was all Magda could do to hold her face still. Elsa had stopped any pretense of smiling.

"I watch you. I've watched you since you first stuck your nose into my family's business. And I've dug around in yours. I've wondered for years what a left-wing agitator's daughter from a nasty little neighborhood like Oberschöneweide is doing playing nice with the National Socialists. I doubt it's to advance the cause. You've got a secret, and I don't like those, and you've got some kind of hold over my father, which I like even less. I'll ferret it out, trust me. And if my family or my Führer is in any way threatened by it, I'll make you pay."

Magda couldn't let that go in silence—it was too close to the truth. She shook her head and, although her heart was hammering, she aimed as hard as she could for outrage.

"That is not only ridiculous, it is an insult. Maybe you've had one too many glasses of champagne. Whatever the reason, I don't need to listen. I don't hate anyone, and I don't have a hold—"

"Oh stop it—spare me the speech. You think you're clever, but you're not: whenever you think no one's looking, the mask slips."

Elsa moved so close to Magda, the heavy rose scent of the Joy perfume Gunther had requisitioned for her in Paris enveloped them both. "I will find you out. The same as I will find out who that dark-haired delight is who sneaks in and out of your cottage at all hours of the night. Don't underestimate me, Magda; don't be that stupid. Gunther is in the SS, which means he's one of Himmler's chosen family—and, therefore, now so am I. You might have my father's ear, but trust me, I have the Reichsführer's."

"Elsa, where are you? Gunther's threatening to send the Gestapo to find you!"

A woman was calling out from the ballroom's gilded doorway, another SS wife from the silver lightning-flash brooch she had pinned to her gown.

Elsa stepped away from Magda with a laugh and a wave and resumed her role as the beautiful bride. She whirled away without another word, leaving Magda alone in the lobby, shivering uncontrollably despite the well-fed fires that flanked her.

It wasn't art, or coal, or cattle. It was people, a thousand of them. The list of Berlin names and addresses—which was headed *Resettlement,* another word with new meanings that Magda would grow sickeningly familiar with—landed on Magda's desk on the afternoon of Wednesday the fifteenth of October. She didn't have time to scan its pages, or to copy it. Himmler pounced the moment the document appeared, as if he had sniffed its arrival out.

"What does it mean?" Magda asked the question as lightly as she could.

Her boss's response was too oblique to make anything from it.

"The fruition of months of hard work and the start of the next phase. A good day for us all."

He took the typed sheets and retreated to his office with a spring in his step Magda would have described in anyone else as jaunty. She itched to ring Walther, to warn him to be on the alert at the factory. To rush through the next batch of identity cards and press the counterfeiters to work double, or triple, time. Himmler, however, kept calling her in and out of his office for the rest of the day and she didn't dare pick up the phone.

I'll go to the villa tonight. I'll slip away early if I have to.

He didn't let her. Himmler kept piling reports on her desk for her to summarize, even though the speed he wanted them completed with meant she had no time to properly study them. All she could do was pull out the headings and figures they contained and hope that would satisfy him. She began to wonder if it was deliberate, if he wanted her head spinning.

By the time she drooped back to the cottage, Walther's home was shuttered and dark. Thursday was the same, and Friday. Himmler kept her working such long hours, it would have been easier to sleep in the office. She was able to call Spandau once, but Walther was in a meeting and Himmler reappeared before she could risk leaving more than a vague message. When she rang the villa on Friday evening, Elsa was reigning over it and wouldn't put her call through.

I'll go on Saturday. The printing press can work all weekend if needs be to get the cards that we need. If nothing has happened on Friday, nothing will happen on Saturday.

It was a reasonable conclusion to come to. Himmler was never in the office on a Saturday or on a Sunday—he was pious about his staff spending time with their families, even if, for him, the definition of family stretched to his mistress. He was also due to return, on Monday at the latest, to the Eastern Front. Magda had spent most of Friday ensuring his beloved personal train, *The Steiermark*, was ready to welcome him. It had taken her until long past nine o'clock to round up sufficient supplies of flour and eggs to make the egg noodle dumplings he adored, and to track down the masseur and the tailor he refused to travel without. Magda had crawled into the car waiting to ferry her to the cottage half-asleep, and crawled into bed half-dressed, convinced that, whatever the lists meant, the danger they hinted at wasn't imminent. She had forgotten about *Kristallnacht* and how fast the National Socialists could move when they had prey in their sights. She had forgotten how carefully they hid their traces, and she had been too overworked and too tired to look as carefully as she should have done for clues.

When the telephone shrilled her out of a deep sleep on Saturday morning, her brain was still dulled. She presumed it was Walther finally responding to her messages and forgot, in her fogged state, how much she had wanted him to call.

"Seriously? You ignore me for three days, even though I did my best to tell you it was urgent, and now you ring when it's barely light and I'm exhausted and finally sleeping? Can't you put me first for once rather than your own gadding about?"

"Forgive me, Fräulein, for disturbing you. And for not being the man you expected. I hope you will judge the interruption to be a worthwhile one, and as important as whatever it is that is *urgent*."

Magda went from muddle-headed to alert in an instant, and everything she had forgotten flooded back.

"Herr Reichsführer, I apologize. It is me, not you, who should be asking for forgiveness. I am, of course, delighted it is you that has called. I think perhaps you caught me in the middle of a dream."

To her relief, the clipped and petulant tone—which was Himmler's default when he wasn't immediately at the center of anyone's thinking—softened.

"A dream indeed. Well, perhaps that is fitting. Today, after all, is the day all our hard work shifts from theory to practice, and I would certainly label that as a dream. I am sending a car for you. Wear something cheery!"

He put the phone down with no further explanation.

What does he mean? And how does cheery fit with lists and costings and resettlement?

Magda knew that it didn't. She knew that there was a line coming toward her she didn't want to cross, a line she had been standing far closer to than she had realized or had been prepared to face. She also knew that she couldn't refuse to attend whatever she was about to attend without raising suspicions that might jeopardize her place at the center of Himmler's office and all the access to information that gave her.

Magda crossed to the wardrobe, refusing to connect together the reports she had summarized, whose hastily scanned words were now popping up like a join-the-dots in her head. *Something cheery.* She pulled out a red-and-blue-checked dress with a pretty bow at the neck, a toning shawl-collared coat with a matching trim and a pair of navy court shoes and hoped that would keep him happy. She dabbed rose-colored rouge on her cheeks to brighten her skin. She darkened her eyelashes and pinked-up her mouth with a subtle amount of lipstick. She doubted the woman staring back from the mirror looked cheery—there was a wariness in her eyes even makeup and bright clothes couldn't hide—but she looked, as Himmler would put it, as if she was "the right kind." Not overdone, not underdone; suitable, proper.

I look the part, but I don't want to play it.

She was reaching for the telephone to call Walther and get him to think up a reason to follow her, when the swastika-crested Mercedes swept up the short drive.

"Here you are, and how charming you look."

Himmler bowed over her hand and clicked his heels as if he was welcoming her into a candlelit ballroom, not a dusty shed at the rear of Grunewald station.

Magda glanced around. Although there were guards outside, there were only two other people present inside the building itself, both of whom were seated in front of the shed's tall windows.

One of them—Himmler's deputy, Reinhard Heydrich—Magda already knew. Himmler introduced the other, whose protruding ears and long thin nose gave him the air of a watchful rodent, as the report-writer Obersturmbannführer Adolf Eichmann, "whose ability with numbers and logistics is quite the match for your own." Heydrich stood up and shook her hand; Eichmann stayed seated.

"This is for you. We've placed you where the view is particularly clear."

The introductions done, Himmler ushered her to a chair next to a table, where a pad and two sharpened pencils sat waiting. Apart from the rain, which had steadily thickened from a drizzle into a downpour, the view out of the polished glass was indeed clear, not that Magda was sure why it mattered. All she could see was a stretch of empty platform and a worn-out-looking passenger train.

"You must record everything down to the smallest detail." Himmler leaned across her and opened one of the windowpanes. A spray of rain immediately danced through it. "I am sorry about that. If you sit to the side, you should avoid the worst of it. It is important, however, that you can hear as well as see, that way you can capture the full mood. The costings you did were excellent, but, for this first trial, we need to balance those against the experience."

Eichmann's snort made Himmler's back stiffen.

"The experience? Why does that matter? As long as it's swift and streamlined and keeps to the timetable, why do we care about what they *experience*?"

"We don't." The ice in Himmler's voice stopped the questions Magda had been trying to work out how to ask. "How they feel doesn't matter in the slightest. But there are honest German citizens in the surrounding streets whose morning coffee should not be disturbed. We chose Grunewald, if I may remind you, Obersturmbannführer, because it is out of the way and the lines are underused here. Which is a piece of information we can thank Fräulein Aderbach's excellent report for uncovering." He smiled down at Magda and didn't appear to notice she had frozen. "Noise, however, carries. So we do not want noise."

There wasn't any. Himmler kept remarking on it, and kept encouraging Magda to note the fact of its absence down. The people—the mothers and fathers and children and grandparents, the young and the old all marked out with yellow stars—who began filling the platform, and continued to fill it until the morning was done, carried themselves quietly and calmly. They stood patiently while they were ticked off. They added their suitcases to the piles on the trolleys when they were instructed to and didn't question why. They climbed up the steps into the waiting carriages without jostling or pushing. There were soldiers, admittedly, at both ends of the train, and dogs on long chains. But the mothers shielded their children from those so the dogs stayed still, and no voices were raised so no weapons were either. Himmler pronounced the whole operation as perfect, and congratulated Heydrich on the care he had taken in crafting the resettlement forms that had brought the passengers "here with such satisfactory compliance." Even Eichmann managed a smile.

"Where are they going?"

It was the first question Magda managed to ask, after two hours of scribbling words she knew she never wanted to reread.

"This one is headed for Poland, to Lodz. The next ones will go there too, and then we will bring Riga and Minsk on stream."

Magda stretched her cramped hand. She couldn't bear to write any more. The only reason she could keep watching was because there needed to be one witness not crowing with delight.

"There are other...departures planned?"

"Of course." Himmler continued to stare out of the window as the last carriages filled. "Now that we have a system in place—and one that, given how easily they follow orders, we can definitely switch to the cheaper transport model—there is no reason to delay.

Except for the need to extend the processing facilities at the other end, obviously, but we are close to perfecting those."

System. Facilities. More bland words thick with shadows. The rain stopped as Himmler nodded to Magda to note them down. The sun appeared, casting rays of light and shadows across the trees. As the train finally pulled out, slow and straining as if its load was too heavy, Magda had a sudden vision of snowy slopes and tangled limbs and had to choke back a sob. The last carriage disappeared round the bend in the track. Himmler turned from the window all smiles. Heydrich got to his feet and shook Eichmann's hand.

"What happens when they get to Lodz?"

"Resettlement of course." For a horrible moment, Magda thought Himmler was going to wink, but he settled instead for a strangulated sound he clearly intended to be an avuncular chuckle. "Or perhaps we should better call it a *cleansing*, of the Reich and all its territories."

Resettlement and *cleansing*; the two words didn't match. Except they did—they always had.

Himmler had his hand outstretched, waiting for her. Magda got up slowly and gathered together the pages of notes that described the smooth and successful removal of a thousand innocent people. People she guessed—from Himmler's face and the pile of suitcases still sitting on the platform—would never return to the city they had been born in and belonged to. Who—if she was honest with herself, and what else could she be but honest in the face of Himmler's smile—would likely never return to anywhere at all.

I will remember them. I will remember every single word that has been said today. I will unleash them on the world.

Magda couldn't look at Himmler, or his henchmen. She stared at her hand instead, the hand that had recorded the events today as carefully as it had recorded a list of twisted calculations a month earlier. She wished it would burst into flames.

"You have done a great service to your country, Magda. You will be well rewarded for that, and for the work that is still to come."

I am doing this to save lives. I am doing this because the more we know about what they intend for the Jews, the more of them we can help.

Except a thousand Jewish men, women, and children had been packed onto a train and sent from everything they knew, and it wasn't them she had helped.

"Lunch, I think. And champagne. A proper celebration."

Himmler's hand was at her back, steering her out of the shed and toward the waiting Mercedes. His fingers on her spine felt like a gun.

PART TWO

CHAPTER SEVEN

Magda, January–May 1942

The processing facilities… we are close to perfecting those.

Magda sank down onto the marbled tiles in the hallway and let the tears come. For what she knew. For where she was. For this sickening life she now lived, which appeared wonderful on the surface but was rotten within. She dropped her head onto her knees and closed her aching eyes. Everything she had read today was printed on them; everything she had read was filled with pain. The desire for ignorance, for a return to innocence, was overwhelming, but that was nothing her surroundings could provide.

The house Himmler had put her in at the Yuletide gift-giving ceremony was beautiful. It was smaller than the rest of the street's grand villas, and tucked in at the bottom of a narrow tree-shaded drive, but that simply enhanced its charm. Outside, the building was perfect: its little round tower, gingerbread-cottage garden shed, and winter roses could have been plucked from a storybook. Inside, it was filled with nooks and crannies and window seats that, once upon a time, Magda would have lost days curled up in. It was a home built from childhood dreams, one she should have loved. She hated every brick of it.

The Tower House was full of ghosts. They were there from the first day Magda had opened the front door—after the Reichsführer had presented her with the key, in yet another ceremony fashioned from a myth-laden view of Germany that was nothing to do with her. The Lieser family, according to the names curling round the edges of a lovingly done family portrait: Johannes and Ruth, bow-haired Minna and baby Isidor. The rightful owners of the place, who, if the photographs studding its walls told a true story, had lived a happy life inside its light-filled rooms. Their footprints were embedded in the Turkish carpets. Their fingerprints were embedded in the ivy-engraved banisters and pressed into the door frames and the cupboard tops. The family was soaked into the building's fabric, and yet they were gone, as all the Jewish families were gone from the houses Himmler had gifted. They had been tossed away as easily as he had suggested the new occupants deal with the furniture and possessions the dispossessed owners had been forced to leave behind.

"Keep what pleases you, if anything does. Or hand over anything of value and burn the rest."

Magda had ignored Himmler's instructions. She had put away the photographs and the portrait it tore her soul to look at, but she hadn't touched a stick of the furniture, or thrown away the personal mementoes that were dotted around. She wasn't going to make this house hers; she wasn't going to love it or call it home. Or "marry and have children in it to honor the Reich," as Himmler had virtually instructed her to do in an uncomfortable echo of Elsa. She was going to guard it for when the Liesers came back. She had made that promise to Christoph when he had knocked on the kitchen door on her third night there, and found her sleepless and pacing the floors.

"I won't profit from their pain. I won't do it."

She had made that oath to Christoph as fiercely as any SS recruit barked theirs. Christoph had held her, swearing that he believed in her; trying to persuade her not to make herself ill over how she might appear to the rest of the world. He had stayed dangerously late that night; dawn was breaking when he finally slipped away to whatever bolt-hole he was staying in. He wouldn't tell Magda where that was, although she guessed, from the snippets of news he brought her about her parents and Kiefer, that some of his time was still spent in Oberschöneweide. He also wasn't Christoph Traube anymore. Since his return from Russia, he had become Volker Kreisel, resident of Moabit and out of the fighting, due—as was carefully noted on his forged *Wehrmacht* identity card—to hearing loss and a badly damaged arm. With his cocked head and his shrugs and his left arm in a sling, Christoph had become as good an actor as Magda. He spent his days now as Walther's invisible aide, helping to collect counterfeit papers from the chain of counterfeiters spread across Moabit and Wedding, combing the city for the black-market rations Walther insisted on supplementing his Jewish workers' pathetic meal allocations with; moving people when people needed moving.

We are all playing parts; we are all living lies.

Except now Magda could no longer believe the biggest one she had been fooling herself with: that there was anyone left to guard the house for. That there was anyone coming back to stake their claim.

Magda had found the Liesers. They had left Grunewald station on the twenty-seventh of November, setting out on the 900-kilometer journey east through Poland and Lithuania to Riga with a thousand other men, women, and children the roll call of names referred to as *pieces*. Magda had searched through the increasing piles of resettlement lists and destinations and invoices for transport that flowed over her desk until she uncovered them. Neither parent had been marked as suitable for work. No one in their relocation detail had been moved out of their lives by passenger train. Nobody cared about the *experience* anymore, not now that cost was king.

The second departure from Grunewald station that Magda had been sent to witness—sitting alone this time in the dusty shed—was a far more brutal affair than the first. It had set the pattern for all those that followed, and it was hard to pretend that wasn't partly her doing. Himmler had switched to the "cheaper transport model." There were no carriages waiting to welcome the travelers with seats and space. There was no pretense that the luggage would follow. People were herded onto the thin platform, squashed into the cattle wagons and sealed in. Dogs snarled at their heels, whips cracked when they stumbled. There had been screams that day, and pleading voices calling for water and for help. There had been bullets—Magda couldn't see if they had been fired above or into the crowds, but it wasn't hard to guess. If the morning coffee drinkers whose mansions surrounded the station were disturbed by the noise spilling out of it, they gave no sign.

The packed train had lumbered away without anyone appearing in the station to comment or question. The soldiers had trudged back to their idling trucks without raising a glance. Magda had wiped her mouth and wiped her eyes and re-emerged onto streets where families were strolling and the flower seller was smiling, and the October sky rolled on above them cloud-free and crisp blue. No concerned neighbor or newspaper had called Himmler's— or anyone else's—office that afternoon, or at any other time in October or November, when sometimes as many as three trains a day had steamed away from the platform at the back of the elegant station. Nobody, apparently, had seen or heard anything worthy of comment. The trains were as invisible as the suitcases and the streams of disheveled people who had been marched into the station to leave them there. It was as if the whole of Berlin had gone blind.

But I won't join them. I will witness every second, and one day I will find their persecutors and make them pay.

The floor beneath her was growing icy. Magda could feel January's hard frost seeping into her bones. She still couldn't move. She still couldn't believe that the hope that they had all clung to through the last months of 1941 and the first frozen weeks of 1942—that what they were doing was making a difference—was so frail it was in tatters. Neither she nor Walther nor Christoph believed that there would be an end to the persecutions and the evictions and the disappearances that hounded Berlin's Jewish community. But they had convinced themselves that their efforts would gain momentum, that more lives would be saved, that more rescuers would join them. Even as Berlin's Jewish residents were cut further and further adrift from the rest of the city and the *resettlements* continued to whittle them out, the trio told each other they were doing good. The reports Magda memorized and copied out and passed onto Eckhart Bühl might or might not have reached an audience—with no way of seeing the foreign press, it was impossible to know—but she had to believe that the SS movements and the camps she reported on might make their way into an Allied battle plan, or influence the path of the bombers.

The Tiedemann workers at least were unharmed. In a world where offering a seat on a bus to a tired old Jewish woman could lead to a prison sentence, that was surely something to be proud of. None of the Spandau employees had been selected for *relocation* to the East. Walther had been promised that, for now, Jewish armament workers in Germany would be exempt from the clearances. *For now* wasn't a lot to hold on to, but it was something. *For now* kept the counterfeiters working and the nearly 3,000 men and women under Walther's care—and, by extension, their families—safe.

But for now *is done, and I have to tell them both that.*

Her teeth were starting to chatter. Magda finally forced herself off the floor. She had no time to waste on tears—what was needed was clear-eyed honesty. She had to call Walther; she had to warn Christoph. She had to tell them both what she knew. That they all had to work faster than ever before and against impossible odds, and, no matter how efficient they were, they wouldn't win. That *we can help individuals escape, and maybe they can go on and help others* was no longer an idealistic dream; it was a cruel joke. And she knew already what they would say, because it was all she was thinking.

How, despite all that is coming, can we stop now? How can we face ourselves if we give up and do nothing?

She couldn't pick up the phone. The moment she gave voice to the horrors crowding her head, the future would take on a shape that was not only terrifying, it was beyond comprehension.

Forced labor with foreign workers will fill any gaps.

This system protects our soldiers; mass shootings is asking too much of them.

The disposal method works at its best with higher numbers.

The sites are chosen, the process has been tested successfully in the mobile facilities; all we need now is sufficient material to feed the bigger machine.

The few sentences Magda had had time to pick out were, as always, efficient and clinical. It was the style Himmler demanded, the one he said—God help her—that she excelled in. There was no emotion in the words. There was no emotion in the numbers that accompanied them: *a target of 2,500 per hour is to be implemented; 60,000 per day is achievable if the transports are guaranteed;* eleven million in total *"needing to be dealt with."* Nothing stood out; nothing had been underlined, or circled, or highlighted in red. Nothing had a question mark against it—not even *ovens* and *gas.* Magda grabbed the back of a chair and refused to let her knees buckle. The scale was monstrous, unthinkable; that did not mean she could pretend it wasn't true.

She hadn't been able to tear her eyes away from the pages from the moment Himmler had dropped the notes on her desk with the instruction to burn them. If he hadn't hovered, she would have copied out every word. As it was, she had fed the papers into the flames as slowly as she dared, trying to memorize every sickening line. She had spent the next hours desperate for him to leave, aware that there was some detail that she was missing. That there had to be a record of whatever meeting these notes had been written in, and why that meeting had been summoned, and that she had to find it. That the whole story needed reporting. She had sat in Himmler's office, taking dictation, finalizing his diary, nodding and not listening, while she scanned his desk for anything she hadn't been asked to summarize or file. In the end, she had less than five minutes to open the folder she'd spotted, the one marked *Minutes of the Wannsee Conference January 20, 1942: Named Eyes Only.* She had barely had time to scan the first page before Himmler swept back into the office from whatever interruption had annoyed him. When he left for the night, the report was gone and the cabinets she normally checked through were locked.

There's no trace of it left, no proof I can offer. But I know what I saw. And I know what "disposal method" and "bigger machine" and the rest of it means; the notes and the numbers translated those. And I cannot allow myself the luxury ever again of believing that the Liesers, or anyone else shoveled away on those godforsaken trains, have gone to a new life they will be allowed to live in.

She was crying again. She allowed herself a moment of tears, and then she made herself stop. She dried her eyes and reached for the telephone.

Final solution. The last words on the page she had managed to read. Of all the new language of lies she had learned—and as bad as *pieces* and *cargo* and *resettlement* were—every fiber in her body told her that this reinvention was the worst.

"It's repulsive, it's revolting. Can't anyone see that it's nothing but lies?"

As if anyone in Berlin can filter lies from the truth anymore.

Magda didn't say it. The days of "tell them what you really think" had long gone. She kept her mouth shut and didn't react as Christoph snarled at the broken-down shack that had been constructed from cracked boards and dirty straw, whose grease-thick walls and filthy floor were described as "normal for Russian housing." Of course it was revolting, and ridiculous, but this wasn't the place to say it. She moved away instead and stood among a small crowd shivering in disgusted delight at a stuffed dog with an explosive-filled belt fastened round its middle. "A starved Russian mine dog trained to destroy tanks," according to its sign. She knew that meeting Christoph inside the Lustgarten pavilion had been a mistake, that he wouldn't be able to keep the low profile that he had promised, especially in such provocative surroundings. She had only agreed because they hadn't seen each other for weeks and she missed him. And she understood his fury, but she couldn't share it, not publicly.

The Soviet Paradise Exhibition was only in its second week, but—if Minister Goebbels' loudly trumpeted figures were to be believed—200,000 people had already visited it. Magda had had to wait almost an hour in the May sunshine to gain admittance, and her queue was the official visitors one and by far the shortest. Everyone inside the specially built display halls, except Christoph, was transfixed by the models and posters that, according to the massive signs hung above the doorways, showed the true "poverty, misery and decay of Russia." There were huge crowds around the squalid huts "where only the lice are missing." There were more at the roofless government shop with its empty shelves and the restaurant surrounded by piles of garbage and unpleasantly lifelike rats. The photographs of destitute children abandoned to live in crumbling caves had reduced many of the more soft-hearted audience members to discreet eye-patting. The air was mostly, however, thick with squeals of mock-horror and the self-satisfied grunt of "animals." The reactions were as repulsive as the exhibition, but Magda still needed Christoph to ignore them.

"I'd burn it to the ground if I had a match left."

He was back at her elbow, his whole body seething.

"For God's sake, keep your voice down."

Magda stepped smartly away and shook her head when he attempted to follow. She was wearing a visitor's badge with her name and *Secretary to Reichsführer-SS Himmler* on it—did he have no common sense left?

"Is this man bothering you, Fraülein? You appeared to be trying to escape his attentions."

The man in the dark coat had appeared from nowhere. His equally silent colleague was already in position behind Christoph.

They can't have heard what he said, or he'd have a gun at his head.

Magda turned to face her interrogator, shaking out the bow on her blouse as she did so to hide her lapel. The man was clearly Gestapo: she did not need him seeing Himmler's name and over-reacting. She assumed a surprised face, and a voice loud enough for Christoph to hear her.

"Goodness, no, not at all. He is one of our soldiers. He was telling me that he had witnessed terrible sights like this himself, when he fought in that dreadful country."

She paused and blinked, as the tears she had been about to pretend unexpectedly sprang up. The wave of superstition that had gripped her was a nonsense Magda wouldn't normally have given air to; in this place, however, and saying what she was about to say, it suddenly seemed foolhardy to ignore it. She stuffed her hand into her jacket pocket and crossed her fingers, not caring how stupid the gesture felt.

"It's just that I've not long lost my brother in the fighting near Demyansk. The gentleman meant no harm, but his words brought my grief too vividly back."

She caught Christoph's gaze the second before she dropped hers and prayed he would follow her lead and act humble.

"My condolences. The men who fought in that battle were heroes."

The Gestapo man switched his attention onto Christoph and demanded his papers. When Christoph, to Magda's relief, remained polite and his documents passed muster, the two men bowed and swept on, scanning the faces trying not to meet theirs as they went. The hall emptied almost immediately.

"What the hell is wrong with you? If they'd caught one word of your grandstanding, we would both have been arrested. How would I have kept my job with that hanging over me?"

She didn't give him time to answer. She left the exhibition hall and stormed across the Schloβbrücke, not stopping until she was off Museum Island, hoping that Christoph, if he followed her, would have the sense to keep a reasonable distance behind.

"I'm sorry."

He was out of breath by the time he caught up with her—he was still not back to full strength since the long walk home from Russia; she wasn't sure he would ever be—and was far more contrite than he had been half an hour earlier.

"I shouldn't have put you at risk. I'm sorry. But I can't bear the lies."

Magda stared at him, her anger still bubbling. "None of us can. Do you think I don't know the truth of what we are doing to the Russians as clearly as you do? Do you think I enjoyed walking round that charade? I know what propaganda and lies are, Christoph. I spend my days with Himmler's obscenities about *clearing out the communists and the Jews* dripping in my ear. And smiling at SS men who carry the massacres out. Do you think that makes me happy?" But then her anger fizzled out in the relief of not seeing him snatched from her, and she slumped onto a bench. "We all hate them, Christoph, but, for now, we have to live in their world. If we don't, if we shout the truth back at them, we die, along with anyone we might have saved."

"It's not enough." Christoph was wound too tight to sit down; his prowling put her nerves back on edge. "We've never been more needed, and we've never been more powerless. There are patrols everywhere. I've only managed to move one traveler through the safe-house network this month. The printers are struggling to source any decent-quality ink. The transports will start going out again from Grunewald once the snows ease, and we know now what they are really heading to: Auschwitz. To experiments with cyanide gas. Or to the *bigger machine* and not experiments anymore. There's got to be a better way to fight back than this pointless chipping."

The energy surging through him was almost tangible. His face and his manner were wild and out of control, a state none of them could afford to be in. Magda forced herself to stay steady. She had to talk him down: no matter how much she wished it was different, there was no such thing as physically fighting back in Berlin, not with the SS and the Gestapo and Hitler's army of informers so firmly in charge. Or not in any way that would keep them alive.

"What about leaflets? Letting people know what we know? We've focused on getting the truth about what's happening here to audiences outside Germany. Maybe we should be spreading it at home."

He managed not to sneer, although that was clearly a struggle.

"I want to believe the same as you do, that the reports you write and Bühl sends out are getting through. His connections are good—there's no reason not to trust in them. The protest and the outrage we need from the Allies will surely come; your bravery, if nothing else, deserves that. But what about here, where people are face to face with the horrors and don't speak out? How do we reach through their fear and make them see? We already tried using leaflets to protest against the exhibition. Didn't you see the ones trampled on the floor as you went in? *The Nazi Paradise: War, Hunger, Lies, Gestapo—how much longer do we let it go on?* Nobody read them; the soldiers knew nobody would. They pulled them down and laughed; they didn't even bother throwing them away. Would anyone believe us if we started writing about ovens and mass murder? The atrocities we know about can't rely on words to make people wake up, not here. They need fighters."

Fighters. Magda could guess who he meant. She knew he was still involved with a small bunch of his old KPD comrades, although she didn't know who they were or what they did, beyond helping move Jewish escapees with fake papers through the underground network. She only knew that because she and Walther relied on their help; she hadn't directly asked.

None of us ask anything. We steal information and move papers and people and hang on to as many workers in Spandau as we can, but I don't ask Walther and Christoph what risks they take, or what it costs them, and they don't ask me. What do our risks matter?

Magda stared out over the flat waters of the river. Christoph's hand was on her shoulder. Anyone watching would see a couple, but she knew he felt as alone in that moment as she did.

He's going to do something dangerous. He's going to take a bigger risk because bigger risks are all there are left to take. I should make him tell me what it is. I should offer to help him.

She didn't. There was no safety for either of them in that.

Magda continued to watch the ripples and the sunlight and the smiling couples strolling past until his hand and then he slipped wordlessly away.

I cursed him. I killed him.

Magda sank onto a low garden wall as the thought hit her again. It was irrational and unfounded, but she couldn't shake it. When she had told the tear-filled lie at the *Soviet Paradise Exhibition* five days earlier, Kiefer had already been dead for a month. He had fallen in April, one of thousands of German soldiers killed outside Sevastopol in the Crimea, besieging a city that still refused to fall. She couldn't have possibly known that, but the guilt stung.

My brother is dead. And now Christoph could be dead. And I never did a thing to stop or save either of them.

The weight of both men pressed as hard on her shoulders as the May sunshine pressed on her neck. She was exhausted, but that was nothing new. This weariness that gripped her now, however, was worse than anything she had weathered before. It wasn't the two sleepless nights and two days without eating that had swallowed her strength—they were physical tolls someone with a life as comfortable as hers could quickly recover from—it was the depths of her parents' suffering. They had lost their child; they were ruined. And Magda had nowhere to take the agony of bearing witness to that but the Tower House, the last place she wanted to go.

I should have stayed in Oberschöneweide and got a job there. I could do that right now—I could turn round and go back to my old life.

Except she couldn't. That life wasn't hers anymore and all the wishing in the world wouldn't change that.

The call had come on Sunday morning just as Magda was about to pick up the telephone and cancel the car Walther was sending to take her to Winkler Straβe. It was a pretty, sun-filled morning and the day would be a long one. She needed to walk through air scented with spring flowers before she buried herself yet again in the factory budgets.

Sifting line by line through them had become a weekly task— the two of them huddled together searching desperately for any pockets of money they had missed. It had also become a pointless task, but neither of them could bear to give up on it. The strain on the Tiedemann Company's finances was starting to show. Funding forged papers and black-market foodstuffs, and the living quarters Walther was determined to build at the Spandau complex to provide safer housing for his workers, had drained the profits he was making from the armaments contracts. As were the lavish dinners he still had to host to keep those contracts coming. Every time Magda visited the villa, there was another gap on the wall where a painting had once hung, or another mantelpiece bereft of its silver candlesticks.

When Elsa—whose visits Magda normally took care to avoid— had remarked on the disappearances and the impact on her inheritance, Walther had hung his head and blamed imaginary gambling debts. When Albert Speer, the Minister for War Production, had called him in to account for Spandau's delayed deliveries, Walther had offered the same defense. The apology that went with it had not been received well. Himmler had dictated a stern letter to Magda, addressed to "My friend who increasingly concerns me" and peppered with "duty" and "disappointment" and "morals." A year earlier, its pompous tone would have made Walther laugh.

When the telephone rang, Magda had assumed it was Walther, checking arrangements, and had hoped it was Christoph. When she heard Ernst's voice, she knew it had to be bad news. Nothing else would have forced her father to seek out a telephone and call a house he suspected Magda—who had told her father she had moved from the Tiedemann guest house, but not the reason why—had no right to be living in, or no excuse for it that he could stomach.

"You have to come. Your mother needs you."

She had waited in vain for "and so do I."

Walther, who she called at once and could barely speak to, had insisted Magda make the journey to the Aderbachs' home in Fontanestraβe in his personal car. Magda knew that was a mistake, but she was in no condition to argue.

As soon as she reached her old neighborhood, she knew her instincts had been right. Although the red and beige BMW wasn't topped with a swastika, its polished appearance—and its uniformed chauffeur—still signified wealth and therefore a Party connection that wasn't welcome in those streets. The raised eyebrows and the curses it attracted made Magda feel as out of place in Oberschöne-weide as she was in Grunewald and Prinz Albrecht Straβe. She sent the car away before she knocked on her family's door; she couldn't face the contempt she knew she would see on her father's face if he caught sight of it.

Her father had aged; her mother had sped past him. Magda had sat down at the worn kitchen table feeling helpless, desperate to take away the misery her mother's frail body didn't seem capable of shouldering and knowing how hopeless that need was. There was never a moment to properly hug Herthe, or to say any more than, "I'm so sorry." An endless troop of neighbors and co-workers full of sympathy and pats and shared stories weaved their way through the small house long into the night. Most of them were women, most of them were wearing black crêpe armbands and had eyes as empty as Herthe's. The few men who came in clutching their caps were as old as Magda's father, or had been made old by their injuries.

The war was everywhere in Fontanestraße. Not in the ways Magda was used to. Not measured out in numbers and carefully crafted reports, or cloaked in secrecy and words with multiple meanings. It sat in the room like a physical presence, one that was very much alive and filled with immeasurable pain. Everyone had lost someone; no one had a body to mourn. Everyone was, on some level, afraid. That the air raids that had kept the city sleepless in 1940 would come back. That the war in Russia would sink under another ice and snow nightmare of a winter and never be won, despite Goebbels' boasts of German valor and victories. That the jobs that at least provided them with some semblance of security would be lost to the influx of foreign forced laborers everyone had heard were coming any day now from the East. No one expected defeat, but, with the United States' armies now firmly in play, no one thought that Germany's promised triumph was as assured, or as imminent, as they had believed it to be three years earlier when Poland fell. Everyone was on edge, and Ernst was broken.

He had been defeated both by a war and a leader he hated, who had given the son he loved a set of beliefs Ernst despised, and then thrown the boy away. He couldn't find peace. He had ripped the letter from the Army Information Center—which had announced Kiefer's death in language full of "the struggle for freedom" and "sacrifice"—in two. He had thrown the scroll with its gold eagle and swastika, which proclaimed that Kiefer had died "A Hero's Death for his Führer and Fatherland" into the bin. When Magda had tried to retrieve it, he had roared at her. He had refused her clumsy attempts at comfort. He tried, but he didn't want to look at or speak to her. And, although it quickly became clear that Ernst had maintained the fiction that Magda still worked for Walther Tiedemann, neither did anyone else. All the visitors who came might work now for armaments companies, but, in their hearts and their consciences, that wasn't the job they had chosen to do. Their factories hadn't chased down arms contracts the way the Tiedemann Company had; their factories had been forced into changing production. They had stayed in their own neighborhood and stayed true to its values and not gone chasing after riches which—in Oberschöneweide's eyes—were tainted. Nobody said any of that, but the sentiments were apparent in each forced smile and turned-away head.

In the end, Magda grew tired of being unfairly judged. She couldn't say much—even in "safe" neighborhoods, there could be watchers and spies and, whatever else they had complained about, no one had raised a voice against the deportations or in support of the Jewish families targeted by them. But she could allude to the "vulnerable" workers Walther continued to make sure were employed and fed. And the personal financial losses, and possible danger, that had led to. The mood toward her softened a little. Then Christoph had arrived with his reputation completely intact, and had held her hand, and more of the tight faces had relaxed.

"You're still their hero, which makes me less of a villain. I could come home again, if you were here. I could leave Himmler's employment and work with you and for the network, and live a more honest life."

She had said that to Christoph when they were finally alone in the kitchen and she could properly cry for her stolen little brother. Christoph had kissed her, but he hadn't replied. When Magda woke a little later, still curled in the high-backed chair but with a blanket wrapped round her, he was gone.

And now I know why and where.

Magda also knew she should move off the wall she was sitting on. There wasn't a resident of Grunewald who would permit a stranger sitting on their property, no matter how respectably dressed she was. Someone was no doubt already phoning the Gestapo or the *Ordnungspolizei*, or whichever type of state thug they felt most comfortable with. Then there would be questions and, if it came out that she had recently been in a notorious red neighborhood, one the security forces were no doubt already combing for troublemakers and traitors, even Himmler's name wouldn't keep an arrest warrant at bay.

"They're looking for communists. And Jews of course. After what they did last night."

Magda had stared blankly at the woman whispering in her ear as the bus she was returning to Grunewald in was stopped for a third time by soldiers and a roadblock.

"They set fire to the *Paradise Exhibition*. A mob of them apparently, with petrol, or a bomb, or one of those, what do you call them? A Molotov cocktail, that's it, which sounds Russian, so that must mean it was communists. The SS are everywhere this morning, trying to hunt down the perpetrators. Surely you heard?"

Magda had shaken her head and refused to answer and eventually the woman grew bored and turned away from her. She had spent the rest of her journey handing over her papers the second she was instructed to, terrified to look out of the window in case she saw Christoph being dragged down the street. She hadn't heard anything. She had spent Sunday and Monday night with her parents and hadn't left the house. She would have stayed longer, but her presence had driven her father into a silence nobody could bring him out of and—although Herthe would never admit it—his withdrawal had worsened her mother's pain.

"He'll come round, when he's less raw. When he doesn't see the Party every time he looks at you." Herthe had hushed Magda when she gasped at her mother's words, and had held her daughter's hand tight in hers. "I know you've got your reasons for what you are doing—Christoph has hinted as much, and he won't stop defending you. We will listen to those reasons, I promise. But not yet."

Magda had stayed in her mother's embrace as long as Herthe had let her, and then she had left. The world had shifted with Kiefer's death—she was no longer a sister; there was no longer anyone who would share the memory of them once her parents had gone—but she had to return to it. And then she had got onto a bus and the world had shifted again.

I'd burn it to the ground if I had a match left.

Even if it wasn't Christoph who had led the attack—and surely it had to be him—the Gestapo agent might remember the man at the exhibition who had caused a disturbance.

I can't lose him too.

The fear tore at Magda's stomach and doubled her over until her forehead was almost touching the cold stones. She heard the crunch of wheels and a car door opening, but she couldn't catch her breath long enough to care.

"Magda, is that you? What in God's name are you doing? Why are you slumped over Frau Prager's wall as if you are a vagabond or a drunk?"

Magda uncurled herself. Elsa was sitting in the back of her Mercedes, wrinkling her nose as if Magda was emitting a sour smell. The sight of the sleek black car with its SS plates was too much. Magda wanted to scream at Elsa to go away, to go to Hell. Instead what came out of her mouth was, "My baby brother died."

"Get in the car."

When Magda didn't move, Elsa climbed out, her body still graceful despite the heavy pregnancy that curved it.

"I said get in the car. I know you don't care for me, and I'm no fan of yours, but that is terrible news, the worst kind. Let me do the decent thing and take you home."

Elsa's tone was as brisk as ever, but there was an unexpected kindness in her face that Magda desperately needed. She nodded and let Elsa help her into the car. The leather seats were soft and smooth and as comfortable as a feather bed. Magda let Elsa give the chauffeur directions to the Tower House and closed her eyes. Home. It wasn't that. But it was safe and suddenly, more than anything in the world, what Magda needed was safe.

"I'll have to follow you in. One of the drawbacks of Junior here is the constant need to be close to a bathroom. I'll assume yours is acceptable—you do have a cleaner?"

The barbs were in place but not Elsa's normally sharp tone. Magda unlocked the door and ushered Elsa inside. She wasn't ready to be alone, and this slightly softened version of her old adversary might be more bearable.

Perhaps we could find a way to be easier around each other—that would make Walther happy.

Elsa, however, was not going to make that step a simple one. She took one look at the heavy oak sideboard that still dominated the square hallway, and the collection of porcelain jugs still cluttering its top, and immediately began tearing through the rooms that ran off on each side.

"Don't tell me you actually chose these tatty monstrosities?"

Magda followed the offended squeal into the main reception room. Elsa was standing between two green silk-covered sofas that had seen better days with her mouth dramatically pursed. Magda said nothing. This was the first time anyone but Christoph and Walther had been inside the property. Magda hadn't had to justify her choices not to touch the Liesers' belongings to them, and she wasn't about to start justifying that to Elsa.

"You haven't got rid of a thing, have you?" Elsa caught sight of a six-branched candelabra Magda had left in its original position on the dining table and flinched. "What is this? A shrine to Judaism?"

Magda stayed in the doorway and refused to react. "I've been busy. I haven't had time to think about how I want the place to look."

Elsa ran a gloved finger over the worn sofa back and sniffed. "Well, it can't stay like this. Heinrich would have a fit if he saw it. And where's your picture of the Führer? Please don't tell me it's next to a *Torah?*"

Magda said a silent prayer for patience and gestured Elsa out of the room, thankful she had got one detail of the house's décor right, no matter how much she detested it.

"It's in the hallway, see? Between the photograph of the Christmas gift-giving and the sketch of the house. And the guest bathroom that you came in to use is on the first floor."

She waved Elsa up the stairs and retreated to the kitchen, the only room in the house beside her bedroom that she spent any time in, her attempt at warmer relations done. She had barely sat down when the handle on the garden door rattled.

"You can't be here."

It was Christoph and he was a mess. One of his eyes was bruised; his chin was covered in stubble and scratches. His shirt was torn at the neck and his jacket was muddy. He looked as if he'd been in a fight or crawling through hedges. He ignored her horrified gasp and flung himself inside, circling the kitchen, pulling open cupboards and piling food into his knapsack.

"I know, I know. I'll be out of here as soon as I've got what I need. Do you have any cash in the house?"

He was jumpier than Magda had ever seen him before, and clearly had gone too long without sleep. The need to get rid of him before Elsa reappeared took second place to the need to know exactly what he had done.

"Was it you? Who attacked the exhibition?"

To Magda's surprise, he shook his head.

"No, although I wish it had been. But it doesn't matter who did it—it's given the SS the excuse they needed to sweep up the city.

They're pulling in anyone with KPD connections, and as many Jewish people still in the city as they can lay their hands on. The executions have already started."

He was clearly running, but that didn't make sense. He said he hadn't done it. The Gestapo men had walked away from him in the exhibition. Even if someone other than the agents had overheard Christoph and decided to report what he'd said, his papers had passed scrutiny and they had no other name for him than the one written there.

"You've got a new identity. No one could match the name Volker up with the KPD. And no one could surely match you up with Christoph Traube."

Christoph grabbed a jar of milk from the refrigerator and gulped it down. "I'm on the search list, I've been warned. Someone betrayed me; someone always does in the end. They give in to the bribes or the—" He froze as water gurgled through the pipes above them.

"That's why you have to go. It's Elsa." Magda picked up his knapsack from the table and thrust it toward him. "She's upstairs. If she sees you here—"

"Well, isn't this cozy."

It was too late. Elsa was standing in the hallway, staring at them both, with a smile on her face that made Magda shiver.

"If it isn't the mysterious dark-haired figure I used to see prowling around our guest house in the dead of night. Have you finally decided to do the right thing and visit our little Magda in the daylight?"

"It's not what you think." Magda eased around the table, away from Christoph and closer to Elsa, ready to grab her arm if she made a move for the telephone. "He's an old friend. He's leaving Berlin and he's come to say goodbye. There's nothing more to it than that."

Elsa kept her gaze fixed firmly on Christoph. "That's a shame— he is rather delicious. So tell me, Mr. Stranger, why are you leaving the delights of Berlin, and where are you heading instead? No, wait, don't tell me, let me guess. You're not in uniform, so it's not to play your gallant part. And you do look a bit of a fright, if you don't mind my saying so. Your clothes are a mess and you've definitely got a...dangerous air about you. Are you *leaving*? Or are you, perhaps, *running*?" She laughed as Christoph stiffened. "Oh, Magda, who do we really have here? Is your *old friend* from your old neighborhood? Is he a communist or—heavens, surely not—a Jew?"

"That's enough. What or who I am is none of your business."

Elsa widened her eyes in mock alarm as Christoph growled.

"Goodness, what a nerve I've obviously touched. But I'm afraid that it is. You see—and feel free to correct me at any point here—I think you might have had something to do with that nasty business at the Lustgarten. You do rather have the look of a revolutionary about you. And I am an SS wife, which brings certain responsibilities with it." The playful tone dropped from her voice. "Go if you want, but I'll have you tracked down and shot if you try."

The instant Magda saw Christoph's hand move toward his jacket pocket, she knew what was coming. She was between Elsa and the gun before he had a chance to raise it.

"Don't."

"Get out of the way, Magda. You heard her. She'll turn me in if I don't stop her."

Magda positioned herself more squarely in front of Elsa.

"Yes, I heard her. But she's pregnant for God's sake."

Christoph's eyes were blank. "With an SS officer's child. That means two of the vermin go down with one bullet, which is a pretty good deal, wouldn't you say?"

"No. I wouldn't. And you don't mean it." She had been wrong: his eyes weren't blank, they were desperate. "You're a better man than this. Killing pregnant women is what they do, not you; never you."

The gun stayed where it was. So did Magda.

"And even if you do mean it, I won't let you shoot her. You're going to leave; she's not going to report you."

He was still clutching the gun, his finger on the trigger, still staring over her head at Elsa. Magda knew if she moved an inch out of the way, he would fire and they would all be done for.

"Christoph, my love, don't make this any worse. You've a chance now; kill her and you've got none. Listen to me. If you love me as much as I believe you do, listen to me."

She didn't know what did it. Whether it was the word *love*, or the sound of it running through her voice, but Christoph lowered the barrel.

"What if she hands you over to them instead?"

Magda answered him with a certainty she knew she had no right to feel. "She won't. I'll be fine, which I won't be if you're dead. Go."

He snatched up his bag and was gone before she could take her next breath. When Magda finally turned round, Elsa was clutching her stomach, her face a twisted mess of fury and fear.

"Why did you do that? Why did you save my life? You hate me."

All the tiredness of the last few days, of the last few years, crept back into Magda's bones. She sank into the chair opposite where Elsa was standing and forced herself not to drop her head onto the table.

"I don't hate you, Elsa. That's too easy a word. Most of the time, I don't think about you at all. But your death, and your child's death, would break your father's heart, and I care very much about him. And murdering you would, in the end, destroy Christoph, and I care about him far more."

"I could report you. I could tell Himmler exactly what kind of people you mix with. I could end you right now."

There was fire in Elsa's eyes again and all the old jealous hatred blazing. Which meant there was no bargaining and no pleading for understanding, or none that would get through to her. Magda knew she had one chance to get this right. That she couldn't spill out the first thing that came into her head: that she had to use the right words, and use them with conviction. She got up from the table, and she took her time.

"You could, but you won't because you're not a fool. Until not long ago, Christoph was on your father's payroll. And once, when he was arrested for activities not so different from what you suspect him of now, Himmler questioned your father about their association. You know why. You know how things are done—one person's crime isn't simply one person's crime: everyone around the accused shares the blame and is guilty merely by virtue of knowing them. If the SS believe Christoph had anything to do with the attack on the exhibition, if they catch him, they'll eventually look at the circle spinning out from him and they'll call Walther in again. Your father isn't as popular as he was—he won't survive another insinuation that he doesn't choose his contacts carefully. And, after they pull in Walther, they'll come after you because you're part of his... what do you call it in the SS? His clan? Tied together by blood and shared loyalties. And you were here today, don't forget—you let Christoph go. I'd tell that to the first uniform through the door." Magda managed to nudge her stiff body into a shrug. "Where would that leave you? Or Gunther?"

The questions hung in the silence that fell as the two women stared at each other, weighing each other up. It was Elsa who broke it.

"I knew I was right about you." Elsa was no longer crouched against the door frame—she was upright and as rigid as Magda. "I knew you were in league with our enemies. This isn't over—you remember that. One day you'll trip up and I'll have you. And I'll get my father out of your claws."

She moved forward suddenly, shoving the table hard and ramming the sharp edge into Magda's leg. "What are you really up to? This isn't about some stupid love affair and saying goodbye to your little revolutionary. There's something much deeper going

on. Are you and your communist boyfriend hiding them, is that
it? Someone is. All the Jews who dodge the transports and don't
turn up to the collection centers when they are called. They
haven't gone unnoticed, but you know that—you see every report
Himmler sees. And they don't do it without help. Is that what you
are? Are you stealing information? Are you and Christoph part of
this underground network the Gestapo are obsessed with? Are you
using my father's factory as cover?"

This was far worse than Elsa's needling on the day of her
wedding. This accusation was so uncannily accurate, it took all
Magda's willpower to hold herself steady. She deliberately didn't
think about her words this time when she answered. She needed
speed and fury.

"Are you mad? Is that what this is? Has pregnancy unbalanced
your brain? You want to be careful, Elsa, or they will think you're
not SS material and they'll take away your baby. I am Himmler's
personal secretary. You are standing in the house he gave me as a
reward for my loyalty. And yet you accuse me of spying? Of using
my position to save Jews? Do you think that the Reichsführer
would have someone on his staff who was capable of that? Do you
think he is so stupid he wouldn't know? What does that say about
your opinion of him?"

She had hit the right mark. Elsa went white and stepped back.

"This isn't over. I'll find out your game and I will unmask you;
I promise you that."

Elsa's voice was shaking; her threat shouldn't have held any
power. She stormed away; Magda stayed where she was. As the
front door slammed, the pain from her leg that she hadn't had
time to notice coursed through her body and she slumped back
into the chair. She had saved Christoph from a terrible decision;
she had saved Elsa's life. She had been brave and unbreakable, and
she had beaten Elsa down. So the threat shouldn't have held any
power, but it did.

CHAPTER EIGHT

Magda, February 1943–August 1944

Time kept shifting and shortening and sliding away.

They've outrun us again.

Magda stared at the two private memos she shouldn't have read, fighting the urge to scream and kick at the hours that had already spun uselessly past her.

"I have to go."

She waved away the assistant bringing in her morning coffee, ignoring the woman's raised eyebrows. Himmler, at least, was away from the office, or she wouldn't have dared leave so abruptly. He was 300 kilometers away in Czechoslovakia, at the Theresienstadt concentration camp, overseeing the first incoming transports of Jewish deportees from Denmark and Holland, and the first transports out to the Auschwitz extermination camp. Magda didn't want to think about that right now. Not about Theresienstadt, the "model camp" that was Himmler's pet project. Or about Auschwitz, whose killing chambers were his life's work. She also didn't want to think about what the "flair for logistics" he found so useful in her had taught her about her boss. That the easiest way to plot the killing sprees, which were rapidly becoming the hallmark of the Third Reich across occupied Europe, was by following the journeys Himmler made in his personal train.

Magda had made a chart of them. The links she had been able to establish stretched back for two years, but she suspected the pattern actually spanned a far longer time period than that. His trip to Latvia and Lithuania in July and August 1941 was the first one she had noted: 18,000 men, women, and children had been shot dead in the regions he visited by the time that he left. The next date that had stood glaringly out was September 30, 1941, when Himmler was in Kiev in Ukraine. On that same day—according to another memo that wasn't meant to be for her eyes—33,000 Jews were massacred at Babi Yar, a ravine less than ten kilometers away from the Ukrainian capital.

After Magda had connected those two trips, and refused to believe they were a coincidence, she couldn't stop digging. His "inspection tours" were never-ending. To psychiatric units; to woodland killing sites; to celebrations all over Eastern Europe with his beloved *Einsatzgruppen*, the SS death squads who implemented his orders. To the extermination camps whose ovens were so much more efficient and final than guns. It had taken Magda months to piece the jigsaw together and really learn what the man was capable of. It had crossed her mind more than once that perhaps she should be the one with the gun, and he should be its target. It didn't help her to think about that now. It also didn't help her to think about the memos sitting on her desk and all the lost chances they contained.

Magda had found the first one—written with Obersturmban-nführer Eichmann's usual economy—tucked into the private correspondence folder on Himmler's desk on the twentieth of February. Even with her knowledge of the conversations that had taken place a year earlier at the Wannsee Conference, its contents were chilling. Eichmann's memo outlined the planned *removal* and *resettlement* of the 27,260 Jews recorded as still living in Berlin. That number seemed huge, but Magda knew it was barely a quarter of the Jewish population who had been resident in the city in 1938, and a tiny fraction of those who had lived there before Hitler came to power. She had no doubt the Party would carry out the plan, and she was no longer in any doubt about what *resettlement* meant. The last of Berlin's Jewish population was about to be murdered.

There were no operational details; there was, however, a projected timescale, which offered one of those tiny threads of light Magda had learned to call hope. It seemed that the *clearances*—another word that still sent shudders through her—were to begin a month from the memo's date. Magda had grabbed on to that and rung Walther, convincing herself yet again that they could work miracles in any gap that they were offered between order and action, even one as short as a month.

Except they hadn't had a month; they hadn't even had a week. The date she had read too quickly was for the clearance's completion not its starting. The letter Magda had opened this morning—which should have gone directly to Himmler but had mistakenly been delivered to SS headquarters instead—confirmed her misreading. The biggest round-up, of the 11,000 Jews still employed in Berlin's factories, was to take place not at the end of March 1943, but on February 27. Which was tomorrow.

Which means it starts in less than twenty-four hours, and I'm still sitting here. Focusing on everything that won't help, and everything I can't do, instead of what little I can.

She jumped up, put the two memos back in the folder on Himmler's desk marked *Reichsführer-SS Eyes Only*—carefully resealing the envelope on the second one with the pot of thin glue she kept hidden in her bottom drawer—and headed out of the building toward Potsdamer Platz and the S-Bahn that would take her to Spandau.

The journey should have taken far less than the hour that it did. Magda, however, hopped on and off trains in case she was being followed, doubling back on herself and switching lines and trains, stepping from one to the next as the doors were closing. Every lost minute grated on her. Every lost minute could be another life. But *I'll find out your game and I will unmask you* sat under Magda's skin and screamed *caution*. For weeks after Christoph had threatened to shoot Elsa last May, Magda—despite her brave words—had expected the summons that would put her in the cells at SS headquarters and not its main office. It hadn't come. Elsa hadn't denounced her, not publicly at least. What Elsa might have done in private, however, remained another matter.

Live as if you are always being watched and you'll survive all this longer.

Christoph had written that in a note that was stuffed under her door two weeks after he vanished. Magda had no idea where he was now, which terrified her. When she had finally braved her father's presence, for a Christmas celebration that was anything but, he had mentioned a rumor that Christoph was in Poland, fighting with the partisans against the German army. It was easier to believe that than to lie awake at night with her stomach churning, imagining him dead. As for the warning, despite his reminder, that was a lesson Magda had long ago learned. Now, however, with Elsa's threat itching permanently at her, she made sure she lived every moment by it.

She entered the Spandau complex by the rear entrance, not through the arched and highly visible front gates, and went to Eckhart Bühl's quiet office, not Walther's busy one. Eckhart's secretary was his wife, and she was as trustworthy as he was. His office was also deliberately positioned next to the accommodation huts, which meant that he could keep a close eye on the Jewish workers they had been built for, and it wasn't overlooked. And nothing ever needed explaining to Eckhart. The moment Magda appeared, he called Walther down.

"The round-up I warned you about starts tomorrow, not next month. All the Jewish factory workers still in employment are its first target. I don't know if resettlement notices will be served, or if the Gestapo will swoop on homes and premises without warning. Whichever way it's done, we've almost no time to act. And there's six collection centers this time—big ones, including the Clou Concert Hall and the horse barracks in Moabit. That means we won't know where our workers have been sent, and, once they go in, there's no chance of getting them back out."

She thought she had been clear—and urgent. Walther simply stared at her. As the seconds ticked by, Magda wondered if she needed to tell him again or shake him.

"Walther, did you hear what I said?"

"I'm sorry." He rubbed his face. He stood up and sat down again. "This makes no sense. We've had no warning. That would be nearly half our workforce—how can they take half our workforce and still expect production to continue?"

"Because, I assume, they're going to replace our Jewish workers with forced labor, the foreign workers we keep getting told will be coming. They must be on their way this time."

Walther continued as if Eckhart hadn't spoken. "That's not even the point. Whatever it means for production, they can't do it. My Jewish workers have exemptions. I fought to get those. Even when the Party said only Jewish men and women under thirty could stay in employment, I pulled all the strings I could to keep the older ones. I fought for every one of them. Because they're not only my workers, they're my people."

His eyes were glistening. Magda knew his heart was breaking, but there wasn't time to let it.

"I know, Walther, I know. No one could have tried harder than you did, but the Party's hatred has always been unstoppable, and now it's reached a new level. There was a word on Eichmann's latest memo I hadn't seen before: *Judenfrei*. That's their goal, exactly as they said it was at Wannsee, and now they've named it—no Jews, anywhere. Berlin, and the Reich, and the whole world if the war goes their way, *free* of them. The killing camps are ready, the machinery is in place to deal with the terrible numbers they were crowing over at Wannsee. This is it, the last phase, the *final* bit of their *solution*. And it starts here, tomorrow."

"What do we do?"

Eckhart was poised, ready to do whatever his boss asked of him. Except Walther wasn't capable of asking anything. He was slumped in his chair with his head in his hands. Magda gave him a moment, but he didn't look up, so she told Eckhart the inescapable truth.

"We make choices."

She hadn't wanted to say that. She knew how callous, how like a loyal Party member, it made her sound. But Eckhart was waiting; the future of the Tiedemann Company's workers was waiting. Every sentence that was about to come out of her mouth could be classed as a cruel one, but wasn't it crueler to stand back and give up, and let everyone die? She took a deep breath and plunged in.

"We phone the other factory owners we can trust and tell them what's coming. We match up the few stolen identity cards that we have left with the workers who look most like the photographs already on them. There's no time or materials to do anything more. We choose the people we think are most able to go into hiding and survive an underground life. We give them cover stories and we move them out as quick as we can into the network and—given how many people it takes to support one escapee never mind dozens—we pray that the network holds." She stopped. "We don't tell the ones we can't help what is about to happen: it would cause panic and then we won't be able to help anyone."

Eckhart nodded at that; Walther groaned.

Magda stared out of the small window at the long barracks filled with men and women who had survived almost ten years of increasingly bitter persecution. Who had no idea that it was their last hopeful day in the world. She swallowed hard as the irony and the enormity of what she was about to say again, and more forcefully this time, hit her.

"We have to make choices, as hard as that will be. We have to select our best chances, and choose life, for them."

What that choice meant for the rest went—as it had to if they were to do what they had to do—unsaid.

*

Thirty-eight. In the end that was what 1,967 workers had been reduced to. Thirty-eight. Twenty-three given new identities, which may or may not stick. Fifteen led to safe houses that could stop being that within hours. All of them dropped with barely any warning into a lifetime of running and fear.

Magda waved away the waiter circling with yet another tray loaded with sparkling glasses. As tempting as too much champagne and the hope of forgetting would be, she needed to keep a steady head and a close rein on her tongue; her nerves were already shredded by the day's events without adding alcohol.

"We can't witness it. We can't be here when the SS arrive and the round-up begins."

By the time Magda had limped back to the factory as dawn was breaking, Walther had been . . . She wanted to say "himself" again, but he had been a long way from that. As immaculately turned out as he was at tonight's party, twelve hours ago when he had insisted that they all leave the factory, he had been as haggard and worn and sleepless as her. And, as polished as he now was, Magda knew that today had irreversibly changed him, that she would never see the old lights dance again in his eyes. In the early hours he had, however, climbed out of the fog Magda's news had thrown him into and been back in control of himself, clear-headed and full of orders.

"I'm not hiding. I wish to God we could all be standing here to bear witness. But I wouldn't normally be at the factory on a Saturday, and you shouldn't be here at all. If there's discrepancies in their lists, which obviously there will be, I would prefer to deal with that on Monday morning when their bloodlust has damped down and they are less likely to start shooting."

Magda had sunk into a chair and fallen on the hot coffee and rolls Frau Bühl set down in front of her. She was so exhausted, it was hard to concentrate on what Walther was saying, but it was vital to the safety of both of them that she knew exactly what he was planning so she had summoned up the last of her energy and asked him.

"How will you do that? What will you say if you're called to account?"

"As little as I can." Walther had shrugged as he replied, a gesture Magda could see came from despair, not from confidence. "My famous gambling addiction is a good cover for bad record-keeping. I'll make sure I'm bleary-eyed and subtly scented with brandy. I'll sound as cold as I can about the increased runaways, and the suicides I'll blame for so many being missing, and I'll be as enthusiastic as a new church convert about the foreign forced labor." He smiled. Its emptiness brought Magda nearer to defeat than all the fear she had endured through the long night. "I'll act, Magda, the way that we always do."

He had waited then and had let her finish the last roll before he asked the question she didn't know how to answer.

"How was it, being a guide? Did you get your six settled?"

Settled. Magda wasn't sure what to do with that word. Nothing about the underground life—the submarine life, as Christoph had called it, where people in hiding lurked under the surface like U-boats—could ever be that. As for being a guide... Magda wished she could say it had been simple, but she had never been more frightened in her life. Copying reports, picking up forged papers and organizing escape routes had felt fraught with danger, but that was nothing compared to the responsibility of actually moving a person. It was also a task she had never imagined herself doing—she was the information-getter, the thief on the inside. But, when Walther could only track down two of Christoph's network contacts from the three they needed to get the job done, what could she say but, "I'll do it."

Two men and four women, each to be led from the factory one at a time. Magda could only risk taking trams and trains on the return leg of the trips, so each round journey took at least two hours, and sometimes twice that. She had changed her hat and coat each time, picking the neatest outfits she could find from the piles the magician-like Frau Bühl had conjured up.

Following the instructions the more experienced guides insisted on, her traveling companions were as respectably dressed as she was. The men's faces were shaved, the women's were lightly powdered and lipsticked; their outfits were smart but not showy. Cleanliness, according to Christoph's contacts, was what mattered: Jews, in the minds of the SS and the Gestapo, were dirty, slovenly creatures and therefore easily spotted. Every decision was made to minimize attracting any kind of attention. No one with black hair, or with a birthmark, or with anything physically remarkable about them at all was chosen. That was one set of criteria. The only others Magda could think of to base their impossible selection on was that the candidate should have retained some aspect of physical strength despite years of poor rations, and have the ability to be quiet and blend in.

Once the choices were made, and their appearance was rendered as bland as it could be, Magda led each of her charges through side streets and alleyways to anonymous buildings in Wilmersdorf and Westend and Halensee. The journeys were silent, nerve-shredding things. Magda avoided busy areas where the security forces could be patrolling. No one spoke beyond names when they opened the safe-house doors to her coded knock. She rode back on trams, where she avoided eye contact with anyone, refusing to believe that anything bad could happen to bright-eyed Helle Herschell. Convincing herself that, even if the Gestapo caught Otto Wirkus, his quick brain would find him a way out.

She went back to her dwindling group and breathed confidence into them, and wouldn't allow herself to think how misplaced that could be. For every one of the sixteen hours she roamed Berlin's streets delivering her *packages*, as the network referred to them, she assumed she would be caught. She wasn't even stopped. But no one was *settled*; everyone was just starting. And six wasn't enough. When Walther asked the question, therefore, she had gulped down her coffee and devoured the last crumbs of her breakfast and realized she had to do more. Which is what she had shouted at him.

"Settled's not a word I would choose, but I got them to the first stage without problems. I never attracted any attention; I wasn't followed. And we've a few hours left before the raids start, which means I can get more people out, I'm certain of it."

"No, Magda, you can't." Walther had let her rage and he had let her argue, but he wouldn't budge. "You've made half-a-dozen trips in one day and got away with them all. That kind of luck doesn't last. This was never going to be enough—how could it be? Another dozen, another hundred, wouldn't be enough. But we've done our best—you have to believe that. There are people now with the chance of a life. I've sent word to the workers who don't live on site not to come in, to get away if they can. There's nothing more now to be done with today except make it an ordinary one."

An ordinary one. His words had sounded hollow then and they sounded laughable now, as Magda stood in the middle of another Winkler Straße reception that had been planned too long ago to cancel, surrounded by the Party's well-fed faithful. Magda had gone home that morning because Walther had made her. She had slept because her body had made her. And now she was dressed in her best lavender silk watching Walther laugh and joke with Albert Speer as if the factory raids had never happened, wondering if it wouldn't be easier to go mad.

"You're doing your weird neck thing again. It really doesn't get any prettier."

Elsa was four or five drinks further on than Magda and her eyes were glittering.

Magda, who was in no fit state to parry Elsa's jibes, muttered something meaningless about needing to go and freshen her glass.

She barely managed a step away, however, before a man, whose suit was too cheaply cut to suggest he was a guest, entered the room and pulled Minister Speer abruptly to one side. Magda wasn't the only one to notice Speer's normally elegant demeanor crack. His loud curse silenced the party.

"Ladies, what must you think of me? Can I beg your indulgence for such an unpleasant lapse?" Speer was a model of good manners once more when he turned, but his jaw was rigid. "Such an irritation when we should be celebrating an important day for Berlin. As I was about to share with you, this morning we finally cleared the last Jews out of our factories. Berlin's war drive can rely on honest workers again."

A hearty round of applause greeted his words, which Magda automatically joined in with.

"The operation to remove them was, do I even need to say it, an efficient one, but—and this was the reason for my unfortunate language—it would seem a few of our targets evaded the net. It is unfortunate; it will be corrected. And now let us raise our glasses and drink a toast to Berlin's cleaner streets and continue with this most enjoyable evening."

Magda lifted her glass in time with the others. She didn't make eye contact with Walther. And she didn't get away from Elsa as quickly as she intended.

"He's putting a brave face on it. It wasn't a few who got away; it was hundreds, maybe thousands. And it was more than luck." Elsa's voice was thick with hatred. "Gunther told me earlier about all the upset that's been caused. Goebbels is beside himself, as is your dear boss, which is probably why they want to land the blame on Speer. He is, after all, in charge of the factories. They also think there's been a leak of some kind, that the runaway Jews got a warning." She paused, long enough for her meaning to sink in. "What do you think, Magda? You work at headier heights than the rest of us, and you do have friends in the strangest of places. Do you know anyone capable of such an unspeakable treachery?"

Magda knew better than to say anything at all. This wasn't the time or the place for the confrontation Elsa was intent on provoking. She smiled across the room instead, as if there was someone she knew, and she walked away, determined, for tonight at least, not to be caught in the tide of Elsa's poison.

Perhaps they are cursing themselves.

This time, the thought of curses didn't crumple Magda onto a wall; it lightened her step. Four exhausting years in and the war was changing: it wasn't running all in Hitler's favor anymore. And, as much as Magda told herself she wasn't superstitious, it was hard not to feel that its course had started to falter with the factory deportations of February 1943.

And even if that's not true, it's comforting to think that perhaps their deeds don't, and won't, go unpunished.

A week after over 10,000 of Berlin's Jewish workers had been marched out of the factories to Grunewald station and loaded onto cattle trucks bound ultimately for Auschwitz, the news of Germany's defeat at Stalingrad in the southwest of Russia had seeped through to the country's horrified citizens. A defeat on such a scale—by an enemy Germans had been assured was depraved and corrupt and incapable of winning—was too big to hide. The Russian city's refusal to be defeated had cost the lives of hundreds of thousands of German husbands and sons, whose bodies were lost forever. For all Goebbels' promise that Germany would go forward with "a war more total than anything we can imagine," confidence in victory at any time, never mind at any time soon, was shaken. That confidence had been further shaken in September when Italy surrendered to the Allies, leaving Hitler and his puppet Mussolini clinging on to the fringes of the civil-war-torn country. And it had been rocked in November, by the devastating bombing raids that had hit Germany's key cities, including Berlin, and brought the war sickeningly onto the home front.

A comfortable home and a well-padded job had spared her from the worst of the air raids and the shortages of food and fuel. None of that, however, had made Magda blind to the misery the fourth year of war had brought with it. She wanted it over, but, unlike her fellow citizens who were still paying lip service to patriotism, she didn't want Germany's ruling masters to win. She knew too well that, whatever defeat might bring, victory was a far more dangerous option. The war might be turning against Hitler, but the massacres hadn't stopped—they had gathered speed. Himmler's experiments with gas had led from a handful of mobile killing centers to six fully functioning death camps. The Jews, and the communists, and every other group designated as "other," were being murdered in one kind of camp and slowly worked to death in another, and nothing seemed able to stop it. Any sign that anyone might try simply made Himmler and his henchmen more merciless.

The Warsaw Ghetto rose in May 1943: Himmler liquidated it and sent the 40,000 Jewish residents not killed in the process to Treblinka. In November, to cement the lesson of Warsaw, he ordered the mass shooting of the remaining 43,000 Jewish forced laborers in Lublin. The pleasure he took in organizing the details of that operation—forcing the victims to dig the trenches they would die in and having loud music played to drown out the bullets and the screaming—had sent Magda praying to the God she had long since abandoned to better target one of the bombs raining down on Berlin and take Himmler, and Hitler, and the whole murdering mass of them out. The bombs, however, found other targets. Himmler and the rest of them escaped. Magda, sickened to breaking point, and in an echo of Christoph's desperation almost two years before, took bigger and bigger risks to make sure others escaped too.

By the summer of 1944, the continued silence from the outside world convinced Magda that no one was listening to all the memos she had risked her life copying out. She carried on passing the worst of them to Eckhart, but she focused more of her energies on direct action to disrupt the Party's schemes. Despite the increasing surveillance, she visited the illegal printshops scattered through Wedding and Moabit every other day, pushing them to turn their dwindling stocks into the magic papers the fugitives needed. She continued to act as a guide, steering terrified men and women from safe house to safe house. And she added the garden shed at the edge of her property to the list of usable places, equipping it with a mattress and blankets and replenishing the small food stores when her unseen visitors used them. There was no one to stop her, or to counsel caution. Magda no longer visited her parents. Walther was taking as many risks as she was. Christoph was still... She had no idea where Christoph was still, although she had to believe that, wherever he was, he was alive there or the grief would unravel her. And even if there had been anyone to beg her to slow down, or to take care, or to stop, she wouldn't have listened. Taking risks was the only way Magda could balance the guilt of spending her days smiling at monsters.

Which might finally be ending.

That was a good thought for a sunny August day; it almost made her feel like the 29-year-old she actually was, not the old woman her soul had turned into. Two months ago, in June 1944, the Allies had invaded France; now they were closing on Paris. Two weeks ago, a group of disaffected officers had planted a bomb that was intended to kill Hitler. They had failed; the reprisals had been terrible. But they had tried, and who was to say that a second group wouldn't learn the lessons of the first one and do the job better?

They can be beaten. This can all end.

She walked through the back gates into the Tiedemann complex more hopeful than she could remember. And with her guard, therefore, although she didn't realize it, dangerously down.

Walther's secretary was nowhere to be seen and his office door was wide open. Magda could see him sitting at his leather-topped desk, poring over a stack of papers and apparently alone. She walked straight in, bubbling with an enthusiasm that needed a moment's thought and a safer place.

"This new printer is the best I've found. Look at these."

The sheaf of forged *Wehrmacht* identity cards was out of her bag before she noticed Walther's horrified expression, or the toddler sitting on the blue rug spread out by the hearth. Liselotte, Elsa's two-year-old daughter, looked up at Magda and beamed.

"For God's sake, Magda. Elsa is in the hall. How didn't she see you?"

Liselotte toddled over and tugged at Magda's skirt, trying to get her attention. Magda, still stunned by her own carelessness, took no notice.

"I came up the back stairs. I wanted to see Eckhart, but he wasn't in his office."

"He's using one up here now—he can't bear to be near the foreign workers. The condition of them is terrible." Walther shook his head and got to his feet, waving at Liselotte to distract her. "Which is the least important thing here. You have to go. You know how Elsa is when it comes to you. Everyone has gone crazy since July's failed plot to assassinate Hitler. Stauffenberg got close enough to put a bomb in the same room as the Führer, which no one should have been able to do. The Gestapo are on full alert, seeing spies and conspiracies everywhere, and that's spilled down to every loyal follower. I swear to God, Magda, if Elsa sees you, and holding those, she'll have a noose around your neck."

It was too late, however, for Magda to go back the way she had come—Elsa's heels were already tapping toward Walther's office.

"Go through there." Walther pointed to the connecting door in the far corner of his office. "Bühl should be at his desk—wait with him till she's gone."

It was a sensible idea. It should have worked without mishap. Neither of them, however, had made allowances for Liselotte's inquisitive fingers. As Magda brushed past her, the little girl reached up to snatch the fan of identity cards. Her tiny fist knocked into

Magda's elbow and the cards shot out of Magda's hand in an arc. They flew through the air and landed all over the rug and the polished floor. Liselotte immediately screamed with delight and began chasing after them.

"Oh my God, I'm sorry. Let me get them."

The heels were barely a dozen taps away. Walther hurled himself around the desk and pushed Magda toward Eckhart's office.

"Go. I'll do it. If by any chance Elsa sees one, I can make an excuse up. I can't do that if you're here."

Magda burst through the door, putting her finger to her lips as Eckhart leaped up. Within a moment of Magda finding safety, Elsa's voice danced sharp and clear through the thin wood.

"Your new girl is useless. I've told her to remake the coffee with the real stuff, not that ersatz muck, or forget about working here. You can't let your standards slip, Father. There's enough talk as it is about your financial problems." She stopped. When she spoke again, Magda's heart sank. "What have you got there, sweetheart? Have you been raiding Grandpa's desk again?"

The silence that followed went on far too long to calm Magda's thudding heartbeat. When Elsa finally resumed speaking, it didn't help: her baby-friendly tone was gone.

"Why does she have these? Why do *you* have these?"

Magda couldn't hear Walther's mumbled response, but she heard Elsa's bitter laugh.

"Don't. That's ridiculous. There are departments devoted to checking for forgeries. Why would anyone ask you to examine them? What do you know about printing?" And then her voice took on the hard edge Magda knew had crossed them all into danger. "This is her, isn't it? I knew she was involved in helping Jews escape—who's closer placed to the information that's leaking than she is? I should have warned Himmler months ago, but he thinks she's a treasure. And I knew she was using this place as cover. What I don't understand is why you're helping her."

And then Magda heard Walther's answer far clearer than she wanted to.

"I'm not. None of this has anything to do with Magda. I am the one who has been helping our Jewish workers, Elsa. Me." His voice wavered, Magda thought it might crack, but he pulled himself back together with a surety that was heartbreaking. "I have been using my friendships to find out information for years. I have been using the factory and paying for forged papers since Hitler launched his evil crusade. That's where my money has gone, not on gambling. It's me. It's no one but me."

Eckhart's hand was on Magda's as she reached for the doorknob. It was over her mouth as she tried to shout.

"Don't. It will hurt him if you rush out there. He's doing this to protect you, to protect all of us."

Magda wanted to argue. She wanted to push Eckhart away and go running to stand beside Walther, but his next words held her where she was.

"Elsa will hate him for this, but he's her father—she won't betray him. She'd sacrifice you, however, without a second thought. You going in there can only make matters worse."

There wasn't a sound on the other side of the door except Liselotte's little-girl chatter.

Magda dropped her hand from the wood; Eckhart dropped his hand from her mouth. No one spoke in either room. There was a rustle, the sound of a child saying goodbye and a slam. He still held Magda back.

"Give Walther a moment before you go charging in—he's just lost his daughter. At least this way he won't lose his life. Hold on to that."

Another thin thread, too fragile for the hopes pinned onto it. As Walther sobbed on the other side of the door, Magda prayed this was the one they would never have to test.

CHAPTER NINE

Magda, February 1945

The thread snapped. Magda had known it would from the moment Himmler let slip where Walther was being held. She still clung on to her desperate hope that something would save him until long after that hope stopped being a rational one.

Plötzensee Prison, the place where Walther was immediately taken on his arrest, was the execution site, the last stop on the torture line. It was impossible to work at SS headquarters and not be aware of what the name meant. Magda had seen the green vans that fed it moving hooded prisoners out of the basement cells in Prinz Albrecht Straße, even though everyone was meant to be as blind to those transports as they were to the rest. She knew about the prison's frighteningly high suicide rate, about the thumbscrews and the lights that burned all night, and the cells that were too small for the inmates to raise their arms in. And about the hooks hanging in a long row whose nooses were considered a more efficient method of killing than the guillotine they had replaced, which had only been able to dispatch one inmate at a time.

Magda had known the truth about Plötzensee. She had walked through its gates on a freezing February morning and felt its menace. Despite all that knowledge, however, until the moment weeks later when she held the letter in her hand announcing his murder, she still refused to believe the prison would be Walther's ending. Even though she had sat in front of the man she had known for almost ten years—the man she had misjudged and relearned, admired and loved—and known that he was broken and past helping, she had refused to believe it. Even though she had felt the pain of his ruin collect like ice around her heart, she had still allowed herself to be fooled. She had still let Walther lull her into thinking there was a different way out for him.

"They'll find a use for me yet, you'll see. I've proved myself pretty nimble at unwinding rope, which is what passes for work round here. Maybe they'll make a shipbuilder out of me—isn't that what they use the fibers for? Or maybe they'll stick me in the *Volkssturm* with all the boys and the old men they've finally forced into a uniform. There'd be a rather pleasing irony in that, don't you think? All these years 'undermining the Fatherland'—which is one of the charges against me apparently—and then off I go, fighting to preserve it in its dying days."

Her visit in February 1945 was the first time she had seen him since his arrest four months earlier in October. As haggard as he was, he was still trying to be the old charming Walther. All they had given her was fifteen minutes. Fifteen minutes was nothing, especially when it was stacked against a friendship spanning ten years, but Magda knew it was a miracle she had been granted any time with him at all. Visits to Plötzensee were such a rare occurrence, the prison guards hadn't known what to do with her when she arrived. They had only admitted her because the letter of access she waved at them bore Himmler's name. She had forged that; she could be punished for that. Magda didn't care. She had been gone from Himmler's side for a fortnight now and, hopefully—given the disaster the war had turned into for Germany—she was gone from his thoughts. The only tie left between them was the Grunewald house she still lived in, and she would be gone from that soon enough too.

"No weeping—I won't have it."

Walther's order was harder to follow than any he had given her before: his appearance alone would have moved a heart far less full of him than hers. He was so gaunt, his long body hung from his wide shoulders, barely a memory of what it had once been. His cheeks were sunken, his dark hair a faded gray that blended in with his skin. He looked like a man for whom sunlight was a distant memory. As for the place he was held in… Behind its elegant red-brick façade, Plötzensee Prison was a mess of animal smells and iron-barred buildings that fanned out in a shadowy maze Magda had had to force herself to enter.

"None of this has come back on you?"

It was a relief that Walther had taken immediate control of the conversation, even if Magda didn't know how to answer his question. Everything she had wanted to ask—*Are you well? Are you being fairly treated? Are the conditions in here survivable?*—had been answered in her first sight of him. And she knew how close she had come herself to the same fate: she had been questioned at length by a Himmler who was smarting at being cast as a fool by a man he thought of as a friend. She hadn't expected to walk away from that meeting as unmarked as she had.

"I'm not in any trouble. Your testimony kept me in the clear." The relief that swept across Walther's face almost filled it out again. "But I'm not working as the Reichsführer's secretary anymore—I left that position in the middle of January. Hitler is as paranoid about traitors as he was during the assassination attempt, and Himmler has been criticized for his close connections to you. So has Speer. Because I came to his office from yours, I was seen as a liability. He did believe I was innocent though, which may have had more to do with your ability to lie, or Himmler's refusal to let anyone think he had let a renegade work so close to him, than my ability to act. The upshot is that I am out of his circle, although not entirely in disgrace. I have been granted a job in the typing pool. I haven't shown up to do it. Nobody seems to care."

"No more digging for secrets then? No more spying?"

Magda instinctively looked round when Walther asked that, but the guards who had marched them both into the bleak whitewashed room—hers with marginally more civility than his—were outside in the corridor and showed no sign they were listening.

"No. There's no more spying..."

And no more helping either, not for now at least. She didn't say that; she didn't know how to, not when faced with the hopelessness of Walther's situation. That was the moment when she came closest to the tears he had forbidden. That was also the moment when he properly smiled and turned back into Walther: the clever, captivating man she had met another lifetime ago. The man who shared her way of looking at the world and her dreams for how much better it could be. The one person she had always told the truth to.

She wanted to do that now. She wanted to tell him that the closer they came to catastrophe, the more vicious the Nazis grew. That Himmler was sick—his heart, ironically, failing him—but that hadn't stopped him pushing Germany further into disaster and trying to grab more power as the country fell. That he and Goebbels had seen the loyalty slipping from Hitler and were fighting like jackals over who would wear the crown next. She wanted to tell Walther that she knew Himmler would never stop, and that the killings wouldn't stop either. That, even though the Russian armies had overrun Majdanek and Auschwitz—and uncovered all the horrors they both knew were happening there—the transports were still going out to the death camps that had carried on working. That, before she left Himmler's office for good, she had seen a memo confirming that one such train was scheduled to leave Grunewald for Theresienstadt on the twenty-seventh of this month, a whole train for eighteen Jewish men and women, because that was how obsessed and insane the Nazis were. Eighteen Jews were going to be sent to their deaths for being Jews, even though the Führer was hiding in his bunker, and Dresden had been burned to the ground, and the Russian army had crossed the Oder and was barely sixty kilometers away from Berlin. Magda wanted to tell him all that, but she couldn't. It was too much horror to tell and too much horror for him to bear.

She struggled for the right words to finish her answer, but then Walther took her hand, cradling it between his huge ones, and she knew she didn't need to.

"But they haven't stopped, have they? And being powerless to do anything is destroying you. And the worst of it is that they won't stop. No matter how badly the war runs, not even when the Russians are ten, or even five, kilometers away. Nothing but this defeat, this obliteration, that is surely now coming would ever have ended their hatred, Magda. You, of all people, know that."

She nodded and her ragged breathing calmed. There was still one thing, however, that she had to ask him.

"Did we do enough?" He winced as her fingers clawed at his more fragile ones, but he didn't pull away. "I'm sorry, Walther, I know it's not fair of me to ask you now, but the strain of it is eating me up. After you were arrested, we—Bühl and I—froze. We didn't know how far the arrests would extend, or who we might put into danger if we were taken. And, with the factory under Speer's direct control, we can't get started again. Now I can't stop asking myself the same thing over and over: did we do enough?"

She had never asked Walther that before; she had never let herself properly consider it before his capture. They had always been too busy doing; it had always felt as if it would be the wrong question. It still was in so many ways, but she had never needed his help so badly.

He smiled and his eyes lightened. The answer he gave her was, she realized, what he also needed to hear.

"We did what we could, Magda, and I am glad of it. We tried. We didn't stand by, or turn away. We did something. That has to count."

She nodded. Now that she had seen the strength he still carried, there was another question surfacing. A question that sickened her and kept her from sleep.

"Was it my fault? I did the sums. I wrote the reports. I gave them Grunewald and the 'cheaper transport method.'"

Her voice cracked. Walther lunged across the table, his chains rattling, and pulled her as close into his arms as he could.

"No! Magda, don't. It wasn't your doing. You wrote the numbers, but you didn't dream up the nightmare behind them. You wrote the reports, but you didn't delight in what they proposed. And you bore witness—you still can bear witness. You did what you had to, to do good." The door suddenly opened and his voice grew urgent. "But now you have to take care of yourself; you have to get clear of this. When the war is done, people will be caught up with rage and guilt and will want black-and-white judgments. We had all the best intentions, but our actions could stand against us."

"Get away from her. The visit is done."

The guard grabbed Walther's arm and whisked him away before Magda could hold him or say goodbye to him, or thank him for keeping her alive. Or ask the other questions that had been burning at her for four long months—"Why did Elsa do it? Why did she betray you?" She shouted it after him anyway, but the only response was a door slamming shut.

"Get in."

The voice was unmistakable. The sleek black Mercedes with its *SS1* plate was also unmistakable. There was no way to avoid the command or the car, which was parked across the prison exit blocking every escape route. Magda slid into the back seat; Himmler didn't look at her.

"Two weeks away from the office and you've grown sloppy, Fräulein Aderbach. You know that Plötzensee is on the visits-forbidden list. You should know that the prison director would telephone my office the moment you arrived, a 'letter of access' or not. Perhaps you do believe you are as innocent and untouchable as your recent performance suggested."

His voice was as bland as all the words he had taught her.

Which means I am in terrible danger.

"I am sorry. I was desperate to see him. I should have asked I know, but—"

"Stop it." His thin voice sliced the air between them. "Don't demean yourself—or me. One thing you must be to have fooled us all for so long, Fräulein, is brave. Be brave now."

The car had raced through the city's streets as only SS staff cars could still do and was already turning into Prinz Albrecht Straße. Magda knew it wouldn't glide to its usual halt outside the arched front door. She sat in silence as it swung through the double gates at the side instead and into a courtyard lined with green vans.

"Get out."

There was no one around to see as Magda stepped out of the car and down the short flight of steps Himmler pushed her roughly toward. She had been worried that her legs would shake and not hold her as she walked, or that her body would tremble and slip off the chair he directed her to. She had been worried her heart would beat so loud she wouldn't hear his commands. She could barely feel her body at all. Now that the moment of her death was upon her—and what could this be if not that—she felt calm, weightless.

I have lived under the shadow of this room, of this threat, since I went to work for Walther. I've never let myself face that in case the fear crippled me. And now here it is, and the fear has gone.

It wasn't because Himmler had called her brave. She didn't care what Himmler thought of her. It was because of Walther. *It wasn't your doing. You did what you had to, to do good.* She could go to her death with that. Whatever Himmler did to her couldn't diminish that.

"Put your hand on the table."

"What?"

Magda looked up, confused by Himmler's order. He had stepped back against the wall, although he was still watching her intently. There was another man standing where he had been. This one was dressed in overalls like a mechanic and holding a small tin box.

"I said put your hand on the table. I know what you expect, but I am not going to kill you, or at least not today. I will do that, once the attention your treachery has turned on me switches to someone else. But, for now, I still have a use for you."

Magda tried to keep her attention on him, but the overalled man had opened his box and taken out a sharp knife and a wad of gauze and her stomach was suddenly tumbling.

"The Jews are still escaping, and someone is helping them do that. We know there is a web of safe houses—we suspect that you know where they are and that you are running one of them out of the back of the Tower House."

Himmler smiled. There was no warmth in it, not even his version of that. There was nothing but a malice so pure, Magda's heart contracted.

"It wasn't quite the way I intended you to use the place, but everything has its purpose in the end. You will go back there, and continue to let your 'guests' come. And we will watch, and we will mop them up. And, in the meantime, you will return to work, to the job I so graciously gave you, that you don't seem to appreciate, with a little warning to anyone else who thinks they can make a fool out of me."

He nodded to the man with the knife, who stepped closer. All Magda could see was the blade gleaming in his hand; its shimmer hypnotized her. She forced her gaze away and tried to keep her eyes focused on Himmler's, but his gaze was as sharp.

"All that writing, Magda. All the reports that proved themselves so valuable. That I have no doubt now that you copied and turned into lies and spread through your filthy communist friends to make a monster out of me. All done with that pretty little hand. You betrayed me with it, Magda. So what better way is there than this to repay me?"

He motioned to the man waiting with the knife. He raised his hand. The room disappeared. There was nothing left to look at but the thin sliver of light bouncing from the blade. Magda wanted to close her eyes; she wanted to scream her fury at what was surely, unimaginably, coming, but she was mesmerized by the delicate arch the knife made as it danced up through the air, by the slight tremble as it paused waiting for the downswing. And then there was a shiver and the blade fell, and the agony flew in, and not even Himmler's mocking laughter could reach her.

CHAPTER TEN

Magda, April 1945

They have killed him.

Eckhart's letter was scrawled in an almost unreadable hand, and seeped through with fury.

> *They hung him from a meat hook and strangled him with piano wire, and sent the factory a bill this morning for "their services." What kind of a death is that? And his body is gone, bundled into an unmarked grave because "that is all traitors deserve." We cannot mourn him properly; we cannot honor him. There are people walking round with so much blood on their hands, who deserve this ending far more than him.*

The letter had arrived the day before, on the last day of a cold gray March that seemed to have refused any idea of spring. The enormity of Walther's loss, the impossibility of it despite the circumstances of their last heartbreaking meeting, had ripped through Magda's body with as much force as the knife had taken away the middle two fingers of her right hand. The pain of both was inescapable, all-consuming.

His body is gone. Magda knew that, if the war had been running in Hitler's direction, Walther's body would have been paraded and his death would have been front-page news, the headlines screaming their disgust at the man who tricked them all. But the war was running fast away from the Führer now and she doubted anyone but her and Elsa would care.

She wandered over to the window, her body automatically hunching round her damaged hand. It had healed—by the time she came to in the cellar, it had been cleaned up and bandaged. The pain of it still took her breath away. Himmler's plan to set her up in the office as a warning, however, had failed. At first, she had been too ill to get into the car he sent to collect her. Then, as February had slipped miserably into March, the car had stopped coming. Magda assumed that meant the Americans or the Russians, or whoever was battling their way fastest to Berlin, were inching closer. She hadn't had the strength in those early pain-crazed days to go out into the world and find out. She had, however, managed to make one fumbling call to the network before the phone lines went dead. Since then, she had twitched the curtain aside two or three times a day to check, but none had come near the shed. She chose to believe that was because her message had worked and kept the submarine people safe, not because there was none of them left in hiding who needed it. She rarely left the kitchen window now, especially in the evening. There was a certain comfort to be had watching the birds flitting backward and forward, their beaks filled with twigs, perfectly at ease in their home-building.

Which this place isn't and never will be. I can't stay here anymore. I don't have to. There's no one watching me; there's no one to care if I leave.

She had thought that thought for a week now, but the news of Walther's death had made her mind up. Walther was gone, Christoph was gone, but her parents were still out there.

You have to take care of yourself; you have to get clear of this.

Walther had been right. Whichever Allied army got here first would look at her in this house with its tainted history and its pictures of Hitler and Himmler and see the wrong woman. This was a house paid for in another family's blood—she couldn't wait out the end of the war in it.

I have to take the first steps into the future.

The deportation trains were no doubt still going out, and would keep going out while there was a single Jew, or communist, or gypsy, or person counted as *other*, left standing. The Party would keep killing until there was no one left to kill, or the last of their own had fallen. There had to be a reckoning; she had to be part of it. She had to tell Walther's story—and Himmler's; she had to tell the stories of all those whose voices were gone. She had been their witness; now it was time to be their mouthpiece. It was time to go home.

She slept that night, although she hadn't expected to. Perhaps it was the relief that came with knowing that nothing more could hurt Walther. Perhaps it was the relief of a decision made. Whatever the reason, it was late morning before Magda emerged from a sleep that had been, for once, dream-free. She was ready to go. She had pulled her small suitcase out from under the bed the night before. Her old winter coat—with her KPD card and a stack of emergency money still sewn into its hem—was hanging ready on the back of her bedroom door. All she had to do now was pack, as practically as possible.

Filled with purpose for the first time in weeks, Magda dressed quickly in a plain blue cardigan and a heavy tweed skirt, and surveyed the rest of her wardrobe. It was full, but there was little in it she wanted. She was going back to a world whose rhythms were dictated not by chauffeured cars and privileged kitchens, but by shortages and the weather, and the terrible bombing raids now pounding Berlin. That life had no space in it for satin gowns and sequinned boleros or office dresses with prettily pleated sleeves. It required clothes that were sturdy and warm, and unremarkable. She worked as quickly as her damaged hand would let her, folding her too-small collection of walking trousers and winter jumpers and warm woolen dresses into her case. When that was done, she crossed to the chest of drawers under the window to hunt out her thickest stockings.

The sun was poking through the gray April clouds, washing them in pale lemon. There were birds balancing on the twists of ivy curling all over the back, and increasingly the front, of the house. As Magda stopped to watch them, a shadow, or a sudden noise she couldn't hear, startled them and the tiny creatures rose into the air, swooping and diving in a brown and gray wave. Magda moved closer to the glass to watch their soaring patterns—and stepped back as quickly. She wasn't the birds' only audience. There was someone in the shed, moving about far more visibly than they should have been doing in daylight. She could see a blurred face at the window peering up at the sky, a suggestion of height in the way the body below it was stooping. And then the figure shifted and—breaking the cardinal rule about staying invisible that was ingrained into every escapee—pushed the pane open and leaned out.

It couldn't be him. Every rational part of Magda's brain told her it couldn't be him. But Magda wasn't listening to the rational parts of her brain. She dropped the pile of stockings; she ran down the stairs, jumping them two at a time. She ran through the kitchen and out the back door, leaving it swinging wide open and not giving that a thought. All she could do was run; her body was nothing but motion. She flew down the path, forgetting about caution and quiet and the possibility that someone might be watching her from one of the taller villas dotted around her little one. She forgot all of that because her mind was filled with the face at the window and the certain, impossible knowledge that it was him.

And then he opened the door and pulled her inside, and her mind stopped working at all.

*

"It wasn't meant to happen this way." Christoph eased himself onto one elbow and stared down at her. "I heard through the network that you had opened the shed up for use by escapers—which, by the way, was crazy and impossibly dangerous—so I came in here first. I wanted to clean up and shave and look less like a wild man before I appeared at your door."

Magda laughed and pulled him back down beside her, running her good hand through his tangled beard and the curls at his neck that were thicker than hers. "As if I care how well groomed you look. As if I care about anything except that you are alive, and you are here." She nestled against his chest and wrapped his arm tighter around her. She was so weightless with joy, her body felt as if it could float. "I was sure you were dead. I refused to believe it, I refused to think about it, but I couldn't imagine how you could still be alive."

"Most days out there, neither could I."

Christoph shifted and she felt the strength ripple through his lean body. The man who had been broken by Russia was long gone.

"There's not many I started with who've survived. Even those who were as brave as you."

Magda pulled her hand back under the blanket as his eyes raked over the damage. She couldn't bear to deal with his fury and his anguish again.

"Where have you been?"

He fell silent. Magda could sense him weighing up what he was prepared to tell her, and what he wasn't, and knew that what he had heard come out of her mouth was "What have you seen?"

Is that what our futures will be now? Constantly pausing and editing our pasts to protect each other?

When he started to speak again, he was slow and hesitant. He spoke in broad sweeps, not details, about Poland and the partisans he'd fought side by side with, who were fearless and spurred on by a murderous, vengeful rage. About the SS officers it had been his mission to kill. His voice when he described those was blank. When he reached the part about the death marches he had encountered in Silesia, however—the thousands of emaciated bodies he had seen frozen in never-ending lines in the forests and on the roadways where they had fallen, as they were driven out of the camps and beyond help— he stumbled and couldn't shape his words. Magda had stopped him then, and held him until his breathing was steady enough to go on.

"After that it wasn't enough to knock the heads off the monster. I had to fight, properly fight, and I didn't care that it was against my own countrymen, so I went off and joined the Red Army." Christoph laughed as Magda gasped. "Why the surprise? I've been fighting on the side of the Russians since you first met me. Luckily the unit I stumbled on was as crazy as I was. I managed to convince them not to shoot. I told them my story and now I am a *ryadovoy*, a private in the Russian army. Look at the patches on my jacket."

He leaned over and dragged a patched and musty-smelling object Magda wouldn't have described as a jacket out of his knapsack. There was a red diamond with two crossed rifles loosely fixed to each side of the collar.

"Not that I'm still with them: I could do a lot of things, but I couldn't march on my own city. Once we crossed the Oder, it was thankfully easy to slip away; the officers were too exhausted and too caught up in politics to watch what we were doing. Both the Russians and the Americans are ready to storm in and put an end to all this, but Berlin's citizens will have to wait like hostages while the generals argue over who gets to be first." His face darkened. "God help us all if the Russians win that fight. They hate us, Magda, with a depth that is visceral. We are going to reap the whirlwind of what we did to them tenfold." He stopped and shook his head as if the fear of that was a solid thing he longed to dislodge. "Anyway, I came back—to find you. To be here when the end starts."

"Another day and you would still be looking for me."

Magda curled into his side on the mattress as the sun slipped down the sky. He had told his story; now it was time for the whole of hers. When she told him about Walther, Christoph broke into a sob he couldn't hold back.

"I thought I had forgotten how to feel. I thought—maybe I hoped—that everything I have seen had eaten away the part of me able to care. And now I hold you, and I hear that, and my skin feels like skin again. I'm not sure I can bear it."

"You can. We both can. We have to feel, or we're no longer human."

She found his mouth before he could answer and let their bodies speak for them instead.

Another hour passed, and another. By the time Magda finally forced herself out of the makeshift bed, the afternoon was heading for twilight.

"We should go back to the house and get my things. I don't want to be on the streets too long after dark—not with the bombing raids and the curfew."

"Let me go first. If there's anyone around, I'll whistle."

Christoph had dressed quicker than she now could, so it was easier to agree.

"Fine, but you can't go out wearing that." He had put the Red Army jacket on for warmth, complete with its red collar patches. "There." Magda pulled them off and stuffed them in her skirt pocket. "Now you'll blend in. They've conscripted any man with enough breath in him to walk, but they can't kit half of them out, which means the streets are filled with all manner of cobbled-together uniforms. No one will care where this came from."

He smiled and kissed her and slipped through the door. She was still struggling to fix her skirt when the gunshot rattled the windows.

*

She was running again, flying up the path. And then she stopped and didn't know if her body would ever start again. Christoph was lying facedown on the grass, a dark stain spreading out like a carpet beneath him. She closed her eyes. It was a trick of the light, a shadow caused by the sinking sun—it had to be. When she reopened them, he would be getting to his feet, cursing the stony path and laughing at his clumsiness.

"He is dead. Wishing it away won't change that. But we can make sure if you want to. It's probably best not to leave any doubts."

It was the second shot that made Magda scream. That crashed her onto her knees beside Christoph's lifeless body.

"Why? Why would you do this?"

Elsa lowered the gun and stared down at her. "Really? Isn't that rather a cliché? The broken-hearted widow—actually, no, not widow; he never did marry you, did he? All right, the broken-hearted whore then, clutching at her lover's corpse and asking *why*? I expected better from you."

She is mad.

Looking into Elsa's wild eyes and seeing that didn't help. But then Christoph was dead, so what could possibly help?

Magda stayed where she was, assuming that the next bullet would be hers. Elsa rolled her eyes.

"Bless you. Kneeling there, accepting your fate, casting yourself as a martyr. I've been waiting a long time to do that to him—which can't be a surprise given what happened the last time one of us had a gun—but I haven't been waiting to shoot you. Oh no. I've got a different plan entirely for you. Stop posing and get up, there's a good girl."

Magda did as she was told, although her legs felt far too brittle to support her.

"Where were you going?"

"What?"

Elsa's question made no sense.

The gun raised again. "I asked you where you were going. What's hard about that? Your door was wide open and there was no sign of you, so I went into the house. I found your case on the bed."

Engage her. Keep her talking. Remind her that she knows you, that you have a connection.

It was what Christoph said he had tried to do the first time he was interrogated by the Gestapo, because he had read in a manual that acting as if he was a person, not a faceless prisoner was a good tactic. Magda knew it hadn't worked—that the Gestapo agent had laughed and knocked one of his teeth out for trying—but she had to do something to turn this dangerous Elsa into someone she could manage.

"I was going home. To Oberschöneweide, to see my parents. I'm the only one they have now that Kiefer is gone and, with all the bombs that have been falling there, I was worried for their safety."

She needed to keep talking, but she needed to move more. She could see Christoph's blood seeping in a slow river from the grass onto the gravel. If it came any closer, if it touched her, she would be sick and start howling. She took a step away from it, but Elsa raised the gun higher.

"You move when I tell you, not a second before. And don't fob me off with sob stories—that's insulting to both of us. You don't care about your parents. You were running away. You killed my father and now you are running away. I knew that's what you would do—it's why I came. That"—she nodded toward Christoph—"was an added bonus."

You killed my father. The accusation was so ridiculous, it wiped away Magda's fear of the gun.

"I killed Walther? That's absurd. How can you blame me? You are the one who reported him to Himmler. You didn't need to do that: you could have walked away and never seen him again or never let him see Liselotte; that would have been a terrible punishment. But you went to Himmler instead. Maybe you couldn't help yourself; maybe being a loyal SS wife meant more to you than your own father. But that was why Walther was arrested and murdered. Because of that. Because of you. I won't stand here and take your guilt."

Elsa was shaking. For a moment, Magda thought it was with remorse. Then she opened her mouth, and Magda realized it was with fury.

"You stupid fool. You haven't a clue. I didn't go to Himmler to denounce my father; I went to save him."

"How could you possibly think—"

Elsa's snarl, and the gun pointed straight at her head, shut Magda up again.

"Isn't it obvious? Because I was terrified someone else would catch him with those forgeries as easily as I did. I told the Reichsführer that my father was weak, that he had fallen in with the wrong company and was being used. And I told him it was you who was responsible for the leaks and the escapes. That was a waste of breath. He wouldn't believe me; he said my accusation was a slur on him. You called that right, didn't you? You weren't so stupid then."

Magda stayed silent—she knew anything she said could lead to a bullet.

Elsa was still talking, her words running one into the other.

"Heinrich was all about protecting himself. He said the factory was already under suspicion, because of some nonsense that boyfriend of yours had been up to with forged papers, and because of all the exemptions Father applied for, and because of the missing Jews back in 1943. And then he brought Father in and Father refused to help himself. He confessed to being a traitor; he said he had always hated the Party. That was what signed his death warrant, not me. And he called you an *innocent*. I should have come and killed you then, but I still had some hope that you would come forward and save him. And now my father is dead, and that hope is gone." Elsa's tirade finally broke. She stopped and lowered the gun, and didn't seem to know where she was.

It was a mistake. She loved him; she truly thought she was saving him. She trusted the SS would look after their own, but she underestimated Walther.

There was pain in Elsa's face, real pain. Magda hated her—she would never forgive her for Christoph's death, or Walther's—but she couldn't ignore the other tragedy here.

"I am sorry. I am really sorry. Your father loved you; I know he did. He loved you right to the end. By taking it all on his shoulders, he kept you as safe as he kept me."

It was the wrong thing to say. Elsa was deaf to the compassion in Magda's voice; all she could hear—all she had ever heard—was competition.

"Don't you dare. Don't you tell me what my father felt. He was my father, not yours. He loved me, not you. You stole him, and you killed him, and now you are going to pay." She stepped off the path and waved Magda past her. "I've wasted enough time on this. Get into the house."

Magda couldn't bear to look at Christoph's body, but neither could she bear to leave it.

"What about him? What about Christoph?"

Elsa pushed Magda forward and stuck the gun in her back.

"Let him rot. I told you to get inside. I'm not going to kill you, but I will hurt you if you don't do what I say."

If I get through this, if I get out of this, I can bury him. I can do that much for him at least.

That got Magda up the path and up the stairs and into the bedroom, where Elsa instructed her to go and fetch her suitcase. As Magda entered the room, she saw the coat hanging on the back of the door.

"I'm cold. Can I take that?"

Elsa shrugged. Magda unhooked it and pushed her shaking arms through the sleeves, resisting the temptation to run her hand along the hem and check that the KPD card she might need if she made it back to Oberschöneweide was still hidden there.

"Don't add any more clothes—you won't need them. What papers can you bring?"

Magda went numb at the question.

How can she possibly know what is here?

"What papers? What do you mean?"

Elsa pushed her back out into the hallway and toward the top of the stairs. "You really are irritatingly slow today. I need documents. Letters from Himmler that you've smuggled back here, memos about the transport trains that you stole from his office. Anything that proves you worked for him."

Magda clutched the banister, ignoring her throbbing hand, her head spinning as she tried to follow Elsa's impenetrable logic.

"I don't have anything like that here."

It was the only answer she was prepared to give until she had an idea of where this madness was going. It wasn't true. The timeline Magda had constructed, which matched Himmler's movements with the long list of massacres, was tucked inside the bottom drawer of her bureau, together with an account of the deportations she had been forced to witness and notes on all the planning that had gone into them. She wasn't about to hand those over to Elsa: all she had done so far was write down the facts without any context or explanation. The documents could be far too easily twisted the wrong way.

"Honestly, I never took anything from his office, or brought anything here. And why would you need them if I had?"

The blow to the side of her head caught Magda off balance. She would have fallen down the staircase if Elsa hadn't wrenched her back.

"That's not good enough; that won't work. Do you really not understand?"

Elsa's voice didn't rise; her calm expression didn't falter. She explained herself to Magda as carefully as if she were explaining a complex, but logical, math problem to a child.

"You're my passage out of this. I've seen the leaflets the Allied planes are dropping; I've heard their filthy propaganda. They don't understand that we were doing good, that we were making the world a better place by taking the Jews out of it. They keep calling us monsters. The first thing they'll do when they get here is go hunting for SS men, and their families, and everyone will turn on everyone else and I won't be safe. Which is where my plan comes in: I'm going to hand you over instead. Himmler's private secretary. The girl with the 'flair for logistics,' as your boss used to call you. Who I know, because I made it my business to know, added up the numbers and watched the trains go out. They won't care about me once they've got their hands on you. Which is why I need papers."

She stopped, clearly waiting for Magda to recant and hand everything over; clearly convinced that what she had said made perfect sense. Magda knew that there was no point in attempting to reason with her. There was no point in explaining that, if it was the Russians who came first into Berlin, the only thing that would matter was that the two of them were both German, and they could be shot simply for that. Or that, if they escaped a bullet then, neither of them would likely survive the battle for the city that was coming. Or that she wouldn't sit nicely in whatever prison Elsa was planning to put her in and play hostage. Magda could see Elsa was long past hearing any of that. There was only one lifeline left she could think of.

"What about Gunther, Elsa? Won't he come back and help you and Liselotte get away? Wouldn't that be a far simpler solution?"

Elsa blinked. Her face filled—for a moment—with an agony that rendered it both raw and brutal. An agony Magda recognized because Christoph's death had flung her into the middle of the same nightmare.

"Gunther is dead. He was murdered by some filthy communist traitor a lot like your boyfriend. It's a nice idea, him coming home to save us; it's what I hoped would happen. But he's dead, so it won't."

Her voice and her face suddenly drifted away to some place where she and Gunther had been happy and in charge of the world. By the time Magda realized that, however, and that there was a window to grab hold of the gun and end this, determined and in-charge Elsa was back.

"Forget papers—those will do." She was pointing to the two framed pictures Magda had hung in the hallway to stand as proof of how loyal she was. "The sketch of the house, and the photograph of you at the gift-giving ceremony standing next to Heinrich. They are perfect."

"But they are heavy, and they'll take up too much room in the case."

It was a pathetic attempt at an excuse.

Elsa sighed and pushed Magda over to the wall.

"Why do I have to explain everything? Take them down, smash the frames, take out the pictures. Easy-peasy, one, two, three."

There was nothing to do but what she was told. It wasn't easy with her right hand so out of action—not that Elsa seemed to have noticed that. In the end, Magda cracked the frames against the edge of the oak sideboard and eased the pictures free of the broken glass as Elsa paced, muttering to herself, the gun rising and falling.

"Roll them up carefully—don't crease them."

She wasn't looking. As Magda spread the drawing and then the photograph out, Elsa briefly turned away to assess whether anything else in the hallway might have any value. Magda didn't miss her window this time: she moved with all the speed she had lacked before and nudged the biggest shard of broken glass into her left pocket. When Elsa turned back again, the suitcase was closed, and Magda was waiting.

"Outside, hurry up. My car is at the top of the driveway. It's already been there too long. I don't want curtains twitching."

It took no time at all, which was the way it had to be. If Magda had thought about what she was going to do, she wouldn't have done it: she would have seen all the pitfalls; she would have remembered Liselotte and wavered. If Elsa had still had the gun pressed into Magda's spine, rather than loosely pointed at her side, she wouldn't have managed it. But Elsa thought she had won and her guard, and her hand, was down.

Magda seized her moment and she tripped, knocking Elsa off balance. The gun clattered to the ground. As Elsa bent, cursing, to retrieve it, Magda pulled the jagged piece of glass out of her pocket and stuck it with all her strength deep into Elsa's back. Elsa screamed and tumbled forward, banging her head on one of the larger stones edging the path as she fell. The blood started to bloom, from her head and from her back. Magda waited for a handful of seconds that passed as slowly as an hour. Elsa didn't cry out again; she didn't move.

Bend down—check her pulse or her breathing.

Magda tried, but she couldn't bring herself to touch Elsa's limp hand or white cheek. The blood continued to pool around the shard that stuck out from beneath Elsa's shoulder blade like a truncated wing. There was a dark bruise spreading across her forehead, and the cut there was still bleeding. There was no movement.

She's dead. She is clearly dead.

Magda picked up her case and stepped back from the body. There was blood on her shoes, and more spotting her coat and her hands. She didn't know if it was Elsa's or Christoph's; she didn't know where else the splatters might be. She couldn't go out into the main street in such a conspicuous state—the only way of escape open to her was through the back garden. She turned to go, and then she stopped.

Elsa needed proof of who I was. I need the same for her.

Magda bent down and, without touching any part of Elsa, grabbed the bag that had been swinging from her shoulder. She fumbled with the catch and tipped the contents out, scooping up Elsa's identity card as it fell. It took another precious moment to wrestle the suitcase open and stuff the card inside.

I need the reports; I need the full list of the killings.

But before Magda could run back into the house, a car horn blared out on the street. She froze. She couldn't imagine Elsa had brought her driver, or that her driver would call for her so rudely if she had. She couldn't, however, take that risk.

Someone might already have heard the shots, or the scream, and gone for help.

Magda couldn't stay in the open; there wasn't time to go back into the house. There wasn't time to do anything but go back through the garden and away.

I won't look at him. All I have to do is get past him. I can do that. I won't think about him being dead, or about Elsa. All I have to do is get home.

She couldn't help Christoph; she couldn't get caught. Someone would find his body, and Elsa's, and realize Magda was gone. They would join the dots, the right way or the wrong way. And if that someone was one of Elsa's SS clan, there would be no escaping.

Which doesn't matter. Whichever way they join them, her death will point back to me—there's too many connections for it not to. An SS wife murdered, one of their own, and this time no one to call me innocent.

There were things in the house that told the wrong story.

So I need to live and tell the right one. For Christoph, and for Walther and for everyone who has been taken so cruelly away.

She brushed down her clothes, ran a hand through her hair. She wanted to run, but she moved slowly instead, determined not to draw attention. Her loss and its agony couldn't matter; Christoph's body couldn't matter. The only thing that mattered was getting herself and her testimony safely home.

PART THREE

CHAPTER ELEVEN

Nina, November 1989

"Get dressed and get out."

Nina jerked awake and jumped to her feet as the cell door slammed open. She stood to attention, arms at her side, thumbs aligned with the stripe running down her tracksuit bottoms, waiting for the rest of the order. It took her a moment to realize that not only was the guard gone, the door was still open.

It's a trick.

It was the only logical thought. Nina stayed where she was, eyeing the pile of clothes dumped on the floor in front of her, presuming she was being watched and listened to.

They are my clothes, the ones I was wearing when I was caught. Perhaps they are letting me go.

It was a nice thought, but it didn't make sense. When her last cellmate had disappeared a...Nina's brain automatically went to *a week ago*, but that was a reflex. Time was as irrelevant an idea to her now as place. All that was certain was that Jana had gone and no one had brought her own clothes in first.

Perhaps I am finally being taken for trial.

It was a possibility. She had no idea, however, what being taken for trial here meant, or if it even happened.

Nina continued to watch the clothes. The light filtering through the square of frosted glass bricks that served as a window was a wispy pale gray, which suggested that outside it was daytime. That could also be a trick. There was a courtyard outside—Nina had seen that on the few occasions they had let her into the mesh-covered cages that passed for an exercise area. They could have easily rigged a spotlight up, it could easily still be night.

She waited, eyeing the clothes as if they might offer a clue. Still no one came. Nina began to count, promising herself she would take some sort of action if she reached a hundred without anything else happening. She was at fifty when she heard the first door creak and the first hesitant set of footsteps moving away.

Maybe they are drawing us out deliberately. We would be as easy to pick off in that corridor as drunks in an alley.

She began counting again, determined to reach her target, convinced that the next noise would be a gunshot. One hundred and nothing. She started again. Another hundred and silence. Whatever this variation of the games the Stasi loved playing was, it was certainly a drawn-out one.

There were more footsteps now, the footfalls too soft to be guards coming. They weren't hesitant anymore: the metal staircase at the end of the block started to shudder. Nina unlocked her stiff arms and legs and went to the window. That was as much of a reflex as trying to work out how long her last cellmate had been gone. Nina was convinced the small square was set there for no other reason than to taunt the prisoners peering hopefully into it: the glass bricks let light in, but nothing else of the outside, not even its shapes.

Do something, anything. Take some kind of control.

That was easier said than done: Nina had forgotten what being in control meant. She had also forgotten how to make her own decisions; she wasn't sure she trusted her ability any more to make the right one.

I'll put the clothes on, see how that feels, see if that makes anyone appear.

Moving slowly, listening carefully, Nina prodded at the pile on the floor. Everything was there: the dark green corduroy trousers and heavy brown jumper, both chosen for warmth; the long-sleeved

T-shirt and thick woolen socks, which felt impossibly soft, and underwear so clean she almost wept at the sight of it; the thickly padded coat—whose seams Jannick had instructed her to cut into and turn into pockets—and her boots, although not her backpack.

For the first time since she had been pushed out of the van back into the prison she assumed was Hohenschönhausen, Nina undressed without being ordered to. She peeled off the threadbare and musty tracksuit and put on her old self. Her old self, however, was gone—the clothes swamped her. The trousers dangled from her hip bones; the sweater flapped round her ribs. When she pulled on the coat, it wrapped round her like a quilt. The clothes didn't fit properly, and they didn't feel right. After the thin material she was used to wearing, these garments felt bulky and awkward, as though they were wearing her. Trying not to worry about what imprisonment had done to the body she had stopped thinking about long ago, Nina focused instead on the coat, running her hands down its seams.

It won't still be there. They've taken my backpack; they'll have gone through this.

They hadn't. The packet containing the West German passport and money was still there where she had stuffed it on the night of her attempted escape, pressed deep inside the lining.

It could still be a trick. Isn't the fact that they left it, or put it back, and I immediately went looking for it, likely to be a trick?

She stuffed the packet back inside the coat, but the damage was done. If there were cameras as well as wiretaps hidden in the cell's walls—which Nina had always suspected there were—the watchers would have captured her holding the package. They would have captured her checking the money. She would have proved herself to be the criminal they had always said she was.

And if they are watching or listening, they will already know that I put the clothes on, which means I could already have failed. Perhaps whatever I do next doesn't matter.

The thought didn't frighten her—it gave her an unexpected surge of courage. The dice were cast. Perhaps, if she was brave and clever enough—and she had survived the Stasi this long, so perhaps she was brave and clever enough—they would fall her way. Nina took a step closer to the beckoning door. There wasn't a sound in the corridor, but there was a breeze whispering toward her. She could feel a faint stirring in the air, which suggested that more doors than the ones to the cells were open. She moved closer again and sniffed. There was still bleach, there was still the dead-earth smell of damp that always lingered in the building, but there was another strand in the mix too: an underlying note that made her think of bonfires and autumn. Nina stepped into the doorway and took a deeper breath. Smoke. The tang was far away. She couldn't feel heat rising or hear the crackle that suggested the cells had only been opened because the prison was on fire, but the smell was, unmistakably, smoke.

The silence was so complete it made her arms prickle. There had always been noise of some sort surrounding her: alarms and barked orders, the clatter of the hatch opening and food trays being shoved through, the peephole swinging. Now there was nothing. There was also no one around. The guard had gone, the cells she could see were all open. Whatever the other prisoners had decided to do with this strange new freedom was done and the only person keeping Nina in her cell was Nina.

She pulled up her hood; she pushed the door wider; she walked out.

The sky was too high; the yard she found herself in was too wide. Nina had lived so long curled up, she didn't know how to fill the spaces now on offer. She also couldn't shake off the feeling that she was being spied on or followed, despite the fact that she had walked down the empty prison corridors and out through the final unbolted door without a single challenge. As she followed the smell of the smoke into a daylight that wasn't filtered or rationed, Nina had kept her shoulders hunched, her arms curved round her body. She wasn't ready to walk head up and chest open and offer them a target. And then she was outside and no one's head turned and she realized there was something far bigger happening than her walking out of her cell.

Unlike its deserted insides, the prison's courtyard was bustling. Not with soldiers rounding up scattering prisoners, but with men and women, dressed both in uniforms and in office clothes, and all scuttling with the same desperate intent backward and forward across the concrete.

As Nina looked closer, she could see that each of them was clutching armfuls of folders and files, which they then proceeded to feed into steel drums, passing the bundles from one person to the next as if they were involved in some macabre production line. The drums were the source of the smoke that had finally forced her out of her cell. There were dozens of them, each with its orange halo of flames; the smut-filled air shimmered with heat. Behind those were the other figures: Nina's unknown fellow inmates who were dressed the same way as she was, in clothes too big for their bodies. They were on the farthest side of the courtyard, in the shadow of the barbed-wire-topped walls and the empty watchtowers. None of the guards or Stasi agents or laden-down women were looking at them. Not even when first one and then another peeled off and slipped out through the square gateway.

No one is stopping them; no one is shooting.

Nina watched another half-dozen leave unchallenged.

I can do this. I can join them.

Her body was ready, but, after so long living without anything to measure the days by, there was still something she needed to know.

"What month is it?"

It was so long since Nina had raised her voice, especially to ask a question, she barely recognized the thin rasp. But she had, at least, asked the question.

The woman trotting past her barely turned.

"November."

It couldn't be November 1988—Nina knew that. She knew more time than two seasons had passed since her capture.

"What year?"

This time, the woman stopped and frowned.

"It's 1989."

"Grete, get a move on. There are piles of stuff still to burn, and we can't count on there being much time left. There are crowds already massing at headquarters and baying for blood. None of us can risk having our names and our personal details discovered if a mob gets here."

The woman immediately forgot about Nina and ran over to add her pile to the drum her colleagues were frantically dumping sack loads of paper into.

Nina stared after her. November 1989. She had been imprisoned for a year and a half, with no explanation, and now she was free, with no explanation, while the guards she had feared for so long ran round as if someone had poured boiling water all over their anthill. Whatever this madness was, Nina had no intention of watching another moment of it.

Crowds already massing... baying for blood... we can't count on there being much time left.

The phrases danced through her head as she ran past the deserted walkways and the rows of fish and linen and bread delivery vans. Whatever was going on, it was clear that the Stasi agents, who were burning their personal folders and releasing prisoners they had spent years mentally torturing, were afraid. There was no other explanation for the fires and the open cell doors, or for the uniform jackets dropped by the wall and the men who were too pink and plump to be inmates trotting away in their shirtsleeves, despite the freezing temperature.

Whatever the reason was, Nina didn't have time to waste trying to discover it. She reached the main gate and plunged out through the gateway and into the street. She ran two blocks down it, gulping at air that tasted so sweet it made her dizzy, before she realized that she had no clue where she was. Nina stopped and stared around as reality dawned: she had made two journeys into this place and one out of it, and this was the first time she had seen the outside. It didn't even help to know, or assume, its name: Hohenschönhausen wasn't on any map; she had no geographical reference for it. Nina leaned against the complex's wall and racked her brain, trying to pluck out any detail from the last journey she'd made here.

I timed it. I checked my watch when they threw me in the van, and then I checked it again before they tore it off me.

She had been desperate to get some sense of where they were taking her, and—given the blacked-out windows and the soundproof cage she had been locked in—timing the journey had seemed the most logical way to do that. Two hours ten minutes. The time span rushed back at her. It had taken around two hours ten minutes to reach the over-bright garage from wherever it was they had picked her and Jannick up.

But what if it hadn't.

The thought knocked the air out of her lungs.

What if they drove round in circles, or doubled back on themselves, to make me think that was how long it took? What if I'm only twenty minutes from where I was caught?

She didn't know where she was. Beyond the fact that the tunnel she had been about to enter would have taken her into Kreuzberg, she didn't know where she had been caught. And she couldn't trust the time it had taken to get from one unknown place to the other. Her heart was hammering. Every moment she spent in the open by the prison wall felt like a moment when a van would screech round the corner and this would all be revealed as an elaborate joke. Nina forced herself to breathe deeply, to think calmly.

I was on the opposite side of the Wall from Kreuzberg, which must have put me somewhere in Friedrichshain. This area is built up and residential; I have to trust it's still in Berlin. And surely they must have moved me north or east, not south. Nothing round here suggests we're close to the river.

It was a logical guess, but it didn't get her anywhere closer to a specific location. She looked around. The prisoners who had left before her were long gone. There were people nearby, one or two on the street, more watching the fires from the windows and balconies of the flats clustered round the prison compound. They were mostly men. There wasn't one Nina dared to ask for directions.

I could follow the prison wall, see if I can spot any landmarks.

She was another block down before she realized that wouldn't help her. That the complex was huge and—because it wasn't meant to be found, or walked out of—there wasn't a street name, or a sign pointing to a subway or a train station. The only sign she could see was an ominous *Restricted Zone: Entry Forbidden.*

This is Berlin, I'm sure of it. I have lived here my whole life. It's a city I know, not a mystery.

That should have been a comforting thought. Except she was standing in the middle of an area that didn't officially exist. Where the residents of the apartment blocks painted the same drab yellow as the prison buildings could easily be Stasi agents. And her body wasn't the strong one she had taken for granted two years ago, the one she was ready to push through a damp and dangerous tunnel. It wasn't the sudden rush of fresh air that had made her dizzy; it was the lack of proper exercise or good food. Three blocks and her breathing hurt, her legs were shaking. Three blocks and the hunger that she had trained herself to ignore had reared up, loud and demanding. She couldn't walk aimlessly; she couldn't walk in circles—she didn't have the strength.

If I could see the television tower in Alexanderplatz, then I could get my bearings.

It was another logical thought—the Telespargel was the anchor everyone in the city used to orient themselves—but she needed height to see the tower, and the only way to get height from where she was would be to climb onto the prison wall. There were risks, and there was madness, and this day was already sliding too far the wrong way.

In the end, Nina did the only thing her body would let her: she stayed where she was, on the corner of a street filled with confusingly ordinary houses, huddled into her coat against the icy wind, waiting for the right face to walk by. When it did—in the shape of an older motherly looking woman pulling along a small fat dog—it took Nina so long to frame the simple question, she almost missed her moment.

"Excuse me, could you tell me where I am?"

The woman stopped and peered at her. "A long way from home from the look of you." She hesitated. "Have you come from in there?" She sighed when Nina nodded. "Dear God, that place. We're all supposed to pretend we don't know it's there, or what it is, but the sounds you hear sometimes…" She coughed. "Anyway, you're not in there anymore. You are in Lichtenberg."

She waited for some sign of recognition, but Nina couldn't give her one: her brain was too tired to make any connections between East Berlin's boroughs.

"It's in the north of the city. If you go straight down that way, in about an hour you'll get to Friedrichsfelde Cemetery, if that helps?"

If that helps? Nina could have hugged her. Friedrichsfelde was where Herthe was buried; she could find her way home from Friedrichsfelde.

"Thank you. That helps a lot."

"Good." The woman made encouraging noises at the dog, which had curled itself up on the pavement. "There's no trains hereabouts, but you might pick up a bus. If you can get on one today of course, given that the whole city seems to be on the move."

Crowds massing. Baying for blood.

Home wasn't an impossible number of miles away, but what if there was a different threat, one that was even worse than Stasi agents and vans, that would stop her getting there? Her captors had let her out; they were burning evidence. Nina's thoughts began racing. What if the war between East and West that she had been brought up to fear had finally arrived? What if the Stasi were hiding their traces because West German soldiers were coming and they feared being treated in the same way that the Allies had treated the Nazis after World War Two? What if Oberschöneweide had already fallen to the invading army and there wasn't any home to go back to?

"What has happened? Are we at war?"

The woman stopped fussing with the reluctant dog and looked up at Nina. "Well, I don't imagine I would be out strolling with lazybones here if we were. You really don't know?"

Nina shook her head. The woman did the same.

"You must be the only person in the world who doesn't. It's not war, my dear, it's the Wall. The Wall has come down."

It had been down for thirty-six hours. Or not exactly down—the Wall hadn't vanished or crumbled to dust, the way Nina's wildly swinging imagination had pictured it. The Wall was still there, but it no longer looked solid. The concrete slabs looked instead as if they had been kicked and punched and pecked through with holes. Everybody was certain that it would never be made whole again; nobody seemed to know what its dismantling meant, or how it had come about.

"Maybe it was the collapse of the communist government in Poland, or Hungary opening its borders up, or the protest marches in Alexanderplatz and Leipzig demanding an end to division that spooked them. Maybe the Russian president Gorbachev told the GDR's stubborn old men to do it. No one's really sure. It came out of nowhere though—there was an announcement late at night on the ninth that the gates were opening, so we all crowded down here to see. No one believed it was actually going to happen, but it did. The guards watched us come; they didn't try to stop us, or shoot us—not even when we pushed the fence down."

Everyone gathered at Sonnenallee's broken crossing point repeated the same story, in the same slightly hysterical, slightly mystified tone. Everyone had been across and had a look at the West, and wandered back again. Everyone was giddy and uncertain, waiting for someone to tell them what would happen next.

Nina had picked her way through the discarded beer bottles and the Rotkäppchen sparkling wine bottles and joined the fringes of a group all eager to describe an event they were slowly realizing was a key moment in history. It was hard, however, for Nina to listen to the accounts of the Eastern Bloc's disintegration and the descriptions of the West's bright neon lights and brimming-over stores when everything in Sonnenallee was so utterly altered.

The last time she had seen this wasteland that was now some kind of festival site, Stefan had been lying in its dirt bleeding to death. The soldiers who had shot him, who she had fled from almost blind with her tears, were gone. Now there was no one in uniform inside the guard hut; instead there was a teenager slumped drunk or asleep in the doorway. Now the metal barriers that had stopped the cars were up, and the metal fence panels that had stopped the people were down. And now there was a group kicking a bottle around on the sandy strips where the guard dogs used to be tethered and a fleeing truck had once crashed in a mess of metal and bodies.

"When I was here before, there were soldiers and good people died."

The girl who Nina said that to shuffled away.

She wasn't the only one struggling to find her place in this new landscape. There were other people like her, watching but not part of the crowd; too disoriented by the speed of the change from forbidden to free to trust it. It didn't take Nina long to spot them. They stood differently, shielding their bodies from the drunks stumbling past and the dancers determined to continue the party. They looked around them before they moved, checking the faces closest to them, checking the alleyways. In a different life, Nina would have taken them for Stasi informants. Now she knew they were as newly emerged into the world as she was and all damaged to some degree, seeing sights no one else apparently wanted to remember. She didn't seek them out—they wouldn't have shared their stories of loss and fear; she wouldn't have shared hers—but, like them, she kept to the fringes of the crowds and kept moving.

"Are you going to go through?" Beer spilled from the bottle the smiling man was waving at her.

Keep your breathing steady, keep going and you'll be fine.

Nina had a sudden flashback to long-lost Jannick, and to a volley of shots that had ended her hopes of freedom.

"I want to. I tried to years ago. It didn't end well then."

She shook herself and tried to push the ghosts away, but the man caught sight of the pain tightening her face and turned away from it.

I'm not ready for this. I want to be happy that the end's finally come, but I'm carrying too many shadows to trust it.

Nina did want to go through to the West; that hadn't changed—dreams about the Tower House there and the happy life she could have in it had been her one solace in prison. Now that she was faced with the opportunity to simply wander through, however, she couldn't. She knew that, if she tried, her feet would freeze and she wouldn't make it, at least not yet. She had come to Sonnenallee rather than going straight home not to cross over but to see the truth. The news of the Wall's collapse wasn't enough—after her treatment at the hands of the Stasi, Nina refused to believe in anything she couldn't see for herself. Well, now she had seen it. She knew that the world had changed for everyone, not just for her. She was, however, still too far behind to catch up. The West would have to wait. It was time to go and do what she had intended when she first left the prison: to go back to her family, to Britte and Holger and Magda, and fill in the blanks where her life had once been.

The whole city seems to be on the move.

That had proved to be as true as the Wall coming down. When Nina knocked on the door of her parents' flat in Kottmeier Allee, the stranger who opened it shrugged.

"I've no idea who you're looking for, I'm sorry. We were allocated this place a year ago. Whoever had it before didn't leave a forwarding address."

Her heart in her mouth, Nina made her way to Triniusstraβe and Magda's house. It was also shuttered and locked up. Nina sank onto her grandmother's doorstep, with no clue where to look next and the last reserves of her energy gone.

"Well, well, Nina Aderbach. So you finally decided to come back. Don't expect the flags to come out."

Nina rubbed her eyes and looked up. Frau Rothberg, the nosiest of Magda's many nosy neighbors, was looming over the communal fence, her arms lodged on top of it and her face set. Nina had never liked the woman who had confiscated every ball she owned as a child, but she was a welcome sight now, cross or not.

"I'm back, but nobody else is. Do you know where my grandmother's gone? She does still live here, doesn't she?"

Frau Rothberg sniffed. "She does, and your parents too. You would know that if you had ever bothered to send them a letter."

There was so much to unpack in the hostile answer, Nina wasn't sure where to start.

"I don't understand. Why are they all living here together?"

Frau Rothberg sucked her teeth and slowly shook her head. "You really need to ask, as if you can't guess? You ran to the West, dear—did you really think no one would pay for that? Your parents protested their innocence of course. They carried on pretending to be loyal citizens, which no one believed, or you would have been better brought up. As for your grandmother, she was arrested so often last year, it was a disgrace to the street. She's lucky the government had bigger problems than her, or she would have lost this place too. Not that you cared, all tucked up in your cozy new life."

Nina's head was spinning; she felt three sentences behind. "Frau Rothberg, I can see you're angry, but I honestly don't know what you're talking about. What do you mean she was arrested? Why?"

"You mean apart from her part in what you did?" Frau Rothberg's sigh was almost tangible. "It was something to do with her past apparently. I don't know the details—your grandmother always was the secretive type. It must be where you get it from. You really are the most selfish girl. I have no time at all for anyone who went against our beliefs here, but you were the cause of at least some of their troubles and you abandoned them all, without even a postcard to say you were well. Your grandmother broke down on her last birthday, right here in the garden, and told me what you'd done. She would have given anything for a letter, censored or not. You never even tried."

Grandma thought I'd escaped? She didn't know I'd been caught?

All the time Nina had been in prison, she had assumed that the Stasi would have told Magda where she was, that they would have used her imprisonment as a lever. That they hadn't was too much to take in.

"I couldn't send anything. I—"

Nina stopped. She'd had enough of being attacked. She was too tired to explain; she was too tired to be anything except on her own.

"Where is she now?"

Frau Rothberg bridled at Nina's suddenly curt tone. "With your father's family in Dresden. One of his nieces, your cousin Ottilie, is getting married there. From what your mother said, I think they are planning to move there and try a new start, which wouldn't be a bad—"

"Do you have a key to the house?"

The day had been too much: too many people, too much information. Nina needed silence if she was going to begin to make sense of this. She realized that, in some strange way, what she needed was the solid walls and solitude of a cell.

Frau Rothberg drew herself up ready for another onslaught, but then she caught the flash in Nina's eye and she tutted away, returning with the key and without any more questions.

Nina went inside. Half a dozen steps into the hall and she couldn't take another. Everything was so familiar—the pale green walls dotted in photographs, the faintly chemical scent of lemon furniture polish, the rack of neatly ordered coats—she was afraid her edges would dissolve.

I can't deal with any of this until I've dealt with myself.

She went into the kitchen and worked her way through the fridge; dragged herself upstairs and peeled off the clothes that were tainted with prison and foolish hopes of escape; drew a bath, filled to the top with bubbles. She covered herself in every pot of skin and face cream she could find. When Nina finished, she was still a long way from feeling back to herself again, but it was a start. It eased her into the next stage: sitting in front of the mirror in Magda's bedroom, looking at herself for the first time since she had been captured.

I've turned into my grandmother.

There was a photograph on the dressing table, a snap of Magda and Herthe taken not long after the end of the war. Magda was all eyes and cheekbones beneath curly bobbed hair. The picture—and her own, very far from satisfactory reflection—gave Nina an idea.

Two minutes rooting through the drawers and she had a pair of scissors. Twenty minutes after that and the dry ragged mess of her hair was roughly clipped into, almost, the same style as Magda had worn forty years ago. The girl now gazing back from the mirror was still far too thin and her eyes were far too old, but she looked more in charge of herself; less bruised.

The next thing she needed was clothes. It was clear from a quick search of her parents' room that Britte had brought nothing of Nina's with them, and Britte's beige sacks were too depressing to wear. The haircut, however, gave her another idea. Magda's wardrobe was full of beautifully patterned old dresses; it took Nina's newly acquired sewing skills—until recently in use only for mending torn tracksuits and rough prison blankets—no time to remake a prettily checked one to fit her new shape. Once that task was complete, there was nothing left to do but decide her next steps.

I can't wait a week for them to come back, not while the world keeps moving at the pace it's suddenly going at and I've spent so long stuck away from it. And I can't face the mess I've made of things for my parents and Magda until I've found us all a way out of this.

Eighteen months ago, Nina had had a plan: to go to the West to build a new life for herself and Magda and uncover her grandmother's story. That had failed then, but it could work now. It could work far easier now. She had no way of knowing if the Tower House was there anymore or, even if it was, whether its new owners would let her in. The need for it, however, for the safe haven that, in Nina's mind, it had always represented, was still there.

And I don't have to run this time, so maybe I could take my time and find something else to help me.

Nina had had so much time alone with her thoughts in prison, she had picked over every conversation she and Magda had ever had about the past, and all the ones they hadn't but should have done. One phrase, said long ago in a fury when Nina was a frightened child, had kept repeating itself: *I told her to burn both of the pictures*

I was stupid enough to bring back. Nina had spent endless waking nights wondering what that second picture could be. Now, with the house to herself, she had the luxury of looking for it, and for the key to the Tower House she was certain must have been one of the ones she used to play with in her great-grandmother's treasure tin. The quest as much as the bath and the food pushed new energy through her.

Starting with Magda's bedroom, she went forensically through the house, room by room, including the cobweb-filled attic. There was no picture; there was no treasure tin or key. By the time Nina found the battered old suitcase tucked in under the eaves, she was ready to give up. She pulled the case open anyway, expecting it to be empty and another dead end.

At first sight it was, but the silk lining was pretty, a pale rose-covered pink that Nina wondered if she could unpick and use as a trimming. She ran her fingers across the pleated pockets and eased their stitching free, and there it was. Something square tucked into the lining she instinctively knew, with a storyteller's certainty, would matter.

The little object Nina carefully pulled out was a fold of cardboard with a black-and-white photograph of a very attractive woman stapled onto one side and lines of cramped writing across the other. It was also very brittle: even though Nina handled it gently, part of the back page instantly crumbled away when she touched it. Terrified the whole thing would disappear before she could decipher it, Nina carried the card carefully back to Magda's bedroom and turned on all the lights.

That it was an identity card was quickly obvious from the layout, which wasn't very different from the GDR one Nina had carried. Except this one had words she had never seen running across the bottom—"Wife of SS Hauptsturmführer Gunther Roth"—and a stamp she had only ever seen in her schoolbooks. Nina turned the card carefully over. The same eagle and swastika crest was printed on the back as was stamped below the picture. It wasn't Magda in the image; Nina was certain of that: the woman captured in it was blonde and had the kind of bone-structure-led beauty that would have lasted into old age.

But it was someone Magda knew.

Nina had no proof of that. She didn't even know if the suitcase was Magda's—it could have come from a second-hand store. Except the card also had part of an address, and the part Nina could read said "Grunewald." And every prickling hair on Nina's neck told her she had found something she shouldn't have.

CHAPTER TWELVE

Magda, November 1989

Nothing was quite what it should be, or where it was meant to be, or there at all. Magda put her suitcase down, carefully closed the front door, and stood in the hallway taking an inventory of what she could, and couldn't, see. Her heavy green winter coat was missing from its peg. The doors to the living room and the kitchen were open, although Magda had checked they were shut before she left for Ottilie's wedding. And, although the house had been empty for almost a week, there were faint puffs of scent lingering in the air—lavender and coffee and toast. Small changes, barely disruptive, but enough for her to begin moving around her house as if someone else owned it.

Each room she went into bore its mark. The cushions on the sofa in the sitting room were flattened and stacked at one end, not evenly distributed. There was a plate lying on the kitchen draining board, and a chair had been pushed back from the table. Magda left everything as it was and went slowly up the stairs, listening for movement, adding more and more displaced items to her mental list and breathing deeply to slow her pounding heart.

Bubble bath bottle almost empty and replaced on the wrong shelf. The source of the lavender smell.

Bedroom door open: another one that was definitely closed.

Bed made, but coverlet not turned back.

Scissors left out on the dressing table.

Strands of what seems to be material dotted over the carpet.

Nobody here.

She went back downstairs and into the kitchen, her senses still on alert. When she sat down at the table, her drumming fingers encountered a fine layer of crumbs.

Who has been in my house?

The obvious answer was Frau Rothberg: the neighbor was the only one apart from Britte who had a key, and Britte was still in Dresden. It was the obvious answer, but, as much as Magda disliked her neighbor, it didn't fit. Gerda Rothberg might well have sneaked in during Magda's absence—the woman was an incurable gossip and a government toady, and Magda wouldn't put a morning's snooping beyond her—but she wouldn't have made herself a sandwich, or taken a lavender-scented bath, and she would have returned anything she touched to its original place. Whoever had come in wasn't worried that their presence would be felt.

At the same time, nothing valuable had been stolen; nothing startling had been done. Magda could have left the doors open and finished the bubble bath and moved her coat, and simply forgotten. Except that she hadn't, and this kind of thing had happened before. Magda looked round the neat room, wondering if the contents of her cupboards had been rearranged, or if the lights were about to flicker. It wasn't Frau Rothberg, so it had to be the Stasi up to their old tricks: unsettling her; reminding her that they had their fingers all over her life; sending a clear message about who was in charge.

It wouldn't be a surprise if they had reappeared. For a year, from almost as soon as Nina had fled, Magda had been a Stasi target. They had arrived at her house, without any attempt at subterfuge, once or twice a week. Sometimes they had questioned her here; sometimes they had taken her into one of their faceless offices and questioned her there. They had made sure her neighbors knew she was a "person of interest." The questions had never varied: they asked her about Nina; they asked her about the house in the West and what Magda had done in the war. Magda never answered. She had learned not to answer Himmler; a couple of Stasi agents were hardly a challenge. When they got bored with her, they had moved onto Britte and Holger, taking away their house, taking away Britte's job. All they had got from Britte was tears and hysterics. Six months ago, they had stopped bothering any of them. Magda assumed that was because there were far bigger problems that needed their attention than a stubborn old woman. She hadn't assumed they were gone for good. Now it seemed like they were back.

Except it can't be them. They're not in charge, not anymore.

Magda stopped pushing at the crumbs and sat back. It was still hard to believe. A new world had opened up a week ago, and Magda still couldn't picture what shape it would take, or trust that the old shadows wouldn't creep back into it again. If the news was true, there was nobody watching her or anyone else anymore. After almost fifty years of somebody watching. That alone—never mind the Wall's tumbling without anyone stopping it or shooting the revelers responsible—was impossible to believe.

Magda had sat glued to the television on the ninth of November, as mesmerized as the rest of the world by the pictures of the crowds drinking and dancing in front of the Brandenburg Gate and swarming like ants all over the Wall. She had watched the guards standing open-mouthed, nervous hands hovering by their rifles. She had flinched at the mob circling the Stasi headquarters in Normannenstraße, shouting for the files held there to be opened and for the invisible men inside to be called to account, and demanding to know where the infamous secret prison was.

That, in Magda's eyes, had tipped the celebrations from boldness to madness. She had fully expected the pack congregating outside the fences and kicking at them like angry mules to disappear under a hail of bullets. She had stayed up all night chasing bulletin after bulletin, her chest tight with fear. She wouldn't have moved from the set, she wouldn't have gone to Dresden, if it hadn't been for Britte refusing to let her stay. Britte was even more convinced than

Magda that reprisals were coming and was terrified by the Wall's collapse, not celebrating its ending. Their fight and Britte's panic had not made for a comfortable journey.

Perhaps they never had the power over us we feared. Perhaps they only ever had any power at all because we rolled over and gave it to them.

Magda had heard that sentiment tried out among the wedding guests, and muttered between couples on the train she'd caught back to Berlin. Everyone who said it had sounded confused, or guilty, or cheated. Magda didn't believe it. She knew only too well that the Stasi had been—perhaps still were—a real threat; that they were clever and manipulative, and dangerous. That the control they had held over the GDR's citizens had been absolute and many-layered, because that was the way the Party and their *sword and shield* had engineered it to be. She had felt the impact of their forensic attention to detail—an industrialized form of cruelty her past made her all too familiar with. She had seen it in the way the Stasi had treated Nina, trying to force her into spying against her own grandmother. And she had seen how deep their hold ran when she had made her hopeless trip to the Friedrichstraße crossing point on the day Nina had sworn she would meet her there. Magda rarely let that memory come—it wasn't one she was proud of—but when it resurfaced the way it was doing now, it was too vivid to brush away.

Come on Thursday. I'll wait all day.

Nina's desperate promise had got Magda to the station that acted as the officially sanctioned meeting point between East and West on the appointed day. She hadn't decided what she was going to do—part of her was hoping that she would catch a glimpse of Nina and instantly know—but she had at least gone. *You'll have no problem getting through* had, however, turned out to be as much of a lie as the elegant building Magda had forced herself to walk into. The reception hall through which citizens with the right paperwork—or enough courage to risk the wrong kind—could navigate the gulf between the city's two sectors was a place everyone in the GDR referred to as *The Palace of Tears* for all the ones that had been shed there.

The building itself, which had opened in 1962—a year after the Wall had closed down the city—was a marvel. It was constructed almost entirely of glass. It was never still. Clouds danced across it; birds in flight and wind-stirred trees were caught and magnified in its reflecting surfaces. From the outside, the hall's bright and airy design promised movement and hope. Inside, however, the glass was a crueler thing. The light shining through it flared as bright as a spotlight onto the walkways where the armed guards stood ready. It made the rows of narrow passageways through which the travelers were scrutinized and processed, one at a time, appear even starker. It magnified worried hands and nervous faces. Everything inside the hall was stamped through with the Stasi. Everything was designed to make those entering it feel exposed, and to make nothing about leaving through it feel safe.

If I could have seen her, it would have been different.

It had been a hopeless wish—Magda had realized that the second she'd stepped inside. It had been impossible to see who, or what, was waiting on the other side of the brown doors that divided the space and the one-person-wide corridors they led to. There were more soldiers than ordinary people, and probably more Stasi agents concealed among them than anyone else. Magda had circled and stood; she had moved forward and back. She had attracted attention; she had left. She had never heard a word since from Nina.

I wasn't brave enough for my brave granddaughter.

Magda got heavily to her feet, feeling the weight of too many sleepless nights in her bones. Wondering as she always did what Nina had found in the West, and what judgments had fallen. Unable to shake the belief that a year and a half of silence meant that those judgments hadn't fallen her way and that the house had done what Magda had always feared it would—given up secrets she should have been there to explain.

Which is why it is time for me to pull up my old courage and find her.

That thought had been with her since her life, and Britte and Holger's, had ground to a standstill. It wasn't just the constant arrests and the questioning that had whittled her down; it was the slicing away of everything that made up a life. As soon as the dark-coated men first appeared on her doorstep, the committees Magda had served on had ordered her to step down. Holger had been constantly passed over for promotion, Britte had lost her job without explanation, and then an eviction notice had arrived. Nobody at the housing office would see them. All three of them had assumed the harassment that dogged them was the result of Nina's leaving; all of them kept waiting for something worse.

Now that the Wall had come down, however, Magda could look up at the world again, and looking at the world meant finding Nina. As the stones tumbled and the bullets didn't come and Magda had allowed herself to believe that the speed of the switch from East Berlin and West Berlin to simply Berlin wouldn't be matched by a similarly fast unraveling, that urge had become a physical need. Free from the weight of the Stasi, it was a need she was ready to act on—her body felt as if it had shed years.

Magda had followed the political turmoil of 1989 as avidly as the rest of the country, switching between the television broadcasts from East and West as she tried to find the truth beneath each side's propaganda. She had seen the Iron Curtain disintegrate. She had watched the demonstrations for peace and unity that had become a weekly feature in Leipzig. She had watched half a million protestors cram into Alexanderplatz on November 4, waving their banners proclaiming *We Are One People*. She had listened to the Russian president Mikhail Gorbachev preach his new doctrines of *perestroika* and *glasnost*—restructuring and openness—and promising an end to the Cold War.

Unlike forty years ago, when words had come burdened with dark meanings, Magda had welcomed these new ones and believed there was truth in them. She hadn't mourned the East's defeat: the ideals she held dear had been corrupted too long ago for her to believe that the GDR's leaders would ever recapture the spirit of them. She also hadn't believed, however, that change was coming to the GDR with the same kind of fervor she saw written on the faces of the crowds celebrating in Hungary. On October 7, the old men who still clung to power had held a parade along Karl Marx Allee to celebrate the fortieth anniversary of the Republic's founding, in the same way they had for its tenth and twentieth and thirtieth. The massed armies and rumbling tanks didn't suggest that the country's gray-haired government was going anywhere soon. Except that, a month later, General Secretary Honecker and the Wall were gone and the new word everyone was trying out and putting their trust in was *reunification*.

Which has to mean no more excuses. Which has to mean it's time.

Magda had already made up her mind, on the train returning from Dresden, that she wasn't going to give up and leave Berlin the way Britte wanted them all to. That she was, instead, going to return to the united Berlin she had known as a girl. She had booked a train the morning after the wedding and left Britte and Holger behind. She hadn't discussed her plans regarding tracking down Nina. Her daughter and son-in-law had seen Nina's escape to the West as a betrayal and had chosen to live as if they no longer had a child. Magda had never criticized them for that: she knew that their blindness came from hurt and fear. She was no longer, however, willing to follow the same path. She had spent too many years holding her tongue, and being fearful, and no one had benefited from that. She had realized far too late that the price—failing Nina—had never been worth it. And now she was seventy-four years old, and whatever years she had left to her would not be lived without her granddaughter. Whatever else came with that decision would have to come. Tomorrow, therefore, she was going to the Friedrichstraße crossing point and, this time, she was going straight through. After tomorrow...

Magda stopped herself: the only thing that mattered about *after tomorrow* was making every next one count. Her bones lightened; her shoulders straightened. She forgot about the subtle, unexplained changes in her house. She reached for the kettle—and she froze. Propped up beside the daisy-sprigged cup that only Nina knew was her favorite was an envelope with *Grandma* scrawled across it in Nina's unmistakable hand.

> *I never made it to the West. I was caught before we got into the tunnel. I have been a prisoner in Hohenschönhausen since the last night that you saw me.*

Magda laid the letter carefully down on the table. She had read its opening lines three times; she couldn't get past them.

I convinced myself she was selfish.

The memory twisted her stomach.

I stood in the garden, full of self-pity. Moaning to a gossip-hungry, hateful neighbor because my "ungrateful granddaughter" had run away to the West and forgotten me.

She should have known better. All that time she had spent thinking that whatever Nina had discovered, it would make her turn her back on her grandmother was shameful. Nina had deserved better—she might have lacked caution, but the girl had never had a single selfish bone in her body. Magda grimaced as the irony hit her: she had been the one wasting years passing judgment, not Nina.

In the forty-four years since Christoph's murder, Magda had rarely cried. That night, in April 1945 when she had finally stumbled back to Oberschöneweide, she had wept. No, not wept: she had howled in her mother's arms like a child caught up inside a pain too big to understand. There were many days after that when she could have given way to despair again, when it was all she wanted to do, but the business of simply staying alive had stopped her. She had, however, cried as bitterly again nine months later: when she had held Britte in her arms for the first time and Christoph's eyes had stared back up at her. She thought she would never stop, but the baby needed her so she did, and she had decided then that those would be her last mourning tears. Nothing had moved her in the same way since, although Herthe's death had come close to it.

Now, clutching Nina's starkly heartbreaking letter, the tears returned. They fell thick and fast and unstoppable, melting her skin to a paste. Nina hadn't spent the last eighteen months safe and happy and living the full life she had longed for, or even being selfish and uncaring. Her vital, sometimes too-alive granddaughter had been a prisoner. She had been caged, cut off from the world she had risked so much to be part of.

If only I had known...

Magda cut the thought off before it could linger. If only she had known, then what? This hadn't been the detention of a child for telling a joke, or a young girl for distributing leaflets: both difficult, and frightening, episodes in their own way but navigable with the right name and the right reputation. This had been an escape attempt. There was nothing in Magda's armory she could have pitched against that. And that prison... Magda couldn't calm the shivering that suddenly gripped her body, or her horribly racing heart. It was the place she had dreaded as a girl, that had reared its head again in the Stasi threats the day they had arrested her. Hohenschönhausen had been a blight on East Berlin since the end of the war. It had been a more secret demonstration of the GDR's power over its citizens than the Wall, perhaps, but it had never been any less dangerous.

Magda ran her fingers down the letter she still couldn't finish. She rarely cried, and she rarely let the past invade the present. She had chosen her path in 1945 and the only way to walk it had been to never look back. But that name, that prison she had once feared would be her own resting place, had dredged up memories that, try as she might, she couldn't hold back. Magda closed her eyes and wrapped her arms around her shaking body. She didn't want to revisit those desperate days, but they were pounding too hard at her and there was nothing to do but let them come.

Magda had walked away from Grunewald on the second day of April 1945 intent on getting home to her mother and getting justice for Christoph and Walther and all the hundreds of thousands who had gone to undeserved deaths at the hands of Hitler and Himmler and all the evil men who surrounded them.

She gave no thought to what that journey might mean—she couldn't. She had barely left the Tower House since the day Himmler had caught up with her, and then she had only made local foraging trips for food and had barely spoken to anyone. Trapped in her impotent worries for Walther, and Eckhart and his family, and the underground networks Walther's arrest might have exposed, and then trapped by her injury, she hadn't been following the detailed course of the war, beyond the fact that it was almost over. When she finally left Grunewald, therefore, Magda knew that the war was in its last dying days, but she had no real understanding of what that meant for the city. Or, more importantly, that she was walking toward the encircling sweep of the Russian armies who were within a fortnight of conquering Berlin, and whose revenge-fueled approach was unstoppable. She had no idea—although she had heard the drone of the planes for the past three weeks and seen the skyline burn—that she was walking toward a devastation that was on a catastrophic scale, caused by some of the largest bombing raids the city had ever endured. She had no idea that the bombardment had turned Berlin into a ghost of the place that she knew. If anyone had told her any of that, she wouldn't have changed course. She wanted home, and she wanted her mother with the single-minded determination of a lost child, so home she went.

As unthinkable as the journey would once have been when her life was lived in limousines, she walked the twenty kilometers that lay between Grunewald and Oberschöneweide, because she couldn't face the station, or the trains that she feared would still be leaving from there. Her feet covered the distance while her mind stayed with Christoph. She refused to let it see Elsa. She moved by instinct and took little notice of her surroundings.

It wasn't until she reached what should have been Potsdamer Platz, after almost two hours of blind walking, that the silence she had walked in finally caught her attention and she stopped. The bustle she had assumed would greet her was gone. The square was filled with skeletons where buildings had once stood. The air was thick with brick dust; the ground was choked with rubble. The walls left standing were too flimsy to hold the ripped-apart rooms still clinging on to them. A finger's push and the splintered window frames and shredded curtains would topple into the chaos below. Magda stood in the middle of what had once been a crush of people and cars and trams and knew she was witnessing the city's death. There was a part of her that wanted to stand still and start grieving; she forced it down in the need to keep moving.

From that point on, Magda continued her journey with her eyes open, circling streets that were so torn apart she could no longer map them. The great centers of National Socialist power—the Reich Chancellery, the Propaganda Ministry, and SS headquarters among them—were shells, the authority they once wielded pounded to dust. Magda had no interest in lamenting them.

The destruction she encountered as she passed through Friedrichshain and Kreuzberg, however, snatched her breath away. The factories were gone; the houses were gone. The streets were smashed beyond recognition, and the people who walked them were as broken. Women stumbled past her pushing wheelbarrows piled with their meager possessions. Children swarmed over their splintered homes, searching for scraps of their childhood. The shell Magda had been walking inside shattered. By the time she reached Oberschöneweide she was horribly awake and half-running, despite her exhausted legs and blistered heels. The only thought she could hold in her head was, *Be alive, please God be alive.*

She almost lost hope. The Cable Works was gone, reduced to a twisted heap of metal. Her parents' home—her parents' street—was gone. It took Magda another hour of frantic knocking on doors and begging strangers who did not want to talk to her to locate her mother. It was almost dark when she finally pieced together the directions she'd been given and matched them to the reworked streets. Two people had shouted at her about curfew as she ran past them; one man had yelled at her about the dangers of being out in the dark and tried to drag her into an air-raid shelter. When she screamed and swore, he backed off.

When she eventually found Herthe, her mother was crammed into one room of what Magda initially assumed was a partially destroyed house but was actually the only floor left of a once five-story tenement. Her father was gone. He had been marched off at gunpoint, and without a uniform, to fight with the *Volkssturm* against the Russians, one of the broken old men and scared little boys Hitler had pinned his last hopes of victory on. Her mother was already quietly in mourning.

On that first night, Magda had been unable to find the words she needed to tell any part of the story she had been clinging to. Then, over the course of the next two days, as American and British bombs continued to fall on the beleaguered city and the rumbling of the Russian guns grew closer, she poured out the truth of everything that had happened. She left none of it out, even when—as she did more than once—Herthe drew back in horror. Her mother listened, and held her, and didn't interrupt with questions. But when Magda started to tell the part with the trains and having to be a witness all over again—trying to make sense of it, desperate to make her mother understand that her soul had taken no part in it—and when she insisted that she had to tell the whole of it to the world, Herthe had stopped her.

"No, Magda, you can't. I understand you want justice for them all, I promise I do, but the story is told, and its telling ends here. If it doesn't, when the Russians come, the fact that you worked so closely with a factory owner like Walther who was tied up with the Nazis and, more especially, with Himmler, whatever your reasons, will end you."

There would be no truth-telling for Christoph or anyone else. There would be no time set aside for mourning. For the next ten days, as April limped on but spring never came, there would be no time for anything but survival.

We are going to reap the whirlwind of what we did to them tenfold.

Christoph's prophecy on the day of his death came brutally true. The victorious Russian armies tore into Berlin in the third week of April, drunk on bloodlust and victory and revenge, and turned the city into a funeral pyre. The battle for the city raged street by street, house by house. Bodies piled up on every corner, soldiers and civilians alike, caught in the crossfire, ripped open by shrapnel. Even when the shells finally stopped falling and the guns went silent, no one was safe.

Russian soldiers sought out German women with the ferocity they had previously used for hunting their men. Magda and Herthe—warned by blank-faced ruined women running from the already-conquered outer suburbs and praying for respite—had squirreled away food and water as the Russian armies approached, hiding supplies in the cellar and in cavities dug into the walls. They spent their days, and their nights, in hiding. They stuck a sign on the front door warning of typhus. They cut off their hair, covered their faces in ash and used their own blood to daub the red spots on their face that were the universal language of fever.

Magda and Herthe escaped the terror that roared in to fill the vacuum left by the end of war and the Russians' disinterest in peace. Many did not.

And then May came and finally brought some semblance of order, or so the loudspeakers attached to the patrolling Soviet jeeps promised the exhausted and beaten citizens. When Magda and Herthe finally emerged—starving and unable to resist the rations the Soviets were also promising, whatever the consequences—it was to a world changed beyond all recognition. Germany was a nation of the displaced and the dead and the broken. Hitler and Goebbels had taken their own lives. Speer was busily reinventing himself as a wrongly used good German. Himmler, to Magda's fury, had fled. The Allies were squabbling over Berlin like dogs at a bone, but in Oberschöneweide, the Russians, the first in, were firmly in charge. There were as many people terrified by that as rejoicing.

Within days, the purges began. This time, anyone with the slightest hint of Nazi connections was being swept up, and anyone with the slightest scrap of evidence against their neighbors was being encouraged to help in the hunting. No one who was taken was told what they were accused of. Houses were raided; men, and women, were snatched off the streets. If rumors were to be believed—and in the absence of radio broadcasts or newspapers, there was nothing else to clutch on to but rumors—the arrested were sent to a prison in the north of the city whose name, Hohen-schönhausen, was already becoming a byword for terror. Trials, or what passed for trials there, were secret things, and no one ever sent out for a defense lawyer. Punishment was swift and brutal: death, or disappearance into the prison's notorious underground cells, or deportation to slave in the mines in Russia.

"If you go to them and insist on telling them about Walther and the rest of it, you will be arrested. I cannot lose you and your father and carry on."

Herthe had been desperate, but so had Magda.

"And if I don't, someone will raise a suspicion and someone will come knocking and I will be arrested anyway. You said it yourself—my story could be my ending, which means I have to tell my version of it first. Even if it won't get the justice I wanted, or turn Walther into the hero he should be, I have to tell it, and tell it in a way that gives me a chance to stay alive, for the sake of the baby I think I'm carrying as much as mine."

The hope of a child—of a link to Christoph that would always keep him, in some way, alive—stopped Herthe arguing and gave Magda a reason not just to keep going but to take charge of her life. She reported to the local *Kommandantura* in the last week of a blazing hot June with no certainty that she would walk out of the Russian administration offices as a free woman again.

It is a performance. I have given harder ones. And it is the truth, or the best parts of it.

She repeated that to herself over and over as she waited for her turn to have her past picked over. She had prepared with all the eye for detail that, if anyone knew the truth, could now be her downfall. She took her battered KPD card with her, and the patches from Christoph's Russian army jacket. She sat in front of a line of stern-faced Russian men, and the German ones who had flocked to help them weed out the occupied neighborhoods, and spoke slowly so that the translator could keep pace. She told Walther's story and filled it with rescued communists. She told Christoph's story and filled it with his bravery and his "martyrdom" and his lifelong love of Russia. She wove hers carefully through theirs. She was calm and confident, and she knew when to stop.

There were men in the room who remembered the rumors about Christoph, the German who was so committed to socialism that he had joined the Red Army, and called him a hero. There were men in the room who had heard whispers about the anti-fascist activities of the Tiedemann Company and suspected that Walther's rumored execution as a traitor to National Socialism could actually be true.

And there were men in the room for whom the name *Aderbach* still carried a loyal socialist pedigree. They chose to persuade the Russians to believe her. And, when Magda told them how skilled she was at factory organization, the one in charge—whose position would stand or fall on his success at reviving local industry to feed Russian needs—employed her. Magda walked away with her reputation intact and returned to her old life as a factory secretary and a loyal party worker. She never discussed her life in the war again, not even within the safety of her home; she learned quickly enough that the regime had changed but not the methods, and that the past was a place no one could safely revisit. She remained a loyal party worker. She didn't question a thing—not the Wall, or the watchers, or why the hopes and dreams that the men in charge had promised to build a new world out of in 1945 had mutated into another dictatorship with its foundations in fear. Magda didn't question anything, to ensure that she wasn't questioned. She became one of the silent architects of the new regime.

I became my granddaughter's downfall.

The past fell away as the truth rushed in.

Nina was never going to be the kind of girl who could stand by and do nothing in the face of injustice. I always knew that, because that girl was once me, but I never had the courage to tell her.

Magda opened her eyes, her head spinning with *I should have left when I saw how things were going; I should have been braver when Nina was born and got them all out.* There was no time, however, to indulge regrets; there was only time to repair what could still be repaired. She looked back at the letter, at the sentences she hadn't yet read. There weren't many; after the first few, there weren't any surprises. Nina had gone to the West; she had gone to find Erdener Straβe; she promised to come back when she had found the Tower House and established whether it could still be a home for them.

And then it will be my turn to be the brave one. To face up to whatever she has found, to make whatever restitution is required.

It was a good thought, a calming one.

Magda stretched her tired shoulders. Tomorrow, she would go shopping and stock up on all of Nina's favorites; today, she would write down everything she wanted to tell. There would finally be no more secrets.

She got up to make the cup of tea she had meant to make over an hour ago. Something, however, was nagging at her.

Magda picked up the letter again.

I'm going to head straight for Erdener Straße and see what, if anything, of the house is still there. As soon as I've done that, I'll head straight back. Maybe you won't even see this; maybe I will be back before you.

She smoothed out the paper and reread the date scribbled at the top: November 13. According to the letter, Nina had left on the day she had written it. *I'll head straight back.* Didn't that imply the same day, or, at the very least, the one after? Except today was November 18. Nina knew no one in the West; she had no one there to stay with. Surely if she had just been released from prison, she also had no money to speak of, or none in the right currency.

Magda sat down again, the tea forgotten. Nina had been gone for five days. Where could she possibly be?

CHAPTER THIRTEEN

Nina, November 1989

Nina had left a note, but she hadn't told the whole truth in it. She hadn't mentioned the identity card, or that she was determined to track its owner down if she could. She had kept her own secrets in order to uncover Magda's.

I've stuck faithfully with our old pattern of silences.

She couldn't worry about that now; she couldn't concentrate long enough to worry about anything. She was in the West, and everything in the West was exhausting and intrusive and loud.

And vivid and vibrant and bold.

Nina sank into her seat on the busy S-Bahn train, watching as the people around her chattered and laughed with no thought of who might be listening or of lowering their voices.

And why would they? What need is there for discretion, or fear, over here?

The casualness of the interactions buzzing around her was both exhilarating and unnerving. It was a contradiction that had summed up her whole day.

Nina had left her grandmother's house early in the morning on Monday, November 13. She had meant to leave far sooner than that, but she had lost most of Saturday to a sleep so deep it had left her groggy, and she had spent the rain-soaked Sunday sitting in front of the television, scrawling through every news channel she could find for news of the Wall's falling.

On her one foray outside, she had bought a backpack and a flashlight and matches. Although she did not expect to be away from home for more than a day at most, she had packed the few wearable clothes she still had, including the made-over checked dress, in with those supplies. She had also stowed both her GDR identity card—which was still in the handbag Magda had thankfully held on to—and the forged West German passport Jannick had given her on the night of her arrest into the pocket of her borrowed green coat. She had no idea when she set out which one she would use to access the West: both felt like a gamble. She also had no idea which of the now open crossing points she should use: the nearest one at Sonnenallee, or the newly opened one that would take her from Treptow into Kreuzberg.

Both of those locations were, however, too thick with the past, so, in the end, she chose Friedrichstraβe, because it had looked the busiest on the news reports she was glued to. That wasn't a thought she welcomed: Nina was unused to crowds, and—despite the newscasters' cheery reassurances about the new openness breaking over the East—she was nervous of who might be lurking in them. For this undertaking, however, blending in with the bustle seemed the safest choice.

When she finally arrived at the reception hall, however, after long waits for crammed busses, the press of people hurrying toward it almost turned her back again. It was even more packed than the television pictures had shown. Streams of travelers flowed through the narrow corridors that led from the eastern side into the West, moving almost faster than the nervous-looking guards could process them.

I'll be waiting at the crossing point. I'll wait all day.

The memory had followed her in and slowed her feet as effectively as the hordes swirling around her. Nina had no way of knowing if Magda had come to the station in 1988, or if she had walked through to the West. She hoped Magda hadn't. The thought of her grandmother standing alone and afraid, surrounded by strangers, and thinking Nina had abandoned her made her eyes sting.

I should have waited for her to come home. I still could. I could go back to the house now and make her come with me when she gets back from Dresden.

Nina turned and tried to push her way back to the entrance, but the crowded hall was moving in one direction only, and Nina was swept up in it.

Follow the strategies that kept you in one piece in Hohenschönhausen: survey the situation, think carefully about the most winnable way through it, and, only then, and always slowly, react.

It was a good idea; it was impossible to act on. She was in the processing corridor facing the glass screen and the demand for her papers before she had time to make a properly reasoned decision about which of the two alternative documents to use. She hesitated, and then, unnerved by the guard's sharp "hurry up," Nina pulled out the first one she touched and trusted to fate.

The man briskly stamped and barely looked at the GDR identity card she had offered him; he didn't look at her at all. No alarms sounded, no prison vans pulled up. He barked at her to keep moving, so she did. Half a dozen steps—that was all it took. None of them crouching, none of them stumbling in the dark. Half a dozen steps and there she was, in the West, surrounded by laughter and noise and people clapping her on her shoulder as if she had just won some kind of a race. It was almost insultingly simple.

The Berlin Nina stepped into was completely the same and completely different from the one she had left. She recognized the language spinning around as her own, but the slang and the inflections made many of the snippets of conversation she could hear hard to decipher. The streets around the station were as busy with traffic and people as the streets around the Ostbahnhof, but there were more varieties of cars than she had names for, and more varieties of people. And the clothes in the West demanded more attention than anyone would have wasted on the outfits worn in the East. Black leather and leopard print hurried past her, and long coats and short skirts and big shoulders, all of those in a kaleidoscope of colors and patterns—blues and reds and greens clashing in blocks and stripes and checks. Unlike in the GDR, where fashion trends were dictated by a five-year plan as rigidly set as the one governing steel production, no one here was anyone's twin. There was also no one moving slowly enough for Nina to stop them and ask for directions, not that she wanted to.

I need a map. Once I have that, I can keep myself to myself and move at my own pace.

She spotted a small shop advertising cigarettes and newspapers and went in. The heavy-set woman behind the counter glanced up as Nina checked through the selection of city maps on display. As soon as Nina opened her mouth to ask for one, the shopkeeper's lip curled.

"Another one from the East, what a surprise. When are you lot going to stop coming? It's worse than a flood."

The question took Nina so completely by surprise, she couldn't think of an answer. All the television coverage of the Wall's dismantling had shown the West Berliners with open arms and wide smiles, not with this hostile sneer.

The woman continued as though she neither needed, nor wanted, an answer.

"Go on then, tell me what the deal is. What is it that you *Ossis* are really after. Where will you start first? With our houses, or our healthcare, or our jobs?"

Nina picked up the map the woman pushed toward her. She had an answer this time. She wanted to say *None of it: I'm from the other side of the same city as you, not a different planet; don't you think we have houses and jobs and hospitals of our own?* She also wanted, however, to avoid attracting attention, so she kept her mouth shut instead. It didn't do her any good: she left the shop with "or maybe what you all need is some lessons in manners" ringing in her ears. Back outside, the wind had whipped up and Nina was hungry. There were cafés around the small square whose neon lights were enticing. There was also a takeaway pretzel stand and a cluster of benches that offered less chance of a bruising reception. Nina was halfway over to those before she realized she was shaking not with cold but with anger.

You have every right to be here. You didn't choose which side of the Wall you were born on. No one has the right to dictate how you live anymore.

She didn't believe that, not yet; she would be repeating it for months until it finally sank in. For now, however, believing it didn't matter: simply thinking it was enough to propel her into the warmth of a café where her money was as good as anyone else's. And to make her decide that, before she could head to Grunewald and lay any claim to this city that was and wasn't hers, she needed to find some sense of its rhythms and not stand so obviously out.

Which means I need to do the opposite of anything I could do in the East and turn, at least for the next few hours, into a good Western capitalist.

Nina moved her drained coffee cup and the plate she had cleared down to the crumbs to the side of the table and spread the city map out. Unlike GDR maps, which had more missing spaces than detail, this one was so comprehensive it had all the tourist sites marked on it. Nina, however, already knew the one she wanted to see: the KaDeWe on the Kurfürstendamm, the fabled temple to capitalism she imagined every GDR citizen who had made the crossing would head straight toward. The famous Kaufhaus des Westens' food hall was, in the East at least, the stuff of legends. The morning was almost gone, the light in November faded early. Given the task facing her, a visit to KaDeWe was time-wasting and frivolous. Nina couldn't think of a better, more Western, reason to go.

In the end, she lost over two hours to the store's delights; if it hadn't been for the other customers finally wearing her down, she could have lost a day. She had run from there and leaped onto the train to Grunewald, swinging her shopping bags full of free samples and, with the money Jannick had given her almost gone, feeling—despite the experience having been as frustrating as it was enjoyable—as daring and impulsive and young as she had felt years ago in the smoky bars where she and Stefan had once put the world back to rights.

Or, in other words, feeling like the 21-year-old that I am.

The thought had made her smile, which made the man in the seat opposite her smile, and both of them laugh. It was obvious from the way he then tried to catch her eye that he wanted to talk, but Nina was too wary still of strangers, and too wrapped up in memories of her day, to respond.

"You have the most incredible cheekbones, and your eyelashes are crazy! Are you a model? Tell me you are—what else could you be with a face and figure as fabulous as that?"

The sales assistant who had called after her had grabbed Nina's arm as she had walked, mesmerized, through the KaDeWe's cavernous beauty hall. Before she could jump back, or protest, Nina was in a chair with a towel around her neck and makeup brushes looming, while the girl kept up a stream of chatter that would have made a battle-hardened soldier surrender. One glance at the price tag on the bottle of foundation she was about to be painted with, however, and Nina's stomach had flipped.

"I'm sorry, but I can't afford any of this."

This time, when she spoke, Nina's accent—which was far softer than the sales assistant's—had silenced the stream of clacking brand names and replaced them with squeals of delight.

"Oh my goodness, are you from the East? Are you Russian? I knew it. Some of the models coming out of there are amazing. Don't worry about the prices. It won't cost you a thing, I promise—I'm drowning in samples—and it will be so much fun."

It was easier for Nina to sit back and let the assistant prattle on and "work her magic" than to argue, or to explain that her "perfect bone structure and to-die-for body" were the result of semi-starvation in a Stasi prison, not rigorous self-discipline. Nina couldn't begin to imagine how that conversation would go. It was easier to put the truth aside and accept the illusion; it was apparently all that was required of her, and the results were, as the girl said, "remarkable." Nina had left the beauty department with a face she barely recognized but rather liked, and more cosmetics than she had ever owned or heard of in her life.

Then she went into the food hall and was too overwhelmed to navigate it properly. There was so much choice, and so much produce, and no one who seemed confused by the abundance but her. She had weaved through the aisles, stumbling over every decision. Thirty different kinds of cereal; more styles of cake and flavors of yogurt than she could count; groaning shelves that were refilled the moment a gap appeared in them. Nina stood in the checkout line staring at her overfilled basket and surreptitiously counting and recounting her money. Then the woman behind her began complaining because they didn't have the brand of fruit juice her bored-looking daughter was demanding, and frustration drove her out of the store.

One People, One City.

The slogan was everywhere, on banners and on stickers and filling newspaper headlines. The more Nina saw of the West, however, the more she knew that the pledge of unity was a long way from coming true; that there were other, more subtle, walls built in the shadow of the physical one, which would be as hard, if not harder, to topple.

"Excuse me, are you from the city?"

The man opposite had leaned forward while Nina was lost in thought. He was still smiling. He was also blond and tanned and almost ridiculously blue-eyed, and clearly used to women finding him attractive. Nina didn't particularly want to answer him; she wasn't interested in his attentions. She couldn't imagine starting a flirtation, not with a stranger, not after so long. And not when her heart in so many ways still belonged to Stefan.

The train began to slow down as he continued to wait, his smile faltering slightly at her silence. Nina glanced out of the window: it was Grunewald, her stop. She gathered her bags together and got up.

"Won't you at least tell me if you're from Berlin?"

Nina turned as the train doors opened. He was half on his feet, ready to follow her if she offered him one word of encouragement. Nina shook her head and jumped onto the platform.

"I can't answer that, I'm sorry. I'm not sure anymore what Berlin means."

The sky was shifting from pearl gray to slate by the time Nina made her way from the pretty flower-hung station to Erdener Straβe. Grunewald was far quieter than the city center, which was a welcome change to the day's tempo. The streets were empty; the white and pastel-colored villas lining them were tightly shuttered. The air was tinged with pine and the faint scent of autumn bonfires. The suburb was sleepy and peaceful and as picture-perfect as Nina had hoped it would be. She couldn't, however, find the Tower House, no matter how many times she walked up and down the street it was supposed to stand on. Nothing matched the drawing whose details she had learned by heart. After three circuits of the neatly swept pavements, it was hard for Nina to discount the possibility that it had gone. Not all the houses she had scrutinized were old and stately: some were modern confections of glass and steel whose construction, for all her hoping that it couldn't be true, could easily have wiped away earlier homes.

Feeling increasingly hopeless, Nina checked her watch for what felt like the hundredth time. A quarter to three. That meant that there was only two hours of decent daylight left at best, a fraction of what she needed to uncover and explore a missing house.

There's nothing to be done but write off today and try again tomorrow. At least I know the route now and won't get distracted.

The thought of giving up, however, made her heart sink. She knew that going back to Oberschöneweide was the rational thing to do, but even with her feet aching and her hope fading, Nina had no interest in being rational. She was looking for a house her grandmother had walked away from over forty years ago—a house Magda had hated—and hoping to dig up a story her grandmother had always shied from telling. She was also hoping to trace an unknown woman from a photograph that was forty years old, with no idea why or even if she was important. Nothing in any of that was rational. Besides, there was another voice chipping at her ear, competing with the logical one. Whispering that there wouldn't be a second chance; that if Nina gave up now, she would be swallowed up by her old life and the Tower House would stay hidden. Nina knew that was a foolish voice to listen to, but she listened all the same.

Magda never wanted me to come. If I go back home and she's there, she'll try to stop me returning.

Nina stopped pacing and stood still, scanning the properties around her again as if one of them might suddenly sprout a clockface and a turret if she could only wish hard enough.

This is ridiculous. It doesn't matter if I come back tomorrow or in a month, it's gone.

The day was running away from her, she had no money for a hotel and, as used to discomfort as she was, she couldn't sleep on a park bench in the middle of November. The rational voice grew louder. The voice whispering *It was only ever a childish dream and now it's done* grew louder. Nina began to make her reluctant way back to the station, dragging her feet, determined to walk even more slowly and look even more carefully. As she did so, conscious that she must look, not just feel, like a disgruntled and disappointed toddler, a sudden movement on the opposite side of the street caught her eye. It was a cat, a small tabby, running in and out of a gap between two barbed-wire-topped garden walls. As Nina watched it, the cat stopped, looked, or so it seemed, straight at her, and then disappeared back into the shrubbery it had first emerged from.

I am supposed to follow it. I am meant to.

Nina was perfectly aware that couldn't be true. That she wasn't a character in a fairy tale; that the cat wouldn't reveal itself as the enchanted guardian of a magical house. She didn't care. She wanted a sign that the quest she was on would be rewarded, so she took the cat as a sign and crossed the road, calling for it to come.

It didn't, but now Nina was closer, she could see that the overgrown space that the tabby had vanished into was far wider than it had initially appeared. A few steps down the weed-choked gravel and Nina realized that the opening wasn't, in fact, a narrow pathway but a drive whose edges were marked by deliberately placed—and now largely moss-covered—round stones. Breath quickening, she followed it through thickening trees that closed off any view forward or backward that there once might have been, prepared to have her hopes dashed, refusing to believe that they would be.

It wasn't an easy task. The driveway was almost impassable in places, where the tangled hedges had sprawled out to meet each other, and the ground was slick with years of fallen leaves. Nina slowed down, although she wanted to speed up, aware that if she tripped and twisted an ankle or hit her head on one of the heavy stones, it could be a long time before anyone found her. Luckily, the drive was short. Nina went round what turned out to be the final bend with her fingers crossed, and to her delight and—now that it had materialized and she could admit it—complete surprise, there it was. The Tower House. Unmistakable even beneath the thick ropes of ivy that smothered it.

Nina stopped to drink it in. It was there, but it was a mess. The shutters hung in splinters; part of the balcony had crumbled away. The clock was almost invisible beneath its layers of grime, and the tower itself was listing where vines had punched through the brickwork. It wasn't a princess's castle anymore, unless Sleeping Beauty had grown old and withered. It was dilapidated, parts of it struggling to stand.

But it's intact, and there's a charm still clinging to it. There's something to build on.

Conscious she was grinning in a very foolish way and not caring at all, Nina began to circle the building, picking her way through the brambles that had knotted themselves as high as the ground-floor windowsills. The front door was black and solid beneath its veneer of dirt. The lock for which she didn't have a key was ornately worked and had acquired a coating of green that suggested there was bronze underneath it. Trying not to flinch at the touch of the sticky spiderwebs, she pushed at the metal in the hope it had worn loose. When that didn't work, she put her shoulder to the wood and shoved. It didn't so much as creak.

Nina stood back and surveyed the windows instead. There were plenty of them, but the panes of glass on the lower ones were tiny and the iron grilles that held them were firmly rusted in place. As she trusted neither her climbing skills nor the strength of the ivy coils, the wider upper ones weren't an option.

Giving up on the front, Nina began to make her way round to the back. There was no discernible path. What must once have been a garden was now a sea of bindweed that stretched down to cover a partially visible and crumbling shed. The rear of the house was as encircled in ivy as the front; the flaking red door, however, was far flimsier. Nina scraped the clinging tendrils away and threw her weight against it. Two sharp pushes and the lock gave; a third and it groaned slowly open. Nina took a deep breath and stepped inside. What met her was a time capsule.

No one has been here but me for years, maybe decades.

The absence of life was thick in the air. It was damp and musty and filled with rot and with so much dust it made her sneeze, but there were no human scents floating in it. There was decay: the kitchen wallpaper had peeled into streamers; mold swirled the walls and the countertops with green and brown patches; the fireplace was filled with a cobweb-thick pile of twigs and dried leaves as if a generation of birds' nests had fallen there. There was decay everywhere she could see, but—apart from what seemed to be a sprinkling of glass in the hallway—there were no signs of damage. Nothing, in the kitchen at least, had been smashed; nothing had been ransacked. The house appeared to have been abandoned—and then completely forgotten.

Nina closed the kitchen door, dropped her backpack and bags, and then wedged a chair beneath the broken lock. If she had found the house, if she had been seen, others could follow. She wasn't ready for others, not until she knew every inch of what she was dealing with. She barely knew how to feel about what she had already seen, although the thought of what the house might be hiding was beginning to push aside her initial excitement.

Determined to get started while there was still some of the day left, Nina began to walk toward the hallway and the series of rooms she could see leading off from that. She barely managed a handful of steps, however, before she stopped, her feet refusing to carry her any further in. The light was wrong. Even taking account of the late hour, it was watery and weak and she couldn't see a thing out of any of the square windows.

It's the same as the prison—that's why it's thrown me. It's a pretense of windows, a pretense of the outside.

Her heart was hammering; the walls were closing in—she knew she couldn't go any further. If she didn't open the house up, it would defeat her.

Nina turned back the way she'd come and grabbed the chair away from the kitchen door. The immediate rush of fresh air calmed her. All the house needed was light, so light was what she would give it. She tore at the vines clogging the ground-floor windows, ripping the stems from as many as she could reach. As soon as they were free, she used first her sleeves and then her whole jumper to rub clear peepholes in the filthy glass. When she finally went back inside, her hands aching and blistered, it had worked: the last of the day's sun had penetrated the interior strongly enough to turn it back into a house.

Feeling rather more in control, Nina went from room to room on the ground floor, looking but not touching anything. Then she made her way carefully up the stairs, avoiding the sags that suggested rotted floorboards. Apart from her footsteps, there wasn't a sound, not even from the birds she had disturbed in the ivy. The silence around her was as thick as the dust, and—although Nina told herself she was being silly and superstitious—just as uncomfortable as the dark had been.

By the time she'd visited each one of its rooms, the house was once again filled with more shadows than daylight. She had found furniture in all of them, although the heavy wooden pieces and the coverlets and curtains were filthy and mildewed and bore the tracks of moths and mice. She had found no trace anywhere of her grandmother. What she had uncovered instead were an awful lot of things she didn't understand. A pile of what appeared to be framed photographs stacked in the corner of a small bedroom. A branching tarnished-to-black candelabra on the dining-room table, whose curving arms reminded Nina of one she had once seen in a book about Judaism. The name *Minna* scratched into the faded flower-strewn wallpaper of what Nina guessed—from the doll's house sitting collapsed in on itself in the middle of the floor—had once been a little girl's room. All of the discoveries were unsettling; one, however, was disturbing: a stained and water-damaged portrait hanging in the hallway of a man who was, unmistakably, and horribly, Hitler.

Discovering that had stopped Nina's searching. She didn't know whether there were belongings left in the wardrobes or the cupboards. She told herself that she hadn't opened those yet because there wasn't enough light anymore and—although there was cold water trickling through the taps—there wasn't any power. That wasn't the real reason, however: the portrait, together with the SS identity card that was hidden in the bottom of her backpack, suggested there might be things in this house best left for morning and not nighttime's discovering.

By the time she finished her exploring, her watch told her it was six o'clock. It was so dark, it could have been midnight, and it was freezing. The sensible thing to do would be to secure the house again and go home. She still didn't, however, want to do the sensible thing. She couldn't do the sensible thing. If Magda had returned earlier than expected and was there to meet her, that would mean asking why her abandoned old house was full of other people's discarded belongings and the only portrait Nina had found was one of Hitler. Nina had no idea how to do that. Not with *There's things I've done, Nina. For the right reasons but that... went wrong, or might look wrong* circling round in her head. Something didn't fit. Even without looking at them and checking for dates, Nina could sense that the photographs and the doll's house and the other forgotten items she'd found had lived in the house before Magda had. Perhaps it was her imagination—she would be perfectly happy to be shown that it was—but they seemed to be part of the fabric of the place, as if they had been chosen with love to fit with the building, and Magda had made it clear that she had never loved this building. So Nina couldn't go back: there was more digging to do.

Instead of leaving, therefore, Nina broke up a rickety cabinet and built a fire in the lounge's huge fireplace. Once that was blazing, she wrenched a pair of the mildew-speckled curtains off their hangings to use as a blanket. Then she cocooned herself in those on one of the room's two sagging sofas and unpacked the purchases she had made in the KaDeWe's food hall. A sweet bread she had never heard of before called brioche; thick slices of ham; a net of jewel-like oranges; and a bar of Milka chocolate that was so creamily divine she licked every last trace from the wrapper. Even with the flickering fire and her velvet nest, the room was too dark and too cold and there were things in the house that were far more disturbing than Nina had expected to encounter. It was still paradise compared to a prison cell.

The rap on the kitchen door woke Nina from a sleep that was thick and free from dreams. After years of interrupted nights that were never allowed to be her own, sleeping had become a pleasure she reveled in and loathed to leave. The second knock came as she was trying to understand where she was. She unwound herself from the curtains and crept slowly toward the kitchen. There was a man standing there, his blue police uniform visible through the half-glassed door. Nina flattened herself against the wall, but he had already seen her.

"You need to open the door, Fräulein. I need to know what you are doing here."

I can't let him in; he'll see the portrait. It must still be a crime to be a Nazi here. He'll arrest me. I'm not going back to prison again, in the West or the East.

"Fräulein, I know you can hear me."

It was pointless to keep on pretending—it might antagonize him. Nina eased the chair away from the doorway, worried that, if she didn't do as he asked, he would kick his way in. Rather than let him inside, however, she went out onto the step and closed the door behind her, blocking the entrance with her body. She did not know if that would make him angry; she did not know if he would simply push her aside and go in anyway. She shoved her hands into her pockets as she turned to face him and stuck on her most confident expression, but it was obvious from his frown that he had noticed her shaking.

He probably thinks I'm a drug addict who's broken in.

To her relief, he looked her up and down, and then he moved a pace back.

"What is your name, and why are you here?"

Nina wondered for a moment about lying. She still had the fake passport—she could hand that over, pretend that she was indeed a drifter looking for a place to sleep, and then find somewhere to hide until he left and she could creep back again. Common sense, however, prevailed over her fear of his uniform. If she, or Magda, was going to stake any kind of legal claim on the house, she had to start by being honest.

"My name is Nina Dahlke. I am from Oberschöneweide in..." she hesitated. "That was in East Berlin; I suppose it still is. This house here belonged to my grandmother forty years ago. I came here to find it, and to get it back for her if I can."

The policeman didn't look particularly surprised at her answer. "Do you have papers?"

Nina handed over her GDR identity card and stayed silent while he checked it. He gave it back and then pushed his cap up and scratched his head in a gesture that suddenly made him—for Nina—ordinary and human.

"This pile was your grandmother's? To be honest, I've been walking this beat for four years and I didn't even know it was here. We got a call from one of the villas at the back, the tall ones you can presumably see from the bottom of the..." He stopped and looked toward the shed. "Well, from down there. Anyway, someone saw lights flickering and thought there might be a fire, in 'the wasteland by the ruin,' as the caller referred to it. It took me an age to find the way in. I assume none of your family have been back for quite some time if you're from the East?"

Nina shook her head. "I don't think anyone has been here since the war ended. And the lights must have been me. I was using a flashlight, and I made a fire to keep warm. I'm sorry, I probably shouldn't have done that." She trailed off, wondering if she was about to be arrested for trespassing.

The policeman, however, shrugged.

"If it really is your family's property, I suppose it doesn't matter. It's not as if you burned the place down. But if you are going to be in it—which, given its state and the weather, I'm not sure you should be—we should probably get ownership established."

This time, the relief was overwhelming. It released Nina's shoulders and her smile.

"Do you know how I do that?"

When the policeman smiled back at her, Nina realized that he was younger than she had thought and nothing about him suggested that he was familiar with blacked-out vans or the finer points of mental torture.

"I haven't a clue, but I can point you toward someone who does. I don't think you're the first person from the East, or from the past for that matter, trying to reclaim property in Grunewald. It's got a bit of a history, this area. Some of the houses around here—especially the big ones—are notorious for the people who once lived in them, and who they threw out to get their hands on a bit of prime real estate. There's a department at the local council office dealing with claims, or a man there anyway. I don't know how it all works, but given there's been no one living here for so long, it might not be too difficult for you." He glanced at Nina's disheveled hair and clothes. "Why don't you come to the station in an hour or so, and, in the meantime, I'll fix up an appointment with the council. The house will be safe enough. Now we know it's here, we'll keep an eye on it."

He scribbled an address in his notebook, tore the page out, and gave it to Nina. As he was turning to leave, she gave in to her confusion and stopped him.

"You're a policeman: why are you being this kind?"

He frowned. "If it's your family home, you've done nothing wrong, so why wouldn't I be?"

It was an impossibly simple and impossibly perfect answer. Nina stood at the door and watched him climb back over the brambles and the bindweed. Her eyes were pricking. She blinked, but a tear still fell; she realized it was fine to let it. For the first time since Nina had been thrown to the ground with a gun at her neck, for the first time since Stefan had died, the tears in her eyes weren't born of fear or shock or despair, but a simple, oh so welcome, delight.

CHAPTER FOURTEEN

Nina, November 1989

Officer Honigmann not only arranged an appointment with the housing claims department, but he also refilled Nina's emptied purse.

"It's called 'Welcome Money.' It's no big deal—everyone who comes from the East to the West is entitled to it. Take your identity card to the processing center on the first floor and they'll see you right."

From the casual way he mentioned the money, Nina assumed the gift would be a handful of Deutschmarks, perhaps enough to pay for some local travel and a meal or two. She would have been more than happy with that. The idea that anyone would give her money she hadn't worked for was so far outside her experience, the amount seemed irrelevant. When Nina reported to the teller, however, and was given not the small change she expected but an envelope containing five twenty-mark notes, she didn't know what to say, or do.

"Is there anything else I can help you with? Do you have friends here, or do you need somewhere to stay?"

The cheery woman had to ask Nina twice before she stopped staring at the money and rediscovered her voice. All it took was a "thank you, yes I do need a place" and a "but I don't know the area" and the teller slipped happily into action. Nina left the office half an hour later, loaded down with the names and addresses of every business in the area, from hairdressers to greengrocers, and a recommendation for an affordable guest house that was "better than anything on either side of the city."

Nina didn't have the heart to spoil the woman's pride in her neighborhood by admitting that she had never stayed anywhere overnight outside the flat she'd shared with Stefan, other than a family member's home, or a prison. The Tower House, however, wasn't anything close to comfortable yet and she had no desire to spend another frozen night there. And if Grunewald was the place she intended to call home, it seemed sensible to know how easy it might be to live there. The answer was: very. By lunchtime, Nina had a spotless room with its own bath in a neat little house, and a locksmith booked to secure the back of the Tower House and open up the front. And a pair of skinny-legged black jeans purchased from another sales assistant who was convinced Nina was a model and who declared—with an irony not lost on her new customer—that she would "die to be the owner of such fabulously thin thighs."

Bathed and dressed and freshly made-up, Nina had gone back to the house determined to tackle all the corners she hadn't been able to face in the dark. By the time she had finished digging, however, none of her new Western luxuries mattered anymore. They were simply the armor she needed to get back up the drive and into Sascha Niedrig's claims office with some semblance of calm.

The first hour she had spent in the house had been perfectly pleasant. The sunshine pouring through the cleared windows wiped away the worries that had crowded it the night before and turned it into a place of possibilities. Nina had wandered back round the downstairs rooms picking out paint colors and imagining the floors strewn with bright rugs; picturing the kitchen scented with coffee and her grandmother's spice cake. She had made her way up the staircase, tracing her fingers over the vines and acorns carved into it, convinced that she would throw open the cupboards and find explanations.

Her optimism was short-lived. What she found was more items that had clearly belonged to another family, and more confusion.

She started with the top floor, determined to investigate the chests she'd spotted pushed against the walls in each room; telling herself they would be filled with items that were recognizably Magda's. They weren't. They were filled instead with delicately crafted children's clothes, with books bearing inscriptions to *My beloved Ruth* and *My darling Johannes* and sets of silver-handled cutlery stamped with a curling capital letter *L*. One of the boxes in the smallest room contained an ivory teething ring and a baby's rattle packed away in a satin-lined box. Another contained a teddy bear and an elegantly dressed doll. In a third, there was a necklace whose stones gleamed when she rubbed at them. Everything Nina pulled out had clearly been precious to someone, and yet all of it had been left behind when its owners went away. Nina doubted that could have been by choice. It took all her self-control not to imagine shadowy figures hovering in the doorways, waiting patiently for her to hand their belongings back.

Feeling far less at ease than she had when the afternoon started, Nina had turned her attention to the rooms on the first floor. It was there—in the room she assumed, from its position facing the garden, had once been the house's main bedroom—that she finally found an imprint of Magda.

The furniture, which consisted of a large wardrobe and matching chest of drawers, was dark and heavy and not at all inviting. Nina approached the wardrobe first, the echoes of the day she had dug through Herthe's discarded dresses and found the drawing swirling round her. The thin dresses she discovered in this one were, however, very different from her great-grandmother's sensible frocks. These were elegant and slippery and had clearly once been beautiful things. Their colors had faded to a watery paleness, and the lace trims and sequins that edged them were yellowed and rusty, but the extravagance that was left suggested a life filled with parties. They were also so unlike the garments the Magda Nina knew wore, she wouldn't have guessed at first glance that they had belonged to her grandmother. There was, however, one shawl-collared faded blue coat still hanging there whose checked trim was in exactly the same fabric, and the same color, as the dress Nina had cut down to fit her and wear in the West. When she shook the coat out, the cut and the trim revealed them as a pair.

Even then, the fact that the evening gowns filling the rest of the hangers told a story of a very different Magda didn't worry her. Her grandmother had been young in the war, no more than thirty when it ended. It wasn't a stretch to imagine her holding on to a collection of pretty clothes when rationing must have made it hard to buy new ones. Finding the outfits, holding them up against herself and seeing how well they suited her, even in their ruined state, made the past seem far less of a different and dangerous place, despite all Magda's nervous warnings, and it made Nina feel close to her grandmother. The wardrobe wasn't the problem; it was the contents of the chest of drawers that punched Nina's breath away.

The top two drawers contained piles of disintegrating material that shredded even further when Nina ran her reluctant fingers through it. The third was the same, although it didn't open quite so easily, and Nina was forced to plunge her hand into the cobwebby fabric to free it. What she found there was thicker with the past than the echoes the dresses had carried. Her fingers encountered not more old blouses but papers, two sets of them, bound with thin strips of elastic that snapped as Nina gingerly eased the bundles out. She didn't try to fool herself that they might be Old Masters or treasure maps; she wasn't that innocent anymore.

Don't read them—nothing good will come of it.

The voice in her head had felt like a wise one, but Nina knew she couldn't listen to it. She had gathered the papers up and took them down to the relative cheeriness of the kitchen, wishing she had a kettle or a teapot or something to distract herself.

Or a drink to numb myself from whatever is surely coming.

She wiped the dust from the table and laid the bundles flat. They were thin folders, both with a few sheets of paper tucked inside. She sat down, opened the first one, and was met with

Magda's unmistakably elegant copperplate hand and a single word: *Massacres*. The title was too stark to make her want to read on. She pushed it away and opened the second. It contained the same handwriting, and a title that brought her no more comfort than the first: *Deportations from Grunewald*. This time, Nina forced herself to keep reading.

> *October 18, 1941*
> *First deportation of Jews from Platform 17, Grunewald station*
> *Number of deported: 1089*
> *Destination: Lodz*
> *Conditions: Wet*
> *Mode of Transport: Deutsche Reichsbahn BB Passenger Third Class*
> *Behavior of transport: Quiet and orderly*
> *Present: Reichsführer-SS Heinrich Himmler; Director of the Reich Security Office Reinhard Heydrich; Obersturmbannführer Adolf Eichmann*

And Magda Aderbach?

Her name wasn't listed, but her presence was there. Nina's mouth was so dry she could barely swallow. She turned the flimsy pages carefully, taking great care not to tear them. Most of the second page was taken up with a mathematical formula that was apparently about *freight*. There was also a short paragraph referring to a "cheaper transport method that will be used in the future now that compliance is assured," the model number of a train referred to as a "cattle wagon," and a list of new destinations, including Riga and Minsk, which were "expected to come on stream shortly, once the facilities to process them at the other end have been perfected." There were more dates after that, more numbers.

It could mean they were moving cattle, or coal, or even food.

She checked back to the front page. It still said Jews.

The report, if that was what it was, seemed incomplete and unfinished. Nina wasn't sure if some of the lines in it were quotations—if they were, they weren't attributed to any of the men Magda had recorded as being there. It also didn't seem to have been compiled all at the same time, or at least the color of the ink used wasn't consistent. More disturbing than that was its unemotional and clinical tone. There was no commentary or personal reflections; Nina couldn't tell if that was deliberate or not. Whatever it was, it was damning. For all the mention of *cargo* and *pieces*, the first page left Nina in no doubt that the items being moved from Platform 17, on that day, and all the others Magda had recorded, weren't *freight* but human beings.

Nina closed the folder, not yet ready to tackle the second one, not sure what exactly to read into the first. She had heard the term Holocaust before, although it wasn't much used in her school. Lessons there had focused on the phrase *fascist atrocities* and the suffering of the millions of *anti-fascist freedom fighters*—which everyone understood to mean communists—who had died at Nazi hands, both in battle and at the killing camps. Persecution of the Jewish race had been mentioned, but never in the systematic way Magda's report alluded to, which pointed to murder on a massive scale. Murder her grandmother knew far more about than she had ever let slip to Nina.

Some of the houses around here are notorious for the people who once lived in them, and who they threw out.

A different family had once lived in the Tower House—that fact was inescapable. Nina had found traces of them in every room in the house; she knew it was their images she would find in the stack of photographs she hadn't yet looked at. What she was certain of was that their last name wasn't Aderbach. What she hadn't known was where they had gone, or why they had left, and why they had abandoned so many cherished objects when they did.

Except now I could hazard a guess. And if Magda lived in this house straight after them, perhaps she stole it herself, or was given it by the person who did.

She wasn't ready to face that thought, or the hazy memory suddenly tugging at her. She turned instead to the second folder, the one titled *Massacres*. This one also started with a list, this time of places that had been new to Nina before today—including Babi Yar, Rumbula, and Riga—and two, Sachsenhausen and Auschwitz, which she recognized from her school history lessons as camps where the Nazis killed communists during the war. There were more numbers; they were frighteningly high—higher than the deportation lists, some of them in the tens of thousands. The ones recorded against the camp names were higher than any Nina had ever heard associated with those places before, and the designation of the victims Magda had recorded as killed wasn't communist, as Nina had been taught, but, once again, Jewish.

The place names were followed by geographical lists Magda had recorded as "train movements" and the note "one links to the other." The name of the traveler each time was the same and one that Nina recognized as a leading member of the Third Reich's ruling elite: Reichsführer Himmler, the same man Magda had recorded as being present at the Grunewald deportation. The tone of this report was as concise and clerical as the first. But why Magda had written it, or made the connection between the killings and the man, or what she thought about any of the facts she had noted was no clearer than why she had written the other.

The house was a reward.

Nina dropped the folder as the nagging memory pushed through and the certainty hit her. Before, whenever she had thought about the drawing, or about the house itself, it was the details of the building she had focused on. Now the inscription written in the corner of the picture leaped back: *For Magda Aderbach, from HH, a gift.* Nina stared at the papers as the short inscription unraveled itself. For Magda Aderbach, who had witnessed the deportations, who had intimate knowledge of Reichsführer Himmler's movements, a reward for her service.

Because she worked for him.

Nina knew that the HH who had gifted Magda the house was Himmler. She didn't need to go back through the reports checking for his first name, although she did, hoping against hope that she was wrong. She wasn't, of course: Heinrich Himmler was written across too many pages to pretend it could be anyone else. Or to pretend that her grandmother couldn't have known him, and known him well, when she had plotted his precise movements across the key years of the war. When she had stood with him at Grunewald station, writing her dispassionate notes as the trains were loaded with people who were considered as freight.

Who I don't believe for a moment ever made it back home again.

Nina sat back from the table and closed her eyes as the room lurched. How could all this be true? How was she meant to reconcile the image of the woman receiving rewards from Himmler with the Magda Nina, and everyone else, knew? The lifelong and loyal SED party worker, the upholder of equality; the opponent of injustice and hate. Or reconcile that with the fact that, at the end of the war and on into the founding of the GDR, the Russian-backed authorities had purged the districts under its control of anyone with the slightest link to the Nazis. It was one of the founding principles the regime prided itself on. How could a woman who knew Himmler apparently so closely have escaped that blood-letting? And then *perhaps I should be investigated and held to account* crashed into *it's always impossible to save everyone* and *who in God's name was my grandmother* and the party dresses hanging in the wardrobe suddenly took on a far more sinister aspect. Who had Magda danced with wearing those? Himmler? Hitler? Nina's breakfast came back in a rush.

It took her so long to steady herself, she was almost late for the appointment she no longer wanted to keep with Sascha Niedrig. If there had been a telephone in the house, she would have canceled it. She couldn't bear the thought of discussing claims to a house that had started to mock her, or a grandmother whose whole existence had now shifted in such an unfathomable way. She certainly couldn't tell a stranger the truth, or what she suspected the truth to be. She considered simply not turning up, but she didn't want Officer Honigmann—or Niedrig himself—to come snooping.

But what if he knows the real history behind the house and it's not what I think? What if he can disprove my suspicions without me having to air them?

She couldn't go back to Magda with another half-story, especially one she was certain her grandmother would rear away from. In the end, she stuffed the reports—and the portrait of Hitler she'd pulled down from the wall the previous night—back into the drawer, pulled out her bag of makeup samples and rearranged herself into a woman who looked less haunted.

She didn't glance back at the house when she left it. She avoided walking past the station with its treacherous platform. She didn't stop to linger and admire any of the stucco-covered villas she passed on the way. The suburb wasn't picture-postcard perfect after all: that was as much of a façade as the flower baskets decorating the Grunewald ticket office. As far as Nina could see, there was nothing in this place she could take on face value anymore; there were far too many secrets lurking.

Whatever he says, whether he is charming, or whether he is intrusive, I'm going to keep my distance.

Nina arrived at the housing department determined to learn what she could and give nothing away. She had spent the walk constructing the housing department man into a nosy and humorless combination of Frau Rothberg and a Stasi agent. From his first exuberant handshake, however, it was clear that there was no one less likely to go snooping through her life than Sascha Niedrig. His welcoming smile was too warm and open, his manner too straightforward. And—although his office was neat and tidy and his master's degree in History hung framed and full of authority on the wall behind his desk—there was something excitable about him that reminded Nina, fleetingly, of Julia. That did not set her at ease, but it made her marginally less guarded.

Sascha—as he immediately insisted she call him—gave a very good impression of a man trying to contain a larger personality than the professional one his office demanded. The way he greeted her, bouncing to his feet and calling her "the most fascinating thing that's happened here in ages" was so genuine, it went some way to restoring her shaken sense of balance. That he was younger than the middle-aged man in a suit Nina had been expecting—in his late twenties at the most—and attractive, albeit in an understated, unaware way, also did him no harm. And then he hurried her into a chair and grabbed a pen and began asking about the house, and the condition it was in, and when her grandmother had acquired it, and Nina's guard flew back up again. Being questioned by a man surrounded by files felt too uncomfortably familiar; everything about the Tower House, and Magda, felt too muddled to share. She cut across his stream of questions without answering one of them.

"Could you tell me about the area? I know nothing about Grunewald."

Sascha put down his pen and pushed his notepad away. "Forgive me. I've bombarded you, which I promised myself I wouldn't do. Unfortunately, give me a new house to investigate—especially one that isn't in any of our records—and I get carried away. What do you want to know?"

Was everyone who lived here in the war a Nazi?
Did all the trains that left the station go to the death camps?
Is anything in this place what it seems?

Nina folded her knotted fingers in her lap, counted to ten, and managed a more reasonable question.

"A little more about the villas, perhaps, and the people who built them. Some of the houses here are quite extraordinary. Are all of them old?"

It was the right thing to ask, the right way to open him up. Sascha pulled a folder from the pile stacked on his desk and passed her a handful of the dozens of photographs bursting from it.

"Many of them are around the hundred-year-plus mark, which counts as old these days, given how much of Berlin was destroyed during the war. These here are some of the best ones, in close-up, as well as the whole building. I've photographed over 200 of them and there's not one that's the same as the rest."

Nina took the bundle he passed her and thumbed through the carefully framed shots of marble friezes and red-tile-topped turrets, and the wide-angled views of front lawns that were dotted with statues and appeared to be the size of a park.

Sascha continued to pass her more pictures as he carried on talking.

"The houses you're looking at are from the 1880s, but the oldest property in the neighborhood is a hunting lodge that dates back to the 1540s. Grunewald has always attracted Berlin's wealthier residents, for its forests and lakes and privacy, I suppose. I've heard it described as a 'seaside resort without the sea' and a place where you can be idle and breathe, which is not something you could say about the center of the city, as much fun as that is. The area's heyday was in the 1920s, when it was famed for its masked balls and parties that ran on for days." He stopped and cleared his throat. "I could give you a tour if you want, show you the ones with the most interesting histories."

When Nina smiled at him, Sascha blushed. She phrased her next question as carefully as her first, not wanting to alert him.

"Thank you—that would be lovely. But what about after that, after the twenties? It's just that Officer Honigmann said that some of the people who lived here were notorious, and he didn't seem to be referring to the parties they held. Do you know what he meant by that?"

Sascha's smile and his blush faded. "I think so, yes. I think he's talking about the late 1930s, and then on into the war. That was when the National Socialists pretty much took over this area: a lot of the villas fell into the hands of the SS, including their leader, Heinrich Himmler. He had quite a mansion here by all accounts, although you won't find any trace of that one still standing."

"How?" The question was too abrupt. Sascha frowned; Nina collected herself. "I mean how did the SS get hold of them? You said *fell*—did you mean that they bought them?"

Nina had already pieced that answer together from the word *gift*, and the left-behind objects and the deportation lists, but she needed to hear how Sascha would answer.

"No. That's not how the SS operated. They stole them, from the rich Jewish families who owned them first."

Nina let her breath go in the relief of his honesty. And then she saw the disgust on his face and realized how quickly that could turn on her if she wasn't very careful.

"Were they the same families who were deported on cattle trucks from Grunewald station?"

Sascha put down the photograph he had been about to hand to her.

"You know about that?"

Nina nodded and framed her response as blandly as she could. "I'm starting to. I don't know much beyond what I've just said."

"It's more than a lot of people would admit to, if they come from here anyway." His face had changed, the boyish enthusiasm replaced by a leaner intensity. "The deportations from the station here, and the fact that this was once an SS enclave, are Grunewald's darkest, and best-kept, secrets. The truth is starting to come out, but it's slow and not everybody wants to listen. There's still fear, and shame, and too many lost people, and no one knows what to do about that. And there are too many, if I'm honest, who don't want to look back at all; who want that part of German history to be done with and gone. There has been talk of a memorial on the platform the death trains went out of, but..." He paused. "Every time a plaque is installed there, it gets stolen. Sometimes I wonder what kind of people are still living here."

And he loathes them, of course he does; it's written all over his face. So I can't let him find out my suspicions. Not until I know more about him; not until I've spoken to Magda and given her a chance to explain herself.

"Is that what you're doing then: trying to find out what really went on here?" This time, her question was rushed and clumsy, but Sascha didn't seem to notice.

"Yes, I suppose so, although it didn't start out that way. I came to the council originally as a sort of keeper of the villas, to prevent the historic ones being remodeled and ruined." He nodded at his degree certificate. "Architectural history was my specialization, which is how I got the job—that and the fact that I knew the area well. At first, it was all overseeing, and rejecting, planning applications—nothing particularly out of the ordinary—and then the focus changed, and people like you started to get in touch."

He paused, but Nina nodded him on before *people like you* could turn into a question she had no intention of answering.

"We got an approach from a Jewish family who had fled to the States many years ago, or, at least, some of them fled—the ones who could. The children had discovered old title deeds to one of the houses here after their father died, and they wanted restitution. Once that dispute became public knowledge, we got more applicants. And with the Wall coming down, I imagine that the number of previous residents like you, coming back to find out if their old property is still standing, will escalate. My main job now seems to be mediating between angry owners who don't want to give up their homes and claimants whose stories would make you weep if you heard them." He paused again. "Which you, of course, may already have done, or which you share."

Even though her stomach was churning at the thought of what he would make of her case—and how different it was to the assumptions he seemed to be making—Nina couldn't help but acknowledge what his eyes were telling her even more loudly than his words.

"And you love it, don't you? That you can help them."

Sascha's face lit up and turned, Nina couldn't help but notice, from attractive to handsome. "I do, yes. For some of the people I speak to, this is the first time they've tried to get any kind of justice, or recognition, for the terrible things that happened to them and their loved ones. There's an honor, and a burden, in that." He shook his head and grimaced. "Which makes me sound really pompous. What I am is actually a very small cog in a much bigger wheel. Or, if you listen to my grandmother, not even that at all, but rather someone with 'a bad case of interfering with matters that are best left undisturbed.'"

This time it was Nina's turn to frown. Sascha laughed. "Grandmother has lived in Grunewald all her life, and she's very protective of it. And since I've lived with her most of mine, she's very protective of me. She thinks all this 'raking up' will get me in trouble. God knows who with, but she isn't always logical, or forthcoming, when she chooses not to be."

The past isn't some star-sprinkled land I'm longing to share.

The similarity between the two women made Nina momentarily forget her intention of keeping her distance when it came to anything personal.

"She sounds as if she would get on with my grandmother. She's a stickler for privacy and letting things well alone too, and she's good at not talking precisely at the point when you want her to."

Magda was suddenly in the room, although Nina hadn't intended her to be.

Sascha stopped collecting up the photographs.

"They've seen things we haven't, that whole generation. It's not surprising that our 'clodhopping over the past,' as Granny puts it, scares them. They carry scars we can't even guess at."

It's not just our grandmothers who are alike. He sounds as if he's had an upbringing not so far away from mine.

The air in the room had tightened; Nina knew Sascha could sense it too. She got up, uncomfortable with how close the conversation had grown. She was out of practice with handsome men; she didn't know if it was a skill she wanted to relearn.

"I should go."

"Or we could have a drink, or dinner, and talk some more?"

It was clearly an impulse born out of the sudden connection they had made: Sascha looked as surprised that he'd asked the question as Nina was to hear it. Her immediate reaction was to say no. She had distracted Sascha from talking about the Tower House in the professional confines of his office; she wasn't sure she could continue to do that with a glass of wine in her hand and her defenses already slipping.

She was about to refuse him, but then another truth unexpectedly hit her: she was lonely. She had been deeply lonely for a very long time, since Stefan had died. Perhaps, if she was honest, since long before that. That wasn't something she could have admitted to herself in Hohenschönhausen—letting in dark thoughts she had no way of calming in that place would have been a sure route to madness. After her release, she had kept herself too busy to let that, or any other real feelings, in. But the loneliness was there, buried deep in her bones and her soul. And now there was Sascha, who was kind and clever, and interesting. Who might be able to wipe away some of the unhappiness she'd carried with her from the prison, and the confusion and shock she'd encountered today, for a few hours at least.

And who I need on my side, if I'm going to get to anything approaching the truth.

So she didn't say no; she said yes.

*

Later, when everything fell completely apart, Nina wished that she'd done more than hold Sascha's hand on the way back from the restaurant. That when he kissed her—which was unexpected and expected and something she knew the moment she felt the touch of his lips that she desperately wanted him to do—and kissed her again, she hadn't forced herself to resurface and pull back. She wished that she hadn't hesitated, caught for a moment in the memory of Stefan. That she had gone home with Sascha instead, and slept with him, and bound him to her with ties that he might have possibly found harder to break. Instead, because part of her was still caught behind prison walls and caught in the past, Nina had held him at arms'-length for long enough to break the spell trying to cast itself over them. He had still, however, got under her skin.

The restaurant he took her to wasn't too dark, or too cozy, or too intimate for a first meal together. Nina could sense that Sascha was feeling his way round whatever might be developing between them as carefully as she was. He gave her the promised tour of the villa colony as they walked from his office, leading her past the floodlit properties on Winkler Straße and Douglasstraße and Koenigsallee, telling her anecdotes about the industrialists and the actors and the bankers who once lived inside homes that looked to Nina like palaces. Nina nodded but she barely listened: she was too busy trying to formulate a story she could weave around Magda. In the end, however, none of the evening was about Magda at all, not once Nina's forged passport fell out of her pocket as the waiter whisked her coat rather too theatrically away.

"Who is Sofie Hass?" Sascha turned the pages of the document he'd picked up before Nina could snatch it. "And why does she have a look of you?"

It was a way out. A way to buy more time. Nina hadn't intended to tell him her story as quickly as this, but it was better than telling him Magda's.

"Because Sofie Hass was who I was going to be."

Once Nina said that—and because she realized she didn't want to spin Sascha any more half-truths than she had to—everything else followed. She told him it all, from the joke that had first tripped her as a ten-year-old child to the spirit-shattering experience of her capture and imprisonment.

The telling took up the whole meal. Sascha's face moved through every emotion from pity to horror. When Nina stumbled or tried to stop, he gently found the right question, and the right tone, to prop her up and restart her. When he took her hand, as she stumbled through as many of the details of a Stasi interrogation as she could bear to tell, she didn't pull back. When she finished, her body felt younger and lighter and more her own than she had ever expected it could. That Sascha was still sitting there, that he hadn't run, or refused to believe her, or suggested that anything of what had happened could be her own fault or an exaggeration, was a revelation. And perhaps a sign that other stories, when she had them better ready, could also be told.

"I didn't know I needed to do that. I didn't know that I could."

That admission had led to the first kiss, in the dark streets outside the restaurant. That had led to the next on the steps of her guest house. When Sascha asked if he could come to the Tower House the next afternoon, Nina's guard had slipped so thoroughly that it seemed a natural thing to let him. She agreed, and he kissed her again, until she finally pulled away from him. Her last thought, as she fell asleep with the imprint of his lips still traced on hers, was, *This is a man I can trust.*

CHAPTER FIFTEEN

Nina, November 1989

Sascha arrived at the Tower House on Wednesday afternoon in a whirlwind of activity, dragging a surveyor in his wake.

"I'm not committing anyone to anything, I promise. But it seems sensible to get an idea of the level of work that needs to be done, and the grants you might be eligible for, don't you think?"

It was, if Nina was honest, not what she was ready for. Letting anyone into a house that could still harbor dangerous secrets seemed rather more foolish in the daylight than it had when she was distracted by the moon and a handsome man's kisses. Sascha's enthusiasm, however, was catching, so Nina agreed, providing all the detailed inspections were exterior ones.

Sascha immediately began tearing round the outside of the house, taking reels of photographs and exclaiming with delight at the features that were still left, as Nina watched with growing amusement. After all the shocks the house had thrown up, it was good to see the place through someone else's eyes and remember that, despite the decay, the building underneath was potentially as stunning as Nina had always hoped it would be. The outside, however, was one thing; letting Sascha loose on the inside was a different matter. Nina had made sure to stage-manage that possibility far more carefully.

She had got up early and removed Magda's reports, hiding them safely in her backpack, which she had taken back to the guest house. On her return, she'd stuffed Hitler's portrait underneath the wardrobe. She had stripped that, and the chest of drawers, of all the old clothes and bundled those into the bottom of a skip she'd found outside a neighboring property. And she had collected all the items she could find that had belonged to the previous family and heaped them onto the table in the large sitting room, in the hope of distracting Sascha from forensically exploring the bedrooms, or the attic she had spied but not yet ventured into. That was a task she needed to complete by herself, without witnesses. When Sascha finally came in, having photographed the house from every conceivable angle, he was as enthralled by the stash of abandoned belongings as she had expected him to be.

"It's obvious that a Jewish family lived here. There's the menorah of course"—he pointed to the branching candelabra that had been still on the table when Nina first came into the house—"but these other objects also prove it."

He picked up one of a collection of engraved and, like the menorah, once silver cups and a thin, intricately carved wooden case with a small curl of paper stored inside it.

"These are Kiddush cups, which are used for wine on special holidays, and the holder with the parchment inside is a mezuzah. Those are fixed to the door to tell anyone entering the house that this is a Jewish household and therefore governed by specific rites and rituals." He stopped and grinned ruefully at Nina. "I'm sorry, I'm lecturing—it's one of my least attractive habits. Of course you must know what all these things are—this was your family's home after all. You can probably explain them better than I can."

Nina couldn't. She had found the cups in one of the heavy chests on the landing and thought they were pretty, and she'd spotted the case rolled into the corner by the front door and thought it was interesting. She had no idea what they were, but she wasn't about to admit that to Sascha. What she was going to do, however, was gather up every scrap of information she could extract from him and take all the details back to Magda. *The more I know, the less she can evade me* had become Nina's main purpose for staying in the house. She was also aware that, if Sascha wasn't going to start getting suspicious, she needed a set of evasions of her own. She was about to mutter something about religion of any persuasion not really being something that was encouraged in the GDR, when Sascha put down the mezuzah.

"You do know what happened to them, during the war? Your relatives who lived here, I mean."

Nina stared at him, caught off guard by the directness of the question, and started to mutter something nonsensical about a distant family branch. Luckily, a set of ivory-handled spoons had grabbed Sascha's attention, and he bounced on.

"Don't worry if there are gaps—there nearly always are. But I think we could find out with a bit of effort. Even if your knowledge is patchy, we've got their first names, and the initial L off the cutlery for their last one. Given all the personal items they left behind, I think we can assume that they didn't plan to leave here and that, I'm afraid, means we can also assume they were deported on one of the trains. It's not the nicest of jobs, but if we go through the deportation lists carefully, I'm almost certain they'll be there."

"There are lists of the people who were sent to the camps?"

The thought of that was such a shock that Nina had to sit down. She hadn't considered for a moment that the numbers, which were dreadful enough, could be translated into actual named people. That the scale of the misery embedded in the *resettlement and transportation reports,* a misery that Magda had recorded so impersonally, could be made worse was chilling.

Sascha was still working his way through the table and didn't notice her distress.

"Not for everyone, no, but for a lot of them. There is some survivor testimony, and some recovered camp and head office paperwork that wasn't destroyed. And the synagogues that are left have started to try to pull the records together. The main one in Berlin—which is called the New Synagogue but is anything but—apparently has quite a collection. It was in the East, but now the Wall is down, perhaps they will open those up to a wider audience." Sascha picked up the baby's rattle and ran his thumb over it. "The lists I have seen are terrible things—they make the whole nightmare personal, but they are also, I suppose, some sort of testimony to those who were lost and a help in remembering them. Didn't you know they existed?"

Nina pulled herself together as he turned and shook her head.

"I know very little about any of this, to be honest. I think that the way the war was remembered in the GDR might be very different to the way it is remembered here."

She stopped. The gulf between what he had been taught to believe and what she had been told to believe was too big, for now, to bridge it. Sascha's frown disappeared as he watched her struggling.

"It doesn't matter; I imagine there will be a lot of areas that will need fresh eyes on them once reunification is done. Anyway, I think we can do it; I certainly have contacts who could try. The only other thing I need is your grandmother's name; I don't think you ever actually told me."

Nina hadn't. Once she realized that Sascha thought her family was Jewish, she couldn't. Now she was faced with another direct question, however, she didn't know what to do. It was one thing not to correct an assumption or garble an answer to buy time; it was another thing entirely to blatantly lie to him. Her silence dragged on long enough for Sascha to stop rooting through the items still awaiting his attention and look properly at her.

"Sorry—have I been talking and not listening again? Did you tell me and I forgot?"

"No, you're right, I didn't. Her name is Magda." Nina stopped again. Sascha's smile faltered. She had no choice but to continue. "Magda Aderbach." His nose wrinkled.

"Was that her married name? Or did she change it? I've seen Auerbach on Jewish records before but not Aderbach. As far as I know, that's an old one from Bohemia or Bavaria, which doesn't quite fit." This time, it was his turn to pause. "When did she come by the house, Nina? I don't think you told me that either."

Nina stared at him, shifting like a child holding stolen candy behind her back, even though his tone had been curious, not accusing. Knowing his attitude toward her would change the moment any of the truth came out.

Sascha's frown deepened.

"Nina, what is it? Is there something you're not telling me?"

"Herr Niedrig, can you spare a minute? There's not a lot of daylight left, and there's a couple of points regarding the condition of the turret and the balcony I'd like to run through with you."

It was the surveyor. Nina could have kissed him.

"Perhaps we should close up in here as well?"

Sascha had started to motion to him to wait, but Nina didn't want to give him a chance to refocus his thoughts back onto her crumbling story.

"He's right: the light is fading quickly. I can hardly make out the faces in the photos, never mind check for any more names on them. Why don't we carry on with this tomorrow?"

The surveyor coughed and went outside again, looking pointedly at his watch. Sascha nodded reluctantly and followed him. He was halfway out of the door when he turned.

"Some friends of mine are having a party tonight. One of them is a writer; he's launching his new book at a local wine bar. Would you like to come?" He was blushing again. Nina rather liked it. "I won't go on about the past and missing families if you do, I promise. I can see that it's hard for you, dredging all these things up. Maybe it would be good, instead of all the serious stuff, for you to forget about all this and just have some fun."

Fun. Nina couldn't remember the last time she had thought about having fun, never mind actually experiencing it. No Tower House, no Magda, no horror-filled manuscripts, at least for one night; it was very tempting. She smiled at him and felt a shiver run down her spine when he smiled back.

"You promise?"

He nodded.

"Then I'll come."

He kept to his bargain, and the party had been exactly what he'd said it would be: an uncomplicated, enjoyable evening. His friends had been welcoming and witty and interested in the fact that she came from the East, but not obsessive or patronizing, or rude, about it. Nina had had one glass of wine too many and, when she and Sascha finally left the bar arm in arm, almost one kiss too many. She woke up with a smile on her face and a warm feeling about seeing Sascha again, which kept thoughts of the Tower House at bay for a while. She dressed carefully in her new black jeans and a less figure-swamping jumper, aware that he would be watching her, gratefully noticing as she applied her new makeup that, despite all the strain she was under, her face no longer looked as taut as it had, and her eyes had brightened.

Maybe that's a good sign. Maybe I'll find something today that will put Magda's actions in a better, more understandable light; something that will let me tell Sascha the whole story.

She went down to breakfast, feeling more optimistic than she had since she'd arrived four days earlier in Grunewald, to find an envelope with her name on it propped up beside the coffee pot. It took the guest house's landlady less than a minute from when Nina sat down to tell her the letter was from Sascha. Nina waited until the woman took the hint and huffed away before she opened it. She was glad that she had: the opening line, although true—the guest house was so perfectly run because Frau Fischler wouldn't permit it to be run any other way—was hardly flattering.

Your landlady is more of a dragon than I expected and no fan of personal phone calls interrupting her business line, so I have opted for old-fashioned methods instead.

I have been called into meetings which will take up the whole day, so I won't, I'm afraid, be able to get out to the property today. I am more miserable about that than I sound. I also have a favor to ask you. I had coffee with my grandmother this morning—she gets up with the dawn and likes to think that I do too—and I mentioned you and the excitement around finding the Tower House, especially given how long it's been hidden away. I have honestly never seen her so interested in my job before—she had a barrage of questions, about it and about you, which I realized I could barely answer, even though I feel like I already know you in many ways so well—I didn't tell her that. Anyway, the thing is that she really wants to meet you. She was quite insistent about it—she wants us both to come to dinner with her tonight. Would that be too odd? She eats early so we would have quite a bit of the night left to ourselves. Which I would like even more.

If it's a yes, I will pick you up at six. If it's a no . . . well, I very much hope that it won't be.

PS: I have arranged for a gardener to come today and start some of the clearing work that's so desperately needed before we can assess how damaged the lower parts of the façade are, and also for an electrician to come in and sort out the power. I know, I know, I'm overstepping, but don't be mad—there's a budget for this kind of thing

if a house is deemed historic, so we won't be billing you.
And I can't bear the thought of you shivering there in the
dark. Digging through the past is hard enough without that.

He had signed the letter with a curly S and a single kiss. The tone was light-hearted, but Nina knew that didn't mean it was casual or quickly thought out. In the brief time they had spent together, she'd got to know Sascha well enough to realize that, if he cared about something, he took great care with it. She knew that *would that be too odd* really meant *please*. She was also intrigued enough to go. If his grandmother had lived in the Grunewald all her life, as Sascha had said, perhaps there would be blanks in the house's history she could fill in. If she had lived there in the war, maybe the name Roth might mean something to her, although that might need a tactful introduction given the swastika symbol and the SS rank.

Despite the challenge of that, Nina finished her breakfast, feeling, if she was honest, calmer about the day than she would have been if Sascha had been coming back to poke about. The last few days had been filled with people and she was still not used to that; the constant engagements still tired her. It would be good to have time on her own, without worrying about whether she was saying the wrong thing, and to finish combing through the house herself for more clues to Magda's involvement with it. She had a feeling it hadn't yet given up all of its secrets, and she badly needed to uncover some that were good.

In the end, the day turned out to be a frustrating one. The gardener was loud, the electrician was intrusive, and Magda remained as elusive as she had been on every previous search. By the time Nina returned to the guest house, she was irritated with Sascha for jumping in and commissioning work she hadn't requested. She was also late getting ready, and the checked dress she'd brought from home and changed into for dinner suddenly seemed odd and old-fashioned, rather than vintage and chic. She would have begged off the whole evening if Sascha hadn't arrived so endearingly excited.

"That she is asking anything at all is completely unexpected. My grandmother has never shared my interest in history—like I told you, she's always been a stickler for 'keeping the past in the past.' I respect that, but it's frustrating. I know almost nothing about my family. She never talks about herself and all I know about her husband, my grandfather, is that he died in the war. I think there was money in the family at some point—some of her possessions are definitely valuable—but I don't know where it came from, or where it went. She's always tight-lipped, and then I mention the Tower House and it's like a dam burst. She'd obviously heard the name before—the first thing she asked me was what state it was in and had it been more recently lived in. And then she wanted to know all about you and your interest in it, and I felt a bit of a fool admitting how little I actually knew."

Nina grabbed his arm to slow him down and stop him asking her any of the questions she had ducked the day before and he was now clearly about to shower her with. She was far more interested in exploring his past than hers.

"Is she your mother's mother, or your father's?"

"My mother's."

Nina waited for Sascha to elaborate, but his normally lively tongue had tied.

"And your mother has never told you anything about your grandmother, or about your wider family?"

He didn't answer immediately. When he did, after a cough and a stumble across the first words, Nina felt dreadful for pushing him.

"The thing is, both my parents were killed in a car crash when I was seven, which is when I went to live with my grandmother. Before they died, I was too young to know I had questions, and now..." He stopped and almost visibly shook himself. "It's not really something Granny and I talk about: I think the loss still pains her too much."

His life has as many closed spaces in it as mine.

Nina looped her fingers through his and squeezed.

"I'm sorry, truly. My parents and I are...I suppose you'd call it estranged, but I can't imagine such a loss. But I'm glad that you've told me: I'll be careful not to ask her anything tonight that might upset her."

They had reached the quiet street his grandmother lived in. Sascha's face cleared, and he smiled as he pulled out his key.

"She wouldn't let you if you tried. She's kind, but she can be quite formidable. But I think she finally wants to talk, Nina. I can sense it—something about you and the house, and your grandmother's name, has got under her skin. If you can get her to open up, I'll be eternally grateful."

He was still talking to her as he opened the door and called out for his grandmother, but Nina didn't hear a word that he said—she barely made sense of his introduction.

"Grandmother, this is Nina Aderbach. Nina, this is my grandmother, Elsa Roth."

She looks like she's seen a ghost. But then so have I.

Whoever she might be now, the woman standing in the hallway staring open-mouthed at Nina was the woman whose face she had last seen on the swastika-stamped identity card.

CHAPTER SIXTEEN

Nina, November 1989

Nina got through the night, although she wasn't entirely sure how.

Her first instinct had been to blurt out, "But I know you." Her second had been to give her apologies and go. Elsa Roth might look like she had seen a ghost; she did not, however, look scared by that. She looked like she had never been scared by anything.

Sascha had carried on talking as he took Nina's coat and didn't seem to notice his grandmother's wide eyes or clenched body, or the stare that followed it: a cold appraisal that swept Nina from her face to her feet and didn't warm.

Perhaps he hadn't expected her to be particularly welcoming. Perhaps she's as aloof with everyone as she was with me.

Aloof was the word Nina had decided to choose as an explanation for Frau Roth's behavior, even though she knew it didn't fit. Aloof would have accounted for the coldness but not for the hastily concealed shock. Nina instantly knew that Elsa had seen Magda in her face; she also knew that the woman wasn't going to acknowledge that. And neither, therefore, was she. Taking her cue from the older woman's control, Nina had decided not to react until she could get a better sense of what, if any, the relationship between the two women had been. She had smiled instead and waited for a handshake; when it didn't come, she had put out her hand anyway. Elsa's fingertips barely touched hers.

"That is an unusual dress, Fräulein Aderbach; it has quite a distinctive pattern."

It was obvious from her tone that the comment was not intended as a compliment. Nina did her best not to bridle.

"It belonged to my grandmother. She had very good taste. I restyled it to fit me."

Elsa said nothing, but her eyes had tightened on the word *grandma*.

"Is everything all right?"

It had taken a few moments for Sascha to realize there was a problem. When he did, however, the enthusiasm with which he had introduced them both fizzled away. He hovered, staring from one to the other.

When she saw her grandson's discomfort, Elsa's recovery had been instant. Her expression had smoothed to a smile. She had made what Nina could tell was a deliberately old-woman comment about never understanding young people's fashions and given a self-deprecating laugh as she ushered them into the sitting room. Sascha had immediately relaxed; Nina—who could recognize an act when she saw it—did not.

"In you come, both of you; let's all get to know each other. Sascha hasn't been able to answer a single one of my questions about you, Nina, which I find a little strange given the impression you have clearly made on him."

Nina had followed Elsa's brittle smile into a room whose furnishings were far more elegant than she had expected the boxy little house to contain. Sascha had been right: some of Elsa's possessions—even to Nina's untrained eye—definitely appeared to be valuable. The dining table was set in a small alcove at the back of the room. The cutlery laid on the pristine white tablecloth was heavy and silver; the candlesticks were gleaming cut crystal; the china dinner service was bone thin and gold rimmed. And Elsa was the consummate hostess. She took charge from the moment they sat down and was clearly practiced in the role. She conducted the service of the food—a very traditional meal of paprika-sweet rabbit stew followed by poppy-seed strudel—and the conversation with the same nonchalant ease, as though the strangeness in the hall had never happened. She asked Nina about her life in the East but steered her away from any mention of politics. She told a handful of charming anecdotes about Sascha and the history of Grunewald but gave away nothing about herself. It wasn't until she served coffee—in porcelain cups that were so fragile, Nina had been terrified of snapping hers—that Elsa had finally brought the subject round to why Nina was actually there. And—as Nina realized now that the night was done—had taken complete command over the revelations that were to follow.

"Sascha said that you have connections with the Tower House. That you have reopened it."

Nina had nodded. "Reopened may be a little ambitious. I'm not sure the place could be classed as habitable—from what I can see, it hasn't been touched inside or out since the war—but Sascha has had an electrician reconnecting the power and a gardener working to remove the worst of the ivy from the front all day, so at least the light can get in and we can properly see the brickwork."

She had thought her answer was a neutral one—that was what she'd intended it to be—but the effect on Elsa was the same as when she had first taken in Nina's bobbed haircut and high cheekbones and her blue-and-red dress. Her face whitened; her jaw clenched. As she rounded abruptly on Sascha, two red spots had flared across her powdered cheeks.

"You are clearing the grounds? All of them?"

Sascha was too busy dismantling a second slice of strudel to notice his grandmother's strained face, or the sharp edge in her voice.

"The first job is pulling the ivy down—like Nina said, it's got completely out of control—but yes, eventually, we'll have to. The back is even more of a disaster than the front: the whole lawn is clogged with weeds and hopelessly overgrown with brambles. It needs completely cutting back so we can do a full survey."

Elsa's color did not return.

She looks like Magda did the day I found the picture.

Nina had realized that she was gripping her coffee cup too tight, and so was Elsa.

"Are you all right, Frau Roth? You don't look well."

Elsa's gaze had swiveled back then onto Nina. It had not been a pleasant experience. Elsa had weighed her up, as if she was assessing what Nina might do if she struck her. Nina had woken in the night with her heart racing at the memory of those cold blue eyes. Even though they were sitting in an ordinary room in a suburban street, she had been frightened. So frightened that her first thought had been, *I need to get out; something I don't want to hear is coming.* Part of Nina now wished she had listened to that, not to the *You're being ridiculous, she's an old woman; get a grip on yourself* that had followed. Instead of scrambling up the way she had wanted to, she'd sat in Elsa's crosshairs, casting about for some witty remark about the thickness of the ivy and feeling like one of Sleeping Beauty's suitors when she first tried to get through it. Before she could find that, however, Elsa had launched her attack.

"You are Magda Aderbach's granddaughter?"

Elsa threw out the name as if she was spitting it.

"Yes."

Nina had stopped at that and made no attempt to fill in the silence Elsa greeted her response with. That was the point when Sascha had finally registered the edge in his grandmother's voice, and the hesitation in Nina's, and looked up.

"And what do you know about her?"

Elsa's question was unmistakably a challenge; Nina knew she was going into battle.

"That she is a good person." Elsa had raised her eyebrows; Nina had refused to react. "She was rewarded by the GDR's government for loyal service. She saved lives during the war. She is well thought of. She is admired."

This time, it was Elsa who decided Nina had to wait. She hadn't responded immediately. She had opened a silver box next to her place setting and took out a cigarette. She hadn't offered Sascha or Nina one. As Elsa drew on it and slowly exhaled, Nina had caught a glimpse of the younger woman from the photograph.

"How nice for her that must be. But I am afraid, Fräulein, that you don't know your grandmother at all. Whose lives exactly did she say that she had saved?"

Sascha had grown very still. Nina had stared at Elsa, knowing that a pit was about to open up underneath her and that she was powerless to stop it.

"It's not something she brags about, so I don't know the exact details. I do know that she worked in a factory and helped the owner there to rescue people who were in danger from the fascists. Communists, I think. And maybe Jews."

Elsa had taken another drag on her cigarette before she answered. She let out the smoke on a sigh.

"What a charming story. But that's all it is, I'm afraid. You poor girl, you've been as tricked by her as everyone else was." Elsa's tone had dripped with concern, but her eyes were shards of glass. "Your grandmother didn't help communists, or Jews, or anyone else. At least not to escape. What she did, Nina dear, was help to kill them."

"Grandma, for God's sake! Why would you say that?"

Neither woman had taken any notice of Sascha.

"That's not true; that is malicious. Whatever your reasons for saying it, you've got the wrong woman."

Nina had managed to keep her face calm and her hands unclenched. She had managed the words without rushing them but had also remembered the hidden reports and the names of the camps and the massacre sites and her voice had wavered. Elsa heard it; her answering smile had not been a pretty one.

"Have I really? You don't actually believe that, do you? I can hear it in the way your voice trembled. A factory worker, what a good and honest profession. But that's not who she was; that was a façade. I am sorry to be the one to tell you this, my dear, but your grandmother's job wasn't overseeing production lines, or at least not the innocent ones you are imagining. Magda Aderbach was Heinrich Himmler's secretary. I don't need to explain who he was, do I?"

Elsa paused and waited for Nina to speak. Nina stayed silent.

"No, I thought not. Some names resonate on both sides of the Wall. That is, in fact, how she came by the Tower House: it was a reward for loyal service. Everyone in Grunewald knew. She was his right-hand woman—she helped him organize the deportation trains that went out from the station here. And goodness knows with what other atrocities."

That was the point at which Nina knew she should have hit back. The point at which she should have asked Elsa to explain why she was so eager to defame her grandmother, and why her own name was on an SS identity card. And how Elsa knew the things that she claimed. She wanted to, but the knowledge that everything Elsa had said could be true overwhelmed her. Instead of striking back, therefore, she had crumbled and the only thing she could manage to say was a shaken, "I won't listen to this. None of it's true."

Elsa had carried on as if no one had spoken.

"Magda had an incredible eye for detail apparently. That was why she was so valuable to him. A wonder when it came to organizing and to saving money. Just what their evil apparatus loved."

"Grandmother, please. You need to stop."

Nina had forgotten Sascha was there. When she turned to him, his face was as full of shock as Elsa's had been earlier. He had reached for her hand as she stared at him; she wouldn't let him take it.

"These things you are saying are monstrous." He had stopped then and frowned at Elsa. "And even if there was any truth in these allegations, how could you possibly know what Heinrich Himmler's assistant was doing?"

All the while he spoke, Elsa's gaze had never left Nina's. Nina had wondered if Sascha's challenge, as hesitant as it was, might have pulled her back. All it did was strengthen her strident voice.

"That is a good question, Sascha. Because, unfortunately, I was there. The factory owner Magda was supposedly working for was my father, your great-grandfather. He was the one, not her, who was helping people get away from the gas chambers, with forged papers and escape routes, and with his fortune. She was the one who betrayed him to her Nazi allies; she was the one who had him executed."

Sascha's shocked gasp echoed Nina's. She had pushed her chair back and jumped up, her words falling over each other.

"No. That's impossible. You're lying. I won't listen; I won't believe a word of this."

Her distress had been real—it still was—but Elsa had simply shrugged.

"Except that I think that you do. You are acting as if this is all a dreadful surprise, but that is all it is—acting. I think that you've found things in the house that prove I'm right and, if you carry on clearing it up, you will find more. You see, your beloved grandmother didn't just kill at a distance, by writing reports and betraying innocent men. She got far closer to her victims than that. Look."

And then the unthinkable had happened. Nina had stared, unable to move, as Elsa had lifted up the soft gray hair that fell over her face to reveal a jagged scar running like a pale seam across the side of her forehead.

"I got this when I fell, Nina, after your grandmother stabbed me. After I had uncovered the last of her crimes. That one's going to come to light now, so you may as well listen. Magda didn't just betray my father, she—"

But Nina hadn't listened—she couldn't. She was still trying to push Elsa's words away now as she roamed the tight spaces of her

room in the guest house. She had shouted then; she still wanted
to shout now.

"That's enough! My grandmother is a good woman, and you
are poison. I don't know what your game is, but I won't let you
twist me like this."

Her declaration had been meant to sound as strong and certain
as Elsa's, but her voice had risen and filled with sobs, and all three
of them heard the doubt in it. Nina had realized, as she heard her
own voice breaking, that staying a moment longer would allow
Elsa to keep making accusations and then she would break down
and confess what was in Magda's reports. She couldn't do that, and
she couldn't hear one more word until she'd confronted Magda.

She had run from the room instead, away from Elsa's mocking
eyes and Sascha's horrified ones. Neither of them had called her
back. It wasn't until she was wrestling her way into her coat that
she had finally heard Sascha's voice rise and his chair scrape back.
Nina had hesitated then, waiting for him to appear in the hall and
tell her that Elsa was deluded, that this was part of some age-caused
dementia he kept pretending wasn't happening, and that he was
sorry and that he should have warned Nina and kept her safe. He
hadn't come; she hadn't heard his voice again.

All she had heard from the dining room after that was Elsa's
measured tones, and then silence. Left with nowhere to turn,
Nina had fled and spent a night caught between a sleep full of
nightmares and a wide-awake horror. And now it was morning,
and the nightmares had to be faced.

That one's going to come to light now, so you may as well listen.

Nina tore through every floor of the house, from the attic to
the damp-soaked basement, with her head full of Elsa's malice. She
found plenty more boxes full of family mementos, but nothing to
exonerate Magda.

I should go back to Oberschöneweide and confront her. I should make her tell me the truth.

It was a plan. At some point, Nina knew she would have to carry it out, but she couldn't face it—not yet. There were still too many unknowns. What she didn't want to do was see Sascha and pick over the bones of his grandmother's story. Or hit him with her suspicions about Elsa: although she still had the identity card, she sensed that was a fight it would be very dangerous to embark on unless she was certain she could win.

The synagogues that are left have started to try to pull the records together.

Nina sat back on her heels and pushed away the box she had been digging through as she remembered Stefan's comment.

Perhaps I need to cast my net wider; perhaps Grunewald isn't the only place holding answers.

Nina couldn't accept that everything Elsa had told her was true—the idea that her grandmother could have directly had anyone killed was unthinkable. Magda had, however, lived in the Tower House, and the Tower House had belonged to someone else.

Perhaps I should be investigated and held to account.

Jannick had arrived within minutes of Magda saying those strange words and there had been no time to decipher what she meant. Now, everything Nina had seen and heard suggested Magda's words might be true.

But what if she could also atone? What if we could find the family who once lived here, or their descendants, and give back the house?

The thought released the weight from Nina's shoulders the reports had put there. She didn't want to live in the Tower House anymore. All the dreams she had of that were gone; all her delight in the house was gone. But if its return could be somehow used to repair whatever cruelty Magda had, at the very least, stood witness to, wouldn't that help balance the scales? Sascha could wait, and so could Elsa. Nina scrambled to her feet. Sascha had mentioned the New Synagogue; Nina hadn't a clue where that was, but she knew someone who might. And once Nina had been there, and uncovered the house's owners as she was sure that she would, then she would go back to Oberschöneweide and confront Magda, and start the next steps.

She tidied herself up and ran down the driveway; when she got to the processing office, the teller greeted her like an old friend.

"That's definitely in the East, in Mitte, as far as I know, and that area is off my map, although I imagine that will all have to change soon. I think your best bet would be to go on the S-Bahn to Friedrichstraβe and ask someone for directions from there. I doubt it can be very far."

It wasn't. It was a ten-minute walk, but it took Nina back through the crossing point and it felt like she should be measuring the distance not in minutes but years. The New Synagogue was an enormous construction, but it looked barely alive. Parts of the exterior were shrouded in scaffolding. The sections Nina could see were pockmarked and blackened and had chunks missing from the walls. It was crowned by a stumpy tower that appeared to be open to the elements, and many of the upper windows were cracked. It looked, Nina knew, no different to many of the old buildings still standing in the East, buildings she had walked by and never noticed before. It looked, however, like nothing she had encountered in the rebuilt West, and with her newly opened eyes, it didn't fill her with confidence.

No one answered when she knocked on the door, not even when she banged. In the end, it was one of the builders who spotted her from the scaffolding and led her to a small side door, pushing it open for her, with the instruction to seek out Dr. Aaronheim. The building's interior was as dark as the bricks it was built with; three steps inside and Nina was swallowed up. It was also sealed off from the street noise and utterly silent. Nina crept down the corridor the builder had pointed her to as if she was a thief; she certainly felt as out of place. It was a relief to find an open door with a pool of light spilling out, although the man sitting behind a desk piled with papers jumped when he saw her and his, "Who on earth let you in?" was hardly welcoming. When Nina explained the story she had practiced on the train—borrowing Sascha's job and pretending it was hers—he did, however, soften a little.

"We do have records, yes, but"—he gestured to his desk and the overcrowded bookshelves behind him—"as you can see, our system isn't anywhere close to what we want it to be. We hope to get better. Now that the Wall is down, we are hoping we might get funding for a restoration and a museum, which we were always denied under the GDR." He stopped and looked round, an instinctive reaction Nina knew it would take her fellow citizens years to break. "Anyway, I will do what I can. You have an initial you say? And a possible deportation date from Grunewald?"

Nina nodded. She had kept the details as sparse as she could; she didn't imagine her story would hold up well if he probed it.

"Wait here. And please don't touch anything. This may look like chaos, but it's the organized kind."

He was gone in the end for over half an hour. Nina sat the whole time without moving, trying not to shrink from the still very much alive history she could feel pressing around her. There was a photograph on the wall of what the synagogue must have looked like in its earlier days, with a golden globe where the broken tower now sat. And another of a building on fire and the title *Kristallnacht November 9, 1938* underneath it. Nina didn't know what that was, but the date and the sign underneath it which said "Lest We Forget" suggested Elsa and her grandmother might.

"I found them!"

Dr. Aaronheim bustled back into the room with a paper in his hand and a smile on his face Nina instantly warmed to.

"The Lieser Family, of Erdener Straße: Johannes, aged thirty-eight; Ruth, aged twenty-nine; Minna, aged six; and the baby, Isidor, who was two."

Minna, the little girl who had played with the doll's house, only six. Isidor, probably just beginning to talk. Nina tried, and failed, to stifle a sob and the doctor's smile vanished.

"Forgive me. I was so pleased I actually located them, I momentarily forgot why we were looking."

Nina managed to get herself back under control. "They were deported then?"

He nodded. "And murdered, all of them, in the ovens at Auschwitz."

The flames on the *Kristallnacht* photograph flickered in the gloom as if they were leaping. Nina shook her head, trying to push away the images of tiny bodies, of a hand reaching out to a mother who was no longer there.

"Is there family? Someone we could contact?"

Dr. Aaronheim scanned the paper again. "There is nothing listed here. Which doesn't mean there is no one but makes it very hard to know where to start. I could make inquiries if you like. There are channels for families trying to rediscover what happened to their lost ones. I can't promise you they will lead anywhere."

Except to the whole story coming out.

He put the paper down. Nina realized he was staring at her far more intently than she wanted him to.

"Forgive me, Fräulein..." He paused. "I realize that I don't know your name, that you never told me it. If you don't mind me saying, you seem unduly upset if this is just your job. Although perhaps that simply means you haven't grown jaded doing it, and I should applaud you for that."

She had been crying, without realizing it. And now she didn't know what to say, except a blurted-out and tearful, "I'm sorry, I'm so very sorry," which immediately put Dr. Aaronheim on alert.

"Is there something I'm missing here? How was the house discovered? You explained that very quickly. And who does it belong to now? Who was given it when the Liesers left?"

"I can't tell you. It doesn't matter."

Nina scrambled to her feet. She knew it was probably a ridiculous notion, but something in the frown that had tightened his face suggested he was about to slam the door shut and hold her there.

"Grunewald was an SS area—did you know that?" Nina froze; Aaronheim's frown deepened. "You did, didn't you. Was the Liesers' home gifted to an SS officer? Do you know who? Please God, don't tell me that family still owns it? The GDR never prosecuted war criminals, but we are one with the West now, and they did; they still do. If you have any information, Fräulein, it is your duty to—"

But Nina was already down the corridor and gone.

When she burst back out onto Oranienburgerstraße, Nina's first instinct was to run to Oberschöneweide and fling everything she suspected and feared in Magda's face. It would have taken her less time to do that than to go back to Grunewald. The only thing that stopped her was the reports. She had left them in her backpack at the Tower House and she couldn't face Magda without them, or risk Sascha coming looking for her and finding them instead. She had a feeling they were exactly what Elsa was waiting for. She went back, therefore, fully intending to leave again straightaway. She had barely been in the house five minutes, however, before Sascha knocked on the back door.

"I was in the garden waiting for you. Where have you been?"

Nina let him in and ignored the question. She steered him into the sitting room, blocking his view of the backpack that was lying in the hall. Not that he would have noticed it: he was bleary-eyed and had clearly had as bad a night as her.

"Was she right? Weren't you shocked? Were you acting?"

It was as if Nina had stepped into the middle of a conversation Sascha had already spent hours inside. She slumped down on the sofa facing him.

"Acting's too strong a word. I was confused, taken aback."

What she hadn't said was louder than what she had.

Sascha groaned and stared as deliberately away from Nina as she was determinedly avoiding any eye contact with him.

"So you knew. Why didn't you tell me the truth, Nina? Why did you let me go on thinking that your family was connected to the Jewish one who had been robbed of their home, when your Magda was the thief all along? Why didn't you tell me who your grandmother was? Were you trying to make a fool out of me?"

He sounded empty, and desperate for her to turn the mess they were caught up in into something manageable. Nina wished she could, but she was done with lies.

"No, not at all. I didn't know what to believe. I still don't. And you came up with an assumption and I didn't correct you to buy myself time to find out the truth, and because of this. Because I knew that once you had a better picture of her, you would have a far worse one of me. It was cowardly; it wasn't meant to be dishonest."

He didn't look at her or respond.

Is he just going to sit there looking defeated? Is he going to judge and convict me, without listening, or trying to see any of this from my side at all?

Nina's eyes stopped tearing; she stopped wanting to apologize, or to make him feel sorry for her, or better about what he had chosen to believe. She was suddenly aware that her heart was hammering because she was angry, even though she wasn't entirely sure who with.

"And because, like I said last night, I know that, whatever it looks like has happened, my grandmother is a good woman. And I don't know if what Elsa said is true."

Sascha's head finally shot up. "Are you saying my grandmother is a liar?"

Nina stared back at him as angrily as he was staring at her. "Are you saying the same thing about mine?"

He frowned, and she realized that he wasn't the enemy, and she didn't want him to be. That she didn't want to do the easy thing and hit him with all the pain the identity card and her suspicions about Elsa would cause him until she knew beyond doubt they were true.

"I didn't do any of this well, I'm sorry. And isn't it the case here that there's still too much that we don't know? Even down to how my grandmother and yours knew each other?"

Sascha wasn't prepared to let her off as easily.

"I think actually we do know that much at least: your grandmother had my great-grandfather killed, remember?"

Nina didn't want to fight but neither was she in the mood for his sarcasm. It would have been easier to shout at him to get out, or to go to Hell, or to leave her alone. Or to hurt him the way he was hurting her. Nina, however, had learned in a harder school than this how to stay quiet, so she bit her tongue and let the Stasi-evading side of her, the cautious side that she had developed during the long days and nights in prison, win the argument instead. She needed to explore all the possibilities surrounding the story before she could face Magda with it, and the only person she could do that with was him. She unclenched her shoulders, and she tried.

"What if the truth is somewhere in the middle, Sascha? What if Elsa only knows part of what happened, or she misunderstood? Or was involved in some way herself? It was a long time ago—memories get muddled. People can't always separate out what they hope or choose to believe happened from what actually did."

Sascha was still frowning, but Nina could see that the historian's part of his brain was, at least a little, engaged.

"Perhaps. When it comes to reasons and motives, they might. But whatever bits you don't want to believe, my grandma was certain about who Magda worked for, and why she was given the house."

He was watching her face too closely for Nina to keep holding his gaze. "And you know that bit is true, don't you? That was what she meant about you not being shocked."

Part of her—most of her—wanted to deny it, but Nina was tired of carrying round the secret of the sketch and the reports on her own. And she needed him to trust her more than he currently did.

He has been trained to read sources, to evaluate them. Maybe he'll be able to see nuances in them that I can't.

His body and face, however, were still hunched and hostile so she decided to give him what he suspected first and approach the rest with more care.

"I do know, yes, that the house was gifted to her during the war, and that the person who did that had the initials HH."

"So it was Himmler. My grandmother wasn't *lying* about that." His voice had hardened again. Nina continued as if she hadn't noticed.

"I didn't always know that; I only recently worked it out. I found a sketch of the house when I was little, and it had an inscription on it. I didn't know what that meant, but I do know that my grandmother was furious that I had uncovered the drawing at all. And that she hated the Tower House, *really* hated it. She wouldn't talk about it, and she never wanted me to come here. And she has this injury to her hand that is too, I don't know... neat maybe to be the accident she said it was."

Sascha shrugged. "Which is exactly how she would behave if she was guilty of everything my grandmother accused her of. She would want the past to stay hidden."

Nina took a deep breath. "I know that. I've already considered that. But what if there's a different way of looking at things than the way Elsa presented them? The *truth* isn't always what it looks like on the surface. The GDR was a dictatorship—citizens were always being forced to do things they didn't want to, like spy for the Stasi or report on their neighbors—"

"Or help with the murder of six million Jews?"

"Don't say that!"

They stared at each other, both of them furious, both of them believing their reading of the situation was the right one; feeling the gap between them yawning ever wider. Nina was the first with the self-control to break the silence.

"My point is that you don't always know why people do what they do, so maybe we shouldn't judge without all the facts. And I can't reconcile the woman I have known, and loved, my whole life with the woman Elsa described. Put yourself in my shoes for a minute, Sascha. Try to imagine your grandmother working for the Third Reich. Or being an intimate of someone as repulsive as Himmler. Or being a killer. You couldn't if you tried." She paused for a second, wondering if now was the time to reveal the card, and realizing how pointless that would be with his emotions flaring so high. "And even if I could prove any of that to you, you wouldn't want to believe me; you probably wouldn't even try."

Sascha nodded, as if he agreed with her, and then he asked her a question that made the ground lurch away.

"But what if the worst of this is true? What if your grandmother did have my great-grandfather killed? What if she was Himmler's secretary, if her fingers are all over the Holocaust—do you think she should walk away without anyone knowing, or do you think she should pay?"

There wasn't an answer Nina could give him. She stared around the room, peering at its peeling walls as if some ghost might step out and tell her the truth of what they had witnessed there. If she answered *no*, she would be a liar; if she answered *yes*, and—God forbid—Elsa was telling the truth, she had no idea what she was condemning her grandmother to. Nina sat on in a muddled silence, not realizing that Sascha was following her wandering gaze and wondering why it kept lingering on the hallway.

"What have you found, Nina?"

His voice was gentle; his question was a simple one. She was worn out, and afraid, and confused. She needed other eyes than hers on what she had read, another voice to make sense of it. The relief of finally telling tumbled her answer out in a rush.

"I don't know. Papers, reports. Notes really, with no context on them. That could prove that what Elsa said happened how she said it did, or that it could be taken a different way entirely. I'm going to take them back to Magda and make her talk me through them and explain them. I'm going to tell her everything Elsa said, and I'm going to get real answers. And then I'll come back, and I'll tell you what I learned—all of it—and we can work out together what we need to do next. For the good of both our families."

Sascha was sitting very still, his eyes on her face. "Can I see them, before you do that?"

Nina nodded, got up and fetched the reports. She passed them over to him with only the briefest outline of what he would find in their pages; then she sat in silence while he read through them. When he finished and looked up, his face was old.

"They are awful, I know that." Nina stopped and swallowed, determined to remove the pleading notes from her voice. "But they don't prove anything either way. We don't know when they were written, or why. She could have been making notes ready to denounce what Himmler was doing, to make sure the German people knew and could act to stop it. She could have been preparing a paper to smuggle out to the Allies. Or writing it all down to make sure the truth came out after the war."

Sascha's face was so full of pity, Nina's throat closed up. Pity wasn't what she wanted; pity suggested he had already condemned Magda.

"She didn't do it, Sascha. This isn't some celebration of achievements. The woman I know isn't capable of that."

He dropped his gaze and closed the reports. "And the woman I know isn't capable of telling malicious and damning lies."

Nina's stomach was spinning. She didn't want him to see her fall apart; she wanted to sit with him calmly and work out a plan. She wanted to show him the identity card so that there were no more secrets. She went to the kitchen, found a glass, let the tap run. When she came back, the front door was open, and Sascha and the papers were gone.

CHAPTER SEVENTEEN

Nina, November 1989

By the time Sascha left, it was too late for Nina to contemplate a return to Oberschöneweide. She knew that there was no point in running after him and pleading; what she didn't know was what he planned to do next. All she could hope was that he hadn't passed the paperwork straight over to Elsa. Nina still believed that Sascha wouldn't do anything to deliberately hurt her, but she doubted Elsa would share her grandson's scruples.

She spent a sleepless night at the guest house and was waiting outside Sascha's office as soon as the doors opened. He wasn't there, or, if he was, he had no intention of seeing her. As polite as the woman on the reception desk was, it was clear that she wasn't about to budge.

"He has meetings all day, some here, some off-site. He left clear instructions that there were to be no calls and no interruptions. I'm sorry."

She shook her head when Nina asked for Sascha's home address.

Nina left the council offices and told herself she was wandering to clear her head. She wasn't. When she knocked on Elsa's door, the woman didn't smile, but she didn't look surprised to see her.

"If you are looking for Sascha, he isn't here. Neither is he answering my calls. And I am not a messenger service."

He hasn't shown them to her yet.

The relief made Elsa look like a harmless old woman.

"It's not Sascha I want to talk to, it's you. Last night got, I don't know, rather heated, and some strange things were said. So I wanted to talk to you properly, about my grandmother, and the past."

Once again, Elsa's face was unreadable, but she did at least step back and open the door wide enough for Nina to follow her inside. This time, Elsa led her into the house's neat kitchen. The air was fragrant with coffee and cinnamon, and there was a tray of freshly baked biscuits sitting on the countertop. Elsa waved Nina to a seat; she didn't offer her anything.

"What do you want to hear? That I'm unwell in some way? That my brain is old and plays tricks on me? That I'm senile and I muddle up who did what and why?"

Elsa laughed as Nina flinched.

"Oh dear, that was what you were hoping. Well, I am sorry to disappoint you, my dear, but my brain is as sharp as a tack, and everything I said to you is true."

"Why did you tell me so brutally?" Nina knew it was pointless to begin another round of arguing about where the truth lay, but she needed to know where Elsa's malice came from, and why it was still so fresh. "Even if half of what you said was true, it was all so long ago. And yet you went on the attack last night as if you'd been waiting fifty years for a battle. I understand that you hated my grandmother then; it dripped from you, but how can you still hate her so viciously now that you would destroy her in my eyes? I could have given you her address—you could have had this fight, if you still wanted it, with her."

"Who says I still won't?"

The threat couldn't have sounded worse if Elsa had shouted it.

"As for why I still hate her, isn't a murdered father enough? Or would you like more?"

Nina didn't want more at all, but Elsa was staring away from her and it was clear she wasn't about to stop.

"She took him away from me long before he died. She took everything away from me. It was men like her who killed my Gunther.

He never came home, so he couldn't protect me and our daughter when everything fell apart at the end of the war. He couldn't, and your grandmother wouldn't. And my Liselotte paid for that."

Something wasn't making sense, but Nina couldn't put her finger on what it was.

"What do you mean, Frau Roth, 'men like her' killed your husband? He was an SS officer, wasn't he? If my grandmother was the Nazi you say she was, why would she, or 'men like her,' want one of their own dead?"

Elsa's stare swiveled back; it was as hard as it had been the previous night for Nina not to recoil.

"How do you know who my husband was?"

Nina was about to say "Sascha told me," but she knew Elsa would tear that apart. She also wasn't ready to reveal the identity card: she was beginning to suspect that Elsa's story wasn't as straightforward as she had pretended it was, and she needed to understand what that meant for Magda. She ignored the question.

"What do you mean about the end of the war? I assume by Liselotte you mean Sascha's mother, but how did she pay?"

Elsa's face suddenly crumpled. It was such a shock to see its hard edges dissolve into pain, Nina almost reached out and took Elsa's hand.

"The things that the Russian soldiers did to women in the last days of the war..." Elsa stopped. Her skin took on a gray hue that turned her lipsticked mouth into a wound. "I begged your grandmother to help me escape them. She didn't. After I got away from her, I couldn't be me anymore. I hid in the cottage that came with our house; I pretended to be the gardener's wife, a nobody. They still got me. They did things that Liselotte saw—that she heard. That broke her, as little as she was, in ways I could never mend." She stopped again and didn't seem to be able to restart.

"I am so sorry. I cannot imagine how terrible that time was, or how you survived it."

This time, Nina reached across the table and took hold of Elsa's thin hand.

Elsa pulled back as if she had put a match to it.

"How dare you. I didn't ask for your pity. I don't want it. You asked why I hate Magda, well, there is your answer. She killed my father, she tried to kill me, and she is responsible for my daughter's death. Liselotte never had a chance: she was damaged, and she made bad choices, and one of those was a drunk who drove their car into a truck and killed them both. That blood, along with my father's, is on Magda's hands. And now you have brought her back into my life and it's time for a reckoning."

There was so much to grasp, Nina's head was spinning. That Elsa was in terrible pain, that her pain had warped her life, was obvious. That didn't mean Nina had to believe her whole story.

"I don't understand, I'm sorry. Never mind your husband's death, but how could Magda have helped you get away from the Russians if she was a Nazi? Wouldn't she have been a target for them, especially if she really had been Himmler's secretary?"

Nina stopped. *I couldn't be me anymore.* She stared at Elsa, whose face had resumed its hard lines.

"Were you going to use my grandmother as your way out? Were you going to bargain somehow with her? Is that why she stabbed you?"

Elsa didn't react, which told Nina she was somewhere on the right lines.

"You were a Nazi yourself—I know you were. You must have been if you were married to an SS officer." Nina reached into her bag and pulled out the identity card. "And I know that was true—I can prove it."

The card lay on the table between them, open on Elsa's photograph. Elsa looked at it in silence, and then she nodded.

"Have you shown Sascha this yet?"

Nina shook her head. "No. I wanted to hear the truth from you first. The more I listen to you, the more holes there are in your story. I do think my grandmother was involved with Himmler in some way, but I'm beginning to think it's not how you describe it. And I don't think you were innocent in this at all. So I haven't shown him. I could have when he came to see me yesterday, but I was hoping we could all find a way through this together, for the good of both our families."

Elsa's laugh was brutal.

"Why would I care anything about your family? The only thing that matters to me is protecting mine. This is all your fault, Nina. You came here, you meddled, and now the past is going to rear itself back up and it won't be me or mine who suffer."

She suddenly jumped to her feet with the energy of a twenty-year-old. Before Nina could stop her, she had turned on the gas burner, and the identity card was ashes.

"I warned you, Nina, that there was something else to come. That the house had more secrets. Give the gardeners another day or two and out they'll all come. If I were you, I'd run now, back to your precious grandmother. She knows as well as I do that the past belongs to the people who tell it, and I'm going to tell it first."

She's insane.

Nina didn't bother to say it—she knew Elsa wouldn't care; that she would probably laugh that horrible laugh again. She grabbed her bag and left, as quickly as Elsa was still telling her to. But she didn't run to Magda; she went back to the Tower House.

Give the gardeners another day or two and out they'll all come.

The garden, and the little shed that sat at the bottom of it, were the only places Nina hadn't explored. She knew whatever was waiting would be worse than the reports; she knew it couldn't be avoided. That Elsa would tell whatever was hiding there to the world quick enough the minute she had to.

The gardener had cleared a path to the shed, but little else had been touched. The building was in an almost derelict state: when Nina touched her fingers to the door, it gave with barely a push. It was clear that someone had been living inside, but Nina couldn't tell when. The mattress and blankets on the floor were sodden with damp and thick with mold where the rain had poured through the web of holes in the roof. When Nina attempted to open one of the cupboards above the filthy sink, the handle fell off. There were no clues to what Elsa had meant was waiting to be found anywhere in the shed, but there was a spade that was still in one piece and a rake that had most of its teeth. Nina wrestled them outside and surveyed the sea of weeds choking the garden. She couldn't tackle the whole thing; that would take days—some of the bramble bushes were taller than she was. All she could do was follow the path that had already been cleared, sweeping from left to right, hoping that something would show itself.

Your beloved grandmother didn't just kill at a distance.

Elsa's words pricked at her as sharply as the brambles. Nina knew what she was looking for, although she was desperate not to find it. Elsa had dropped too many hints for the prize at the end of this twisted treasure hunt to be a folder of documents or another battered suitcase. Even clearing the ground a foot on each side was back-breaking work, but she pressed on, lifting away the leaves and the bindweed and the thick stalks of long-dead plants. Perhaps it was a good thing that it didn't take long, that her arms still had some strength in them when she found it. That her legs could still hold her when she sank down.

They are twigs. Nothing more. A bundle dropped by a bird building a nest.

Except twigs wouldn't be so perfectly placed.

And they wouldn't be wearing a sleeve.

CHAPTER EIGHTEEN

Magda, December 1989

"The house is still there, but it's an abandoned wreck. And Elsa Roth told me that you were Heinrich Himmler's secretary and that you killed her father and you tried to kill her. I believed her, and then I didn't, and then I found a body and I don't know what to do anymore."

Nina had tumbled through the door and tumbled out her words and then fallen into Magda's arms and wept like a child. Magda had held on to her, pretending a strength she didn't feel as the world unraveled around her. That Elsa was alive, that Nina had met her, that the mess of Magda's past had come out in such an unforeseen way, could have robbed her of her mind. Nina, however, needed her, so Magda kept going for the hours it took to piece together her version of the past with Elsa's and didn't fall apart until she was finally alone.

"She hates you, and she is quite mad. And if Sascha does give her those papers that make you look like the monster—although I can't believe that he would—"

"Then we will deal with whatever she does. The important thing is that we are in this together, and you believe me, not her."

Most days, Magda knew that was true, but then there were the other days, when she caught Nina wordlessly watching her and wondered how fragile that belief really was.

As long as she doesn't lose faith in me today, or when the deeper investigations start.

It had taken two weeks for the rest of the world to catch up with Magda's story, or at least the version of it that Elsa had chosen to tell. Magda had tried to use the waiting time to fill in the gaps in Nina's story, but with the very real threat now hanging over them, Nina had no appetite to discuss the threats that had disappeared with the Stasi. Magda had also used the time to try to warn Britte what was coming—not that her attempts had done any more good there. Britte—who was already struggling to accept the end of a country whose rules she had clung to so faithfully—had been far harder to convince of Magda's innocence than Nina. Every time Magda had tried to explain the truth of who she had been and what she had done, Britte burst into tears. Once the publicity and the headlines and the accusing stares started, she had run.

"I want to believe you, I do, but everything you're saying makes me feel sick," was, in the end, the best Magda knew she could expect from her frightened and confused daughter. It was kinder to let Britte go back to Dresden and the life she was now desperate to build there.

Elsa had lived. It was the one possibility Magda had never imagined. And Elsa—with her back against the wall and knowing the last secret the house would throw up—had told her story first.

From the moment Nina had blurted out the wrecked state of the house, Magda had known that Christoph was still there. That it was Nina who had found him—and left him again, undisturbed—was heartbreaking. And she had also known that Elsa—no matter how many times Nina insisted that "Sascha won't let it go any further, not until I've spoken to you, and spoken to him"—would do everything in her power to ensure it was Magda who paid for his death.

Guessing what Elsa would do was simple enough. The unknown element was Sascha. From the little Nina had told her about the young historian—from the little Nina seemed to know once the stars in her eyes dimmed—Magda knew any claims Nina had to his loyalty were far outweighed by his ties to his grandmother. And Sascha had the notes she had written, the notes that looked like finished reports but were so far from that. They had turned Nina's stomach with their clinical language, and Nina loved her. It wasn't hard for Magda to imagine what a stranger would think. And as for when Elsa got her hands on them... Whatever she had said to calm Nina down, Magda knew she had left her worst enemy a weapon as deadly as any gun.

BODY UNEARTHED IN GROUNDS OF MYSTERY HOUSE!

The headline made the morning edition of every Berlin newspaper and was the high spot of the television news. Christoph was still curled beside the path where he'd fallen, his body hidden by the bindweed and the brambles for over forty years. Or *Tragic Christoph Traube*, as the later editions dubbed him when the body's identity was revealed, *an innocent man shot dead by a lover with desperate secrets to hide.*

Magda read the reports over and over while the pain washed through her as new and sharp as the day he had died. Nina stormed round the house in a fury.

"Elsa must have given the press his name to throw everyone off the scent. The last thing she needs is the police investigation pointing at her, so she's pointing it firmly away. She knew I went to look for more secrets—she virtually forced me to do it—and the newspaper report said his hand was visible, although the gardener swore he'd not seen it before. That could make me look complicit and less plausible as a witness when I stand up for you."

There was nothing Magda could say to make Nina feel better.

Elsa was as clever as she had ever been. She remained, as the papers delicately put it, an "anonymous source." She dripped out the hints for another week before she stopped playing and opened the snare. The stories stopped; the speculations were replaced by "arrest imminent."

Magda knew the story's teasing out was deliberate—she could feel the hatred Nina had told her was there in every new tidbit that the papers lapped up. Her only surprise was that Elsa didn't spin the torture out longer. Nina, however, thought the days passing without a phone call or a summons was a good thing; she saw it as proof that Sascha had intervened. She even called his office twice, although he was always unavailable. Magda didn't try to dissuade her; she knew the importance of hoping.

The strain on Nina of the truth unfolding had been terrible to watch; the constant unpicking of the past had been a fraught and tear-filled thing. But Magda had done it. She had told Nina her story down to the tiniest detail; in the end, the relief of unburdening herself had been almost freeing. With the past about to be dragged into the light, Magda had wanted an ending, and she was ready to face it. She had offered to go to the police herself when Christoph was found, to finally get justice for him. That, as she kept insisting to Nina, was the missing piece; the lack of it the one thing left she could properly put right. Nina had refused to let her. So Magda had waited instead for the knock on the door that she knew was coming. When it did, it was Nina who flew between tears and fury. Magda walked down the snowy path to the squad car with her best coat neatly buttoned and her head held high. She had been very proud of that.

"Frau Aderbach, are you listening?"

She hadn't been, she had been picking over the past, something she spent too much of her time lately doing; she knew that wouldn't help her here. She wanted to get to the truth and to get justice, not to have the police think she was a dithering, or evasive, old lady. Magda smiled politely at the detective sitting opposite her and apologized.

"I was asking if you understood what you have been accused of."

Magda nodded. "Yes, I do. I am not clear, however, if I am under arrest."

The detective—whose name she now remembered was Gerber—shook his head. "Not at this present time, no. But I have to make you aware that there is no statute of limitations on murder anymore, and there is no statute of limitations at all on crimes against humanity. We have grounds to proceed against you on both of those charges. The file on Christoph Traube's killing has been passed to the Office of Public Prosecutions. The Himmler information—the notes that a member of the public provided and you have confirmed that you wrote—has been passed to the Office for the Investigation of National Socialist Crimes in Ludwigsburg. They have already requested a meeting."

Crimes against humanity. Magda knew that term. She had first heard it used at the Nuremburg Trials, where the words used to underpin it were *purposeful* and *systematic*. It was a horrible term, a perfectly fitting term for the atrocities that came under its umbrella. To hear it turned against her made Magda's heart ache. She was about to say as much, when Nina cut in.

"Doesn't this make you uncomfortable?"

It was the first time Nina had spoken since she and Magda had been led into the interview room. It was clear from the detective's scowl that her interruption wasn't a helpful one.

"Nina, please, that isn't the point here."

Nina ignored her and carried on, her voice rising. "Seriously though, interviewing old women about crimes that are so horrific, it is unacceptable for anyone who lived through them to have to remember them. Crimes that she is completely innocent of. Doesn't doing that make you uncomfortable?"

The detective put down his pen and straightened his cuffs. He stared back at Nina.

"No, Fräulein Dahlke, it doesn't. It makes me *uncomfortable* that my children do not have grandparents, or uncles, or cousins, or aunts. It makes me *uncomfortable* that my family doesn't have graves to mourn beside. Do I need to explain to you why? I am more than happy to."

There was a pause that, this time, Nina didn't attempt to fill. Detective Gerber, however, hadn't finished with her.

"It does make me uncomfortable, however, to think that anyone—no matter how young or old they are—would want to forget these crimes simply because they are unpleasant to remember. Maybe instead I should tell you what makes me *comfortable*, because that is simpler. Making sure criminals are brought to justice and have to face up to the miseries they have caused, no matter how good a life they've managed to build since they committed them. That not only makes me comfortable, Fräulein Dahlke, it makes me happy."

Nina sank back into her chair and wouldn't look at Magda when her grandmother reached out and took her hand.

Gerber tidied his folders together and turned back to Magda. He made no attempt to hide the disdain in his eyes.

"That is all for today. Perhaps when we call you in again, Frau Aderbach, which we will, and more formally, you should bring your lawyer with you, not a chaperone. You are going to need a far stronger defense than any your granddaughter can offer."

We have played our parts so perfectly, they believe we're the same as them. What if no one ever believes we were not?

The fear that had filled her at the gift-giving reception had finally come true. Gerber's disdain wasn't for Nina; he had dismissed her completely. His disdain was utterly reserved for her. Magda knew then that, despite the way the war had ended, the shadows she had feared in 1941 had caught up with her. That, until the end of her days, she would see the same contempt that Gerber felt for her in other faces, no matter how this fight with Elsa played out, or who else but poor silenced Nina believed her. It was a worse sentence to face than any judge could impose.

*

The press pack descended in a storm. Magda woke two days after the police interview to a cordon of cameras and a stream of journalists rattling her letter box. She was all set to march out and confront them and release her story to the world, but her newly appointed, and resolutely no-nonsense lawyer, Karolina Beitel, would have none of it.

"Nina called me and told me what was going on, which is why I am ringing you. Do not, under any circumstances, go outside. As I told you when we first spoke, there's not much appetite at the moment for Nazi hunting—it hardly fits with the whole push for reconciliation, especially as East and West have always dealt so differently with war crimes and the question of where guilt stops. The whole thing is a political minefield that most politicians would rather had never reared its head. Your case, however, is a hard one to overlook. Himmler is one of the big fish who got away, and now you appear and there's someone to pay for his crimes, or so plenty think—speaking to the press will only feed that. If I were you, I'd go somewhere quiet for a few days, at least until we know where we are with the charges. You've got a whole city to choose from; it shouldn't be too hard to hide."

That she was the one who had to disappear was an irony not lost on Magda. That Karolina offered to find her a safe house—"in the West, mind, because that's all I know"—was a blessing. Magda sat in the back of the car Karolina sent—alongside Nina, who refused to allow her grandmother to go anywhere alone—her mind wandering between the journey she was on and the ones she had made so long ago it felt as if someone else had lived that life. The place names they drove through—Wilmersdorf and Halensee and Westend—were horribly familiar. The places themselves, however, were not. The landscape had altered so much since Magda had dodged with her charges through its suburban streets, it could have been a different country. She felt no loss in that.

Schloβtrasse in Charlottenburg, where Karolina had found them a guest house, was tree-lined and peaceful; the houses nestling in it were quiet and neat. Despite the strain she was under, and the strain of what was coming, it was a far more comfortable return to the West than Magda had ever pictured herself having. Once it was clear that no journalists had followed them, she began to breathe a little easier. And at dinner on their first quiet night, away from the imprint of the East and the pressure of the press, Magda found herself finally able to talk properly to Nina again. About college and the possibility of Nina becoming a journalist. And about Christoph, who had been the love of Magda's life and impossible to replace. Neither of them mentioned the Tower House, which was less than half an hour's drive away. Neither of them mentioned Elsa. It was a pretty bubble to live in; it lasted almost three days.

"The representative from the Nazi investigation office in Ludwigsburg is here. He has agreed to hold the meeting with you at the Town Hall in Charlottenburg rather than a police station, as that is out of the public eye. I do think they are building a case against you, Magda. If they do, the Public Prosecutions Office will follow suit. I am sorry, but there it is. Be ready by ten. I will collect you."

Karolina was brusque but not uncaring. Magda didn't know if the lawyer believed her account of what had happened in the war or not—Karolina had been clear from their first engagement that innocence or guilt wasn't part of the discussion. Her main concern continued to be that Himmler's suicide in 1945 would turn Magda into a scapegoat. From the newspaper reports Magda had read—fed, she had no doubt, by Elsa—that seemed like a reasonable fear. The headlines were prolific, the articles lurid. Magda read accounts in which she was described as an *eager witness to genocide* and *Himmler's Handmaiden* and *the girl who costed out the Holocaust*. She had been physically sick at what the papers said, but she couldn't stop reading them. Then the photographs had appeared: there were so many, old and new and some she had no memory of being taken, that it was hard not to see the Stasi lurking.

Magda adopted a rich-woman's uniform of headscarf and dark glasses and refused to let Nina anywhere near the Town Hall.

"I didn't protect you in the past, Nina, when I should have. The secrets I was holding stopped me. Now you have another chance at a future, but that won't happen if you shackle yourself too closely to mine."

Nina was still arguing when Karolina refused to let her get into the car and sped Magda away.

The interview room Magda was led into was comfortably appointed. The chairs were padded and placed at careful, non-confrontational angles around the long table. There was a glass and a small water jug set beside each place. It was still an interview room.

The man sitting waiting didn't get up when Magda entered, or shake her hand. He was holding files and opinions; she was the one whose testimony wasn't to be trusted. He was the one in control of the questions, who chose the first one, in his words "to establish the facts," but really to put Magda firmly in her place: "Can you confirm that you were, as has been alleged, Reichsführer-SS Heinrich Himmler's secretary?"

It took Magda most of the morning to steer him back to Walther Tiedemann, and to what the two of them had been trying to achieve, not what it looked like she had done. By the time they broke for lunch, Magda could feel the cracks in her version of Elsa's story widening. Even Karolina had begun to look tired.

"You are doing well, Magda. You were clear and consistent, even when he pushed back and insisted that everything you told him could be seen in the exact opposite way. That wasn't easy, holding your temper the way that you did. If it was just a question of *you said, she said,* there wouldn't be much of a case, or not a simple one. But it's the reports you wrote that are the problem. I know you described them as notes, not the finished article, but I can't lie and say they're not damning."

Magda knew that better than Karolina. The sight of those pages again, the realization of how clinical and cold their contents sounded without the context and explanation, and the emotions, she had intended to add, had turned her stomach. She knew—when faced with the language and the attention to detail stamped through them—how hollow her excuses must sound.

"Do you think he is going to recommend prosecution?"

Her voice sounded so frail in the high-ceilinged dining room that Magda was ashamed of it. Karolina's attempt at a smile was equally weak.

"It's a possibility, yes, but we're not there yet. And if he does, there's a long way to go. It's one thing for Elsa to make these accusations in writing, and in private, but who knows if she can hold her own at a trial?"

Magda couldn't bear to tell Karolina that she did know, and that this Elsa, who seemed no different to the old one, most definitely could.

The lunch hour ended without Magda being able to eat a thing. They went back to the interview room, both of them pretending their shoulders were still up. It was empty.

Half an hour ticked by and still no one came.

"This is ridiculous. This is rude."

Just as an irritated Karolina was about to storm off and start snapping, the door opened and the prosecutor came in. He was no longer blank-faced; he seemed—to Magda's surprise—uncertain.

"I am sorry for the delay. I appreciate how impolite it must look. But there has been a development. We're not entirely sure yet what it means, but it certainly changes things. Frau Aderbach, there is a woman downstairs who insists that she knows you. Who says that, during the war, you saved her life."

Magda stared at him. His face had softened; he seemed to be smiling. She swallowed hard and made sure, this time, her voice was steady.

"Did she give her name?"

The prosecutor nodded. "She did. She said you would be sure to remember it. She is Helle Wendell now, but when you knew her, she was called Helle Herschell."

Beautiful bright-eyed Helle Herschell.

One of the few from the factory we were able to save; dear God, she made it, and if she got through those years alive...

For the first time in over forty years, Magda Aderbach burst into tears.

CHAPTER NINETEEN

December 1989

Nina woke up late with a throbbing head and a sandpapered throat. Helle Herschell—who had read the newspaper reports and tracked Karolina down through her office—had turned out to be an exuberant, unstoppable woman, determined to "celebrate the life your wonderful grandmother allowed me to go on living." Nina had arrived at the restaurant Magda had summoned her to and found her grandmother and Helle toasting each other with champagne and behaving more like teenagers let loose on the town than a pair of respectable-looking pensioners.

A short while after the second bottle had disappeared, Karolina had breezed in, fresh from holding a press conference Magda had refused to have anything to do with, and the champagne had carried on flowing. Nina remembered Magda admitting defeat at around eight o'clock and wobbling off into the night with Helle. She remembered agreeing to go on to another bar, and then to a club, with Karolina. After that, the rest of the evening was a bit of a blur.

She crawled out of bed and groped for her watch. Ten thirty, which at least meant breakfast was done and she wouldn't have to pretend that her stomach could hold it. Hopefully Magda had slept late too. The last weeks had taken a savage toll on Nina and she was only twenty-one; the potential effect on a 74-year-old was frightening, no matter how young Magda might have thought she was last night. The ordeal was also not over: Christoph's murder hadn't gone away; the truth about Elsa was sure to emerge. Magda's moment in the spotlight wasn't over.

Try to imagine your grandmother working for the Third Reich. You couldn't if you tried.

Well, now Sascha would have to do even more than that: Sascha would have to reimagine everything. Elsa wasn't only responsible for Christoph's death; she was also responsible for Walther's. And she wasn't a simple German housewife who had muddled through the war as best as she could—she had been wedded to the SS as strongly as she had been wedded to her husband.

Everything he knew is a lie.

Nina sat back down on the bed again, her legs suddenly shaky. She knew what he would be suffering better than anyone could; she could help him find a way through it better than anyone could. Part of her desperately wanted to. But Sascha was the architect of Magda's fall—he had to be. He must have given the reports to Elsa; he might have been the one who had gone to the police. At the very least, he hadn't stopped his grandmother.

If only he had waited. If only he had talked to me first.

But he hadn't. So Sascha was done with—Nina had no choice about that. She made herself get up again before she gave in to a bout of self-pitying tears. She needed coffee. Maybe she could persuade Magda to go to one of the elegant old cafés Karolina had said still lined the Kurfürstendamm. With a bit of fresh air maybe she could manage that—it would be a way to continue the celebration Magda deserved.

She dressed and went to knock on Magda's door. There was no answer. Assuming her grandmother would be waiting in the small residents' lounge, Nina went downstairs. According to the manager at the reception desk, however, Frau Aderbach had already breakfasted and left.

"At least an hour ago, I believe, but let me check."

Nina waited, her stomach sinking, while he checked through the appointment book.

"Here we are, I remember now. There was a telephone call for her—she took that and then she requested a taxi. That came for her shortly after nine o'clock."

Nina already knew where her grandmother had gone, but she asked anyway. The manager smiled, clearly delighted to demonstrate how efficient he was.

"Grunewald. Erdener Straβe. Apparently she was meeting an old friend there."

"I don't care how busy he is, he is going to see me."

Sascha was once again unavailable; this time Nina paid that instruction no attention. She stormed past the receptionist and into Sascha's office and refused to let her heart soar when he looked up. Luckily for her he didn't smile. He shook his head, instead, and said, "No." Nina didn't give him a chance to say anything else.

"You need to listen to me. Magda has gone to meet Elsa at the Tower House and it was Elsa's idea. Unless we go there and stop them, something really bad is going to happen—I know it."

She waited for Sascha to jump up, but he just sat there, staring as if she was the one who was mad.

"They are two old women. What on earth do you think they're going to do, lock horns and wrestle?"

"Don't you dare dismiss me." Her voice came out in a snarl that made him sit back. "Don't you get it, Sascha? Your grandmother is a liar and a killer. Any day now the police will be coming for her, and she will have to stand trial. Do you think she will voluntarily do that? Do you think she will allow anyone to unpick the story she has lived her whole life by and reveal the one that makes her the monster?"

When Sascha finally got to his feet, Nina could see he was trembling.

"Do you think she's going to hurt herself?"

"If she does, it will only be to put the blame back on Magda. How can you still care what—"

Nina stopped. Of course he still cared—Elsa was his grandmother. And he still hadn't made the jump from seeing her as a loving old woman to a killer that he needed to. Nina wasn't sure if he ever could. All she was certain of was that picking a fight with him wouldn't help Magda.

"I don't know, but it's a possibility. Or she plans to hurt Magda, which will hurt her in the end too. You are the only one she cares about, Sascha, the only one she will listen to." She paused, although she was desperate to be away, sensing he needed a moment to catch up with her. "Will you come with me please? Will you help me stop anyone else getting hurt? Haven't we all been through enough?"

He nodded, grabbed his coat, and followed her down the corridor, his urgency finally matching hers. When they got outside the building, they both broke into a run. But by the time they got to the driveway, the sky had turned orange.

*

The Tower House was a wreck. Magda had walked very carefully down the path, not wanting to risk her old bones on its cracks and clumped gravel, waiting to see the beauty Nina had insisted it still had, despite its neglected condition. She came around the corner and couldn't find a single trace. The façade was stained and crumbling where the ivy had been stripped away. The clock was so filthy, its face was unreadable. The pathway and the grounds had been partially cleared, but they were still knotted with nettles and weeds, and dotted not with the cornflowers and roses Magda remembered but discarded strips of red-and-white crime tape. The whole place looked as miserable as Magda had felt living in it. A part of her was glad. It finally looked the way it should.

She didn't bother trying the front door. She assumed that Elsa would have arrived first. She assumed she would be waiting at the back, in the garden, knowing that would be the hardest place for Magda to be. None of her assumptions were wrong. She was about to ask Elsa how she had tracked her down, but Elsa jumped in first.

"You got away with it."

No hello, no time wasted on pleasantries; it was as if the last forty years had passed in a moment. Magda waited for Elsa to elaborate on *it*; she had no intention of asking what she was being accused of.

"All the things you did, all the misery you caused, and the lying; you got away with it all."

There was so much hatred in Elsa's voice, Magda was glad that she'd kept her distance.

She's still beautiful. She's seventy-one, but blink and the elegant woman from the war is still there. I imagine she still attracts admiring glances.

It didn't matter. The inside was still rotten. Magda knew—because Karolina had been very clear about the next steps—that, at some point today, the police would arrive. That Elsa would soon be sitting on the wrong side of the table. She could, therefore, let Elsa still be beautiful, but she couldn't let her lie.

"You're like a stuck record—you always were. Well, if you can repeat yourself, so can I: I didn't do anything wrong, except defend myself against you. No one could convict me for that; no one will try once the truth finally comes out. As for you…"

Magda let the sentence fall, suddenly wondering why she'd come. It had seemed so urgent this morning to face her. To tell Elsa that she wasn't afraid of the past anymore, that she was ready to embrace—and, one day soon, celebrate—all that she and Walther had done. That she didn't care where that left Elsa. Now the impulse seemed pointless. Elsa hadn't changed, and Elsa was the past. Standing in the ruined gardens of a house she had never wanted, Magda realized that the only thing that mattered now was what was left of the future.

She had already decided to walk away when a sharp wind sprang up and a drop of rain fell, and she saw Elsa shiver.

"This is a waste of time. We should leave. We have nothing left to say to each other."

Elsa frowned. "That's it? It's that easy for you to go? I thought you would want to be here, in the place where you left Christoph. Maybe I shouldn't be surprised: you walked away from him the last time easily enough."

She was still full of barbs, but the barbs had no sting left. Magda shook her head. "Why would I want to stay? He's not here. If he's anywhere, he's in my granddaughter. That's all I need, Elsa; I've got the best of him with me every day."

She turned and began to pick her way back through the weeds. Unlike everywhere else she had seen in the West, Grunewald hadn't changed. She could find her way back to the main street, find a taxi; go back to Nina and start planning.

"Wait."

Magda stopped. Elsa—who seemed to care less about her bones and the clinging bindweed than Magda did—quickly caught up with her.

"There are still things I don't know; that only you can help me understand. Can't we go inside, at least for a moment? Aren't you at all curious to see what it looks like in there?"

Magda wasn't interested at all, but she was tired and in need of a seat before she began wandering through Grunewald. And maybe, if Elsa really wanted to talk, there might be something worth hearing. If nothing else, Magda was curious to know how she had survived.

She followed Elsa along the path and in through the open kitchen door. It was too hard, however, to go any farther. It was also too hard in here to fight off the memories. To not see Christoph leaning against the countertop and grinning. Or crashing through the cupboards on the day that he fled. Or holding a gun. Magda groped for a chair and sat down; she was vaguely aware of Elsa locking the door behind them.

"Did someone find you?"

Elsa looked at her and frowned. "When?"

Magda wondered if Elsa's memory was going.

"When I hit you, when you fell."

Elsa snorted. "When you stabbed me, you mean? You didn't do a very good job of that. There was a lot of blood, but the cut wasn't deep enough to do any real damage. You should have checked me better. I came to; I wasn't in great shape admittedly, but I got myself up and got help. You're lucky that I was concussed and the doctor thought I was rambling and put me under sedation or I would have given your name up right away. As it turned out, by the time I could tell anyone, nobody cared. Why does it matter now?"

She was prowling round the small room, too much on edge.

Magda shook herself out of the fog she was in danger of falling into and began scanning the kitchen, trying not to look too obviously at the cupboard drawers or wonder if there were still knives in them.

"What did you want to talk to me about?"

Elsa wasn't listening. She was peering through the window, pacing back and forth between it and the door. Magda watched her, trying to remember what the kitchen had been like the last time she was in it. She could sense that something was out of place, but she couldn't think what.

"I suppose they'll come for me now. Then the whole story will come out, never mind the fragments from the press conference that have already been in the papers. Everything about Gunther and the SS. Everything about me and my father. No one will believe I was trying to save him. Sascha will hate me. I don't want that."

There was a pile of what looked like towels and curtains on the floor, which was odd. But then the whole kitchen was such a peeling, moldy mess, perhaps that wasn't odd at all.

Magda forced herself to focus on Elsa.

"No. I don't suppose you do. Maybe the kindest thing would be to go now and speak to him, tell him the truth and give him time to at least try to adjust before the police arrive."

Elsa ignored her. She left the kitchen and began to head down through the dusty hall toward the sitting room.

Not trusting what she was up to, Magda followed. There were more curtains, or towels, or tablecloths, piled up around the front door. Magda's neck began to prickle. There was some connection her brain wouldn't make, something she knew instinctively was a warning floating around on the edges, but Elsa was still talking, and she couldn't latch on to it.

"So I'm not going to let them."

"Let them what?"

Magda's straining nerves made her voice loud. Elsa jerked as though she'd forgotten Magda was there. Then she stopped her pacing, and she beamed. Magda's heart lurched: Elsa's smile was so sweet and so sunny, it looked positively crazed.

"I'm not going to let them take me, silly. The police. I'm not going to let myself be arrested like some common criminal; I'm not going to go along with that ridiculous charade." She was suddenly behind Magda, ushering her into the sitting room. "Now sit down—you'll be far more comfortable. No need to make this worse."

Her hand was on Magda's shoulder, pushing her onto the tattered green silk. Magda instinctively moved to grab her wrist, but Elsa was too quick.

"Now, now, don't make a fuss. Don't try to fight it." Her tone had hardened, and so had her face. The smile and the air of amusement was gone. Vicious and dangerous Elsa was back. "It will be quick, you'll see. This place will go up like kindling. There'll be nothing to find when I'm done but our bones."

The curtains on the floor, the locked doors. She's built a fire trap.

Magda's brain finally connected, but it was too late. Elsa, moving as spritely as she had done in the garden, was gone from the room.

Magda flung herself after her, but the door was wedged shut. She banged and yelled; there was no answer. First there were footsteps, and then there was silence. And then there was the unmistakable smell of material burning.

She's trying to frighten me, that's all this is. Maybe she's hoping I'll have a heart attack and then there'll be no witness against her.

Magda wanted to believe that, but the smoke curling through the keyhole and under the door frame made it a lie. Fear pumped strength through her. She ran to every window and set her weight against them, but the panes were too thick to break and too small to climb through, and the iron grilles that held them were all rusted into place. Elsa had stripped away all the curtains—there was nothing to stuff into the gaps where the smoke was crawling in.

Magda could hear crackling now, and smell bubbling paint and charred wood. She had a sudden recollection of a night fifty years ago, when the streets had burned so fiercely she had thought the forests were on fire. Of standing next to Walther and watching the flames and realizing that no one was coming, watching the smoke thicken in the sky the way it was thickening now. Her eyes were tearing; her throat was starting to rasp. She needed air.

Go to the fireplace—it's wide enough to hide in. Curl up in there.

The voice in her ear sounded like Christoph's. It could be. He had been in this room. He had held her here and dried her tears when she'd sworn she wouldn't profit from the Liesers' pain. He had loved her in here, and she had loved him, and she had done that every day since.

Magda dragged herself across to the fireplace, her arm over her face. It was full of ashes. She scraped those away and pulled off her sweater to use as a mask. When she pressed herself inside the opening, a draft whispered down the chimney, kissing her skin, playing with her hair. She was so tired. She could hear the house groaning as the fire licked through it. She had no more strength left. If she listened hard enough, perhaps she would hear Christoph again; she was sure she could feel him. Wasn't this warmth his arms around her? Wouldn't it be easiest to sink into them?

"Magda? Magda, where are you?"

The cry was faint, but it meant he was there, just as she had known that he would be.

Magda closed her eyes and let go.

"Magda, Magda, wake up. Come on now, sweetheart, don't let us all down."

It wasn't Christoph—it didn't sound a bit like him. And she wasn't curled up in the fireplace anymore but lying down, with too many layers and straps holding her in place. As Magda struggled to get up and pull off the mask that was choking her, the man in the green helmet cheered and Nina, who Magda realized was the one clutching her hand, burst into tears.

"Take it slowly now—you inhaled a fair bit of smoke."

The man, who Magda now recognized as a fireman, eased the oxygen mask off.

Magda coughed and gagged and gulped at the air. It still stank of smoke, but it tasted impossibly sweet.

"Elsa?"

Her voice came out in a croak.

Someone else in a uniform fetched her some water. She sipped it as slowly as she was directed to and tried again.

"Where is Elsa? Is she dead?"

Nina sank down on the edge of the gurney. "I can't believe that you care after what she tried to do. No, she's not dead, which is a miracle according to the firefighters. They found her in one of the upstairs rooms, still clutching a box of matches. She's very poorly—she's suffered some burns, as well as smoke inhalation—but she's alive. They're going to take her to hospital first and then come back for you. Which is the wrong order, but nobody will listen."

This Traube has as many lives as a cat.

Himmler's words from years ago were now better suited to Elsa.

"She didn't want to die. Nobody does when it comes to it."

Magda caught Nina's frown and stopped. Her granddaughter's emotions were running too raw to spare any speck of understanding for Elsa. Magda couldn't blame her: she wasn't about to waste any time either praying for Elsa's return to good health.

"Help me get up; let me see."

"Grandma, no, you're not ready…" Nina sighed as she realized Magda was going to do it anyway and loosened the tightly wrapped blankets. "Here, go slow."

There was an ambulance parked at the bottom of the driveway; two men were loading a stretcher into it. Another man, the only one Magda could see who wasn't in uniform, was standing a few paces away watching.

"Who is that?"

"Sascha, Elsa's grandson." There was a catch in Nina's voice Magda knew, at some point, would need tending. "I went to see him this morning when I worked out where you'd gone. I was afraid that meeting her could be dangerous. I wish I hadn't been right."

The ambulance began to move slowly away, its lights flashing. Sascha stayed where he was. Magda swung her legs carefully over the side of the gurney and sat properly up.

"You said that they were close, that she raised him, and yet he's not going with her."

Nina took hold of Magda's hand again. "I doubt he can bring himself to. He knows everything—I told him it all, but he doesn't quite believe it yet. He doesn't know what he's meant to do with it." She stopped and shrugged and looked, to Magda's searching gaze, as if she was on the edge of running over to fix Sascha's dejected shoulders.

Elsa might have survived, but she hasn't escaped punishment: her grandson knows who she is. He'll never see her as she wanted him to again and she will have to live with the burden of that.

Magda squeezed her granddaughter's hand.

"Do you want to go and be with him? I would understand if you do."

Nina hesitated for the briefest moment and then she shook her head. "No, I don't. Whatever I thought might have been possible between us ended when he took the reports and gave them to Elsa. Nothing that has happened here today changes that."

They sat in silence, holding each other, watching as Sascha waited for the ambulance to leave. He looked over at them once. When Nina didn't move, or show any sign that she wanted to speak to him, he walked slowly down the drive and away.

"Frau Aderbach? I understand that you are the property's owner?"

It took Magda a moment to refocus. When she looked up at the fireman and reluctantly nodded, his smut-stained face was grim.

"I'm sorry, but we can't save anything meaningful of it. The damage is too extensive to—"

He stopped as a low rumbling filled the air, followed by a long drawn-out crash.

Magda swiveled round as Nina gasped. She had been so busy thinking about Elsa, and Sascha and Nina, she hadn't given one thought to the building she had just been pulled out of. It wasn't a building anymore, or not one she could recognize; it was a blackened shell. The roof was half gone; water seeped down its front and through the exposed floors. The clock had disappeared; the iron window grilles were twisted like barley sugar. And the turret was falling, tumbling in a cascade of bricks that smashed into the walls like shrapnel. There was a shout of "stand clear" from the firemen. There was a moment when the turret seemed to steady itself and make one final attempt to hold on to its shape. And then the last bricks gave up and fell, and there was nothing left but silence and a stack of smoking ruins.

Magda drew a deep breath that filled her whole body as the burden she had never wanted to bear finally let go of her. The Tower House was gone.

EPILOGUE

January 27, 1998

Nina stepped out of the shot and let the cameraman focus on Magda. She was standing alone, with her faithful Helle a few places behind, gazing along the overgrown and tree-lined gully where the cattle trucks had once run. Her face was still; her hands were clasped in front of her. It was the perfect closing image.

The rest of the now unused platform was emptying. The mostly old men and women swaddled in their thick coats and scarves—some of whom had once worked in the Tiedemann factory—were more than ready to swap the morning's bitter wind for the warmth of a restaurant. Nina nodded to her parents, who were standing apart from the others, still uncomfortable with aspects of Magda's story but doing their best to rise up to it. Her job was done. The report on the unveiling of the Platform 17 Memorial to the murdered at Grunewald station would be the evening news's main item. She was proud of it, although she had ditched her script and had, in the end, said very little of what she had planned to. The 186 iron grates edged with the date of a deportation, its destination, and the number of the dead that train had contained, which ran the whole length of the platform's sides hadn't needed clever words to describe them.

Nina had stood next to the first plaque, which was labeled 1941, and next to the last, which was labeled 1945, and let the sweep of the camera do the talking. The only words needed beyond that belonged to Magda and the survivors. The dedication had been heartbreaking and dignified and, perhaps, a closure of sorts.

It was also a fitting end to the series of documentaries she had made since her dream career had become a reality, all of which had centered on the Holocaust. Perhaps it was now time to move on to a different subject. Perhaps it was also time—as Magda had pointed out more than once—to start investing as much effort in her personal life as she had in her professional one. What she was ready for now, however, was hot coffee. And Magda—despite her protestations and her refusal of an arm or a stick—was worn out and had already stayed out in the cold far too long.

Nina was about to tell Karl to stop filming and call her grandmother back from her grieving when a sudden movement caught her eye. A man in a dark coat was standing at the other end of the platform, dropping red winter roses onto the stones. As Nina watched, not wanting to disturb his ritual, he bowed his head and rubbed his eyes, and turned.

"Sascha?"

She barely said it aloud, but the air was still, and he heard her.

He passed his hand over his eyes again and then he walked slowly toward her.

"I knew it was you. I didn't know whether to come over or not." He was still holding a rose in his hand. "They are for my great-grandfather. There was never a grave, so this feels…" He stopped, the eight years of silence that stood between them swallowing his words.

"Fitting?"

He nodded. "Thank you, yes, fitting. Are you filming this for *Tagesschau*?"

It was Nina's turn to feel lost for words. She nodded.

"I saw the documentary you made, about the Tower House. I'm glad the land is in better use now—a children's home seems fitting. And I saw the one about the Tiedemann Company and your grandmother. You were kinder to mine in that than you needed to be."

He has changed. He's more worn than eight years should have made him.

Nina could see Magda talking to Karl and looking her way. The wind had grown even sharper. Eight years was a long time, enough to forget someone, or to put them gently away. Nina knew that the simplest thing to do would be to say goodbye to Sascha, wish him well and leave the past where it was. But she hadn't ever expected to see him again and now here he was, and she wasn't quite ready to do that.

"I wasn't sure that I would be, when I started making it. I was carrying so much anger. But in the end, I didn't want the story to be about blame. That had already caused too much damage. And from what I heard, Elsa was still in a bad way and too ill to be charged with…well, with anything—it didn't seem right to hound her."

"She thought that you believed her. That's what she took from the program and the fact that you didn't pursue her." Sascha's face twisted. "She told me that; she refused to be dissuaded. And you were right, she was ill—she had a stroke after the fire. She recovered better than her doctors expected her to—her body is impaired, but her mind is still strong—but never enough to face trial. The prosecutors thought someone so frail would win too much sympathy." He took a deep breath. "She lives in a home now. She's not sorry; she carries no guilt or responsibility for any of it. I no longer see her."

Nina could hear from the pain in his voice how much that had cost him. She sensed there was more that he needed to say. She stared at the train tracks poking through the fallen leaves and waited while he found it.

"I thought I was in the right. I thought I knew who the victim was and who needed punishing. I didn't stop, I didn't listen, and I made the wrong choice. It's a poor defense, especially when it's made standing in a place like this, but it's the truth. And, for what it's worth, I am deeply sorry."

It meant more than she was ready to tell him.

She heard her name and turned round: Karl was coming, his arm looped through Magda's. Nina put a hand on Sascha's elbow before he saw, sensing he would back away if he realized it was Magda.

"You made a mistake. I would have made the same one if the tables had been turned; I nearly did. Isn't it time to be done with the past and move forward?"

He looked down at her, his face losing its lines. His smile hadn't changed, and neither had Nina's response to it.

Magda was waiting, watching them both, her hand out ready to take Nina's.

There could be healing in this.

Nina stepped back and let Magda's outstretched hand meet Sascha's more hesitant one. She let their eyes meet. When she saw the recognition flare in Magda's, she spoke and hoped they could both hear the hope in her voice.

"Magda Aderbach, I'd like you to meet Sascha Niedrig, Walther Tiedemann's great-grandson."

A LETTER FROM CATHERINE

Hello,

Firstly, and most importantly, a huge thank you for reading *The Secretary*. I hope you enjoyed reading it as much as I enjoyed writing it.

If you want to keep up to date with my latest releases, just sign up at the following link. I can promise that your email address will never be shared, and you can unsubscribe at any time.

catherinehokin.com

As anyone who has read my previous novels will know, I spend a lot of time in Berlin and love to walk where my characters walk. This book took me to Hohenschönhausen prison, where ex-prisoners act as guides—a visit I won't easily forget. This is a place whose stories are still being told and it is presented very much in that spirit, as a living thing rather than a museum. Go there if you can, and also, if you are in the city, make time for the Silent Heroes Memorial Center, which is housed in the building overlooking the courtyard where the German officers involved in the 1944 plot to assassinate Hitler were executed. It drips with history.

If you have a moment, and if you enjoyed the book, a review would be much appreciated. I'd dearly love to hear what you thought, and reviews always help us writers to get our stories out to more people.

I hope too that you will let me share my next novel with you when it's ready—I have a new set of characters waiting to meet you…

It's always fabulous to hear from my readers—please feel free to get in touch directly on my Facebook page, or through Twitter, Goodreads or my website.

Thank you again for your time,
Catherine Hokin

@cathokin

cathokin

14552554.Catherine_Hokin

www.catherinehokin.com

ACKNOWLEDGMENTS

Magda is not a real character, but the events I have immersed her in, including the costing mechanisms used for the Holocaust, very much were. As readers of my previous books will know, a huge part of my process involves research, including visits to key sites where possible, and a lot of reading.

As ever, I have used too many resources to single them all out, but those I would like to particularly mention are: *Heinrich Himmler* by Peter Longerich, which is an incredible study of a very complex man; for background to resistance to the Third Reich, *Resisting Hitler* by Shareen Blair Brysac and *Sophie Scholl and the White Rose* by Annette Dumbach and Jud Newborn; for Grunewald and the deportations, *Die Grunewald-Rampe* (Edition Colloquium), *Transit, Captivity & Witnessing the Holocaust* by Simone Gigliotti; for background to the last days of Berlin, *Berlin the Downfall* by Antony Beevor and *Berlin at War* by Roger Moorhouse; for the GDR, *The Berlin Wall* by Frederick Taylor, *Stasiland* by Anna Funder, *After the Wall* by Jana Hensel, *Red Love* by Maxim Leo, and *A Generation Divided* by Thomas Davey. I found Nina's joke on the brilliant website *Iron Curtain Kid*.

One small historical note—Hedwig Potthast, who was Himmler's secretary, left his employment in 1940 not 1941, and remained his mistress.

I owe thanks to many people. I always say it, but I always mean it. Those thanks in particular go to Tina Betts and Emily Gowers, my wonderful agent and editor, for their insight, patience, and hard work—this book has, once again, been a great collaborative experience. To the whole team at Bookouture who got behind it, especially Kim and Sarah in the marketing team. To my son and daughter, Claire and Daniel, for their never-failing love and support, and to the wider writing community I'm lucky to be part of who cheer on every success. And, lastly but never least, to my husband, Robert, who I couldn't do a step of this without. Much love to you all.

READING GROUP GUIDE

Discussion Questions

1. Does the title *The Secretary* prepare the reader for the content of the story? What were your expectations going into the book?

2. The novel is constructed around a dual timeline. Were both storylines equally engaging or were you more invested in one than the other? Why?

3. In Chapter 2, when Tiedemann first tells Magda the reason why he began to work with the National Socialist regime, he says, "Maybe I'm a coward, trying to justify the road I chose." Do you think there is any truth in that statement?

4. Is Nina the author of her own misfortune? If yes, how so?

5. At the end of Chapter 4, Magda remembers the warning that "Being with men whose values are as twisted as Himmler's corrodes a little piece of your soul." Does that corrosion happen to her? How much of Magda is truly herself by the end of her story?

6. Magda worked physically very close to Himmler. Should she have attempted a more permanent way to stop him? What else could she have done?

7. "All I've done is build another layer of secrets." Nina realizes this at the end of Chapter 5, but she continues to do it. Of all the secrets she keeps, which is the most dangerous one?

8. Does the novel have a satisfying end? Could there be the healing that Nina hopes for?

Author Q&A

Q. What inspired you to write *The Secretary*?

A. I think like most writers, I try not to dwell too much on the process of idea generation; it's not always clear where they come from and there is always a nagging fear that they might dry up. To put it in the words of the wonderful Leonard Cohen, *"If I knew where the good songs came from, I'd go there more often."* Most of my books come out of a nugget I've discovered while researching another one, or from something I discover on my travels. In the case of *The Secretary*, I think there were three main strands involved. One is my fascination with the language that the Nazis used to cloak their brutality. When Magda talks about *freight* and *cargo* and *discounted rates*, these are actual terms used in the paperwork. There is something utterly terrifying in the way the lives of millions of people were reduced to a dry accountancy exercise. The second was a visit to Grunewald and to the station where many of Berlin's deportation trains began their journey. The platform with its memorial plaques was hard enough to look at, but what was worse was the proximity of the area's beautiful villas. They are so close to the station that what was happening there cannot have gone unnoticed. And I really did find a derelict one, which became the Tower House. And the third was also a research visit, this time to the Silent Heroes Memorial Center in Berlin where I realized that the scale of resistance in the city was far bigger than I had previously realized.

Q. There are three strong female voices in the book; were any of them more challenging than the others to write?

A. First, I enjoyed writing all of them. Nina's timeline in terms of her age is close to mine, and I really wanted to write from an older woman's perspective, which is why Magda's voice was so important. Of all of them, however, I think that Elsa was the hardest. She is a horrible person and intentionally very much Magda's opposite. But she couldn't be a caricature, so there had to be the odd flash of humanity in her. It was also important to me that she didn't soften but became a more hardened version of herself as she aged. She was motivated by jealousy as well as her political beliefs, and then by the horror of what she had done: I don't think she ever believed that her father would go to his death, and she is never able to face up to her responsibility for that. She is thoroughly dislikable but also very sad—or at least that's how I hope she comes across!

Q. Was there any unique research you did for this book?

A. Yes, there was. I visited Berlin's Hohenschönhausen prison, which is both a museum and a memorial and one of the most remarkable places I have ever been in. The site has been a prison since the Russians took over the area in June 1945. It was a truly horrific place then: the living conditions were inhuman, and it is estimated that up to 3,000 people died there between 1945 and 1946. As part of the tour, you visit the cells the Russians used, and it is not an experience for the fainthearted. In 1951, the newly formed Stasi took it over and a new building was added, which included 200 prison cells and interrogation rooms. The type of physical torture used by the Russians fell out of favor and was replaced instead by psychological methods, which were equally as brutal. Because the prison was inside an exclusion zone, many of East Berlin's citizens didn't know of its existence, never mind what happened there, which is one of the reasons why it wasn't stormed in 1989 when the wall came down. The site has been open to visitors since 1994 and many of the guides are ex-prisoners who are still coming to terms with what they suffered there. I cannot recommend it highly enough if you want to understand what repression in the old East really meant.

Q. World War II novels can often mean writing about horrific situations; when you were plotting the book, did you discard any ideas because they felt too dark or bleak?

A. The answer to that is always yes. Concentration camps and prisons are spaces where terrible harm was visited on real people, and there are things I have read in my research that have no place in the pages of a novel. One aspect of *The Secretary*, however, posed a different challenge, and that was how best to get across the character of Himmler without going to some very strange places. As I indicated in the prologue, the SS had many aspects of a cult and Himmler himself had a morbid fascination with black magic. He set up the H-Sonderkommando—*H* standing for *Hexen*, the German word for witches—whose job was to collate as much material as possible on the supernatural and prove Himmler's quite mad theory that the widespread witch-burning in the 1600s had been a deliberate attempt to destroy the German race. His 13,000-volume library consisting solely of occult publications was recently discovered in Prague, and he also set up Wewelsburg Castle in North Rhine-Westphalia as a kind of Nazi Camelot, complete with swastikas and occult symbols on the walls and a crypt with an eternal flame at the center. As I said, strange places, and better left well alone.

Q. This is the second time you have written about the German Democratic Republic (GDR); what are the challenges of writing about this particular place and period?

A. The main issue—which is also the same for anyone trying to write about Russia under Stalin—is that so much of its history has been lost or rewritten or hidden from view. The fascination for me is that, apart from the fact that the GDR was born in 1961, which is the same year that I was, it is also a country that—in the brief not-quite-thirty years of its existence—had so many facets. Yes, it was a state based on repression and surveillance and censorship, but it was also a country where workers had access to incredible cultural programs through their workplaces and where women were granted the right to equal pay in 1949 and where there was generous maternity leave and free childcare. I am, of course, very aware that much of what sounded good had a downside, that nurseries, for example, were the first step in ideological indoctrination. But it's difficult not to be interested as a writer in a state that emerged so fully-fledged with its ideas about how life should be lived and was, in the end, so fleeting.

Q. Why do you set your books in Berlin?

A. I do get asked this a lot, especially as I live in Glasgow in Scotland! One reason is that I am very interested in the German experience of the war itself, as well as in the run-up to it and its aftermath. And Berlin is the most wonderful city—it faces up to its history, both in the 1930s and 1940s and during the period of division, and there is a constant dialogue with the past, which it is not afraid to re-examine and question. It has a wealth of museums, which is a writer's mecca, as well as a great food scene and a language I am finally cracking. And my son lives there, which is rather nice.

The Real Face of Resistance in WWII Germany

"It doesn't matter if one man fights or ten thousand; if the one man sees he has no option but to fight, then he will fight, whether he has others on his side or not. I had to fight, and given the chance I would do it again."

This quote is from the German novel *Alone in Berlin* by Hans Fallada, which is one of my favorites and one I reread when I was researching the background to *The Secretary*. Although this book is a piece of fiction, it is based on the true story of a working-class Berlin couple, Otto and Elise Hampel, and their campaign of protest against the National Socialist regime during World War II.

The Hampels' method of resistance was a very individual one. For two years, starting in September 1940, they wrote a series of 287 postcards urging people to refuse to cooperate in any way with the Nazis and asking them to find a way to overthrow Hitler. They left the completed cards in stairwells and mailboxes in public and domestic buildings all over Berlin. It is highly unlikely that the cards had any impact—people were frightened of being caught with anything subversive, and few, once they saw the message, would have picked them up. The Hampels were eventually caught, and they were executed at Plötzensee Prison on April 8, 1943. Theirs was an odd little campaign that had no wider circle of involvement than them, it produced no results, and it ended in death. It was also an incredible act of bravery and far more typical of the kind of resistance to Hitler encountered in Germany than the campaigns waged in the countries that the Nazis occupied.

When we think about resistance in World War II, I imagine that most of us conjure up images that have their roots particularly in France and Poland. Secret armies of partisans or spies gathering intelligence for the Allies, destroying communication lines, distributing anti-Nazi literature, helping escaped POWs, and attacking the German armies once the tide of the war had begun to turn. That type of resistance was essential to the Allied war effort and also demanded a phenomenal level of bravery from the men and women putting themselves on the front line. Resistance was extremely dangerous and the reprisals for those who were caught—or for their fellow citizens who were made to pay—were brutal. This type of coordinated action was not, however, replicated in Germany, and it is important to recognize that resistance in Germany was not, in fact, a movement at all—it was rarely even united. Protest against the Third Reich machinery was slow to organize, and it was more often carried out by individuals who were isolated from each other or by small groups who were easily flushed out and dealt with. That, however, does not mean that opposition to the Nazis didn't exist. During Hitler's twelve-year reign of terror, it is estimated that over 800,000 Germans were arrested by the Gestapo for resistance activities and, of those, at least 15,000 and possibly as many as 77,000 were executed.

Although accurate figures for the individuals who were murdered for their bravery are hard to come by, some of the groups involved and the acts they committed are well-documented. The attack on the Soviet Paradise exhibition in May 1942, which is referenced in *The Secretary*, did include a sticker campaign and an incendiary bomb attack, which left eleven people injured. It was coordinated by a group of friends and resistance fighters, which centered around the Luftwaffe officer Harro Schulze-Boysen, the economist Arvid Harnack, and his American-born wife, Mildred.

They were part of a wider, although very loose, network of around 400 contacts whom the Nazis named Die Rote Kapelle, the Red Orchestra. Their activities included circulating resistance pamphlets and leaflets that, among other things, called for a popular uprising; collecting and sharing information on German war preparations; and encouraging disobedience of Nazi officials. Over one hundred members of the groups prosecuted under the Red Orchestra banner were executed in 1942 and 1943, including Boysen and his wife, Libertas, and the Harnacks.

Die Weiße Rose was another group of like-minded individuals whose resistance campaign has been told through both books and films. The White Rose was founded by a handful of students at University of Munich, including brother and sister Hans and Sophie Scholl, and produced a series of pamphlets during 1942 that advocated sabotage of the Third Reich's machinery and provided very clear advice on how to do it. One leaflet in particular, which declared that "the day of reckoning has come, the reckoning of German youth with the most abominable tyranny that our people have ever suffered," caught the wrong kind of attention and led to the group's arrest. Like the Boysens and the Harnacks, its leaders were put through a mock trial and all of them, including twenty-one-year-old Sophie, were guillotined.

Another, and perhaps the most well-known, act of resistance within Germany was Operation Valkyrie. The plot in July 1944 to assassinate Hitler was led by German army colonel Claus von Stauffenberg, a committed nationalist who believed that it was his patriotic duty to kill Hitler and save Germany. He placed a bomb in a briefcase under a table during a meeting at the Wolfsschanze (the Wolf's Lair), one of the Führer's military headquarters, as close as he could to Hitler's chair. The bomb went off, panic followed, and many officials believed their leader was dead. Unfortunately, the case had been unwittingly moved by someone else sitting down and Hitler, now protected by a heavy wooden table leg, sustained only minor injuries. Stauffenberg and five other conspirators were executed.

There was no shortage of brave individual and group acts of resistance in Germany during the war—to date, historians have uncovered at least forty-two other plots to assassinate Hitler and they will no doubt uncover more. The hundreds of thousands arrested on anti-government charges included people from every walk of life, from the military to church pastors and trade unionists, from lawyers and professors to students and Jews, as well as ordinary men and women like the Hampels. The question therefore has to be, with all that determination, why was an organized movement never achieved? To answer that, it is essential to look at what happened in Germany not during, but before the war.

By the outbreak of World War II, Germans were living in a totalitarian state; in other words, they were ruled by a government intent on asserting total control over the lives of its citizens.

When Hitler came to power in January 1933, he wasted no time setting up the kind of state he was determined to rule over. The Enabling Act removed all constitutional restraints on government power. Emergency ordinances gave the police the ability to ban public protest and to control the press. By June, all opposition parties had been banned and forced underground. It was a systematic and ruthless program of repression that wiped away both the voice of protest and any possibility of legal challenge to the new regime. It was also a program that created a climate of fear. Arrests were carried out on a mass scale. The Dachau concentration camp was opened in March 1933, and anyone believed to be a threat to Hitler—and the new parameters defining a threat were wide ones—was sent there. The security forces were massively expanded, as was their network of informants, including children who were educated to inform on their parents. And as the Nazis' stranglehold strengthened, mass deportations and the principle of collective reprisal—which could extend from families to whole communities—were added to the mix. People were afraid. They were watched, weighed up, taken. There was no appeal. That anyone had the courage to speak up at all is, I think, remarkable.

Would I resist? It's a question many of us ask ourselves when we look back at this war, or at any other conflict people have suffered or are suffering through. Would I stand up and be counted? I don't have an answer. I have lived my whole life in a democracy and I have done and still do my fair share of shouting, but I have never been in a position where the lives or the freedom of the people I love have been put at risk by a machine that crushes the voices that dare to shout, "*No.*" There is a remarkable museum in Berlin called the Silent Heroes Memorial Center, which contains a huge catalogue of individual courage. I felt humbled by the stories I read there. There is also a remarkable film called *The Restless Conscience* about the many now forgotten people who fought back. That made me cry.

So would I resist? We all hope that we would be as brave as the Hampels or young Sophie Scholl, but we don't have a clue. And this, I think, is why the stories and the accounts of what could be done and what couldn't matter. They help us to praise those who did act and to remember them, but, hopefully, they also teach us not to judge those who, for reasons I hope we will never have to face, were forced to keep their hate silent.

YOUR
BOOK
CLUB
RESOURCE

VISIT
GCPClubCar.com

to sign up for the **GCP Club Car** newsletter, featuring exclusive promotions, info on other **Club Car** titles, and more.

 @grandcentralpub

 @grandcentralpub

 @grandcentralpub